Train  ctress, Barbara Nadel ... .
Born in the East End of London, sh ... n
a visitor to Turkey for over twenty years. She received the Crime Writers'
Association Silver Dagger for her novel *Deadly Web* and the Swedish
Flintax Prize for historical crime fiction for her first Francis Hancock novel
Last Rights.

Praise for Barbara Nadel:

'Nadel's evocation of the shady underbelly of modern Turkey is one of
the perennial joys of crime fiction'
Mail on Sunday

'The delight of Nadel's books is the sense of being taken beneath the
surface of an ancient city. . . We look into the alleyways and curious dark
quarters of Istanbul, full of complex characters and louche atmosphere'
Independent

'Wake up and smell the coffee, the tobacco and the other rich smells
permeating the huddled streets of Istanbul, the superbly drawn backcloth
to Nadel's intelligent bestsellers featuring grumpy Inspector Çetin İkmen'
Peterborough Telegraph

'Nadel's novels take in all of Istanbul – the mysterious, the beautiful, the
hidden and the banal. Her characters are vivid. A fascinating view of
contemporary Turkey'
Scotland on Sunday

'Another atmospheric thriller from a talented author and detective team'
Lancashire Evening Post

'Crime fiction can do many things, and here it offers both a well-crafted
mystery and a form of armchair tourism, with Nadel as an expert guide'
Spectator

'The strands of Barbara Nadel's novels are woven as deftly as the carpet
at the centre of the tale. . . a wonderful setting. . . a dizzying ride'
Guardian

BARBARA NADEL

BODY COUNT

An **INSPECTOR İKMEN** mystery

headline

First published in 2014
by HEADLINE PUBLISHING GROUP

First published in paperback in 2014
by HEADLINE PUBLISHING GROUP

1

Cataloguing in Publication Data is available from the British Library

ISBN 978 0 7553 8894 3

Typeset in Times New Roman by Palimpsest Book Production Limited,
Falkirk, Stirlingshire

Printed and bound in Great Britain by
Clays Ltd, St Ives plc

Headline's policy is to use papers that are natural, renewable and recyclable
products and made from wood grown in sustainable forests. The logging
and manufacturing processes are expected to conform to the environmental
regulations of the country of origin.

HEADLINE PUBLISHING GROUP
An Hachette UK Company
338 Euston Road
London NW1 3BH

www.headline.co.uk
www.hachette.co.uk

To Elsie and Lütfü who took me to Mexico. And to the Maya, without whom this book would not have been written.

Cast List

The Police

Inspector Çetin İkmen – middle-aged İstanbul detective
Inspector Mehmet Süleyman – İstanbul detective and
  İkmen's protégé
Commissioner Ardıç – İkmen and Süleyman's boss
Sergeant Ayşe Farsakoğlu – İkmen's sergeant
Sergeant Ömer Mungan – Süleyman's sergeant
Dr Arto Sarkissian – police pathologist

Other Characters

Fatma İkmen – Çetin's wife
Nur Süleyman – Mehmet's wife
Muhammed Süleyman – Mehmet's father
Peri Mungan – Ömer Mungan's sister
Gonca Şekeroğlu – a gypsy and Süleyman's ex-mistress
Şukru Şekeroğlu – Gonca's brother
Hadı Şekeroğlu – Gonca and Şukru's father
Tansu 'Sugar' Barışık – an aging prostitute
Selçuk Devrim – a telecoms engineer
Hatice Devrim – Selçuk's wife

Faruk Genç – a health spa manager

Hande Genç – Faruk's wife

Professor Cem Atay – Hande's brother

Leyla Ablak – a wealthy socialite

General Osman Ablak – Leyla's husband

Sezen İpek – Leyla's mother

Rafik Efendi – Sezen's Uncle

Abdurrahman Şafak – an elderly aristocrat

Suzan Arslan – Abdurrahman's maid

John Regan – a British academic

Arthur Regan – John's father

Hamid – a gypsy boy

Şeftali – Hamid's mother

When Şukru saw him, the kid was poking a stick in the man's wound. It made the body's head move almost as if it were still alive. For a few moments Şukru just watched, mesmerised by the child's apparent lack of either fear or empathy for the dead man. Ever since İstanbul's Roma gypsies had been evicted from their traditional quarter of Sulukule three years before, life had been tough and it was the kids who had suffered the most. This kid, like Şukru, was Roma. Şukru knew him – he knew the whole family. His mother, once madam of a good-sized brothel back in the old quarter, now sometimes sold her body to poor immigrants on Taksim Square. The mother had little pride and so she beat the child, taking it out on the son, who in his turn poked a corpse with a stick.

The child – he was twelve at the most; no one including the kid himself knew his age for sure – didn't see the middle-aged man approach. It was still dark and the ground was covered in a thick wadding of newly fallen snow – powdery, pure white and silent. As Şukru moved closer, he saw that the child was shaking. Was he cold, or frightened, or both? The government were moving the Roma on from this district, Tarlabaşı, now too. Houses were being demolished to make way for 'better' homes for people who were not Roma and everyone was scared all the time. Just as they had been back in Sulukule. As a child with no father and a whore for a mother, this kid was shunned and

Şukru felt sorry for him. The boy poked the man's wound again, but this time with his finger. Şukru cleared his throat. The kid, alarmed, looked up at Şukru Şekeroğlu, one-time grease wrestler, one-time king of the gypsy dancing-bear men. Trembling still harder now, he raised a hand in greeting. 'Şukru Bey!'

Şukru Şekeroğlu tried not to show on his face how much he pitied the boy. He put his phone to his ear and waited for an answer.

'Who you calling, Şukru Bey?' The child, still apparently oblivious to how macabre his situation was, spoke with a frozen frown on his face.

'You'd best get away from here now,' Şukru said.

'Why?'

No one was answering the phone, but Şukru persisted. 'Well, do you want the police to think that you killed Levent Bey?' he asked.

The child frowned. 'I didn't. I've killed no one.' He put his head to one side and regarded Şukru closely. 'You calling the coppers now?'

'Yes.'

'Why?'

'Because sometimes that is all that is left to do,' Şukru said. And then as someone finally answered his call he said to the boy, 'And Levent Bey was not one of our own; he was one of theirs. Now they have taken him back.'

Chapter 1

Police sergeant Ayşe Farsakoğlu knew that all she had with and of the man who was making love to her was sex. No words of affection passed Mehmet Süleyman's lips as he took her up against the wall of her shower room. When he came, it was Ayşe who panted with spent lust – he simply grunted and then immediately washed himself without looking at her. She, however, looked at him. Although middle-aged now – Ayşe had first met Inspector Mehmet Süleyman when he was twenty-nine – he was still slim, handsome and very aware of his power over women. The scion of an old Ottoman family related to the sultans, Süleyman was as mercurial as he was beautiful and Ayşe had been besotted by him for over a decade. Less than a year ago she'd passed up what might have been her last opportunity to marry a man who had really loved her for Süleyman. She was forty, and although she was still beautiful, her face was lined. Her eyes, for just a moment, became sad. But he didn't notice. Married unsuccessfully twice and with a trail of failed affairs and one-night stands behind him, Mehmet Süleyman was unreliable, promiscuous, obsessed with his job and a thoroughly bad prospect. She loved him.

As he stepped out of her shower room, his phone began to ring. It had to be the station. No one else called before six in the morning. Ayşe walked back into her bedroom naked, hoping that maybe the sight of her tall, slim, slightly bronzed

3

body would arouse his passions once again, knowing that if she had to compete with his work she was on a hiding to nothing. And she did have to compete with his work. She heard him say, 'OK, I'll be there' – he looked briefly down at his watch, which was lying on her bed – 'in ten minutes at the most.' He didn't tell whoever was on the other end where he was coming from and she didn't know where he was going. Leaning against the door frame of her bedroom, Ayşe watched him dress quickly and tried to remember how many times she'd seen him do that in the past. Eventually she said, 'What's going on?'

'A partially decapitated body in Tarlabaşı,' he said.

She said nothing. He continued dressing with care, making sure that his shirt was crease-free, his tie just so. He used cologne on his face and through his hair and he even ran a finger across his teeth to make sure that they were perfectly clean. How could such self-absorption be attractive? And how could Ayşe concentrate on such irrelevances when apparently someone had been killed over in the poor district of Tarlabaşı?

She sat on her bed. 'Who called?' she asked.

'Sergeant Mungan.' He lit a cigarette. 'I have to go.'

He didn't bend down to kiss her goodbye and it wasn't just because he was in a hurry. He rarely kissed her. Since their on/ off affair had resumed in December 2011 when Ayşe had given up İzzet Melik, the man who had loved her so much, there had been sex but no passion. Even when he was inside her, he was as cold as winter. She watched him leave the room and then stood by her bedroom window so she could see him get into his car in the snowy street below.

Mehmet Süleyman didn't like Tarlabaşı any more. From a professional point of view it had been trouble for years. Anywhere that was poor had problems. But the district's poverty notwithstanding, and including its great brotherhood of drug dealers, was not why he disliked it. He objected to how it was being changed, which was against the will of the majority of its people.

Those who wanted to redevelop the area – construction companies approved by the government – had tried to put a positive spin on the demolition of an established nineteenth-century central İstanbul neighbourhood. But they'd failed. The locals – mainly Kurds, foreign immigrants, Roma, transsexuals and prostitutes – were not easily convinced. They knew that the brand-new flats they were being offered as compensation were in tower blocks thirty kilometres outside the city, because that was exactly what the deal had been when the Roma had been evicted from Sulukule. And that was why so many of them had subsequently moved out of those new flats and into the urban stew that was Tarlabaşı. In spite of the presence of the very obvious wrecking balls and earth-movers, Süleyman didn't blame them. He'd heard stories about those tower blocks; about how people cried when they moved into them because they missed their communities. And what was it all for anyway?

He pulled off Tarlabaşı Bulvari on to some nameless street he knew would take him where he needed to be and briefly looked over his shoulder towards the back of İstiklal Caddesi, the very heart of the vibrant part of İstanbul known as the 'New City'. Land there was worth a fortune. Land there was what Tarlabaşı, once it was remodelled for the new urban middle classes, was going to become. His car bumped down what quickly turned into an unmade track, past a shop selling nothing but plugs, which was next to a derelict house that had clearly been decorated by Tarlabaşı's only recent new tribe of residents, street artists. What once had been a kitchen was now spray-painted with images of government ministers dressed as Nazis. Süleyman shook his head. Not so many years ago the only people ever portrayed as Nazis were the military. Now contained and curtailed by the Islamically inspired government of the AK Party, the army were not the bogeymen any more. In fact, an ongoing investigation into Ergenekon, a plot that had allegedly been devised by the generals to undermine the AK government, had made those who had once ruled into those who were now hunted. The military coups that had happened in the past in defence of Atatürk's secular state were now no longer possible. But what had taken their place was, it seemed to Süleyman, gradually turning sour also. That was certainly the view from somewhere like Tarlabaşı, as well as, he imagined, from the prison cells of the generals who had already been locked up pending trial for treason.

He got out of his car and walked over to where a group of people – police officers and civilians – stood and squatted in the snow.

'This man found the body.'

Ömer Mungan was new to the department as well as to the city, and he was eager to please. He had a tendency to pull Süleyman towards whatever it was he wanted him to see, whoever he needed him to meet. It didn't help to endear him to his new boss.

'Yes, thank you, Sergeant,' Süleyman said as he extricated himself from Ömer's nervous grasp. He walked alone towards the very tall, grizzled man, whom he knew, if not well, then well enough. Şukru Şekeroğlu had always had something of the look of his sister Gonca. Coming upon him and that look suddenly made Süleyman's heart squeeze. Gonca the gypsy artist had once – and in reality, still – possessed his soul.

'Hello, Mr Şekeroğlu,' he said. But he didn't extend his hand in greeting.

Şukru looked up at him from underneath tangled eyebrows. 'Inspector Süleyman,' he said.

'You found the body.'

'Half an hour ago.'

'Where were you going?'

'You know how cold it's been.' As if to illustrate this point, he stamped his feet on the snow to warm them. 'This place is a building site now; I was out collecting anything I could burn to keep my kids and my father warm. Then I saw this . . .' He waved a hand towards what was now a small white tent. 'Him.'

Süleyman rubbed his gloved hands together and looked up into the lightening grey morning sky. 'My sergeant says you knew the dead man,' he said.

'I knew of him,' Şukru corrected. 'Everyone round here did.'

'So he was a local . . .'

'He was a nutter.'

Süleyman lowered his gaze and looked into Şukru Şekeroğlu's eyes. They were just as hostile as he remembered. Back when Süleyman had loved Şukru's artist sister, Gonca, Şukru had used those eyes as a weapon in his armoury to try and terrify the policeman away. He'd never succeeded. When their affair had finished it had been because Gonca, finally bowing to family pressure, had ended it. Even in the bone-freezing cold of a January morning, with a dead body awaiting his attention, Süleyman knew that in spite of everything, he'd still smile if he saw his old gypsy lover turn the corner. He looked back at her brother. 'Mad.'

Şukru shrugged. 'He made films. Not with a video camera, with an old film camera.'

Süleyman took out his notebook. 'Films of what?'

'Of Tarlabaşı. The streets, the people, I don't know.'

'Do you know his name?' Süleyman asked.

'Levent Devrim. Did you know him?'

Süleyman frowned. 'No. Why should I?'

7

Şukru shrugged again. 'He was like you.'

In view of the fact that Şukru had recently described the dead man as 'a nutter', this was hardly complimentary.

'Posh,' Şukru said.

'In what way?' Out of the corner of his eye, Süleyman saw a car draw up and then a large, very familiar figure haul itself out of the driver's seat.

'Spoke nice. I dunno,' Şukru said. 'Talked about stuff people round here don't know anything about.'

'Like?'

'Books . . . art . . . alternative things . . .' He shook his head. 'Like those kids who come and graffiti walls with anti-government slogans. All about saving the district. It's impossible. Why bother?'

A lot of intellectuals and artists had become very vocal about the fate of Tarlabaşı and its inhabitants in recent years. They knew that since the razing of Sulukule it was the only place actually in the city where Roma and other poor people, including a small long-standing Syrian Christian community, could afford to live.

'Do you know how long Levent Devrim had lived here?'

'No. But it was well before the rest of them came and scrawled up pictures of Che Guevara and politicians dressed as fascists on old brothel walls.'

'Do you know anyone who might know?' He heard footsteps behind him, heavy and weary as they trudged through the snow.

'Sugar'd know,' Şukru said. 'She's an old whore, a Kurd, lives up by the Syriani church.'

'Do you know her address?'

Şukru tipped his head back. 'No. But you can't miss her place. She can't work any more because she's too old, so now she sells sex stuff – underwear, dolls, things like that. Look for a ground-floor flat with whips hanging in the window.'

It was an exotic thought. 'Thank you, Mr Şekeroğlu, I will,'

Süleyman said. Then, in response to a light touch on his shoulder, he turned and looked into the face of Arto Sarkissian, the police pathologist. 'Good morning, Doctor.'

The Armenian shook his head. 'Well it is morning, Inspector, although whether it is good or not . . .' He looked over at the small tent that had been erected over the body of the dead man. 'Throat wound . . .'

'His head's almost off,' Şukru put in baldly.

'I see.' The Armenian didn't ask how he knew or even who Şukru was. He headed out across the snow-capped rubble and into a building entirely devoid of frontage. On one of the few pieces of masonry still standing was the image of a man Süleyman recognised as one of the high-profile developers involved in the district's 'regeneration', dressed as Mussolini.

Süleyman turned back to Şukru Şekeroğlu. 'Did you see anyone in the area when you found the body?'

'No,' he said. 'It's snowing, if you notice. If I hadn't been desperate for fuel, I'd've been in my bed. People round here don't have too much to get up for, especially when it's this cold.'

Şukru's hostility wasn't easy to stomach, especially so early in the morning. But as a resident of Tarlabaşı, he did have a point about having little to get up for. Few people in the area had legitimate jobs, and the wrecking ball that acted as a soundtrack to their lives had robbed them of whatever hopes they might have had for a future in the city. As Gonca's brother, however, he aroused less sympathy in Süleyman, who knew that, left to herself, Gonca would still be with him and he, consequently, would be happy. But the father for whom Şukru Şekeroğlu had gone out collecting wood had forbidden it, and his lover had had to comply or be killed.

'You called us immediately?'

'Yes. Why wouldn't I?' Şukru said.

'I don't know, Mr Şekeroğlu,' Süleyman replied. 'Maybe—'

'Maybe you don't trust me. I don't know.'

The implication was that Süleyman didn't trust him because he was a gypsy. He ignored it.

Süleyman looked away, across the other side of what passed for a road, at Ömer Mungan, the thin, hook-nosed young man so recently promoted, who had come to him from the far eastern city of Mardin. Once, a few years before, Süleyman had been sent to that city in pursuit of an escaped prisoner. What he'd found when he got there had been a marvellous honey-coloured hill town full of old mosques and ancient churches and with its very own indigenous pagan goddess, the Sharmeran. He wondered whether Ömer loved 'his' Sharmeran as they all seemed to out there, or whether the civil war in nearby Syria and the refugees who had poured across the border into Turkey had shaken his faith in everything he had ever held dear.

Süleyman said to Şukru, 'I'd like you to give a statement to Sergeant Mungan.'

Şukru shuffled his feet in the snow and said, 'What are you doing?'

'I,' Süleyman said, 'am going to look at what you've already seen, Mr Şekeroğlu. A man with his head almost severed from his body.'

Nobody, except for the very poorest, had a soba any more. The large wood-burning stove that stood in the middle of the İkmen family's hall was a constant bone of contention. Fatma İkmen, a stout but shapely woman in her mid fifties, was nearly always the one who got up early in the morning to feed the soba with wood, and she was sick of it.

'Peasants in the country have sobas,' she shouted, knowing that

10

her husband Çetin, who was in the shower, wouldn't be able to hear her. 'People in cities have central heating.'

She threw some logs into the belly of the beast and then shut the fire door. She sniffed. And it smelt – mainly of smoke, which was to be expected, but she still didn't like it. To be fair to him, her husband probably didn't even notice the smell. He smoked more cigarettes than Atatürk himself was reputed to have done. Although because in recent years they had gone up in price so much, he was trying to cut back – when he remembered.

'Çetin!'

He didn't answer. All she could hear of him was the sound of the water from the shower and some tuneless singing. She went into the kitchen and poured herself a glass of tea from the samovar. From her kitchen window she could see three of the major İstanbul monuments – the Sultanahmet or Blue Mosque, the Hippodrome, and, just about, Aya Sofya, once the greatest church in the world. Fatma lived at the very heart of the old city in a large apartment with her husband, who was a successful inspector of police. In many ways she was a fortunate woman. So why did she not have central heating?

A short, thin middle-aged man with wild grey hair burst into the kitchen simultaneously knotting his tie and smoking a cigarette.

'Çetin.'

'Yes?' He smiled and she almost, *almost* felt herself fall into the charm of his smile.

'Çetin, why do we still have that soba? Please tell me.'

Çetin İkmen rolled his black, heavily lashed eyes and puffed on his cigarette. This was an old and to him boring conversation. 'I've told you, Fatma,' he said, 'that once I have retired we will get central heating.'

'In a year's time.'

11

'Yes, in a year's time,' he said. 'One more winter, that's all. Allah, if I could be here now I would have it put in today! But what do you want to do, eh, Fatma? You want a house full of workmen pulling up floorboards all on your own?'

'Well, no . . .'

'And this place is full of stuff.' He sat down at the kitchen table and she brought him over a glass of tea into which he threw four sugar cubes. 'We've had nine children here, Fatma, most of whom seem to have left the majority of their possessions behind them in this apartment. We have to plan. We have to get the children to take their things away.'

'Mmm.' She leaned against the cooker. She knew that he was right about the clutter, but she also knew that he didn't want to tackle it any more than their children did. It was a massive job and he always had something better to do and somewhere else to be. His phone had rung at just after seven, which had to be to do with his work. He had also sung in the shower, which usually meant that some sort of challenge was on the cards.

'So what was your call about this morning?' she asked him.

İkmen put one cigarette out and then lit up another. 'An incident, possibly a murder, has taken place in Tarlabaşı,' he said. 'Mehmet Süleyman's out there now.'

Fatma shrugged. 'Tarlabaşı. What is it, gypsies?'

İkmen turned towards her, fixing her with one of his disapproving stares. 'I don't know,' he said. 'Does it matter?'

'Eh.' She turned away from him to cut bread into slices. Fatma İkmen was a good, kind woman – a pious Muslim, too – but she had prejudices that İkmen found unacceptable. Roma gypsies was one. They had no recognisable religion and they drank and so they were automatically 'bad'. Over the years he'd tried to talk her out of such nonsense, but she had stoically refused to change. Just like he had refused to change his mind about people he liked to call 'holy sheep', pious people who did whatever the Koran, the Bible or whichever belief they adhered to told them, without question or thought. To İkmen, an avowed agnostic, their apparent mindlessness was not only incomprehensible; it was also, he felt sometimes, dangerous. Those not like oneself could all too easily become 'the other' – despised creatures to be casually discarded, ignored or blamed.

İkmen threw what was left of his tea down his throat and stood up.

Without turning around, Fatma said, 'If this is Mehmet's case, why are you involved?'

He didn't respond, but she knew what his answer would have been had he given it. He was always 'involved'. She turned to look at him. 'Çetin,' she said, 'are you really going to retire at the end of the year? Are you?'

Çetin İkmen put his jacket on, stuck his cigarettes in his pocket with his car keys, smiled and failed to answer her question. 'As the great Sherlock Holmes once said, Fatma, "The game is afoot!"'

Chapter 2

The late Levent Devrim was, or had been, fifty-five years old, according to his identity card. A spare, almost ascetic-looking man, he had also been rather handsome before someone had tried to hack his head off. Arto Sarkissian put a hand inside Devrim's coat, under several layers of woollen jumpers, and felt the dead man's bare flesh. He was as cold as the snow underneath and on top of him. He looked at the wound again, photographed it and then took a small sample of desiccated blood from the very far left-hand side of the cut. Both the carotid artery and the jugular vein had been severed, which was what had killed him, but then the murderer had gone on to apparently saw at his neck vertebrae too. When the gypsy had told Mehmet Süleyman that someone had tried to decapitate Devrim, he had not been lying.

'Morning, Arto.'

Sarkissian looked around; crouched uncomfortably in what was only a small tent, there was little room for an overweight man like the doctor to manoeuvre. But he could move enough to see that Çetin İkmen had just arrived.

'Çetin, what are you doing here? Inspector Süleyman . . .'

'Oh, I was just—'

'Passing? No you weren't,' the pathologist said. 'Who told you about it?'

'Mehmet.'

'Mmm. Inspector Süleyman still on your leash.' He turned

uncomfortably to look at him again. 'He's a big boy now, you should leave him be.'

'I'm not interfering.' İkmen held his hands up in the air, all innocence.

'Much.' The Armenian turned back to the dead man. He and Çetin İkmen had been friends for many years, even before they started working together – in fact, since childhood – and Arto probably knew more about the inspector than anyone else, including his wife. He didn't believe for a minute that İkmen was going to retire. He'd find some way to stop the process, even though he was, like Arto himself, well past retirement age already. But then something caught the doctor's eye that took his mind quite away from Çetin İkmen. There were fragments in Levent Devrim's wound. He picked up a pair of surgical tweezers from out of his instrument roll and gently nudged at one of these anomalies.

'What is it?' İkmen asked as Arto lifted the tweezers up to the light.

The Armenian squinted. 'I don't know,' he said.

Sugar's real name was Tansu Barışık, and she said she was seventy years old. Süleyman thought that perhaps she was being a little bit economical with the truth, but he didn't ask to see her ID card. Everyone, after all, knew who she was. Following Şukru's tip, he'd been brought to her door by a man dressed in the full ecclesiastical robes and regalia of the ancient Syriani church, who had been rather less fazed than Süleyman himself had been by Sugar's whips, rubber dolls and dildos and a strong smell of cat pee.

Sugar set a tiny cup of coffee down in front of the policeman and then sat in a vast, broken armchair. She was fat, with feet that spilled over the sides of her flowery carpet slippers. 'Levent was odd but harmless,' she said. 'But then often that's the way with very clever people, isn't it?'

'He was clever?' Süleyman took a sip from the cup. Turkish coffee – hot, thick and medium sweet, just the way he'd told her he liked it.

'He went to Galatasaray Lycée,' she said, as if there was some sort of connection between İstanbul's most famous school and natural intellectual acuity. Süleyman, who had also been to the Lycée, knew for a fact that it was not necessarily the case. All you really needed were parents who were willing and able to pay the enormous fees. At least that was how it had been when he had attended the school and also, probably, when Levent Devrim had been there. But however clever or otherwise he had been, one thing was for sure: Devrim was no run-of-the-mill Tarlabaşı resident. What had brought such a person to such a place?

'I heard that Levent Bey liked to make films,' Süleyman said. 'Was that his job?'

Sugar smiled, idly and thoughtlessly fiddling with a nearby dildo as she said, 'Levent didn't work. I don't know what he lived on. The camera was a hobby. Just little bits of film of the kids in the street, the buildings and the market, you know. He thought he was Stephen Spielberg, I think, but . . .'

'Did anyone ever object to him filming their home or their children?'

'Not that I know of,' she said. 'He was just Levent Bey, you know? A bit strange, spoke a bit posh – bit like you, as it goes – wore clothes even the Roma beggars wouldn't touch . . .'

'He didn't care about his appearance?'

'It meant nothing to him!' Suddenly realising what she was doing with the dildo, Sugar threw it down. Süleyman saw a rat scamper past where the sex toy had landed. His hostess appeared completely oblivious. 'Levent didn't want or need nice clothes, just like he didn't want or need nice food, drink or women.'

'So what, Sugar Hanım, did he need?'

Before she spoke, she paused, and then she said, 'You say he's dead, right?'

'I'm afraid so.'

She sighed. 'Levent liked a smoke, and I don't mean tobacco. Allah alone in His wisdom knows what brought him to Tarlabaşı in the first place, but I know what kept him here.'

'Cannabis.'

'I've never known such a massive pothead! Day and night! I don't think I can remember him straight in what has to be twenty-five years since I've known him.'

'He was young when he came here?'

'Yeah. But as I say, I don't know *why* he came. That's one of the great things about this place: no one asks you where you've been, where you're going or what you do. It's the end of the line, or it was until they started knocking it down.'

'Do you know who his dealer was?'

She shrugged. 'Pick any kid on a street corner,' she said. 'Drugs were never my thing. I spent time with Levent, but I never smoked with him.'

'What *did* you do with him?'

Sugar looked at the very handsome man sitting in her house and she said, 'We talked, and sometimes, yes, I fucked him. When we first met, I didn't look like this and he was a nice-looking young man. He didn't treat me like shit and I could talk to him, which was nice.' She leaned forward, her shoulders straining as they pushed down against her enormous bosoms. 'I told you that Levent was clever, but I'm no slouch myself. I finished high school, even if it was in the back of beyond.'

17

'Where?'

She named some town he didn't recognise, which she told him was in the far eastern province of Van. Kurds often came from places no one else had ever been to except other Kurds.

'Then when I got sick, he looked after me,' Sugar continued. 'In 2003 I got diabetes. Speak to people here and they'll tell you that if Levent Bey hadn't looked after me, I would have been dead. He took me to hospital, wouldn't leave me until they'd found out what was wrong with me.' For the first time since she'd been told of Levent Devrim's death, Sugar's eyes filled with tears.

Süleyman let her have a moment to herself, and then he said, 'Did he have any enemies?'

'No.' She wiped a couple of tears away from her eyes with the sleeve of her holey cardigan. 'Or rather, not that I know of. Maybe one or other of the dealers had a grudge because he couldn't pay for his smoke, but I never heard anything like that.' She shook her head. 'He was always kind and polite, he never robbed anyone, never slept with anyone's wife, never lost his temper . . . Oh, except for once, but that was years ago.'

'It must have been significant for you to remember it,' Süleyman said. 'Who did he lose his temper with?'

'I don't know. A man, about sixty I suppose, came to see him one day at his flat. I didn't recognise him and he wasn't from round here. I'd baked Levent Bey some börek, which he always loved, and I was taking it round as the man was leaving. Levent was like a lunatic, shouting at the man to fuck off and leave him alone. The man didn't reply; he just went.'

'Did you ask Levent Bey who the man was?'

'He pre-empted me,' she said. 'Took the börek from my hands, told *me* to fuck off and then I didn't see him for days. When he did finally surface he was his old self again and so I never asked. But the man was well dressed. It has to be twenty years ago now. I wondered whether he was Levent's father.'

'Did they look alike?'

She thought for a moment, and then she said, 'I don't remember. Maybe? Maybe not? I've seen a lot of men in my life, Inspector; a point comes when they all start to look the same.' But then, fearing that she might have offended him, she added, 'Present company excepted, of course.'

He smiled. In spite of her large size, and her age, he imagined that Sugar had been quite a looker and a charmer in her youth. He might even have paid for her services himself back in her heyday. He'd always been turned on by amusing women, even if they were streetwalkers. In fact, some of the best sex and the most fun he'd ever had with women had been with prostitutes. Briefly his thoughts turned towards Ayşe Farsakoğlu and the empty sex he'd had with her that morning. Her eagerness was beginning to repel him.

'Have you been to his flat yet?'

He looked up at her and said, 'No.'

'Well, I've a key if you want to use it,' she said. 'Save you kicking the door in.' She hugged herself against the cold that, in spite of the hissing soba in the corner of her shop, wound its way around legs and up into fingers, chests and faces.

'That would be very useful.'

'OK.' She stood up and walked over to a shelf that held fur-covered handcuffs and a bowl decorated with the image of a woman giving a man oral sex. She took a large black key out of the bowl and handed it to him. 'Whatever you find in there will be interesting,' she said. 'But it won't necessarily be pretty, and I won't be able to tell you what it means.'

* * *

19

The way the Tarlabaşı kids behaved was familiar to Ömer Mungan. Even in the snow they still begged, hassled and dogged the steps of every outsider they could find – just like the poor kids in Mardin.

'You're a policeman. You have a gun. Let me see your gun,' one hoarse-voiced young Roma kid begged.

Ömer walked on in spite of the children; he knew better than to react.

'You have money. I'm poor, give me money for food. Allah will bless you!'

'Please, brother, a few kuruş.'

Then a tug at one of his sleeves. 'You see how cold it is? I have no shoes!'

Briefly he looked and saw that the child did have shoes. Inadequate and probably leaking, but he was far from barefoot.

'You have shoes,' Ömer said.

The child looked up at him with big brown eyes. 'Do you have no heart, policeman bey?'

Ömer didn't answer. Sure he had a heart, but he employed it sparingly. Walking to meet up with Süleyman, who was now apparently inside the dead man's apartment, he was also trying to get out of his mind the vision of how Levent Devrim's head had looked when the orderlies from the mortuary had put him on a stretcher. For a moment the wound in his neck had stretched and opened, and Ömer had feared that his head might fall off. Dr Sarkissian, seeing the look of horror on his face, had assured him that it would not, and he had been proved right, but it had been an uncomfortable moment. Another one to add to all the others.

When the kids finally gave up on him and Ömer was alone, he allowed himself the luxury of morbid thought. There was no getting away from it: in spite of being lucky enough to have a sister living in İstanbul who he could talk to, Ömer was lonely and homesick. He'd known everyone in Mardin – Turk, Kurd, Syriani, Christian, Muslim, fire-worshipper. He'd even known some of the Turkish troops stationed in the city. Everyone had known his name and he'd known theirs. He'd also known a bit and sometimes a lot about the people. He had understood them.

But here in İstanbul, he was lost. In İstanbul there was not just the odd eccentric or aggressive person to deal with; there were thousands of them. What was more, he didn't know them or their families and so he was completely incapable of predicting their possible behaviour. But then that went for his new boss, Mehmet Süleyman, too. A good-looking, arrogant, clever but also sad man, he felt. Ömer had caught whispers around the station that Süleyman had fallen out with his last sergeant over a woman. He'd overheard one constable say that the woman was Ayşe Farsakoğlu, Inspector İkmen's sergeant. But that could merely be gossip.

It hadn't just been ambition that had brought Ömer Mungan to İstanbul, although that was certainly part of his motivation. Mainly it had been about money. Like his sister, the higher wages in the city had not only attracted him but had been necessary to help retain his ageing parents' big house in Mardin. Now that his father had arthritis and couldn't work any more, it was up to the Mungan children to secure the family home and, if necessary, pay for their parents' medical treatment too.

When Ömer had flinched as the dead man's head had looked as if it might fall off, Inspector İkmen had put a reassuring hand on his shoulder. He was a nice man, old – he was retiring at the end of the year – but easier to approach than Süleyman. Sometimes speaking to his boss if he was agitated or upset was hazardous. First there would be a dark glower, a look of disdain, and then, if he was lucky, a barked-out order. If he wasn't lucky he'd be treated like a servant, sometimes for painfully protracted amounts of time. As he walked towards the address Süleyman had sent him on his phone, he hoped that this day would be a good one.

Some people lived in a state of ordered minimalism, some in complete chaos, and some – a few – in a fantasy world. Süleyman had seen one or two of the latter over the years, but never one as extreme as Levent Devrim. Ömer Mungan arrived to join him and together, for a moment, they looked around the apartment, saying nothing. After about a minute of this, Ömer said, 'Did he work with numbers, do you know, sir?'

'He worked with nothing, unless you count an old camera,' Süleyman said. 'He was unemployed.'

'So what is all this about?'

They both looked at what to them was just an endless succession of numbers. Pencilled on walls, scratched into the surfaces of ancient chests of drawers, painted on the ceiling and on probably thousands of pieces of paper scattered all over the tiny apartment, even in the bathroom and kitchen. Many were expressed in the form of equations, and neither Süleyman nor his deputy had the slightest idea what they were meant to be solving – if anything.

'He lived here alone, sir?' Ömer asked.

'Completely.'

'Did he have visitors?'

'I've been told rarely,' Süleyman said.

'Do you think he might have been one of those mathematical geniuses you hear about sometimes, a sort of . . . I don't know what you'd call it . . .'

'Savant.' Süleyman shrugged. 'I don't know.'

Süleyman walked over to one of the pencil-scarred walls and said, 'What on earth was he trying to work out?' He turned to look at Ömer. 'It's times like this I wish I'd paid more attention in mathematics classes at school. Do you . . .'

'No, sir, sorry,' the younger man said. 'History and Turkish, yes, some English . . .'

'Doesn't matter.' Süleyman waved a hand. 'It's easily organised.'

Ömer made a point of looking at things in the room that were not equations. There was some thin bedding, a few clothes, a plate, a tea glass, some blank sheets of paper and several pairs of slippers. On top of a short row of what looked like leather-bound books was a large movie camera.

Süleyman's phone rang. 'Hello, Doctor,' he said, 'what have you got for me?'

While Süleyman talked to the pathologist, Ömer Mungan looked closely at the camera. On the case was one word, *Zeiss*. A book underneath the camera was called *The Homeopathic Bible* and was written in English.

'Thank you, Doctor,' Süleyman said. He ended the call and turned to Ömer. 'Levent Devrim was killed by a straight-edged blade – a cleaver or a machete. The doctor thinks the murderer was either disturbed before he could remove the head completely or he lost the stomach for the job. There are also small wood fragments in the wound that were inserted post-mortem.'

Ömer shrugged. 'By the gypsy? Why?'

'Şukru Şekeroğlu? Why would he do something like that?'

'To see if he was dead?'

Süleyman shook his head. Şukru Şekeroğlu might be a man he didn't like, but he was neither mindless nor a fool. 'No.'

'So . . .'

'So who might disturb a dead body and not call us? Who

might even have seen something that could prove significant? A street urchin? A madman? A drug addict?'

'That's a wide field in this area,' Ömer said. 'Doctor say anything else, sir?'

'Devrim had some furring of the cardiac arteries.'

'A heart condition.'

'In its early stages.' Süleyman turned back to look at the equations on the walls. 'We had better leave here soon and return to the streets.'

Chapter 3

The water was ice cold, so in no way did it soothe her as the hot shower had done. But it closed the pores of her skin, which prevented both breakouts and the ingress of infection. It was also a punishment.

Although intellectually Leyla knew that her vast family wouldn't even exist were it not for lust-filled men and sexually ambitious women, she knew that what she'd just done had been wrong. She had a husband; why did she need to take someone else's too? But then she knew the answer to that question. She looked down at her beautiful body, floating naked on top of the water, and was pleased with what she saw. No man, unless he was gay, could resist her charms, even at her age. But simply contemplating her actual years, as opposed to the ones she admitted to others, depressed her. As if blocking out the truth, she closed her eyes.

Ageing was horrible. On the rare occasions when her husband undressed in front of her, it was like watching an ancient snake shed its skin. She tried to focus on the sex she'd just enjoyed with someone else, and to anticipate, possibly, more sex to come that night, but she couldn't. Suddenly she repelled herself, and with her eyes still closed, she turned over in the water, exposing her breasts to the sharp bite of the cold water in the pool. Shocked at the frigidity on her nipples, she turned quickly on to her back again and tipped her head lightly backwards.

Was it self-indulgent to consider how people would feel should she drown in the plunge pool? Leyla wondered. She decided that it probably was. Besides, if she died, especially in such erotically charged circumstances, her husband's enemies would enjoy it all too much. They'd talk about 'the traitor' and his 'immoral' wife, and how she'd probably killed herself because she couldn't take being married to such a person any longer. Then they'd go on about how she'd finally seen the light of religion, which had left her no choice but to commit suicide. Leyla shook her head. No, that would never do! She might not want her husband sexually any more, but she would never tire, for as long as he had it, of his exalted position in life or of his money.

With her eyes still closed, Leyla heard one of the patio doors that surrounded the pool open, and her thoughts immediately jumped to other things. More pleasure. She straightened her neck and swished her hair through the water. Then she smiled.

The equations meant nothing. Colleagues versed in the ways of mathematics told him so, as did a professor of mathematics from İstanbul University. Levent Devrim's only living blood relative, his brother, Selçuk, confirmed what had already been said when he finally arrived at police headquarters almost four weeks later, just as the snow was beginning to melt. He'd been in Russia, supervising the cabling of some Siberian city on the edge of nowhere, and had been snowed in.

Five years younger than Levent, Selçuk Devrim was a smart, well-spoken man who worked in the booming Turkish telecommunications industry. There was also, Süleyman felt, something familiar about him. Like Levent, he had been to the same school as Mehmet Süleyman, but was too old to have still been at the Lycée when the policeman joined.

'He was mad,' Selçuk Devrim said simply. 'Delusional. Thought he could do all sorts of things that he couldn't.'

'Like mathematics?'

'Yes.'

'And film work?'

Selçuk Devrim rolled his small blue eyes. It had been quickly established that there was not and had never been any film in Levent's old Zeiss Super 8 camera.

'My father went to his grave in despair.'

'Over Levent?'

Selçuk looked out of the window at the frigid grey sky outside. Even in this weather, his dead brother had been kept in a freezer. 'He got to eighteen quite normally, and then he went mad,' he said.

'In what way?' Süleyman asked.

'Every way. Promiscuous behaviour, bizarre beliefs in nonsensical theories, the mathematical rubbish . . .'

'Do you have any idea what your brother thought he might be calculating, Mr Devrim?'

'Nonsense.'

'Like?'

He breathed out and shook his head. 'Can't say I really know, except that it was something to do with astrology. He believed in all that Aries, Pisces rubbish. I can't tell you anything more than that. My brother was big on destiny.'

'His own, I take it.'

'Inasmuch as he felt he had one, yes. I saw him once or twice going into some of the trendy bookshops on İstiklal Caddesi that peddle New Age rubbish. Such nonsense! Personally I think that life is just what you make it yourself.'

There were echoes in Selçuk Devrim's description of his brother of fatalistic, possibly Islamic thought. 'Was your brother religious?' Süleyman asked.

'What, with Gemini and Sagittarius on his mind? I don't think so. No, it was all sort of hippy cod-philosophy with him. Why do you think he left the nice comfortable home my parents provided for him and went to live in that shithole?'

'Tarlabaşı?'

'Inspector, if you ever find a place more tightly packed with nutcases, thieves, charlatans, prostitutes and drug addicts, I'd like to know so that I can avoid it. I visited him there a few times. Once, when my father had just begged him to come home and Levent had abused him, I went there to give him a piece of my mind. When I turned up, though, he was off his head on I don't know what, curled up in the arms of some ancient tart, and so I left. What was the point of talking to him in that state?' He shook his head. 'On the other hand . . .' He looked up, and Süleyman noticed for the first time just how grey his face was. 'Levent, to my knowledge, never hurt anyone. He was a gentle soul and I would have taken him into my home, much as my wife would have hated it, had he ever asked. He was my brother, and I loved him.'

'Did no one ever think of getting him psychiatric help?'

'Oh, we thought of it, but my mother wouldn't have it,' he said. 'She had a bit of a thing about psychiatrists, mainly because her father had been put in an institution when she was a child. No, Inspector, Levent was "eccentric", according to my parents, and only that.'

'You can't think of anyone who would have wanted to hurt your brother?'

Selçuk Devrim's eyes glittered, then tears trickled down his cheeks. But he didn't sob. 'I don't know who he mixed with in that awful place, who he took drugs from or with. All I saw was that old woman he was—'

Sugar. 'We've spoken to the lady I think you refer to,' Süleyman said. 'She was very close to Levent, and in fact it was . . .' he consulted his notes to find Sugar's real name, 'Miss Barışık who gave us the key to your brother's flat. We found a sum of money underneath the bed in a tin box, just under three hundred lira. There was also a bank card . . .'

'Yes, Akbank.' He wiped his cheeks with the back of his hand. 'Our father used to put five hundred lira into his account every month.'

'In spite of their row?'

'He loved him, he was his son. One of the things I had to do when Father died was make sure that what little money he had left went to Levent. Then when that ran out, I paid it.'

'So that was your money?'

'Yes. As you probably know by now, Levent had a heart condition, which complicated matters still further. How could I leave him without money? What if he fell sick? It wasn't as if I couldn't afford it. I earn well. And in spite of the money I gave to Levent, my wife still managed to give up work last year. Money isn't an issue.'

'Did your brother know that you were funding him?'

'He knew that Father had died. Allah alone knows where he thought the money was coming from.'

'And yet your father bought him what I am told was, in its day, a very fine camera. And you both attended Galatasaray Lycée.'

Selçuk Devrim smiled. 'Oh Inspector,' he said, 'what can I or any of us say about the impoverished former elites in this country, eh? My father bought expensive cameras and didn't buy a house. He was a silly, silly old man who lived in the past.'

And then Süleyman knew exactly why Selçuk Devrim had seemed familiar.

That no one in Tarlabaşı admitted to having seen anyone or anything unusual or suspicious either before or after Levent

Devrim's death was not wholly unexpected. Ömer Mungan knew that in general the police were not welcome in the district and people limited contact with them as far as they could. However, most locals admitted to at least some affection for Levent Devrim, which meant that they probably did care about whether his killer was caught or not. But nothing was forthcoming, and the heavy snowfall on the night of his death had covered any footprints that might once have existed. Forensic evidence was scant. A hair on Devrim's shirt that was not his own had turned out to belong to Sugar Barışık.

As was his apparent custom, Devrim had been stoned when he died. He'd also had a small quantity of rakı in his system. There had been no alcohol, or even any empty bottles in his flat, and Sugar Barışık had stated that she hadn't given him any. She hadn't seen him the night he'd died at all. Where had he got the rakı from?

As Ömer walked the streets of Tarlabaşı, he wondered how a man could have been almost decapitated and no one know about it. While he was still capable of doing so, Devrim must have howled in pain or fear – probably both. He hadn't been *that* stoned. Dr Sarkissian had stated in his report that the victim had soiled himself before he died and so had been clearly very afraid. Ömer felt rather than saw hostile eyes on his back. The woman at his side, apparently oblivious to the eyes, said, 'I don't get it. Why are they knocking this place down again?'

Peri was Ömer's older sister. She'd come to İstanbul three years before to work as a nurse in the German Hospital in Taksim. Like her brother, she was multilingual in the languages of the far south-east, and they conversed, as they usually did when they were alone, in Aramaic, the tongue they had grown up speaking.

'The government want to develop the area,' Ömer said. 'Knock down unviable buildings and replace them with family homes.'

'Mmm.' Peri frowned. 'Nice homes for "nice" people.'

'The current residents will be relocated.'

Peri looked at a very tall man dressed in a woman's fur coat smoking a joint on a broken doorstep. 'Like him? Where's he going to find work away from the clubs of Beyoğlu?' She shook her head. 'When they moved the gypsies out of Sulukule to make way for "nice" families, they relocated them so far outside the city they couldn't afford to commute, and so most of them came back into the city centre to live in squats. There's nothing for anyone to do out on those new housing estates. No work.'

'I know,' Ömer said. 'But what can you do?'

Peri pulled her coat tightly around her body and said nothing.

'This murder hasn't helped.'

'You think?' Peri shook her head. 'Ömer, you have to get out of the habit of stating the obvious. This is İstanbul; we know. We're quick.'

He ignored her slight. 'Nobody's actually said anything, but there have been plenty of implications, particularly from the gypsies.'

'That Mr Devrim may have been killed by shadowy agents of progress?'

'Yes.'

'You can see their point.' She looked in the window of a tiny basement shop entirely filled with screwdrivers slung in at every conceivable angle. To Peri and her brother, Tarlabaşı was very familiar territory. Very Mardin. 'The people here are happy in what some may consider their poverty. If you're a transsexual or a gypsy or a recent immigrant, you can live here unmolested by those who might think you immoral, and that's worth something.'

'Yeah, but don't romanticise it too much. Drug dealers and gangsters live here too.'

31

'True.'

'Where you from?'

A small girl, her hair tied up in thick brown bunches, spoke to them in perfect Aramaic. Without even noticing, they'd found themselves in the vicinity of the Syriani church of St Mary the Virgin. And because it was Sunday and they had just been to church, all the Syrian Christian children looked especially, neat, clean and smart.

Peri smiled. 'We're from the city of Mardin,' she said. 'Where are you from?'

'Here.' The girl sucked her thumb.

'That's nice.'

She pointed at Ömer. 'Is he your husband?'

They both laughed. Angular and tall, Peri was almost the image of her brother.

'She's my sister,' Ömer said.

'I'm a Christian,' said the child. 'What are you?'

And it was then that Ömer and Peri became aware of the difference they knew their ID cards belied. Even in rackety, multicultural Tarlabaşı, suddenly they felt very alien.

Chapter 4

There were worse jobs than pandering to the health and beauty fancies of the rich. In the past, Esin Nadir had waited at tables and even worked in the hotel's kitchens. Now all she was doing was placing hot stones on rich women's backs and stomachs, repeating parrot-style what Faruk Bey had told her about chakras. There was nothing on chakras in the Koran; it was apparently some Hindu thing and so they couldn't really exist. But while rich women paid a hundred dollars an hour to have them aligned, who was Esin to argue?

Another day at the Great Palace Hotel's Wellness Spa dawned. Esin turned all the lights on and made sure there were plenty of towels and robes for the customers, and that the aromatherapy jars were topped up with essential oils. Faruk Bey the chief masseur and director of the spa, would be in soon, and he was a stickler for detail. She'd have to turn the steam on in the steam room, top up the magazines in the waiting area and make sure that the plunge pool was clean before he arrived.

Esin put the steam on and then went to the broom cupboard to pick up a mop and a net. The plunge pool, an ice-cold artificial pond used for closing the pores after they had been opened by either the sauna or the steam room, often needed skimming for flakes of dead skin and hair. The tiles around it also needed mopping frequently, even when the pool hadn't been in use. Unmopped, they looked dull and could appear grubby. She opened the door to the pool room and smiled as the thin February sunlight haemorrhaged through the curved glass patio doors that made up three quarters of the wall space. At this time of year the pool was not terribly inviting, but in the height of summer there were few places better to be, and Esin had been known to get into the pool after work almost every day in July and August. She rested the mop against the door – she'd wash down the tiles once she'd finished everything else – and moved towards the pool with the net. Then she stopped.

Originally from the rough city-wall district of Edirnekapı, Esin was no stranger to tragedy and violence, but when she saw that body floating in the pool surrounded by a cloud of its own blood, she couldn't stop herself screaming.

Çetin İkmen watched Arto Sarkissian, together with two of his orderlies, lift the woman's naked body out of the pool and place it on a plastic sheet they had spread on the tiles. Standing in the open patio doors, İkmen smoked while noting with a feeling of revulsion that the woman's breasts did not fall down flat as they laid her on her back. Implants beneath the breast tissue showed themselves for what they were: oval bags with distinct edges. He wondered how old the almost waiflike figure in front of him might be, and decided that there was probably no way that he could know.

The pathologist hunkered down on his knees and put a gloved hand up to the woman's throat. Before anything else could happen, he had to declare life extinct, which he now did. He then began a slow visual examination of the body while directing the police photographer to record every aspect of the subject in minute detail. After watching him for almost ten minutes, İkmen said, 'Any idea about age, Doctor?'

There was a pause before the Armenian said, 'Forties or fifties, but well maintained, I'd say. A lot of work on the face, particularly around the chin.'

'So well off?'

'Or rich husband or boyfriend.'

Ayşe Farsakoğlu, who was standing beside İkmen, said, 'Doctor, the blood . . .'

Still looking down at the corpse, he said, 'There's a wound to the forehead. I think that's the source. Or rather, it's a possible source.'

Esin Nadir had completely bypassed her superiors at the Great Palace and called the police as soon as she'd seen the dead woman floating in the plunge pool. When Ayşe Farsakoğlu had briefly interviewed her, she'd said she knew the woman by sight but didn't remember her name. All she knew was that she was a client rather than a member of staff.

Arto Sarkissian rose heavily to his feet and instructed his orderlies to turn the corpse over.

'My rough guess, and it is rough, is that she's probably been in the water at the most five hours,' he said.

'So she died today.'

'In the early hours of this morning.' The doctor lowered himself down again with a grunt and began looking closely at the woman's back.

İkmen turned to his sergeant. 'Who has keys to this place?'

She consulted her notebook. 'The therapists, Esin Nadir—'

'Who found the body.'

'Faruk Genç, who is also the manager, Maryam Eminoğlu, who runs fitness classes, a British aromatherapist and homeopath called Suzy Greenwood and the hotel security guard, Bülent Eğe. Greenwood and Genç are already here.'

'Good. We'll need statements from all key-holders.'

'Sir.'

İkmen looked back towards the pool. 'So, Doctor, accident, suicide or—'

The Armenian held up a hand, which İkmen knew of old was his cue to fall silent. Several minutes passed during which the inspector had another cigarette and Ayşe Farsakoğlu looked with some admiration at the hotel's grounds. When she was a child, this part of old Sultanahmet had been the almost exclusive preserve of drug addicts and backpackers on what had remained of the old hippy route to Kathmandu. The Great Palace, if she recalled correctly, had been an old fleapit boarding house called the Hotel Stay. The spa had been a hamam which must have been derelict for twenty years before the owners of the Great Palace converted it. Now equipped not just with the spa, but a gourmet restaurant and Wi-Fi too, the place was one of the chicest venues in town. How long it would retain its good reputation when word got out about a dead body in the plunge pool, Ayşe didn't know. It probably depended on the circumstances of the death, whether it was accident, suicide or . . .

'Murder,' the Armenian said. He looked up into Çetin İkmen's eyes. 'Possibly. I may be wrong, but she's got heavy bruising on the back of her neck which I think may well have happened as a result of her head being smashed down forcefully on a hard surface.'

'Like tiles.'

'Like tiles, yes,' he said. He stood up slowly. 'No guarantees until I get her on the table, but I don't think your journey has been wasted this morning, Inspector.'

Sometimes İkmen's fluency in the English language could work against him. This was one of those times. Suzy Greenwood, the hotel's resident homeopath and aromatherapist, didn't speak much Turkish, and so it was only sensible that he should interview her. However, although he wanted to hear her evidence, if she had any, he didn't want to hear about her job, which he regarded, along with religion, as nonsense. He therefore went into his interview with her somewhat tentatively.

It was quickly established that Suzy, a woman in her mid forties, hadn't been at work for a week because she'd been on holiday.

'I went to Greece,' she said. 'You can check my passport.'

He did. She wasn't lying.

'I went to a homeopathy conference in Kavala,' she said. She looked İkmen up and down. 'I smell you are a smoker, Inspector; you know that I could help you with that.'

'Could you.' In retrospect, he should just have cut her off there, but Suzy Greenwood took his response as an invitation to climb aboard her hobby horse and ride it for all it was worth. A deluge of 'facts' followed – to İkmen entirely lacking in any sort of scientific veracity that he could recognise. Apparently the key to his smoking cessation lay in the idea that water, somehow, had a 'memory'. He'd never viewed water as a sentient being before and he wasn't sure that he did so now. Sadly for Suzy, her words just served to enhance the prejudices İkmen already had against homeopathy.

'Inspector!'

Mercifully, Ayşe Farsakoğlu had come into the small conference room the hotel had given him to interview staff.

'Excuse me, Miss Greenwood,' İkmen said with a smile. 'Sergeant Farsakoğlu?'

'Sir, I think you need to hear something,' she said.

'OK.' He looked at the Englishwoman and extended his hand. 'Well, thank you very much for your assistance, Miss Greenwood,' he said. 'I don't think we will need to speak to you again, but of course I will contact you if anything changes.'

She smiled. 'Of course.' And then as he began to leave with Ayşe Farsakoğlu she added, 'And don't forget I'm always here if you need a consultation.'

'Thank you.'

Ayşe led İkmen along a corridor back towards the spa. He said, 'Why are "alternative" people such damned hard work? That woman was like some sort of religious fanatic. And it was all rubbish.' His phone rang and he stopped and answered it. 'İkmen.'

He listened to the caller for a few moments while Ayşe stood in front of a door and watched him. When he finally ended the call he said, 'That was Dr Sarkissian. Our victim was murdered. He has confirmed it. He reckons her head was smashed against the bottom of the plunge pool.'

'It couldn't have been an accident?'

'No. Her neck was held and constricted while her forehead was forced down on to the pool floor.'

'So we're in business.'

'So it would seem.'

Ayşe opened the door of the spa manager's office, where İkmen saw a man of about forty sitting behind a very 'designed' glass desk.

'Sir, this is Faruk Genç.'

İkmen tipped his head. 'Mr Genç.'

'This is my superior, Inspector İkmen,' Ayşe said to the spa manager.

After over forty years in the İstanbul police force, İkmen knew a worried expression when he saw one, and Faruk Genç had one all over his face.

'Please, do sit down, Inspector,' he said.

İkmen sat.

'Could you tell Inspector İkmen what you told me?' Ayşe said.

Genç sighed. 'I know the dead woman. I wondered what had happened when I saw that her car was still here this morning.'

'What's her name?' İkmen asked.

'She's called Leyla Ablak,' he said. 'You'll find her clothes and ID card, car keys, handbag in one of our lockers. I have a master key.' He looked down at his blank glass desktop.

'How did you know Leyla Ablak?' İkmen asked. Out of the corner of his eye he saw Ayşe raise an eyebrow.

Faruk Genç did not look up. 'She was a client and, er, we'd been having an affair for almost a year,' he said. 'She's, er, Leyla was married, and so am I.'

To say that İkmen was shocked by Genç's candour would have been an overstatement. But he was surprised. Men who were unfaithful to their wives didn't usually own up to their infidelity so readily. But then death had become involved here, and Mr Genç, sensibly, probably wanted to get his story out before anyone else did.

'Were you here with her last night?' İkmen asked. There was little point in minutely investigating their relationship until he had established where Genç had been when Ablak died.

'Yes,' he said. 'The spa closes at seven. We met at midnight. I gave her a massage, she liked that.'

'Did you also make love?'

He looked up. 'Of course.'

'So how did she end up dead in your plunge pool, Mr Genç?'

'I don't know.' He put his head down again. 'When I left her, she was alive.'

'In the plunge pool?'

'No, in the shower.'

'You left before her?'

'Well we couldn't leave together. We might have been seen. We always met late as it was, in the hope that most people would be in bed around here, especially at this time of year.'

Those bars and nightclubs that did exist in Sultanahmet were quiet during the winter months and tended to close early.

39

'But you manage this spa, Mr Genç,' İkmen said. 'Why did you leave Mrs Ablak here alone?'

He sighed again. 'She had a key. I gave it to her. Sometimes she would be able to get away before me. The key enabled her to let herself in and wait for me. Last night I had to get home. I left Leyla to have her shower and then jump in the plunge pool. That was her routine. She did it to close her pores. We were . . . I cared for her, you know. I would never have done anything to hurt her.'

'Mmm.' İkmen put his chin in his hand. Genç didn't really give the impression that he was particularly heartbroken by Leyla Ablak's death. There were no tears in his eyes. 'You say you had to get home, Mr Genç. Why was that?'

'My wife called. She has cancer, Inspector. I know it sounds bad.'

The small office became silent for a moment, and then İkmen said, 'So tell me, Mr Genç, how did you manage to get away from your very sick wife to come here and have sex with Mrs Ablak?'

He loosened his tie. 'Well, er, Hande, that's my wife, she . . . we sleep separately now and she goes to bed early. She, um, she takes a lot of pain medication. If she wakes and she needs more in the night, she calls my mobile phone and I go and give it to her. We keep our phones by our beds.'

'Yes, but you weren't at home, were you, you were—'

'Hande knows that I have friends and she is aware that I have to see them sometimes. I . . . I told her I was out. She knew I'd be a little time.'

'In pain,' İkmen said. 'She knew you'd be a little time while she was in pain.' Again the small office became silent around İkmen's anger, and then he said. 'Well, Mr Genç, I will need the clothes that you were wearing when you came here last night, plus a sample of saliva for DNA testing. As you had sex with Mrs Ablak, I will also want semen. There may be some residual seminal fluid inside her body we can compare it to. I will also need to speak to your wife.'

'My wife?'

'In order to discover when she called you and what time you subsequently arrived home.'

Faruk Genç jumped up from his chair and began to walk backwards and forwards very quickly behind his desk. 'Can't I just bring you her phone?' he said. 'She's very sick.'

'No, her phone won't do,' İkmen said. 'It may tell us when she called you, but it won't tell us when you got home.'

'Yes, but I can work that—'

'No, sir, we need to be precise,' İkmen said. 'Our doctor will determine a time of death for Mrs Ablak, and in order to eliminate you from our investigation, we will need some proof that you left here before that time. We will have to speak to your wife.'

Ayşe Farsakoğlu regarded the expression on İkmen's face and detected in it something she could only describe as satisfaction. A weak man, who might or might not be a murderer, had done a bad thing and been caught out in it. And now İkmen was making him pay.

It was midday by the time the news broke about the death of Leyla Ablak. And although the dead woman's name was not released to the press, Inspector Mehmet Süleyman's mother, Nur, knew exactly who the victim was.

'She is your Great-Uncle Hüseyin's granddaughter!' she said as she told her son all the details with breathless excitement. 'Leyla İpek, that was her name before she married Osman Ablak. You know the elderly man she married after she divorced that American. Of course General Osman Bey is very wealthy – in property, her mother told me. She wasn't pleased about it, though, because Osman Bey is no one. And now with this scandal . . .'

Süleyman had just come out of one of the few places that the late Levent Devrim had definitely frequented socially, the Ada bistro and bookstore on İstiklal Caddesi, when his mother had called him. According to staff at the Ada, the mysterious mathematician had spent most of his time reading, usually books about what they described as New Age subjects. This covered topics as diverse as yoga, homeopathy, spiritualism and conspiracy theories. He'd talked to other people, but only really when they spoke to him. No one had actually *known* Levent Devrim.

'I remember Hüseyin's brother, Great-Uncle Rafık,' Süleyman replied as he walked back down İstiklal towards the side street where he'd parked his car.

'A true prince, yes. He never worked.'

'He was creepy.'

'Mehmet! He was not!'

'But Leyla İpek—'

'Oh, Mehmet!' His mother clicked her tongue in aggravation. 'Leyla İpek! Hüseyin Efendi's last bayram, 1970, you remember! Leyla was quite the young lady then . . .'

'Yes, and I was a child,' Mehmet said. 'I remember an old man who looked like my grandfather, a younger man who gave me the creeps, and I remember sweets.'

'Well anyway, you must do something about it,' Nur Süleyman said.

'Do something about what?'

'About Leyla İpek. She's family, she's been found dead and you are a police officer.'

'Mother, I am not working on that case.'

'Well then you must tell your superiors that it has to be assigned to you.'

'It doesn't work like that.'

Infuriated, she put the phone down on him. Now that his father,

Muhammed, had drifted away into the further reaches of dementia, his mother spent all her time discussing her husband's imperial background with anyone who would listen. Mehmet's brother Murad had even found her doing it at Sirkeci railway station, accosting complete strangers at the Orient Restaurant. Now that a distant family member had died in mysterious circumstances, she was going to be abuzz. But Mehmet was still working the Devrim case and Çetin İkmen had already been assigned to this new incident.

Mehmet Süleyman turned left off İstiklal and on to Hamalbaşı Caddesi, where he'd left his car. Down the hill in front of him and across Tarlabaşı Bulvarı was the district of the same name, where Levent Devrim had once chosen to live. Why anyone who wasn't an immigrant, transsexual, Syriani or Roma would choose to settle in such a place, he couldn't imagine. As far as he could deduce, Devrim had had no sexual kinks that would have set him apart from the mainstream and he had been well educated and well brought up. But then he had been odd – eccentric, as his parents had apparently put it; more likely he had been mentally ill.

Faruk Genç's wife, Hande, had guessed that her husband had been seeing other women, even though she said she hadn't known who. When İkmen had asked her to corroborate her husband's story, she had done so. She'd never told Faruk about her suspicions, but then as she said to İkmen, 'He was happy thinking that he was saving my feelings, and I am a pragmatist. What can be wrong with that?' There had however been a light in her eyes that İkmen recognised as malice, and he wondered whether she had known more than she was letting on.

İkmen and Ayşe Farsakoğlu's meeting with Leyla Ablak's husband Osman did not go so smoothly. In his eighties, Osman Bey, a military man, was a veteran of the Korean War and of the 1974 Turco-Greek war over Cyprus. He was not a man easily persuaded that what he believed could in any way be wrong. And Osman Ablak, soldier and latterly successful businessman, did not believe that his wife would have been unfaithful to him.

'The truth, Inspector,' he told İkmen as he motioned for him to sit down opposite him, 'is that my wife had an arrangement with that spa. She could use it any time she liked and sometimes she liked to do so at night.'

'Sir—'

'General.'

'General, I know this is very difficult for you, but . . . Look, General, a man at the spa has admitted—'

'They're all queer in those places.' Osman Ablak waved away with one large hand the notion of straight men in spas. 'My wife was a woman of taste and refinement; she wouldn't have been attracted to some fruit.' He lit a cigarette but without offering one to either İkmen or Ayşe Farsakoğlu, to whom he hadn't even proffered a seat. 'Did you know that my wife was a member of the Imperial family?'

'No, I did not.'

'Yes, her grandfather was a prince. Now whatever you may think of them, that family did not rule this country and its empire for five hundred years without knowing a bit about human nature. Corrupt and appalling they may have been, but they were no fools. My wife would never have gone with a queer.' He looked at İkmen sitting and Ayşe standing with a challenging expression on his face. However, like Faruk Genç, General Ablak didn't cry over Leyla's death. Maybe, İkmen thought, Leyla Ablak wasn't a woman that anyone would cry over. He also wondered what, if any, relative she might have been to that other son of the Ottomans, Mehmet Süleyman.

'As I say, a member of staff at the spa has made a statement to the effect that he was sleeping with your wife—'

'Preposterous!'

'General,' Ayşe Farsakoğlu cut in, 'our pathologist is performing tests on your wife's body now. Once he has finished, whether your wife was having an affair or not will be proven. In the meantime, we have a man under investigation who tells us that he was having a relationship with her. What do you expect us to do? Ignore him?'

A bitterness and an anger that İkmen knew wasn't entirely the fault of this opinionated old general told him that Ayşe was tired and probably agitated too. She thought he didn't know about the resumption of her affair with Mehmet Süleyman and how deeply hurt she was by the way the Ottoman simply used her. But İkmen had known both of them for many years and had learned to read the signs a long time ago.

It took the general a few moments to gather his thoughts after her onslaught, time during which İkmen said, 'General, what my sergeant is saying is that we cannot afford to ignore any evidence, be it physical, word of mouth or whatever, in our hunt for your wife's killer. This is a dangerous person. He or she held your wife's neck with one hand whilst smashing her head against the bottom of the hotel's plunge pool. That's a very violent act. We need to catch this person before they do something like this again.'

General Ablak didn't move or make any sort of comment. For the first time since the officers had arrived he looked a little sad. Eventually he said, 'Well what about this, er, this man at the spa who says he . . . with her . . . Couldn't he have . . .'

'Killed her? We're in the process of investigating his story,' İkmen said. 'That gentleman is of course most definitely of interest to us. However, we also need to know about anyone who may have disliked or had some sort of grudge against your wife. Can you think of anyone who might have wanted to harm or even kill Mrs Ablak?'

The general looked İkmen straight in the eyes. 'Women can be very jealous of one another, Inspector, and my wife was a very wealthy, beautiful and fortunate woman.'

İkmen, who had been expecting him to elaborate on those words, waited in vain for clarification. Eventually he said, 'Do you have any particular woman in mind, General?'

Ablak waved a hand dismissively again. 'Leyla had a lot of friends who were not really friends. She played golf; there's a lot of rivalry in that game.'

'Do you play golf yourself, General?'

'No! Hateful game! No, we both belonged to the Kemer Golf and Country Club, which was where my wife played and where we would both sometimes go to meet friends for drinks. As you will have noticed, Inspector, there was a considerable age gap between myself and my wife, over twenty years, and so Leyla did a lot of things on her own. She also visited her family on her own.' He looked down.

İkmen said, 'Why was that? Didn't you get on with her family, General?'

For a moment he remained silent, and then he said, 'Her father was fine. Until he died last year I had a good relationship with him. But her mother and the rest of them?' He shook his head, then looked up again. 'I was never good enough, not for Princess Sezen.'

'That's her . . .'

'Mother. Good enough for her daughter to take my money but not good enough to be a member of that family. What can I say? If my wife was having the affair you claim she was, then why did either of us go through the hell that bunch of Imperial bastards put us through, eh?' He looked at Ayşe and said, 'I suppose you think I killed her, don't you?'

Caught off guard, Ayşe said, 'General, I can—'

'Oh, don't worry . . . Sergeant,' he said. 'If I were you, I'd suspect me too. After all, I could have been lying when I told you that I didn't know my wife was having an affair, couldn't I? And in view of my pending arrest . . .' He looked them both in the eyes; İkmen did not lower his gaze. Now at least that particular elephant in the room had been acknowledged: the fact of General Ablak's alleged involvement in Ergenekon, the plot to overthrow the government. İkmen should have raised it himself, but then it was probably irrelevant.

'General,' he said, 'your involvement, or not, in a possible plot to overthrow our current government is not something I have any interest in. All I want to know about is who killed your wife.'

In terms of door-to-door inquiries, searches and forensic investigation, the police had done Tarlabaşı to death. And yet Ömer Mungan still believed that there was more he could do. However because he felt comfortable in the area, where so many people spoke Aramaic, he was all too aware that he could just be deluding himself. Unlike his sister, Peri, he was homesick. This wasn't helped by the fact that his boss, Inspector Süleyman, appeared to want to keep him very much at arm's length. He didn't know why this was, although the gossip back at the station was that the inspector had become too close to previous sergeants, who, it was said, he believed had always let him down. Whether this was true or not Ömer didn't know, but as he sauntered past a small sex shop up by the Syriani church of St Mary the Virgin, his mind was not on his job but rather on how he might be able to get posted back to Mardin. In spite of wanting desperately to keep his parents in their old home, he knew that his father at least would be mortified if he knew how unhappy his son was.

'Hey, you!'

For a moment he didn't think the voice was anything to do with him. But then he felt a hand on his shoulder.

'You!'

He turned and found himself looking into a fat face he recognised as that of the old prostitute Sugar Barışık.

'Where's your boss?' she asked. She was wearing clothes that were hardly adequate for a cold February day, and her legs were bare.

'Inspector Süleyman?'

'Yeah. Where is he? Has he forgotten about Levent now that some woman's been killed?'

Ömer had heard that a woman's body had been found at a posh spa in Sultanahmet and that she had been murdered. But he didn't know anything else – except that Süleyman wasn't involved in that case.

'No,' he said, 'we're all still working really hard to find his killer. But so far . . .' He shrugged. 'No one saw or heard anything.'

She leaned in towards him. 'You need to threaten these bastards round here. Don't ask a gypsy nicely; he'll just laugh in your face, which is what they are doing. Come with me.'

She pulled him into her shop, which, Ömer noticed, smelt strongly of cats. She sat him down in a chair between her soba and an inflated rubber sex doll. Then she locked the shop door and lowered herself into her own chair, which was almost as large, battered and hairy as she was.

'Now look, son . . .'

'Sergeant Mungan.'

'Sergeant whatever,' she said with a wave of her hand. 'Listen, something's come to my ears lately and so I'm passing it on provided you never say to anyone that it came from me. OK?'

Ömer didn't like making promises that he probably couldn't keep, but what else did he have? Levent Devrim had been dead for over a month, and no information had been discovered that shed any light on who might have killed him. 'OK,' he said.

Even though the shop door was locked, Sugar looked around warily. Then she said, 'There's a family of gypsies live up by the Bulvarı. I don't know what their family name is, but the mother is called Şeftali, she's a prostitute. You can't miss her: she has a purple birthmark on her face the size of a shoe. She's got a little girl looks fleabitten all the time, but it's her eldest you need to talk to, a boy called Hamid.'

'Why?'

For a little while Ömer didn't think that she had heard him. He was just about to repeat his question when she said, 'Well let us say that maybe Şukru Şekeroğlu didn't find Levent's body first.'

'This kid did?'

Sugar Barışık held up her hands. 'Oh, I know nothing! But the child is a thief and a thug and he pimps his own mother – so it is said.'

'I can't bring him in for being a kid from a rough area, Sugar Hanım . . .'

'Ah, but you can bring him in for picking my pocket,' Sugar said.

'Picking your pocket? When?'

'About half an hour ago,' she said. 'In the market.'

'How do you know it was this Hamid?'

'Because I was in the market, he was there and then my purse was gone,' Sugar said. Then she leaned across her vast stomach and whispered, 'Look, kid, work with me here, will you? I saw the boy in the market. I'm giving you an excuse straight from heaven.'

Chapter 5

Leyla Ablak's mother, Sezen İpek, didn't cry, even though a group of family members who sat with her wailed incessantly. One of them İkmen recognised as Süleyman's mother, Nur Hanım.

'If it is any consolation, our pathologist is of the opinion that your daughter died instantly and without pain,' İkmen said. What he didn't say was that Leyla Ablak had struggled prior to her death and so must have had some notion about what was about to happen to her.

'What was she doing at the spa in the middle of the night?' Sezen İpek asked, more of herself than of İkmen. 'What?'

'Well, Sezen Hanım, if we could possibly talk alone . . .'

'Without my family? Impossible,' she said.

There were a lot of her family. In İkmen's experience, Ottoman dynasties related to the Imperial family were even more numerous than peasant clans out in the east. The large, shabby drawing room in the İpeks' crumbling Ortaköy yalı was crowded with people. All but one – a man who looked old enough to have remembered the last sultan – were women.

'Sezen Hanım, I have to insist,' İkmen said. 'Sergeant Farsakoğlu and myself . . .' He briefly caught sight of Nur Süleyman looking in his direction when he mentioned Farsakoğlu's name. Then he saw her look at his sergeant with pure hatred. He was well aware of the fact that she knew about

Ayşe and her son, and that she didn't approve. '. . . really need to speak to you in private.'

For a moment Sezen İpek looked outraged, and İkmen feared that she might just throw them both out of her house. Then she turned to a tiny woman sitting beside her and said, 'Get these people out of here, will you please, my dear sister. I appreciate their concern, but I have a headache coming on.'

The tiny woman didn't speak, but simply ushered the women and the ancient man one by one out of the room. As they left, they all carried on crying, and even when the door was closed behind them İkmen could still hear their wails coming from other parts of the house. When they'd gone, Sezen İpek looked at İkmen and said, 'Well?'

She was, İkmen reckoned, about seventy-five years old. Of medium height, she was slim and upright and she had a face that could frighten God. If Leyla Ablak had been brought up by this woman, then she had been either a frightened, shivering leaf of a woman or an Amazon. From what he knew of her so far, she had probably been the latter, which meant that Leyla and this woman must have had some terrible scenes. He got straight to the point. 'Sezen Hanım, did you know that your daughter was having an affair with the manager of the spa she attended at the Great Palace Hotel?'

Her face didn't change at all. 'Yes,' she said calmly. 'I did.'

'Do you know the gentleman?' İkmen asked.

'No, but I knew that Leyla was seeing a man rather younger than her husband.'

'And did you approve?'

'What could I do?'

'Did you tell her husband?'

She shrugged.

There was a silence, and then she laughed.

51

'Sezen Hanım?'

'That dry old stick! Ha! Do you know who Osman Ablak is, Inspector İkmen? He is the son of one of those people who sold our empire out and made this country into the rudderless mess it is today.'

The general's people had been republicans, followers of Atatürk.

'My daughter married him for his money. Even for that reason, I disapproved. But she was an adult, so what could I do?' She shook her head and for the first time looked as if she might be about to cry, but then she pulled herself together. 'Anyway, she spent his money on ridiculous things: t'ai chi retreats, spas, acupuncture – anything crazy, New Age and quackish that she could find. I know the general didn't approve of such things any more than I did, and he must have known that she was being unfaithful to him. At his age! My daughter was beautiful . . .' Her eyes brimmed.

'Your daughter had a lot of cosmetic surgery,' İkmen said. 'Which I assume the general paid for . . .'

'Of course he did! Where else would she have obtained the money for surgery! Why not from one of the people who took it all away from her family?' Now she began to cry. 'The only consolation I had was that she was taking his money while he was alive, so he could see it going.'

'Maybe making your daughter look nice made him happy?' İkmen said.

'No! No, it didn't make him happy, because she was unfaithful to him!'

'Maybe he didn't know that she was being unfaithful.'

'He did know!' she said. 'He did!'

'And how do you know that, Sezen Hanım?' İkmen said. 'Was it because, in spite of your almost-but-not-quite denial earlier, you really did tell him?'

She leaned towards him. 'So what if I did?'

'You may very well have put your daughter's life in danger,' İkmen said. 'Did you think of that?'

'I wanted him to hurt!' she shouted.

İkmen stood up and leaned down to shout right back at her. 'Well you may have hurt him so much that he killed her! Or not!' he added. 'But whatever he did or didn't do, you acted for reasons that make me want to be sick!'

When they eventually left the İpek family's yalı, İkmen said to Ayşe Farsakoğlu, 'You know, Sezen Hanım is the sort of person who makes me even more grateful to Atatürk for bringing the Ottoman Empire to an end. What an absolute—'

'Sir, I saw Inspector Süleyman's mother,' Ayşe said. 'I suppose . . . maybe they're related to the İpeks . . .'

'Oh, probably!' İkmen lit up a cigarette and got into his car. 'They're all related to each other; it's like one big miserable club for overprivileged malcontents who choose to live in a psychic museum of their own creation.'

Ayşe got in beside him. She couldn't think about Mehmet Süleyman, not now. Last time they'd been together he'd made her cry. 'So do you think her husband did know about Leyla's affair with Faruk Genç?'

İkmen shrugged. 'I think if he did, he behaved rather stupidly when he didn't tell us the truth,' he said. 'Knowing that we'd have to come and see the mother-in-law from hell.'

'What's he done this time?' In spite of the disfiguring birthmark on her face, which was enormous, Şeftali the gypsy was a good-looking woman. About thirty-five, she was tall, slender and had the kind of curly red hair that an art historian would no doubt have described as 'Titian'.

Ömer Mungan had taken two constables with him to visit the

53

three cramped rooms where the gypsy and her family lived just behind Tarlabaşı Bulvarı. Sugar's tip-off about Hamid, whether it came to anything or not, had been too tempting to pass up.

'We've had a complaint about pickpocketing,' Ömer said.

'What? Hamid?' She shrugged. There was a heap of ragged clothes lurking in a bowl of water at her feet. Şeftali crouched down to agitate them. As she rolled her sleeves up, Ömer saw the track marks up her arms and at her wrists. She'd been using for a long time. 'Who says he's been pocket-dipping?'

'Is he here?'

He wasn't. The two constables had already searched the place, such as it was. There was only one child present, a tiny girl standing in a corner looking at them with suspicious eyes.

'No, he isn't,' Şeftali said.

'Do you know where he is?'

She looked up at him. One of her eyes was completely surrounded by a dark bruise. 'No,' she said. 'Why would I?'

'You're his mother.'

She shrugged.

'He should be in school.'

Şeftali went back to her washing. 'He's Roma, why do you care?'

'Because it's the law.'

'It used to be lawful for us to live in Sulukule.' Şeftali stood up in one smooth movement. 'But then suddenly it wasn't lawful for us to be there any more and so we moved to this shithole. Now you're knocking this down and soon it won't be lawful for us to be here either. You Turks make it up as you go along! Don't talk to me about what I can and can't do with my kids. And anyway,' she added, 'what are you doing interesting yourself in some pocket diving? You're one of them who's been trying to find the killer of the old man with the camera. Still haven't found him, have you?'

'No.'

'Well then I suggest you stop going after my son and do that,' she said. 'You may think we're all scum round here, but we don't deserve to live in a place where people get their heads chopped off, do we?'

'No.'

'No. So do something about it, then.'

When he left, Ömer Mungan felt chastened by what Şeftali had said. The Roma did get a poor deal in the city, and what had he expected but hostility? Sugar Barışık's information about the boy Hamid had only been hearsay.

But what Ömer didn't know as he and his constables left Şeftali's tiny flat was that she was already on the phone to her son, telling him not to come home.

There were days when fate – or whatever one believed in – was clearly against one. General Ablak put his telephone back in its cradle, slowly. The call he'd just received had not come as any sort of surprise. Leyla's death, if not her infidelity, had been the biggest shock of the day. This, however, was not something that he could just ignore. He had Murad to consider, and the possible besmirching of his only son's good name. That could not be allowed to happen. Murad's mother had died thirty years before, and now that Leyla was dead too, there was only the boy, if a man of fifty-seven could be called a boy . . .

The call had come from someone who didn't identify himself, but then that was standard practice. All he'd said was 'They're coming for you,' because that was all he had needed to say. Who *they* were was something that the general knew anyway. As to *when* they were coming, it could be any minute, or the next day; maybe even the following week, although that was doubtful. If they were coming, they were coming soon. The

55

general walked over to his office door and locked it. His phone rang again, but this time he left it unanswered. When it stopped, he very calmly reviewed his options. If he went to court and was convicted – which he would be, because that was what happened in cases like his – then Murad would be dishonoured. His father would be a known traitor and his own career, not to mention his family, could suffer. Before that, though, there would be prison to contend with, and the general knew that for all his tough military training, he couldn't deal with that. Better men than he had succumbed to prison violence, heart disease or just despair in those places. General Ablak, proud follower of Atatürk, believer in modernity and the beauty of rational thought, sat back down at his desk and worked through in his mind what might be left for him to do.

His son had known what was going on right from the start and the general had said everything he had wanted to say to him. Murad knew that his father loved him. He believed and would continue to believe in his innocence. And now that there was no trophy wife left, there was no one else. A thought came to the general and he took a sheet of paper out of his desk drawer and picked up his Montblanc pen. It only took him five minutes to say everything he needed to say. He put the note into an envelope and addressed it, then laid it beside his telephone.

The general took a few moments to remove his mobile phone, his keys and his loose change from his pockets. He arranged them all neatly on his desk. Then he put his hand into his desk drawer again, took out his old service revolver and shot himself through the head.

'I thought the kid was just messing around,' Şukru Şekeroğlu said to Şeftali the prostitute. They were both in the small yard at the back of his house with her son, Hamid. Even though he was nearly sixty years old, Şukru wouldn't allow his aged father to see him with a woman like Şeftali. 'I assumed he was shaking because he was cold. If I'd known he'd seen someone when he came across Levent Bey's body, I would've had him speak to the police.'

Şeftali held her son by his collar. 'He didn't see someone, he saw some*thing*,' she said. 'Like a . . . a . . . What was it?' She shook the boy. 'What?'

'A monster,' the boy mumbled.

'A monster! Yes! It was a monster that he saw, and so of course he's going to be too frightened to tell the police or you. I had to beat it out of him. Crying at night like a baby because he thought the monster might come for him. I couldn't have it when I was trying to work.' The boy squirmed to try and get away from her and Şeftali smacked him on the head. 'And now today the police come round asking for him. They say they want him for pocket-dipping. But the copper who come was one of them working on Levent Bey's murder. So they know he knows something.'

'How do they know?' Şukru asked.

'I don't know! Maybe he's been telling people!' She agitated the boy hard again.

Şukru said, 'You're making assumptions.'

'So what if I am? He can't tell them he knows something after all this time; they'd beat him to death! You know how they are!'

Şukru got down on one knee and looked into the boy's face. 'Hamid,' he said, 'did you really see who killed Levent Bey?'

The boy looked at him for a moment with steady eyes, and then he said, 'Yeah.'

'And was what you saw a monster? Really?'

Şukru knew that some people in his community believed in

57

all sorts of supernatural beings up to and including monsters. But he didn't. He only believed in what he could see. 'Hamid?'

The boy broke his gaze and said, 'There were feathers, like a bird.'

Şukru felt cold. 'Where?'

'On its head, down its back.'

'What else?' Şukru asked. Suddenly he felt colder.

The boy shrugged.

'What?'

'Nothing,' he said.

Şukru said, 'Well it must've had a face, this monster of yours. And what size was it? Was it big, small . . .?'

'It was big . . . like, like tall big, but it never had a face,' Hamid said.

'It didn't have a face?'

'It was a monster, just like he said,' Şeftali said. 'You told my boy to leave Levent Bey's body and run away before the police come, but now he's in trouble because of it.'

'I didn't know that he had seen anyone, much less a "monster",' Şukru said. He stood up. 'The kid told me nothing. How do you know he didn't just make it all up, Şeftali Hanım? Eh?'

'Because the police come for him!'

'For picking pockets, which you and I both know he does,' Şukru said.

But Şeftali shook her head, her breath coming short and hard in the frigid February air. 'No, no, Şukru Bey, they know something, I know they do!'

'But if only you know . . .'

'Well, and the boy and . . . I might have told Fındık about it . . . His crying at night and . . .' She looked up into Şukru's face. Şeftali's best friend, Fındık, was a notorious drunk and gossip. Anyone in Tarlabaşı could know about the boy and his 'monster'. That wasn't good. Şukru suppressed an urge to hit her.

Instead he shook his head and then shrugged. 'So . . .'

'So you'll have to look after the boy until the police go away,' Şeftali said. 'You encouraged him to just get up and leave Levent Bey's body before the police came.'

'I didn't know about his "monster", did I?'

'No, but . . .'

'I can't look after your son; I've got kids of my own and I don't need the aggravation,' Şukru said.

'I'll pay you. You know, in . . .'

He curled his lip. 'No.'

'Oh, so what do you suggest we do, then, Şukru Bey?' Şeftali said, her hands on her hips. 'You told the boy to hop it, and now—'

'He hopped it without saying a word about what he might have seen!' Şukru said. 'I'd suggest you take him to the police yourself, Şeftali Hanım. Explain that the boy is having nightmares . . .'

'And what do I say about you, Şukru Bey?' she said. 'Do I tell them that you knew that my boy found Levent Bey's body before you did? That's withholding information, isn't it?'

Şukru Şekeroğlu looked at her beautiful ruined face and wondered what he should do with Şeftali the prostitute. Although illiterate and uncultured, she was in many ways like his artist sister, Gonca. Lovely and yet sly, Şeftali always had her eye on the main chance, just like Gonca. And in common with his sister, she knew how to manipulate men. Much as he loved her body from time to time, he hated her for that sly mind. But he also knew that her silence was essential to him.

'OK,' he said. 'How much to buy a small revision of history, then, Şeftali Hanım? I didn't see the boy; he came and went before I arrived.'

He watched her turn it over in her mind, and he resolved then and there that when all of this was over, he would first fuck her and then beat her until she couldn't stand, as a punishment.

She said, 'For a start, you can take him off me. Get him away from here so I can work. I don't need coppers on my doorstep; it puts people off.'

Şukru considered this for a while, and found that it actually wasn't such a bad idea.

Chapter 6

Mehmet Süleyman watched Çetin İkmen open up the envelope and then read the letter inside.

'What does it say?'

İkmen, seated at his office desk, perused the document for a few moments before he answered. Ayşe Farsakoğlu was out at lunch and so the two men were alone. 'Well, he asserts his innocence with regard to the accusation of treason that was levelled at him, and he also says that he didn't kill his wife either,' he said. He put the note that General Ablak had written down on his desk. 'One either believes that a man about to commit suicide cannot lie, or one does not. You know I telephoned him; it must have been just before he died.'

General Ablak's body had been found in his office the previous evening by his son. Clearly suicide. The only note he'd left had been for Çetin İkmen. İkmen handed the document to Mehmet Süleyman.

After reading through it once, Süleyman said, 'He liked you.'

İkmen shrugged. 'He hardly knew me.'

'So the treason charge, do you think that's related to his death?'

'How would we know?' İkmen said. 'All that, er, that political stuff is not what we do.'

Both men became quiet until İkmen said, 'I need to go out for several cigarettes. Do you want to come?' He picked up his jacket from the back of his chair.

'Yes.'

Since smoking in public places had been banned back in 2008, İkmen and Süleyman had been obliged to go outside every time they wanted a nicotine hit. İkmen particularly found it hard. Once outside and lit up, he said to Süleyman, 'In answer to your question about General Ablak, we've all heard his name bandied about in relation to the Ergenekon investigation . . .'

Süleyman looked over his shoulder and then said, 'Yes.'

'Whether he was involved or not, I can understand why he took his own life if he was under suspicion,' İkmen said.

'You don't think he killed himself because he murdered his wife?'

'No, I don't. If you murder someone, you might just get away with it. But if someone thinks you're involved in treason . . .' He shook his head.

The governmental investigation into the so-called Ergenekon plot to undermine both democracy and the rule of law appeared to be endless. But did such a plot even exist? It was an issue so contentious that people like İkmen spoke about it only in whispers. Even army officers who had once been chiefs of staff had been arrested, and several of them had committed suicide already. Whether such suicides were tacit admissions of guilt was a moot point. İkmen, as an avowed secularist, was deeply conflicted on the subject.

He sucked hard on a rather unsatisfying Marlboro Light. Trying to cut down was not really working for him. 'Leyla Ablak's killer wasn't her husband, and nor do I think it was her lover, either.'

'No?'

'No, he admitted to that affair far too quickly,' İkmen said.

Süleyman let smoke drift slowly out of his mouth. 'Hiding in plain sight . . .'

'Oh, I admit it is a valid and sometimes successful technique, my dear Mehmet, but I don't think that it is so in Mr Genç's case. By the way, can you tell me anything about Mrs Ablak's family? I believe you are related . . .'

Süleyman sighed. 'You saw my mother at Sezen Hanım's house in Ortaköy; she told me.' He shook his head. 'Leyla and I are distant cousins. Through my father and Leyla's mother we are both related to the Imperial family, as I am sure you are bored with being told. I am bored with knowing it. To my knowledge I last saw Leyla İpek in the 1970s, when I was really more interested in model trains than in girls. I'm told she was pretty.'

İkmen smiled. Nur Hanım, Süleyman's mother, had apparently telephoned their boss, Commissioner Ardıç, to see whether he could reassign her son to the Leyla Ablak case. He had replied, most emphatically, that he couldn't.

'Sezen Hanım didn't approve of General Ablak,' İkmen said.

'No, he was a "nasty" republican, a destroyer of the Empire and therefore beyond the pale.' Süleyman shook his head. 'You can't please old Ottomans, Çetin. They don't like the secularists, and they mistrust the present government because they are far too common and Islamic for their taste. Mind you, money always changes things. Ablak's dirty Kemalist money was good enough for my family.' He glanced down at İkmen, who looked back at him with a question on his face. Süleyman, who knew him very well, knew exactly what it was. 'But no, I can't imagine even my most insane relatives killing anyone.'

'I didn't think so,' İkmen said. Although Süleyman had no doubt that Sezen İpek and her family would be minutely considered by him. 'No, my mind is on the lover's wife.'

'Faruk Genç's?'

'Yes. I felt that his dying wife, although freely admitting her

63

own pragmatism about her husband's affair, was rather *too* pragmatic. There was no passion there, where I think most people would have expected it. There was some barely suppressed malice, too. I must say I am also drawn towards the world that Leyla Ablak was apparently so attracted to,' İkmen said. 'The "alternative" health scene.'

Süleyman frowned. 'Oh?'

'Yes, aromatherapy, chakras, homeopathy – she did a lot of that.'

'Really. I didn't know.'

'Ah, the appeal of the weird,' İkmen said as he lit one cigarette from another.

'Well that's very interesting, Çetin.'

İkmen laughed. 'What, pseudo-science? The outer limits of human credulity? I mean, I know I say this as the son of a woman who was a witch . . .'

'Yes, but you believed in your mother, didn't you?'

'My mother clearly had something, even if I can't really say what that was.'

'It's interesting because my victim, Levent Devrim, was into alternative therapies too,' Süleyman said. 'Apparently he read copiously on all sorts of "weird" topics – aliens, stone circles, the Mayan 2012 prophecies – at his favourite bookshop, the Ada on İstiklal.'

'Can't imagine your cousin consorting with the great unwashed at the Ada,' İkmen said.

'Maybe not, and maybe the fact that Devrim and Leyla were both into these therapies doesn't mean anything,' Süleyman said. 'But I tell you, Çetin, I am struggling to find a motive for Levent Devrim's death. As far as I can tell he was a quiet eccentric obsessed with numbers. Although what numbers meant to him, and why, I have no idea. The calculations we found scrawled all over his apartment were meaningless. Then today Ömer was told by Levent Devrim's old paramour Sugar Barışık that Şukru Şekeroğlu didn't in fact find his body. A gypsy kid found it. But of course the child, Hamid, was nowhere to be found.'

'Did Ömer speak to Şukru Şekeroğlu?' İkmen knew the gypsy brother of Süleyman's great love, as well as the rest of the Şekeroğlu family, rather well, and had always been aware of the fact that back in his native Sulukule, Şukru had been a local celebrity for decades. He wondered how he was dealing with the comedown that Tarlabaşı had to be for him.

'No,' Süleyman said. 'We're going after the boy Hamid on the pretext that he picked Sugar Barışık's pocket. Once we get hold of him, we can also question Şekeroğlu again. In the meantime, I'm going to have Şukru watched.'

İkmen raised his eyebrows.

'Yes, I know Tarlabaşı is a tough place to stake out, but I've got a few old Sulukule contacts over there, and I've got the budget for it.'

'Sulukule contacts who will tell you the truth about Şukru Şekeroğlu?'

'Ah, well that could be moot,' Süleyman said.

'Friends or enemies?'

'Oh, enemies.'

'Then you'll have to be careful.'

'Of course. But what can I do? A strange face in that quarter would be headline news in all the coffee houses and brothels within minutes. One of the many things that really puzzles me about this case is how the murderer managed to get in and out without being noticed.'

'Unless he was local.'

'Unless he was local, which is a terrible thought, because if that's the case then I'll never catch him.'

'Unless he upsets one of the local drug dealers, or his neighbours.'

Süleyman lit another cigarette. 'Absolutely. But I don't think he is local.'

'Why not?'

'Because Tarlabaşı is agitated. Since Devrim's murder, people are afraid. Admittedly half of them think it's a conspiracy on the part of the government to get them to move out of the area more quickly and with less bother . . .'

'Well . . .'

'While of course some more "progressive" types outside the quarter believe it was an inside job to frighten away the developers.'

'Yes, I've heard that,' İkmen said. 'What do you think?'

'I think Levent Devrim was murdered by someone and I think we have too many conspiracies in this country.'

İkmen smiled. 'Poor Mehmet.'

'At least with Leyla Ablak there is, or could be, a cogent motive,' Süleyman said.

İkmen looked up into the foggy February air and coughed. Then he said, 'Yes, possibly. Her late husband hinted at jealousies amongst his wife's friends. Don't you think it's amazing how so often it is highly privileged women who harbour truly vicious feelings about each other?'

'They have little else to think about,' Süleyman said.

'The only people my wife is jealous of are folk who have central heating.'

Süleyman didn't answer. Apparently, once he had retired, İkmen was going to have central heating fitted in his apartment. Why he hadn't had it put in before was a bit of a mystery.

'So I must make the acquaintance of the Kemer Golf and Country Club,' İkmen said. He lit another cigarette, then looked up at Süleyman. 'What do you think they'll make of me, Mehmet?'

With his frayed trouser turn-ups and very unfashionable haircut, not to mention the general grey ashiness of his demeanour, there was very little about İkmen that Süleyman thought the good people at the Kemer Golf and Country Club could allow themselves to like. But then, he thought, that was really their problem.

Hande Genç watched and listened in silence as her husband grovelled around her like a penitent.

'Hande,' he said, 'do you want me to leave the television on or do you want to read?'

The news had already started and it was full of depressing stories. Did he imagine they were upsetting her? She said, 'Leave the TV. I'm dying and you've been unfaithful to me; how much worse can things get?'

He didn't say anything. She saw him very obviously busy himself making room on her night stand. She wanted to hurt him but she knew she didn't have the strength to do that physically. That didn't matter. Instead, she said, 'I told the police a lie.'

His face drained of blood. 'What about?'

'I knew you were having an affair with Leyla Ablak.'

'No you didn't. How could you?'

'Younger women with old husbands can't resist boasting about any toy boys they might pick up,' she said.

On the TV, the news from Syria was bloody and grave, as usual.

Faruk Genç put the book Hande had been reading underneath the tray that contained all her medications. 'You didn't know Mrs Ablak,' he said.

'*I* didn't, no,' she said. And watched his face as he went through a mental list of people who visited her who might have known Leyla Ablak.

In the end he said, 'Who do you mean?'

But she just shrugged. He moved towards her, his hands outstretched, 'Hande, who do you—'

'Don't you touch me, you son of a pig!' She cringed away from him. She looked elsewhere, her eyes eventually coming to rest on the television screen. On it she saw a face she recognised.

'Hande—' her husband began.

'Shut up!' she snapped. Then she pointed at the television. 'Look.'

The picture of General Osman Ablak was no longer on the screen, but the newscaster was obviously talking about him. '. . . veteran of the war in Cyprus, currently under investigation in connection with his role in the 1980 *coup d'état* and subsequent alleged actions prejudicial to the democratic process. General Ablak was found dead at his home in İstanbul last night. A police spokesman said that the death was not suspicious.'

Hande looked at her husband and said, 'That means he probably killed himself.'

Still looking at the TV screen, Faruk Genç said, 'They didn't say that and you don't know it. He was old.'

'So then the shock of finding out that his wife was slagging around stopped his heart,' she said. 'Either way, you and your lover killed him.'

'No we didn't. He was involved in Ergenekon.' Even though he had once loved her, and she was dying, he couldn't look at her without feeling true loathing. How had she known about Leyla? Why wouldn't she tell him? Was it just a lie with which to taunt him?

68

'Maybe he killed her and then killed himself,' she said. The look on his face was so horror-struck that she was inclined to go even further, which she did. 'Or maybe I had her killed, with General Ablak's blessing.'

Before he knew what was happening, he found himself on top of her with his hands around her throat. 'You tell me the truth, you fucking bitch! Stop playing with me and tell me the truth!'

Horrified by his own violence, he threw himself off her and stood looking down as she coughed and heaved her way back to normality. Once she was herself again, Hande Genç pointed at her husband, and then she laughed at him.

Chapter 7

He was sure that one of those little shits who hung about around the entrance to Tünel had taken his wallet. There were often small groups of Roma kids waiting at the end of İstiklal Caddesi for tourists to get off at the top of İstanbul's historic funicular railway. Then they'd nick their wallets or bags or anything they could get their hands on.

But how could he prove it? He hadn't noticed his wallet had gone until he'd got back to his apartment in Karaköy. And anyway, it sounded just so politically incorrect, and John Regan was nothing if not politically correct. Luckily he'd left his credit cards at home, and so the kid had only got away with about two hundred lira in cash. That was about eighty-five pounds. Spitefully John hoped that the stolen money only brought the thief pain in some way. Maybe he'd buy dodgy drugs with it that would land him in hospital. But then he let it go. He had stuff to do.

The computer he used to write his book on was in the bay window overlooking his street, Büyük Hendek Caddesi. Across the road was one of the city's many Sephardic Jewish synagogues, while at the end of Büyük Hendek was the famous Genoese-built Galata Tower. In the past, Karaköy, or Galata as it was known in Ottoman times, had been a very cosmopolitan area. But the Latins and most of the Jews had left decades, if not hundreds of years ago. Now John, an Englishman from a very English town in East Anglia, was the most exotic creature that Karaköy had to offer.

He sat down in front of the machine and, after a brief look at his emails, brought up the document that he hoped one day was going to change his life. He had only started actually writing his semi-fictional romance – set in Yıldız Palace at the time of Sultan Abdülhamid II – a few weeks before, but already he felt that he had something. When he'd tried to work on the book back in the UK, it just hadn't gelled. Although he could visualise Yıldız Palace, which he had visited as a tourist many times over the years, he couldn't find the context in which the sultan's real-life lover, the Belgian glove-seller Flora Cordier, had lived. Her shop had been on İstiklal Caddesi back when it had been called the Grand Rue de Pera, and at first sight he couldn't place her in such a youthful, twenty-first-century milieu. However, living in the area had opened his eyes, and he'd begun to find all the little nineteenth-century streets that Flora would have known, all the tucked-away churches she could have walked past every day. As the historian he had trained to be, John was delighted that now it was just his literary skills that were open to question. But how would he know whether he was any good unless he tried? He read through what he had written and then looked out of the window into the street.

Was it just his imagination, or was the man standing outside the synagogue looking up at him? Thirty-something, young – and good-looking. No. Or if he was, it was just because John was a new boy on the block, as it were. Since coming to İstanbul to live, John, whose Turkish-language skills were minimal at best, had made friends with a couple of English-speaking local people, including Sırma, a publicist who lived just up the hill in Cihangir. When he had told her he reckoned that people were staring at him in his local area, she'd said, 'Oh John, Turks always stare. When someone new moves into a neighbourhood, they stare. Eventually they'll get used to you and then you'll complain that they're ignoring you.' But he'd been in town since

3 January and it was now almost March. How much more time did they, and he, need?

One of the women wouldn't stop talking, while the other one just cried.

'Leyla Ablak was a dear friend and she will be very badly missed,' said the one who talked all the time. 'Of course nobody here believed the rumours about her husband the general, although now he's dead too, it does make you think. Suicide, wasn't it?'

A week had passed since General Ablak's death, and everyone now knew that he had taken his own life. İkmen, who had been waiting for these friends of Leyla Ablak to return to İstanbul from their winter golfing breaks abroad with their husbands, tried to get a word in edgeways but failed. Had Ayşe Farsakoğlu been with him, she might, as a fellow woman, have had more luck, but she was back at the station doing the ever-increasing paperwork the state demanded. The stuff İkmen always shunned. For a moment he felt both guilty and stupid.

'As for Leyla, who would want to hurt her? And at a spa? At a spa you relax, you don't get your head bashed in or whatever it was that happened to her. Although Latife Hanım told me that she was at the spa at night. Seems strange. What was she doing there at night? Do you know?'

Although Leyla Ablak's infidelity had not been reported, İkmen got the distinct impression that this woman, Verda Kavaf, already knew about it. She just wanted him to say it.

'Mrs Ablak had gone to the spa to meet someone,' he said.

'Oh,' Verda Kavaf said. For a moment, the other woman, Latife Özen, stopped crying. 'Who was she meeting, Inspector?'

İkmen smiled. 'I'm afraid I can't say,' he said. Latife Özen began crying again.

İkmen had been up to the club these women belonged to, the

Kemer Golf and Country Club, two days after Leyla Ablak's death. Contrary to his expectations the staff and management had been very helpful. They'd told him that Mrs Ablak had been a good golfer, an adequate horse-rider and a very frequent user of the fitness facilities. She also, together with Latife Özen and Verda Kavaf, belonged to a monthly book-reading circle. Other members who came and went included the wife of a judge and a female airline pilot. According to Verda Hanım, Leyla Ablak had favoured erotic books, usually by foreign authors. When she'd told him that, İkmen had noticed a slightly sour look creep on to her face. He remembered what General Ablak had told him about Leyla's friends. But then, from the little that he knew about it, didn't competition always exist between rich and powerful women? Did anything mark these women out as particularly toxic?

'Do you think Mrs Ablak had had too much cosmetic surgery?' İkmen asked.

There was a stunned silence.

'You see, our pathologist found a lot of small, neat scarring on Mrs Ablak's face and body,' he said. 'I wondered what you thought about that?'

Latife Özen stopped crying.

Verda Kavaf said, 'Oh, well clearly if it made Leyla Hanım happy . . . I have never resorted to it myself . . .' She had; İkmen could see the scars on her face even through her make-up. 'But then she had her reasons . . .'

She looked at İkmen as if she was expecting him to ask her about those reasons. He didn't disappoint her. 'What reasons?'

'Oh, well . . .' She was trying to look grave, but İkmen could see the small smile that lay beneath her assumed expression.

Latife Özen sniffled. 'Oh, Verda Hanım, you cannot . . .'

'Cannot what?' İkmen asked.

'You cannot . . .' Latife Özen shut her mouth. Where Verda Kavaf was pin-thin and elegant, Latife, who was clearly her acolyte on some level, was a small, round bundle of nerves and lack of style.

'Leyla liked men, Inspector,' Verda Kavaf said. 'She enjoyed male attention and she went out of her way to make sure that she got it.' She laughed, but without warmth. 'When Leyla walked into a room, nobody else could get a look-in, nobody else was allowed to.'

'What did her husband think about that?' İkmen asked.

'I don't know,' Verda Kavaf said. 'He appeared not to notice. He always smiled when she made eyes at other men, pouted her lips and generally put herself at the centre of everything.'

'He didn't want to see what she was,' Latife Özen interjected.

'Which was?'

There was a pause, and then Verda Kavaf said, 'She was very taken with a foreign book she found online. *Fifty Shades of Grey* – have you heard of it?'

'No,' İkmen said.

'It's an erotic story about a young girl who allows herself to be sexually dominated by a rich and powerful man. Leyla was besotted by it. She said she wanted to find a man who would dominate her.'

'And did she?' İkmen asked.

The two women looked at each other for a moment, and then Verda Kavaf said, 'I don't know whether she found her Christian Grey – that's the character she was so taken with in the book – but she did meet somebody, that I do know.'

'How do you know?' İkmen asked.

A look of sourness settled on her features. 'Because she was happy again,' she said bitterly. 'I've known Leyla most of my life, and I know that she is only ever happy when she's in the throes of romantic love, and I know she didn't have that with the general.'

'She was having good sex,' Latife Özen added. And then, realising what she'd just said, and to whom, she put a hand up to her mouth and her face went red.

Şukru Şekeroğlu was the type of man who had always played his cards close to his chest. Even amongst what remained of the Sulukule gypsy community, he was an enigma. Nobody, not even his ex-neighbour Necati Hallaç, knew exactly how many children he had or by how many women. But then the Şekeroğlu family had always been a law unto themselves, and that was why Necati hated them. They had money, through Şukru's artist sister; they had fame; and years ago, and most significantly, Şukru had smashed Necati's nose across his face in a fight over a woman. After that Necati had left Sulukule, only coming across Şukru Şekeroğlu again when they both found themselves living in Tarlabaşı.

Şukru, for his part, had welcomed his old adversary as a long-lost friend and Necati had pretended to respond in kind. But he hadn't either forgotten or forgiven Şukru Şekeroğlu for the beating he had given him thirty-five years ago. Since leaving Sulukule, Necati had supplemented his income as a shoe-shine man with the occasional selling of information to that policeman who had once loved Şukru's sister, Inspector Mehmet Süleyman. However, what he was doing now was providing more than just information, and it was much better paid. This time he had to watch Şukru Şekeroğlu and find out where he went, what he did and who he met. He had to keep an eye out for a kid, too – the eldest son of the whore with the birthmark on her face. Usually the boy was everywhere, but Necati hadn't seen him for well over a week.

It was well known that Şukru Şekeroğlu had multiple business

75

interests. Not that he gave the appearance of being a busy man. He only appeared on the street before midday if he was collecting fuel, which he did infrequently, and most of his time after that would be spent in his favourite coffee house. Later he would go to the bar owned by his father. But he'd be doing business all day long, and Necati knew that one of the people he'd been talking to at the coffee house lately was a Roma from Bulgaria who ran a pocket-diving ring up in Beyoğlu. What the arrangement with the Bulgarian was, Necati didn't know, but he told Süleyman, 'In the past, once he couldn't wrestle or dance his bears any more, Şukru would go into the city with his kids and dive pockets and bags. Then Gonca got rich and the family became respectable. But times are hard again now, even for the Şekeroğlu, so maybe Şukru has gone into business with this man.'

Süleyman had asked, 'In what way?'

'Well, maybe he supplies the Bulgarian with kids,' Necati had said. 'They speak the language and they know their way around.'

Faruk Genç didn't look like the sort of man who knew his way around a whip. İkmen, sitting opposite him, clarified what he had just said. 'I'm not asking whether you beat Mrs Ablak up because you lost your temper; I'm asking whether she ordered you to act in a violent and dominant way towards her,' he said.

'No! Why do you want to know these things?'

İkmen leaned on the table that stood between them. Faruk Genç had never been inside a police station before and he clearly wasn't enjoying the experience.

'Because, Mr Genç,' İkmen said, 'I've reason to believe that Mrs Ablak may have harboured a desire to be dominated, and people who like that kind of thing are generally masochistic.'

'Well she wasn't,' he said. 'Anyway, I wouldn't have smacked her or whatever those people do even if she'd asked me.'

Apart from the bruising on her neck, Leyla Ablak hadn't sustained any sort of injury to other parts of her body that Dr Sarkissian had been able to see. But in light of what her 'friends' had told him about her preferences, İkmen had been obliged to check it out.

'Do you know anything about Mrs Ablak's fixation on a book called *Fifty Shades of Grey*?' he asked.

'That!' Faruk Genç snorted. 'What woman isn't fantasising about Christian Grey?'

İkmen felt it doubtful whether his wife was. In spite of an improvement in the weather, she was still firmly focused on the hated soba.

'So she—'

'Oh, she talked to me about it, but we never did any of those things,' he said. 'Leyla wanted good sex, not violence.' He looked down. 'I gave her good sex.'

According to Verda Kavaf, Leyla Ablak had been happy, which Latife Özen had put down to her having good sex. It all made sense, and İkmen had never seriously thought that Leyla had died during the course of a masochistic sex game. Also, albeit reluctantly, Genç's wife Hande had supported the alibi he had given, which was that when Leyla had died, he had been on his way home. There was no forensic evidence to implicate him either. But what if Leyla Ablak had found herself another, more adventurous lover? What if she'd stayed at the spa that night in order to meet him?

'Do you know whether, apart from her husband, there was anyone else in Leyla Ablak's life, Mr Genç?' İkmen asked.

He looked back down at the floor again. 'No,' he said. 'There wasn't.'

'Are you sure?'

He looked up, angry now. 'Well of course I can't be certain!

77

We didn't live in each other's pockets! We were having a very private affair! For all I know she could have been sleeping with half the city. But I don't think she was.'

'I'm sorry I have to ask you these—'

'Oh, are you?' Faruk Genç said. 'Are you really?'

İkmen didn't say anything. He had been harsh in his judgement of Faruk Genç as soon as he'd admitted his affair with Leyla Ablak, because he had never approved of infidelity. As a man without religion, people often assumed that his values were impossibly liberal, but they never had been and never would be. However, Genç had shown courage in coming out with information that had naturally aroused suspicion immediately.

'Mr Genç,' İkmen said, 'my only concern is to find who killed Mrs Ablak and then lock him up for as long as the law allows. From the start you have been most accommodating and I thank you for that. I am truly sorry that your wife had to hear about your affair in the way she did, but I really had no choice.'

Faruk Genç didn't say anything.

'I was also most distressed to learn of General Ablak's death,' İkmen said. 'Although of course, that is quite separate from his wife's murder . . .'

'You know my wife thinks the general killed himself because of my affair with Leyla.'

İkmen shook his head. 'I think that's most unlikely, Mr Genç. General Ablak was involved in an investigation into . . . well . . .'

'Ergenekon,' Genç said.

'Into the kind of political issues that I am very glad do not concern me or my officers,' İkmen said.

They both sat in silence for a few moments, individually wondering at the seismic political shift that had taken place in Turkey that allowed once revered military men to be vilified as traitors.

78

Then Faruk Genç said, 'So where do we go from here, Inspector?'

İkmen smiled. 'I expect you will go back to work, and so will I, sir.' He stood up and put his hand out to Faruk Genç who took it but then seemed to have a moment where he appeared to be wondering what to do next.

İkmen said, 'Mr Genç? Is there anything wrong?'

'Well, er . . .' Then he seemed to pull himself together, and smiled. 'Oh no, no, Inspector, nothing is wrong, everything's fine.'

John had decided to call the daughter many authorities believed Flora Cordier had borne the sultan Tirimujgan. It was the name of Abdülhamid II's Circassian mother, who had died when he was a child; like Flora's little girl, the sultan's mother had been blonde. 'Tirimujgan 2', as he was referring to the child, had lived in the imperial harem at Yıldız Palace long after her mother had somehow faded out of history. It was unlikely that Flora had adapted well to harem life, and she had probably gone back to Belgium. But she'd had to leave her daughter behind, and the child had eventually become a woman. What was more, she was the sultan's favourite and was allowed to do just about anything she wanted – within reason. And that had been her problem.

John looked up from his computer screen and glanced out of the window. It was dusk – he'd been working all day – and Büyük Hendek Caddesi was completely deserted. He suddenly felt a twinge of homesickness. Back in the small Cambridgeshire village he'd lived in ever since he'd left university, people he'd known for years would be settling in for the evening with dinner and the TV. If he happened to see David, the vicar, walking his dog, he'd pop in for a brandy and a chat and it would all be very safe and warm and civilised. In İstanbul, he had failed to get the hang of the coal-fired thing called a soba that was supposed to keep the apartment warm. He'd asked the barely conscious kapıcı, the building concierge, several times how one was supposed to first light the thing and then keep it going, but the man had just shrugged and muttered something in Turkish that John could not understand. To keep warm, he wore all his outdoor clothes, including a hat and fingerless gloves. Then there was the rattling, humming plumbing and the electrical wires that hung out of the walls like architectural spaghetti. He turned away from the window and regarded his shelf of books all about learning Turkish. If anything, the language seemed more alien to him now than when he'd first arrived back in early January. Yet he had been out and had spoken to people, albeit usually reluctantly, and he had made friends. But it wasn't home and it was never going to be.

Cooking something for his dinner was a task John knew he should tackle. He'd managed to master the gas-bottle-powered oven and he had some lamb chops in the fridge. But he just didn't feel like it. Maybe it had something to do with how the girl, Tirimujgan, had died – or rather how it was said she had died: tied up in a sack and thrown into the Bosphorus. The story went that she had fallen in love with her half-brother, Prince Selim, and had been found with him in flagrante by the palace staff. The sultan, of course, could not put up with that and the girl had been killed, while Prince Selim had been exiled to some backwater of the Empire to think on his misdeeds. It was a really sad little story, this tale that he was going to inflate into a grand, doomed romance, and John suddenly wondered whether he should be doing it. But then that was a ridiculous idea and he dismissed it immediately. This project had been years in the planning, against all the odds he had a publisher, and he'd taken a sabbatical from his very comfortable fellowship at Cambridge to do it. Anyway, it was personal.

A ring on the doorbell brought him back to full consciousness, and he jumped up from his chair, left the apartment and ran down the stairs to the front door of the block. There were no intercoms in the building, and so every time he had a visitor, he had to run all the way downstairs to open the door. Often he got there, as on this occasion, to find that it was no one, probably some passing kid mucking about with doorbells.

He returned to his apartment and his front window, with the intention of pulling the blinds. Out on the street the figure of a man caught his eye. Just like the time before, he was young and attractive, and he was standing outside the synagogue. Although John couldn't see him properly through the early evening fog, he thought he could possibly be the same man he'd seen out there before. Had he rung the bell and then drifted into the grey background of Büyük Hendek Caddesi? At that moment the man looked up and stared straight into John's eyes. John backed away from the window and scuttled to the far side of his living room. Then he sat down on his sofa and stayed there in the darkness until he got the courage together to go back to the window and pull the blinds, without looking down into the street.

Chapter 8

'I know a man,' Çetin İkmen said to Mehmet Süleyman, 'who is not going to be happy.'

What felt like an eternity of false leads, irritating paperwork and the usual petty station-based in-fighting had passed, and now – this.

It was difficult to know where to stand in that room. It was like an abattoir. Ömer Mungan had gone outside to be sick.

'I don't think Dr John Regan is exactly ecstatic,' Süleyman said. 'Ardıç is something of a side issue.'

'With three murders, all unsolved, on the city's books, I'd hardly describe our commissioner as a "side issue",' İkmen replied. 'And this victim's a foreigner. You know how he hates a non-Turkish death.'

Ayşe Farsakoğlu, though rather more robust than Ömer Mungan, stood over by the open window that overlooked Büyük Hendek Caddesi and breathed in deeply. She was accustomed to her superiors' banter, if not the foul surroundings she was in. One of her old colleagues, Balthazar Cohen, had used to live on Büyük Hendek until al-Qaeda terrorists had blown his apartment to pieces and nearly killed his son. Berekiah Cohen, the son, was married to one of Çetin İkmen's daughters and the whole clan now lived across the Golden Horn in Balat, which had also once been a Jewish quarter. What Cohen would make of this latest outrage Ayşe couldn't imagine. He was old and sick and in all probability it would make him cry.

The victim, who wasn't easy to spot in amongst the blood that stained and dripped from every piece of furniture that was still intact, was, the kapıcı had said, an Englishman. He was called Dr John Regan and he was, or had been, a middle-aged writer. The kapıcı hadn't been able to get access to Regan's apartment. He'd wanted to deliver the Englishman's bottled water, but when he couldn't rouse him, he'd used his duplicate key to let himself inside. What he'd found, just in the hall, had been enough to send him screaming into the street. A local uniform had responded to the incident, but then İkmen had been called. He had in turn called Süleyman. Now they were both waiting for the pathologist to arrive.

As usual, Arto Sarkissian was not long in coming. As he entered the room, he said, 'Good God.'

'Yes,' İkmen said. 'Like you, Arto, I thought I'd seen it all. Good morning.'

The Armenian blinked as if he was trying to wash something out of his eye. 'I don't know about "good",' he said. 'So where's my victim?'

İkmen pointed to a blood-soaked bundle that lay on the floor in front of a small sofa.

The Armenian shook his head. 'You know what this reminds me of?'

'It reminds you of something?'

The doctor put his medical case down on the sofa and said, 'I read a book, years ago, about the Jack the Ripper murders in London back in the nineteenth century. Jack was never caught, but his last victim looked like this. There was a photograph in the book. It was unrecognisable as a human being.'

83

They all looked at the thing on the floor, and Arto Sarkissian wondered where he was going to start.

Hande Genç was dead. Her mother and her sister were in her bedroom, washing her body. Her husband, Faruk, sat tense and alone in their living room, looking out of the window at the small and distant view his apartment had of the Bosphorus.

As stubborn as ever, Hande had endured her pain until the early hours of the morning, when, finally, she'd allowed her husband to call out her doctor. He had recommended immediate transfer to hospital, but Hande had always been determined to die at home. She'd asked him to give her more diamorphine, which, much to Faruk's dismay, he had.

Faruk had known she was in the final hours of her life before the doctor arrived, and so he had begged her to tell him the truth about whether she had been involved in Leyla Ablak's death. Not a day had gone by since Leyla's murder without Hande taunting him about it. One day she and Leyla's late husband had planned her death together; another time it had been Hande alone; and on other days still she denied even knowing that Faruk had been having an affair with Leyla. She was punishing him for being unfaithful to her, but as time had gone on and she had moved ever closer to death, Faruk had begun to panic. What if she died taking the truth with her? He needed to know whether his actions had, directly or indirectly, led to Leyla's death. If they had, he didn't know how he could ever atone. But he was desperate to find out so that he could at least try. Maybe Hande or the general or both of them had hired someone else to kill Leyla, and if that were the case, Faruk needed to find that out too. All he could do for Leyla now was help to discover her killer, and if Hande could give him a name, he could pass that on to the police.

The previous night had been one of horror for Faruk. First Hande had vomited blood, and although he'd pleaded with her to let him call the doctor at that point, she'd just rasped at him to clear it up and then whispered her bile about Leyla. Faruk had done as she'd asked, trying to ignore her vicious taunting, but eventually it had got underneath his skin and he had hit her. He'd regretted it immediately, especially when she'd drawn him close and said, 'I will never tell you, Faruk. I will go to my grave and you will remain here, in hell.' He'd run around the apartment, crying and banging his head against the walls in frustration. But then the doctor had arrived. Just before he gave Hande her first injection of diamorphine, he had asked her whether she wanted to say anything in private to her husband. All three of them knew what this could mean. But Hande didn't even look at Faruk with her bloodshot, jaundiced eyes. She just said, 'No,' and then the needle went into one of the exhausted veins in her arms and she became a living corpse. Later she began to fit. It had only taken one more dose of pain control and then she was dead.

Now, alone with a body that would never tell him its secrets, and her family, who despised him, Faruk wondered how he was going to be able to get through her funeral.

'May Allah give you patience.'

The unexpected voice made Faruk jump. But it was only Cem, Hande's brother. When Faruk had called his mother-in-law to tell her that Hande was dead, Cem had driven her and Hande's spinster sister, Nilüfer, over to the apartment. Faruk attempted a smile. Unlike the women, Cem wasn't his enemy. Maybe it was because he was a man and therefore understood infidelity. More men than women did it. Or maybe it was just because he was a rational academic who did not believe in religion – his appeal for Allah to give Faruk patience was a standard response spoken to the bereaved – or in monogamy and other outmoded or oppressive forms of human relationship.

'Hande's pain is at an end,' Cem said.

Cem Atay was a lot older than his sisters. In his mid fifties, he was an historian who had fronted several popular television series about Anatolian civilisations and the Ottoman Empire. These days he was single, but Faruk didn't doubt for a moment that he had lovers.

'Yes.' Faruk's answer was tardy and he was barely conscious of giving it. Now that Hande's mother and sister were washing her body, the funeral was only hours away. In line with Muslim custom, they would want to have her buried before sundown if possible. As women, they wouldn't go to the graveside, as Faruk would be expected to. They also wouldn't have to respond to the discharge, which was when the imam asked all those present whether the deceased had been a good person and, more crucially, whether those still living forgave the dead person for his or her past misdemeanours. Just thinking about it made Faruk sweat. He wasn't a religious man, but there was something about lying to Allah that did not sit well with him. But then what else could he do? Could he actually say that he didn't forgive his wife for taking to her grave what might be her involvement in a murder?

Cem, seeing his pain, tightened his grip on his shoulders and said, 'You won't get over Hande's death, Faruk, but you will get used to it. Trust me on this. When my father died, I was just as shell-shocked as you are.'

Arto Sarkissian washed up as best he could in a tiny bathroom at the back of the apartment and then went to join Ayşe Farsakoğlu and the group of senior police officers, which now also included the commissioner, Ardıç, in the kitchen. When he walked in, they all looked at him expectantly.

'Well, Dr Regan didn't die a natural death . . .'

'I think that even we could see that, Doctor,' Ardıç growled. Overweight, tired and distinctly grey around the cheeks, Ardıç was due to retire just after İkmen. Like the inspector, he didn't really want to, but that was not because he loved his job so much as that he feared the man who would replace him. The rumour mill had it that the man his superiors had in mind was of a very pious nature. And although Ardıç was not averse to religion, he found that when it entered public life, its influence sometimes led to favouritism along sectarian lines. This sat badly with Ardic and his personal philosophy regarding his department. His own religion was and always had been a private matter.

'To give him credit, the Englishman fought,' Arto said. 'That's why there's blood in the living room and in the hall. I'd say that the attacker came in through the front door.'

'He let him in?' İkmen asked. The kapıcı had said that when he tried to deliver Regan's water, the door had been locked.

'That will be for Forensics to decide,' the doctor said. 'But it's very possible.'

'So he could have known him?'

'Maybe.'

'Çetin, did the kapıcı see anyone come to visit Dr Regan last night?' Süleyman asked.

İkmen shook his head. 'He was out. Drinking.'

'Until when?' Ayşe said.

'He doesn't remember.'

'Time of death?' Ardıç asked the doctor.

'Anywhere between about ten last night and two o'clock this morning.'

'Cause?'

'Ah well, that's where you're going to have to be a little bit patient with me,' the doctor said. 'The victim has sustained so many wounds, administered I would say by a very sharp, long-bladed knife . . .'

'A machete?'

'Not really, but something like that. However, that was only at the beginning. Later on I think he used a smaller knife. I'll tell you why in a moment. Basically he has multiple wounds and it's going to take me some time to work out exactly which one, if any of them, was responsible for his death.'

Süleyman looked confused. 'If any?'

'He could have died from simple blood loss,' the doctor said. 'However, what I can tell you is that if my observations are correct, whoever attacked him tried, and failed, to cut his heart out.'

There was a stunned silence. Then Çetin İkmen said, 'Cut his heart out? Are you sure?'

'His chest cavity has been cut open, probably with the large knife, his ribs broken and separated and the vessels around the heart hacked at and in some cases severed,' the Armenian said.

'But the heart is still in the chest?'

'Such as it is, yes. Where it's been cut about, there isn't actually that much of it left.'

Süleyman said, 'If the murderer wanted to cut out Dr Regan's heart, why did he stop?'

'He could have been interrupted,' İkmen said. 'By a noise that made him fear he was about to be discovered, or maybe even by a person entering the apartment. We've got officers going door to door—'

'Or,' the doctor interrupted, 'what I think is the most likely reason.'

Ardıç frowned. 'Which is?'

'Well, from a medico-butchery point of view, I'd say that our murderer had very little knowledge of anatomy. For some reason he wanted this man's heart, but when it came to the reality of obtaining the organ, he was up to neither the job nor the sight of what was revealed when he opened up the chest. I think he just stopped because he couldn't go any further.'

'Mmm.' Ardıç nodded his head up and down. 'Doctor, I recall you said something similar about the Tarlabaşı semi-decapitation.'

'Yes, that was a possibility in that case too.'

'So we could be looking at the same offender in both this case and the Tarlabaşı murder?'

'Possibly, yes.'

'Mmm.'

'Very different victims, however,' Süleyman said. 'A crazy, drug-addled fantasist in Tarlabaşı, a foreign writer with a doctorate here.'

'Yes, although the Tarlabaşı man was well educated, as I recall,' Ardıç said. He cleared his throat, and when he spoke again, his voice had a much harder tone. 'But whether one person is doing these things, or twelve, the fact remains that they're happening and they shouldn't be.' He looked across at İkmen. 'Movement on General Ablak's wife?'

İkmen shrugged. 'We've ruled out the lover. The husband?' He shrugged again. 'I've been back to see the lover's wife a few times, but she's terminally ill and so I've had to tread carefully.'

'Well then maybe now it's time to tread heavily,' Ardıç said. 'You say the woman is terminally ill, but that wouldn't stop her arranging the death of her rival even if she didn't do it herself. Put your boots on, İkmen, go back to her and squeeze her – hard.'

'Yes, sir.'

'And in the meantime, Doctor, I assume you've arranged transport for the body to your laboratory . . .'

'Once I have permission from Forensics and the photographer, yes.'

'And then I suppose I'll have the delightful task of telling the British Consul that one of his nationals has been murdered,' Ardıç said. 'I hate it when we lose a foreigner.'

The old man, who gave his name as Deniz Ribeiro, was one of the very few Jews still resident in Karaköy. He was also, apparently, one of the most observant. 'There's not much I miss around here,' he told Ömer Mungan. 'And so when I tell you that there was a gypsy hanging about around the synagogue, I expect you to believe me. For weeks, on and off, same man or similar, hanging around. Until Selim Bey – he owns the bakkal on İlk Belediye Caddesi – told me that the place was infested with Bulgarian gypsies, I thought it was some jihadi type. But then I heard him speak into his mobile phone. I can speak Arabic and five other languages, but I didn't know that one.'

'If you thought the man might be plotting something against the synagogue, why didn't you call us?' Ömer asked.

The old man didn't answer. But Ömer knew that the subtext to his silence was his probable belief that because the synagogue was a place of worship for Jews, the police didn't care. Ömer said, 'So this gypsy, what do you think he was doing hanging around the synagogue?'

'Nothing. Looking at the buildings opposite.'

One of which was where John Regan had lived.

'How long did he do this for?' Ömer asked.

Deniz Ribeiro shrugged. 'A couple of weeks. But on and off, not every day.'

'Did you tell anyone about this, Mr Ribeiro?'

He laughed. 'For what it was worth, I told Hasan Bey – he's the kapıcı of the building opposite the synagogue entrance.'

'What did he say?'

'What does he ever say! "Leave it to me! I'll take care of it!" He does nothing, takes care of nothing. Two of his tenants were robbed in their own apartments last year and what did he do? Nothing. He's a drunk, but who else is there to tell, eh?'

Hasan Bey had said nothing to İkmen about any lurking gypsies, as far as Ömer knew. But that didn't mean that Deniz Ribeiro was making it up. Hasan Bey was a drunk, which was precisely why he'd been out of the building when John Regan had died. But then apparently so had all of the other tenants, apart from the old Syrian lady who lived in the basement.

'Did you see the gypsy outside the synagogue yesterday evening?'

'For a bit, yes,' Deniz Ribeiro said. 'But when I looked out of my window at about eight, he'd gone.' Ribeiro lived next door to the synagogue, which gave him a very good view of John Regan's building.

'Did you see anyone go into Hasan Bey's building?' Ömer asked.

'What, you mean the murderer? Is it true that the Englishman's head was chopped off? You know, like that man in Tarlabaşı?'

'Can we please stick to the facts, Mr Ribeiro? Did you see anyone going into the building?'

'No,' he said. 'I saw people leave. That drunk who goes out with Hasan Bey sometimes, who lives on the ground floor. He wobbled out at about seven. The couple who live next door to the Englishman went out much earlier, at about five. The Syrian woman in the basement never goes anywhere. Apart from the Englishman's place and Hasan Bey's apartment, the rest of the building is empty this time of year.'

Much of the building was used for short-term holiday lets for people visiting the city for a week or two in the summer.

'So the gypsy was outside the synagogue when the other tenants left?'

'I suppose so, yes. Although Hasan Bey went out later, but then he always does. You can set your clock by his addiction to the rakı bottle.'

'Can you describe this gypsy to me, Mr Ribeiro?'

'I can, although he's so typical you'll think I'm making it up.'

'Try me,' Ömer said.

'Well, medium height, dark, hawkish sort of features, scar on his left cheek, leather jacket, mobile phone stuck to the side of his face all the time. A gypsy on the make? Yes, like a fucking cartoon character, I swear to God!'

Marko was good to him, but he did make him work. Every day he was taken all over the city, everywhere that tourists went, and every day he had to make at least a thousand lira. If he didn't, then Marko would tell Şukru Bey, who would tell his mum that he wasn't pulling his weight. Şukru Bey had got him out of Tarlabaşı and so his mum was now in his debt. He had to keep on being good both for his own sake and for his mum. But then Hamid was a brilliant pocket-diver. He'd got used to snatching bags, but that wasn't quite so easy. Even so, provided there were enough tourists around and the other boys didn't beat him to it, he always met his target.

But Hamid was homesick. Going back to the apartment in Fener with Marko and the other kids wasn't much fun. Marko spoke some Turkish but none of the boys did. This, as well as the fact that the Bulgarians were Christians and he was a Muslim, excluded Hamid from their play. He missed his mother and his sister, even though they'd irritated him. And all for what? Because he'd seen a monster standing over the body of mad old Levent Bey. But then it wasn't just because of that, and Şukru Bey, if no one else, knew it too. Just thinking about Şukru Bey made Hamid shudder, and so he stopped doing it. He was doing well now, and that was all that mattered. Marko seemed to be unusually happy this morning, so clearly no one, including Hamid, was doing too badly.

Chapter 9

'A biography of Sultan Abdülhamid II could be contentious,' Çetin İkmen said as he leaned back into his office chair. 'But would a person kill somebody for writing it?'

Ayşe Farsakoğlu, whose grasp of English was not nearly so good as İkmen's, put one of the bloodstained pieces of paper from John Regan's apartment down on her desk and said, 'I don't know, sir. Maybe. People get offended by all sorts of things, don't they?'

İkmen shook his head. 'Don't they indeed. Hah! I get offended by people who moan continually about smoking, but somehow nobody cares what I think. The wonderful world of selective offence.'

Ayşe smiled. This was İkmen's code for the belief he and many other secular Turks now had that their views were becoming subordinate to the new Islamic elite. Ever since the religiously rooted AKP Party had come to power in 2002, Çetin İkmen had felt what he interpreted as the cold hand of the pious on his shoulder. And even though he knew that he was probably overreacting, he was also aware of a change in the tenor of his country that did not entirely favour people like him. Some of the new elite even expressed admiration for the long-gone Ottoman Empire, and that included the much-maligned last autocratic sultan, Abdülhamid II.

'Abdülhamid killed a lot of people mainly because he was

obsessed with his own security,' İkmen said. 'He was clearly as mad as so many of his ancestors had been, but that doesn't excuse the thousands he had put to death. Well, not in my eyes. I don't know what Dr John Regan's thesis was with regard to Abdülhamid, but I can't see how, as an academic, he can have avoided criticism.'

'There's some sort of partial manuscript on his computer, but until the—'

'Unfortunates.'

'The technical people . . .' She looked up at him and smiled. He always called the police department's team of technical experts 'the unfortunates', on the basis that they supposedly had poor social skills. '. . . have had a chance to examine it, then we won't really know.'

'Well, it'll keep them safely away from women,' İkmen said. 'Or rather women will be safe from their inept—'

His phone rang. 'İkmen.'

While he took the call, Ayşe went back to looking at some of John Regan's research material. As far as she could tell, he'd been more interested in the sultan's personal life than in his actual reign. There were notes about his mother, his brothers and also about his harem and his children. Mehmet Süleyman was a descendant of the man secular Turks of a certain age, like Çetin İkmen, still called Abdul the Damned. He'd been sent into exile for his crimes against his own people and had been replaced by first one brother and then another, both puppets of the post-Ottoman regime known as the Young Turks. They'd not been much better than the Empire, but then had come Atatürk, and although Ayşe didn't hold with the idea that he was the be all and end all of Turkish political life, he had undoubtedly transformed the country for the better. Or rather, that was what she believed. Not everyone held to that view; the Ottoman Empire was back in favour with some people. Politicised religion Ayşe could at least understand, although she didn't agree with it, but to want a creaking and corrupt and – more to the point – dead empire back seemed like madness.

İkmen put his phone down slowly and said, 'Hande Genç, wife of Faruk Genç, is dead and in her grave.' He shook his head. 'Poor woman, she suffered.'

'Then maybe, sir, she was glad to go.'

'Oh, I've no doubt of it,' he said. 'When one is riddled with cancer and has been betrayed by one's partner, life must be bleak to say the least. But now her husband wants to come in and speak to us again. Apparently he has something he wishes to tell me.'

'What do you think it's about?'

İkmen put an unlit cigarette into his mouth and leaned back in his chair. 'I don't know. When he was first speaking to me I wondered whether he was perhaps planning to confess to the murder of Leyla Ablak, but I don't think it's that.'

'You think that maybe he's going to implicate his dead wife?'

'I don't know.' He shrugged. 'But he'll be here in an hour. We'll just have to wait until then to find out what he has to say for himself. The way things have been going in the city since the beginning of this year, I'm not prepared to speculate on anything.'

'Three murders in three months.'

'Yes,' İkmen said, 'and do you know what I noticed about that when I first got in this morning, Ayşe? They all took place on the twenty-first of the month. Levent Devrim was killed on the twenty-first of January, Leyla Ablak on the twenty-first of February and Dr John Regan on the twenty-first of this month.'

Ayşe raised her eyebrows. 'Have you told the Commissioner, sir?'

'Oh yes,' he said.

'What did he say?'

'Well you know Ardıç; at first he berated me for not having seen this pattern earlier and then he said that we really must not fall into the trap of ascribing occult meanings to what could be mere coincidence. I said that as far as I could tell there was nothing occult at work here, but then he said that with serial killers it was always, and I quote, "some sort of religious or magical mania".'

As Ayşe knew only too well, Commissioner Ardıç, for all his good qualities, was a man given to generalisation. İkmen had said of him before that his knowledge of a lot of serious crime came from the television and films.

'Anyway, at the moment, the connection to a specific date is just one element in a very complicated picture,' İkmen said. 'I can accept, on Dr Sarkissian's evidence so far, that there could be a connection between the deaths of Levent Devrim and Dr John Regan. But Leyla Ablak's case has an entirely different profile. That death, to me, is more personal. But maybe Mr Genç will tell us more when he arrives.'

The tears just wouldn't stop. He tried to control them but he couldn't. Eventually, given the obvious embarrassment he was causing to the man sitting next to him, Arthur Regan asked the cabin crew if he could please move to a seat where he could be on his own. Luckily the flight was half empty and so this was easy. Arthur cried on in peace, although somewhere over the Alps the crew did ask him whether he wanted chicken or pasta for his meal. He said he wanted nothing, just a large glass of whisky, which they brought to him immediately. Had it only been the previous afternoon that the British Consul in İstanbul had called to tell him that John was dead? Had it really been less than a day?

Usually a bad flier, this time Arthur didn't give a toss about all the bangs and jerks that were always a part of any flying experience. His son was dead at the age of forty-six, taking with him the last familial relationship that Arthur still possessed. He wished that he too could die, right there in that seat, in that aeroplane, but he knew he wasn't going to. The consul had told him that the İstanbul police believed John had been murdered. Until he found out who had done this, and why, Arthur knew he had to keep on living. Who would kill a gentle academic man going about the business of writing a work of romantic fiction? But then had John just been doing that, or had he availed himself of what was now a very vibrant nightlife scene in İstanbul? Back in Arthur's day, the 1960s, the only nightlife available outside the big hotels and traditional meyhanes was confined to the brothels of Karaköy and the beer houses in the gypsy quarter of Sulukule. That was, he'd been told, all very different now. Now the city had hundreds of clubs and bars catering to almost every taste in music, dance and sexual orientation one could imagine. İstanbul had a big gay scene, and Arthur wondered whether John's loneliness had driven him to bring someone unsuitable back to his flat. All the consul had told him about his son's death was that he had been killed in his own apartment, opposite the Neve Şalom synagogue.

Arthur recalled the streets of Karaköy that John had come to know well. Back in the 1960s, when he'd been working for a tiny English school in Beyoğlu, he'd explored the area around the Galata Tower extensively. It had actually been outside the Tower that he'd first met Betül. She'd been drinking coffee at a tiny café where a small group of self-identified bohemians met. As classic romantic fiction would have had it, their eyes met and the rest was history. It still hurt Arthur that he'd had so little time with her. They'd married in 1965, John had been born, in

England, in 1966, and then in 1967 Betül had died. No preamble, no terrible illness; she'd simply dropped dead in the bathroom. Her heart, according to her doctor, had just stopped. Afterwards, Arthur had never wanted to go back to Turkey, although John had been on several occasions and had always been fascinated by his mother's country. So much so that he'd decided to live there and write a book about it.

Arthur looked at his diary to remind himself of the name of the person who was going to meet him at the airport. Inspector Mehmet Süleyman. He knew that surname. Even though it was over forty years ago now, he remembered the day Betül had pointed to a large empty piece of land in the now chic suburb of Nişantaşı and said, 'Oh, Arthur, that is where the house of the sad Princess Gözde Süleyman used to be. All her life she mourned the death of her fiancée, then when she died, her house burnt down. It's one of the saddest love stories in the whole of Turkish history.'

A Bulgarian gypsy was featuring large in Ömer Mungan's life, even though he didn't know his name. Not only had old Deniz Ribeiro told him about a gypsy – local gossip had it that he was Bulgarian – hanging about outside the Neve Şalom synagogue, but apparently Şukru Şerkeroğlu had some sort of business deal going on with a Bulgarian gypsy called Marko.

A lot of kids, some gypsies and some not, dived pockets and bags in and around İstiklal Caddesi. They rarely worked alone and were usually organised by adult gang masters. It had been going on for years. Very rarely were any of the adults arrested, and the kids who were nabbed red-handed never snitched on their handlers; it was more than their miserable lives were worth. Ömer thought how strange it was that parts of İstanbul had grown so rich while other parts remained back in the nineteenth century. He looked at a group of young boys hanging about around the entrance to Tünel and wondered whether one of them was the elusive Hamid, son of Şeftali, the birthmarked prostitute. He moved in close to them and tried to listen to what they said, but they weren't talkative types, and when they did utter one or two words, he couldn't understand what they meant. Ömer moved away again, but not far.

Inspector İkmen's Tarlabaşı informant had told him that Şukru Şekeroğlu could very well have spirited the boy Hamid out of the quarter and given him into the care of his Bulgarian friend. But even if that had happened, it didn't bring them any closer to the kid or to a Bulgarian man whose description, according to Ribeiro, was so 'typical'. All they knew, again through Süleyman's informant, was that a particularly favoured beat for Bulgarian gypsy pickpockets was outside Tünel funicular railway station at the bottom end of İstiklal Caddesi.

The Bulgarians and the Turks had had a difficult relationship over the centuries they had been involved with each other. Ömer had seen a TV programme about it once, by some eminent professor. The Bulgarians had been ruled by the Ottoman Empire until 1878, but when the country had become part of the Warsaw Pact bloc after World War II, relations between the two countries had all but ceased. In more recent years, a lot of Bulgarians had migrated to Turkey, particularly İstanbul, where they had a reputation as hardened criminals. This of course was a generalisation, but a lot of İstanbullus stood by it, and Ömer Mungan, as a new resident, was in no position to argue with them.

He looked at the children again and wondered what they were thinking. Unlike the pocket-divers of the past, these kids were fairly clean and tidy; only their eyes, Ömer thought, were in any way suspect. The way they looked everywhere all the time, checking their world out for opportunities in the shape of tourists, the vulnerable and the unwary. They hung around in groups of three at the most. More often than not, however, they were in pairs. Only one kid stood on his own, and he was the only one who didn't look shifty. Maybe he wasn't with the others. But if that were the case, why had he been standing alone outside Tünel for over an hour? Beyond the music shop opposite the station, there wasn't much to interest a kid of eleven or twelve.

Whoever ran these kids almost certainly wouldn't put in an appearance. And when the boys finally finished their shift, there'd be little point in trying to follow them, because they'd all split up. Or rather that was what Inspector Süleyman had told him they would do. It was all quite sophisticated. Back in Mardin, the pocket-diving kids just went home to their parents and got arrested there.

Although he tried not to, in case the kid noticed him, Ömer found himself focusing on the boy who was on his own. From his vantage point at a café just inside the Parisian-style Tünel Pasaj, he watched him through one of the wrought-iron gates that closed the tiny alleyway off at night. Although some of the other kids spoke and sometimes shouted unintelligible things to each other from time to time, the lone boy remained silent and even, possibly, a little wary of the others. Occasionally shifting from foot to foot, he didn't, as far as Ömer could tell, even try to take a tourist's watch or a cripple's wallet. The others were successful, on and off, but, as per his instructions from Süleyman, Ömer just watched and waited either for a man to turn up to move the kids on, which was unlikely; or to follow at least one of them if and when they did move on.

He drank his coffee and carried on watching.

'I think Hande might have been taunting me, but I can't be sure,' Faruk Genç said.

İkmen looked across his desk at him. Genç was pathetic and the inspector was sorry for him, but he was also angry. 'Mr Genç,' he said, 'if your wife told you that she, together with General Ablak, killed your mistress, then you should have told me immediately.'

'But she was angry! Which I can understand. She was trying to make me suffer!'

'So if you didn't believe her, why are you here now?' İkmen asked.

'I don't know.' He put his head in his hands and then raised it again. His eyes were black underneath and bloodshot. 'Hande never went anywhere. I can't believe she could have found out about Leyla and me, and anyway, how would she have made contact with General Ablak?'

İkmen sighed. 'Secrets are dangerous creatures, Mr Genç,' he said. 'We keep them at our peril. Just because your wife was housebound doesn't mean that she had no contact with the outside world. If you want to know whether Hande Hanım and General Ablak jointly or separately killed Leyla Ablak, then you have to look at who might have been jealous of your affair with her. Maybe someone you work with, a friend, maybe a—'

'But I told no one! We were always so careful! We met in the middle of the night!'

'And yet the killer, whoever he or she was, knew you were at the spa that night, and so, by extension, others might have known it too. Do you know how likely it is that Leyla Hanım was killed by a wandering psychopath who just fancied the idea of murdering her? Almost zero. She was executed by someone who either knew her or knew of her and who had a reason to want her dead.'

'Yes, but Hande—'

'Mr Genç,' İkmen said, 'your wife is dead and so is General Ablak. Unless further evidence comes to light linking them to

102

Leyla Ablak's death, I will have to continue my investigation as if you never came here today. Both of them remain suspects even though they are deceased. But if you want to find out the truth about your lover's death, you are going to have to help me.'

'By doing what?'

'By thinking seriously about who might have known about your affair.'

'I've told you, I—'

'Ah, but I don't think you have really told me, Mr Genç,' İkmen said. 'I want to know about *all* your little secrets, your every slightest suspicion, your darkest fears. Think, Mr Genç: who might have taken a fancy to you in the last year? Female or male, I really don't care. You're a good-looking man with a good job; somebody must have had the hots for you at some point. And Mrs Ablak was a fine woman, wasn't she? I can't believe that others weren't jealous of her. I've met a couple, although I don't think either of them can be seriously considered because neither was in İstanbul when Leyla Ablak died. And don't think that you can discount the family, either.'

'Whose family?'

'All of them,' İkmen said. 'Your own, Hande's, the Ablaks. Although they do not know it, Leyla's own family are not off the hook. That old Ottoman rubbish doesn't impress me one bit. I trust that this time, Mr Genç, I can rely on your full co-operation.'

'Yes, Inspector.'

'Because let me tell you, Mr Genç, you are not off the hook either. I am not impressed by what I imagine you thought was your loyalty to your dying wife. If she was a killer, dying or not, you should have brought her to me. Justice is not selective; it doesn't care if you have a slight cold, a broken leg or terminal cancer. It expects, quite rightly, to have you in the end.'

* * *

Mr Arthur Regan was a man in his late seventies who didn't need to know the full horror of his son's death. But he insisted.

'You can tell me all of it,' he said to Mehmet Süleyman once the driver had wrestled the police vehicle they were travelling in out of the airport.

'Mr Regan . . .' But then he'd need to know because he'd have to identify the body, and there was a limit to what could be done to make John Regan look anything other than butchered. 'Your son was stabbed repeatedly,' Süleyman said. 'I am afraid, sir, that his body is very badly damaged.'

'Oh. I see.'

There was no way that he could go into detail, though, and Süleyman knew it. When he'd first met Arthur Regan, the older man's eyes had been red and wet from crying. John had been his only child and Süleyman couldn't even begin to imagine what that felt like. Even the thought of his own son, Yusuf, dying brought tears to Süleyman's eyes. To outlive a child was a parent's worst nightmare.

'You know that my son was gay, Inspector,' Arthur Regan said.

'No, sir, I did not.'

'It isn't a judgement,' he said. 'Just a fact. Do you have any idea who might have . . . killed him?'

It was almost impossible for him to say the words.

'We have, um, some routes to look at,' Süleyman replied. He had never been as fluent in English as İkmen was, not even when he had been married to an Irish woman.

'Leads?'

'Yes.'

As usual, the airport had been packed. Süleyman had had to stand with all the hotel drivers and the travel reps, holding up a board saying 'Mr Arthur Regan' – it hadn't been his finest hour.

'Your son, Mr Regan, he was writing a book?'

They passed the vast collection of hotels and conference facilities that had grown up around the airport in the last decade and headed into another knot of traffic which consisted mainly of yellow taxis. Some of them had the Turkcell bug's antenna on their roofs, an advertising step way too far for Süleyman.

'Yes. My son has written many books over the years. He is . . . he was an historian. His speciality was Victorian London. He taught at Cambridge, you know, until he decided he wanted to become a romantic novelist.'

'But here he was writing a history of Sultan Abdülhamid II, I think.'

The old man shook his head. 'No,' he said, 'he was writing a novel. It was to be about Abdülhamid but it was about his personal life. There's a legend about how he was involved with a Belgian woman who bore him a daughter. It's said that he eventually killed the girl because she seduced his eldest son.'

Mehmet Süleyman had a vague recollection of the story, but he'd never known whether it had any basis in fact.

'John was always fascinated by that tale.'

'An unusual fascination for an Englishman,' Süleyman said.

'Oh, he's always been interested in Turkey and Turkish history,' Arthur Regan said. 'Although she died when he was a tiny child, his mother is behind most of it. She was Turkish. And I must say that I also encouraged his interest. It's . . . it was part of his heritage. Coming here to live and write his book was the fulfilment of a dream he'd had for years. There wasn't anyone in his life, if you know what I mean. Hadn't been for years. So his work and his interests became his life. Do you think, Inspector, that my son was killed by someone he knew?'

'That is what we must determine. There is no evidence of a

forced entry into the apartment and so he may have known his killer. We have to look closely at his contacts in the city.'

The traffic began to move. Their driver gave a small grunt of satisfaction. Arthur Regan looked down at his own hands before he spoke again. 'When my son was younger, he did sometimes pick men up to sleep with. I don't know whether he was doing that here.'

'Our pathologist found no sign of recent sexual activity,' Süleyman said. 'But of course, Mr Regan, we will investigate all possibilities.'

They spent the rest of the journey into the city in silence. Arthur Regan looked out of the car window while Süleyman wondered how, when and where he'd met his Turkish wife. John Regan had been forty-six years old when he died, so Arthur and his wife must have first met back in the 1960s. Süleyman just recalled that decade himself, although he'd been a child at the time. Back then, the only foreigners who came to İstanbul were English teachers and hippies en route to India. He wondered which group Arthur Regan had belonged to. But he didn't ask him anything about it. It didn't seem appropriate. In less than an hour Mr Regan would have to identify the body of his mutilated son.

The lone boy eventually stole something from a man's back pocket and then almost immediately walked away from Tünel and made his way down the hill towards Karaköy on Galipdede Caddesi. Ömer Mungan took the decision to follow him. If the kid was alone, he had a chance of being able to track him to the adults that ran him. He walked past the Dervish tekke on the left-hand side and down between the musical instrument and CD shops. The road was steep and cobbled but Ömer was used to that. Every street in Mardin was cobbled, and so steep that domestic rubbish had to be collected by donkey.

The boy loped along, a hand in the pocket where he'd put what he'd stolen. From time to time he looked in shop windows, and Ömer found himself wondering what, had he just been working for himself, he might have purchased with his newly acquired wealth. But he only looked. Eventually he turned off Galipdede into a small street that Ömer felt probably led to somewhere near the Galata Tower. He knew that had he known the city better, finding a different route whereby he could pick the boy up later on would have been preferable. But he didn't know the city well and so he walked, admittedly some metres behind him, into a street that was almost silent. The boy couldn't help but hear his footsteps.

He didn't turn around completely and look straight at Ömer. It was more of a slight turn of the head accompanied by a quick glance with one eye. But it was enough. Ömer saw his body tense, and although he knew without doubt what the boy was about to do, he didn't increase his own pace. The boy began to run. For a moment Ömer wondered what he should do, then he ran too. The fact that he had no clear idea about what he might do if he caught the kid did not assist his pace, which, in comparison to the boy's, was risible.

And then things got even worse for Ömer. As if suddenly powered by a jet engine, the kid increased his pace and flew across the pavements and roads of old Galata like a gazelle.

Chapter 10

John Regan had only really had one friend in İstanbul, a female publicist called Sırma Alper from Cihangir. It was she who had told the police that one of the things John liked to do was have coffee and a snack at the Ada bookshop on İstiklal Caddesi. This had led Ayşe Farsakoğlu to an assistant at the shop called Derviş Güler.

'Yeah, the British guy was cool,' Derviş said. He was the sort of fashionable, hip, funky, bearded man who made Ayşe Farsakoğlu feel old. 'Liked to read all the historical stuff.'

'Did he meet anyone in particular when he came to the shop?' Ayşe asked.

'Not that I saw. I don't think his Turkish was very good.'

'But you spoke to him.'

'Yeah, I can speak English.'

'You remember we were asking questions about another of your customers back in January? A man called Levent Devrim?'

'Oh yeah, a guy police officer came.'

Mehmet Süleyman.

'You don't remember whether Dr Regan, the Englishman, had any contact with Devrim, do you?'

Derviş thought for a moment, then said, 'Don't think so. The scruffy dude was into a lot of New Age stuff. The British guy was much more fact-based, you know.'

Discovering possible connections between multiple homicide

victims was a dark art that didn't always deliver the desired, or indeed any, result. John Regan and Levent Devrim had enjoyed going to the same bookshop but they hadn't been friends. Leyla Ablak and Levent Devrim had been interested in alternative health and New Age philosophies but they hadn't apparently known each other. The only thing they all really had in common was that, so far, no one actually knew why they had been murdered.

Ayşe walked out of the Ada, on to İstiklal and almost into Mehmet Süleyman's arms.

'Oh, sir, I . . .' she stuttered. 'I . . .'

He ignored her discomfort. 'So were Levent Devrim and Dr Regan friends, or is that a ridiculous question?' he asked.

'It's a ridiculous question, sir,' she said.

He shook his head. 'I asked Dr Sarkissian whether John Regan had any illicit drugs in his system, but like Leyla Ablak, he didn't. Only Mr Devrim was stoned and slightly drunk, and he, it seems, smoked and drank alone.'

They began to walk down İstiklal in the direction of Taksim Square. Ayşe was going back to her car, which was parked in a side street.

After a moment she said, 'Where are you going?'

'Oh, John Regan's father has rented an apartment on Zambak Sokak; I'm going to take him to see where his son died.'

'That must have been tough for him yesterday, the state of the body and . . .'

'He bore it well,' Süleyman said. 'He says he wants to stay on here in the city for as long as he can. Wants to be here when we "catch him".'

'That puts the pressure on, doesn't it?'

'It's his choice,' Süleyman said. 'It's up to us to fulfil his expectations.'

Ayşe smiled. He was being very proper and 'on message' with the new image of a friendly, results-orientated Turkish police force that was plugged by the organisation at every opportunity these days. 'How corporate of you,' she said.

He shrugged. 'We get corporate, as you say, or we perish,' he said.

She saw the street where she'd parked her car coming up on her right. 'The car's just here,' she said. And then she moved slightly closer to him. 'Will I see you tonight?'

He gave her that look he sometimes could that was so cold it almost burnt her eyes out. Ayşe felt herself shrink beneath it.

'It depends how work goes,' he said. Then he added, 'I expect it's the same for you.'

'Er, yes . . .'

But she knew it wasn't. And so did he.

Hamid was back in Tarlabaşı in his mother's tiny flat with Şukru Şekeroğlu, who was murderous. Unfortunately for Hamid, his mother was out.

'How did the police know it was you?' yelled Şukru as he smacked the boy around the head. 'What did you do to call attention to yourself?'

'Nothing!' Hamid put his arms across his head to try and help deflect Şukru's blows. But they just kept on coming. 'Anyway, I got away from him, didn't I? I never led him to Marko, did I?'

Şukru, panting now, stopped hitting him. 'No, but he doesn't want you if you're marked by the police. Why did he chase you, this policeman?'

'I dunno! I was leaving Tünel, I walked down Galipdede, peeled off down some little road to the Galata Tower and then I heard footsteps behind me. So I looked and there he was. I recognised him. He was that copper that speaks Syriani. He was always over here when Levent Bey got topped. But he never knew me, I swear it!'

'Well he had to be running after you for a reason!'

'I'd just dipped some old man's pocket.'

'Then if he was just going after you for dipping, why didn't he call for help, eh? That's what they do usually, isn't it, call for assistance. You said he just chased you until you lost him.'

'Yeah.'

Şukru shook his head. 'I don't like it,' he said. Then he turned on the boy again, this time kicking him. 'Why the fuck didn't you tell me you'd seen someone with Levent Bey?'

'Ow!' the boy screamed, and then, 'Because I never saw no one killing him, I saw a monster with feathers and a face like—'

'You said you saw it killing him!'

'Yeah, well, maybe it . . . No . . . Yes, I did, but . . .'

Şukru kicked him again and then, exhausted, stopped. 'I can't work out whether you're a mad kid or you've been smoking your mother's crack,' he said. 'There are no fucking monsters.'

'There are, I've seen one, when I saw Levent Bey.'

Şukru sat down and put his head in his hands. The kid could probably be coached to go to the police and tell his monster story, leaving Şukru out. But his mother, Şeftali the whore, had been getting free childcare out of Şukru while the boy was with the Bulgarian, and she wouldn't want to give that up without some persuasion. Şukru was not a naturally violent man, but there were times when it was necessary, and this was probably one of them.

It was a nice photograph of John Regan; he was smiling and looked healthy, fresh and a lot younger than his forty-six years. The man sitting next to Çetin İkmen took it from him and sucked contentedly on his nargile while he looked at it. As the rose-scented tobacco snaked its way out of his mouth and nostrils he said, 'Nice.'

İkmen, who was smoking an altogether less floral tobacco, said, 'You know him?'

He'd come to the Tulip Nargile Café in Tophane, the centre of water-pipe smoking in İstanbul, to meet a man he'd been acquainted with for many years but whose real name he didn't know. To many, including İkmen, he was simply Pomegranate.

'No,' Pomegranate said, 'but if you'd like to introduce me . . .'

'He's dead,' İkmen said.

'Oh.'

'You should try reading the papers, or rather the ones that are worth reading, sometime,' İkmen said. 'His face has been all over them.'

Pomegranate shrugged.

'Anyway, look,' İkmen said, 'this man, an Englishman called Dr John Regan, forty-six, has been murdered and in a way that would give you nightmares. I won't go into detail. In short, he was living in Karaköy on Büyük Hendek Caddesi, he was writing an historical novel and he was gay.'

Pomegranate looked at John Regan's photograph again and said, 'What a waste.'

'Absolutely. We've got his aged father staying on in the city on the off chance that we manage to catch this lunatic . . .'

'You've not caught more than a cold lately, have you?' Pomegranate said archly.

İkmen could allude to the İstanbul police department's lack of success regarding recent murders in the city, but he didn't like it when others did so. He pointedly ignored Pomegranate's comment. 'His father has told us that his son was effectively outside of the gay scene back in the UK. But he doesn't know

112

whether he was still keeping himself to himself here. When he was younger, he was apparently partial to casual pick-ups.'

'Did he know the city well?'

'No. Spoke minimal Turkish and he only arrived in January. His mother was Turkish, but she died when he was a kid. He's been fascinated by all things Turkish ever since.'

Pomegranate looked at the photograph again. 'Mmm. Know what his preferences were? Did he do chicks with dicks?'

Tall, slim, groomed and with the most chiselled jaw İkmen could imagine, Pomegranate had been involved in İstanbul's gay scene for almost four decades. He'd started out in the 1970s with one tiny, very closeted café in Beyoğlu and built up to the two clubs, one gay and one transsexual, that he owned now.

'I believe he liked men to be men,' İkmen said. 'But in this city, who knows?'

'Well we do have the best trannies in the world,' Pomegranate said, 'even if I do say so myself.'

'We certainly have a lot of them,' İkmen said. One of them was his own cousin, Samsun. 'But look, Pomegranate, I need to know whether this John Regan was on the scene in any capacity. If he was, I want to know with whom and for what.'

'Well, sex . . .'

'Maybe, maybe not,' İkmen said. 'I'm not sure. But what I am sure about is that I don't want to come stamping into your clubs, or anyone else's, with a load of knuckle-dragging constables in tow. You people get enough of that.'

'Oh, İkmen, you are so gay-friendly!'

Again the inspector ignored the acid dripping from Pomegranate's voice. 'Look, there'll be money in it and you can feel all nice and warm and fluffy having done your civic duty.'

113

Pomegranate puffed on his nargile and then said, 'How can I resist?'

This time İkmen couldn't ignore his tone. He liked Pomegranate and he respected him, but the whole arch atmosphere just wasn't appropriate. He leaned across so that he could whisper in Pomegranate's ear. 'This man, John Regan,' he said, 'somebody tried to cut his heart out.'

And then he watched as Pomegranate's mouth fell open and his face went white.

Most of the national dailies were unimpressed by the İstanbul police department's response to first two and now three unsolved murders. Faruk Genç had spread the papers out on his desk and was looking at them with both confusion and the obsessive type of interest that can only come from being involved in something. To make up for the paucity of gory details from the police, some of the more hysterical publications were making a big thing out of the fact that all three victims had been killed on the twenty-first of the month; one of them had even dubbed the supposed single murderer 'the Twenty-First Killer'.

Faruk Genç was not a man given to superstition in any form, and so he found the whole notion of the Twenty-First Killer ridiculous. He imagined that Inspector Çetin İkmen did too. A knock at his office door took Faruk away from his papers. 'Come in.'

The door opened. It was Suzy Greenwood, the English homeopath.

'Oh, Mr Genç,' she said, 'could I have a word?'

She stood in that way that English people did sometimes when they would really rather not be doing what they were doing and so felt the need to apologise in some way for it. Suzy, with her

114

skin the colour of porridge and her habit of endlessly popping her own homeopathic pills, was a bit of a tragic case.

'Of course. Please sit down, Miss Greenwood,' Faruk said.

She sat, but only on the very edge of the chair.

'How can I help?' Faruk asked.

'Oh, well I know that it's very soon and everything and that you probably don't want anything to do with anything connected to the horrible events of the last few weeks, but . . .'

'But?'

She bit her lip. It was hugely irritating. Faruk Genç reiterated, 'But?'

'But Mr Genç, when Mrs Ablak died, she had an outstanding bill.'

'To you?'

'Yes.'

Most of the therapists worked for themselves, paying the spa for the office space and other facilities that they used. Most of them invoiced their regular customers either after each treatment or on completion of a course.

'How much did she owe you?'

'Well, I was treating Mrs Ablak for depression,' she said. 'That's a long course and so I would invoice her once a month.'

He tried not to let his feelings show on his face. The only reason why Leyla had been depressed was because she was worried about her husband being accused of treason, or rather she was concerned about how that would affect his finances. Also she had become nervous about her infidelity in the last few months of her life. Although her husband might be a traitor, she didn't want to be branded a scarlet woman. It was nothing to do with falling in love with Faruk or anything like that; she hadn't loved him and he knew it.

'So how much did she owe?'

He saw her cringe. She was one of those English people who didn't like to talk about money. How ridiculous!

'Two hundred euros,' she said. 'And you see, with Mrs Ablak dead and her husband dead too, I don't know who to recover the money from.'

'No, of course you don't.'

'I mean, it is a lot of money, Mr Genç, and I could really do with it. Do you think the police would know how I could get it back? Or is there maybe a lawyer or somebody?'

For someone who was so nervous about talking money, Suzy Greenwood was a very anxious creditor.

'You see, Mr Genç, although I know you've just been through a terrible time, what with Mrs Ablak's death and then your dear wife . . .' Like all the spa staff, Suzy Greenwood knew that he'd been having an affair with Leyla Ablak. Everyone in Turkey knew that the general's wife had died after having illicit sex. She was being, as she could be, consciously obsequious. '. . . I know I can trust you to help me,' she added.

Not for the first time, Faruk Genç was aware of the way that Suzy Greenwood made his skin crawl. He bit down on his revulsion and said, 'Of course, Miss Greenwood, I will do everything I can to help you recover your money. I will speak to the police.'

'Oh, would you? That would be so kind!'

'It is my pleasure,' he said.

She giggled a little and for a moment they both sat in silence looking at each other. He wanted her to go but she, apparently, wanted to stay where she was. Eventually he said, 'Was there anything else?'

'Oh, no, sorry,' she said. She stood up. 'I shouldn't take up your time.'

'It is no problem.' He smiled.

'That's very kind.' She moved towards his office door and opened it, then turned back to look at him once again, 'You know, Mr Genç, if there is anything I can do for you, you only have to ask,' she said.

As she closed the door behind her, Faruk Genç felt a shiver run down his back. Was he only imagining it, or had she had a playful glint in her eyes when she'd offered to do 'anything' for him? Ugh, it was a terrible thought, but it was not the first time he'd had it. İkmen had asked him whether any members of staff at the spa had nursed a passion for him, and of course there had been, from the start, the unwelcome flirting of Suzy Greenwood.

The informant, Necati Hallaç, had already told Süleyman that the boy Hamid had been seen at his mother's flat in Tarlabaşı with Şukru Şekeroğlu. When the gypsy brought the boy in to the police station, Hamid was dirty and covered with bruises, but he was definitely the same boy that Ömer Mungan had chased the previous day.

Şukru Şekeroğlu pushed him in front of Süleyman and Ömer and barked at him, 'Tell them what you told me.'

The child looked cowed and Süleyman noticed that he flinched every time Şukru moved towards him.

'Just speak,' Ömer said. 'Tell the truth.'

The child looked up at Şukru, which was not an encouraging start, and then he said, 'I saw something standing over Levent Bey back in the winter.'

'That is Levent Devrim,' Süleyman said.

'Yeah.'

Süleyman frowned; he was interested in the boy's use of the word 'something' as opposed to 'someone'. But he didn't prompt the child in any way. He told him to sit down and then he said, 'Tell me everything.'

117

The boy looked at Şukru Şekeroğlu, who nodded his head.

'It was proper early in the morning,' Hamid said.

'What were you doing away from home at such a time?' Süleyman asked.

'Collecting firewood.'

Şukru Şekeroğlu had given exactly the same reason for being out on the streets when he'd found Levent Devrim. But then of course it had been snowing.

'Tell us what you saw, Hamid.'

The boy took a moment to apparently compose himself, and then he said, 'I went to where they're pulling down the buildings because there's always wood there. They just knock it out and then chuck it about so you can get hold of it easy. But 'cause it'd been snowing, all the stuff outside was wet and so I went inside.'

'Inside?'

'One of the old broken houses. I went inside to get wood.'

There was a pause, and then Süleyman said, 'What happened next?'

Hamid looked at Şukru again, and this time Süleyman said, 'Don't look at him!'

The boy snapped his head around to the policemen. 'I saw it through a doorway in the old house,' he said.

'Saw what?'

'The monster.'

'Monster?' This time Süleyman looked up at Şukru Şekeroğlu. 'What's this? Some kind of joke?'

The gypsy shrugged. 'The boy came to me with something he wanted to get off his conscience. I don't know, I just brought him. Maybe he's mad.'

Süleyman looked at the boy again and said, 'All right, so if we accept that there was a "monster", tell me what it looked like and what it was doing, specifically, to Levent Devrim.'

118

The boy did look scared, that was beyond doubt. He said, 'It had arms and legs like a man but on its head and down its back it was like a bird.'

'It had feathers?'

'Yes.'

'And its face?'

'Oh, that was like it was melted or something,' he said. 'A nose that was falling down its face and a mouth that hung like a . . . I don't know . . . I didn't see its eyes.'

'It didn't see you?'

'No.'

'So you didn't see it from the front?'

'No. From the side.'

'What was it doing to Levent Devrim when you saw it, Hamid?'

'Nothing.' He shrugged. 'Standing over him.'

'So you didn't see this thing kill Levent Devrim?'

'No.'

'How long did you watch it for?'

'Dunno.'

'Seconds? Minutes?'

The boy shrugged again. 'A bit.'

'A bit. So then what did you do? What did it do?'

'It went away,' Hamid said.

'Just like—'

'It walked past Levent Bey and then it went off into the wrecked house next door and then it disappeared.'

'Disappeared?'

'I couldn't see it no more.'

'OK, so what did you do then, Hamid?'

'I went to look at Levent Bey. I saw that his head was hanging off. I poked him with one of me sticks to see if he was still alive, but he weren't.'

To Süleyman and Ömer Mungan it seemed that a man who had been effectively decapitated had to be dead, but then neither of them was a young gypsy boy raised on myth and magical thinking.

'Then what did you do?' Süleyman asked.

'I legged it,' the boy said.

'You went home?'

'Yeah. But I never told me mum nothing. I never told no one nothing till I told Şukru Bey today. He brought me here because it was the right thing to do.'

As well as hearing the rehearsal in the boy's voice, Süleyman knew what Sugar Barışık had told Ömer Mungan before the boy disappeared: namely that he'd been telling people that it had been him and not Şukru who'd found the body. He looked up at Şukru Şekeroğlu. Still with his eyes on the man he said, 'So what were you doing up at Tünel yesterday, hanging out with a load of foreign boys?'

'Oh, I wasn't hanging out with them boys. They was just there.'

'Pocket-diving.'

'We all was, but I was on me own,' Hamid said. 'I run away from home after I saw the monster.'

'Why?' Süleyman asked.

For a moment the boy looked confused, and then he said, 'Because I thought it might get me.'

'It didn't see you. How could it get you?'

The boy said nothing.

Later, when he let Şukru Şekeroğlu and the boy go, Süleyman asked Ömer Mungan, 'What did you make of the monster story?'

Ömer thought for a moment and then he said, 'You know,

sir, that was one of the few things the child said that I did believe.'

And Süleyman smiled, because that was exactly how he felt about Hamid's story too.

Chapter 11

'All right, I didn't like her,' Suzy Greenwood said to İkmen. 'Is that what you wanted to hear?'

'I want to hear the truth,' İkmen said, 'and if that is the truth . . .'

'Leyla Ablak was seducing Mr Genç away from where he should have been, which was at his dying wife's side,' she said.

İkmen looked across at Ayşe Farsakoğlu. He wanted to see her reaction to this – her English was up to it – but she just yawned. He'd seen Süleyman in the car park earlier, for a couple of cigarettes, and he'd been yawning also. A busy night for both of them, then. İkmen only just managed to stop himself from scowling. Ayşe should have forgotten about Süleyman years ago; he was no good for her.

'And what was Mr Genç's dying wife to you?' İkmen asked. 'Did you treat her with your homeopathic medicine?'

'No. I didn't know her.'

'Then why were you so concerned about what her husband was doing with Mrs Ablak?'

Suzy Greenwood sat up straighter. 'Because I thought it was wrong,' she said.

'How did you know about their affair?' İkmen asked. 'Did somebody tell you?'

She thought for a few moments, and then she said, 'No. No,

I just . . . I know Mr Genç quite well, and so I notice things about him.'

'You are in love with him.'

'No!' She looked up at him and he saw that her eyes were filled with tears.

'What made you think that Faruk Genç and Leyla Ablak were having an affair, Miss Greenwood?'

She shook her head. 'Oh, it was . . . Well, they flirted,' she said. 'Whenever Mrs Ablak came to the spa, she seemed to seek him out, she pursued him – or rather, that was what I felt. But I didn't know that they met at the spa after hours and I didn't kill her. Why would I?'

'Why indeed?' İkmen looked down at a piece of paper on his desk and said, 'When Mrs Ablak was murdered, you were at a conference in Kavala, Greece. Is that correct?'

'Yes. I told you when you first asked me where I was.'

There was no doubt that she had left the country before Leyla Ablak died and returned after she was dead. But she could still have ordered her murder. Her and Hande Genç, maybe General Ablak . . . But it was an outside chance and İkmen knew it. There was no record of Suzy Greenwood ever having met or even telephoned Hande Genç. The only reason she was at the station at all was because Faruk Genç had always, he said, had the feeling that she had the hots for him. In that he was probably right, but it still put Suzy a long way away from killing his lover.

'So what did you know about Mrs Ablak?' İkmen looked down at his notes again. 'I believe that you were treating her, or whatever you call it, for depression.'

Incensed by what she saw as a slight on her profession, Suzy Greenwood said, 'Homeopathy is treated with respect in my country, I'll have you know! The royal family swear by it!'

İkmen smiled. 'With respect, Miss Greenwood, am I supposed to be impressed by the beliefs of a dysfunctional German family?'

For a moment she was speechless. She'd only come in because, when he'd called her, she'd thought that it meant İkmen was getting her two hundred lira back for her. She said, 'Mrs Ablak was depressed because her husband was under investigation and also because of some childhood issues.'

'What childhood issues?'

'That is confidential between the therapist, myself, and the patient . . .'

'She's dead, Miss Greenwood, and you are a suspect. Tell me what her issues were; I don't have time for this.'

Her face drained. Maybe it was actually hearing the word 'suspect' in relation to herself. She said, 'She talked a lot about her mother. Her mother is a member of your former royal family, and apparently she overwhelmed Mrs Ablak with her past when she was a child.'

'In what way?'

'Oh, slavish following of outmoded etiquette; her insistence that no man was ever good enough for her daughter. Mrs Ablak had a history of broken relationships, which she put down to the fact that her mother refused to let her marry the first man she ever loved, years ago. And her father, who wasn't royal, was weak. She felt that her mother had ruined her life.'

'Is that it?' İkmen asked.

'Yes.'

'But then what are spas but places for the worried rich to come and pay someone to talk to them?' He shook his head. Fatma had nagged him about the soba all the while he had been trying to drink his morning tea, and it had put him in a foul mood. It wasn't even cold any more, and besides, every time she talked about the soba, he had to think about the fact that he was retiring at the end of the year. And he really didn't want to.

'To be honest, she wasn't a bad woman so much as a selfish one. She was always civil to me. I just couldn't abide her behaviour around Mr Genç.'

İkmen, who had made an inventory of Suzy Greenwood's clients the previous evening, said, 'You told me earlier, Miss Greenwood, that you had never met the late Mrs Genç.'

'That's right.'

'And yet you treated her brother, didn't you?'

'Her brother?'

'Cem Atay,' İkmen said.

'Professor Atay? He's a friend of Mr Genç.'

'He's also Mrs Genç's brother,' İkmen said. 'What does he come to see you about, Miss Greenwood?'

This time she didn't even bother to try and protect her client's confidentiality. 'Professor Atay is in the public eye. Sometimes he suffers from camera fright.'

'And homeopathy helps him with that, does it?'

'He says it does, yes,' she said.

İkmen smiled. 'So we have to thank you, I imagine, Miss Greenwood, for Professor Atay's latest excellent documentary about eastern Anatolian myths and legends.'

But Suzy Greenwood didn't smile. She just said, 'I guess you do, Inspector, yes.'

And then his smile dropped. 'You didn't tell Professor Atay anything about Mrs Ablak, did you?'

'Of course I didn't.' She sounded exhausted, because she was. She'd had to get out of bed at the crack of dawn to come and have questions barked out aggressively at her. 'Why would I?'

*   *   *

125

Sezen Hanım laid a rug over the old man's knees and then went back to her embroidery. She had a frame in front of the soba at which she sat creating a silk representation of the Sultanahmet mosque. She looked back at the old man again. Her uncle, Rafik Efendi, whose house she shared, was the last member of her immediate family who could remember the Ottoman Empire. And even he only had the vaguest of recollections.

Rafik had been born in 1918, just before the end of the Great War, and had been little more than a toddler when the Republic had come into being in 1923. He wasn't really an Ottoman at all, but he was the nearest thing that Sezen had, and she loved him. It was just a shame that Uncle Rafik had always preferred men. None of his marriages had lasted, he'd never had any children, and keeping his homosexuality quiet had sometimes placed a strain on the whole family. He'd been priapic in his youth, and in later years, when people interested in the life of one of Turkey's last princes had come to visit him, it had been impossible to trust him with male guests. Even at his advanced age he still 'entertained' occasionally, much to Sezen's disgust.

Sezen sewed and thought about Leyla. The police still didn't know who had killed her, but then they were probably not that worried about it. Republicans – or, even worse, Islamists – to a man, what did they care about a woman who should have been a princess? Had they really cared, they would have allowed Mehmet Süleyman Efendi to investigate Leyla's murder. One of their own. But they hadn't. Instead there was that awful little man İkmen, who was now also involved in an investigation into the murder of a foreigner. News reports said that the father of the foreigner, an Englishman, was staying on in the city until his son's murderer was caught. So of course İkmen would give that his full attention. Leyla would just be sidelined.

She began to feel tears invade her eyes and pulled herself

together. Sezen Hanım didn't cry; she had too much dignity. But for all the waywardness of Leyla's early years, and the resentment that had characterised their later relationship, she missed her daughter bitterly. The final year of Leyla's life had probably been the worst: her husband coming under suspicion in the Ergenekon investigation, and then the unhappy little affair she'd had with that married man at her spa. The spa where she had died. Although she didn't know him, Sezen Hanım didn't trust that spa manager, and she wondered why the police hadn't arrested him. He'd had sex with Leyla after hours and then, after hours, she was murdered. How hard could it be to work out what had happened there?

But then her thoughts were distracted when she accidentally speared her thumb with her embroidery needle. 'Ow!'

As she looked down at her hand, blood began to ooze from the wound. In the corner, the old prince stirred briefly and then went back to sleep again.

'It's Miss Barışık,' Ömer Mungan said as he handed the telephone over to Mehmet Süleyman.

The older man took the call. 'Yes?'

'Hello, Inspector,' the old woman said. 'I hear you've had the boy Hamid and Şukru Şekeroğlu in your no doubt loving embrace.'

He smiled. 'You know I can't comment on that, Sugar,' he said. 'But I won't insult your intelligence by telling you that you're mistaken.'

'You are as gracious as you are handsome, Mehmet Bey,' she said. 'It warms an old woman's heart and I thank you for it.'

'You're welcome. Now what can I do for you, Sugar Hanım? If it's in my gift to help you, I will.'

'Well actually it's more what I can do for you,' Sugar said.

'Oh?'

'A little snippet for you, Mehmet Bey, about Şeftali the whore, Hamid's mother.'

'What about her?'

'She's doing her shopping with two black eyes and a lot fewer teeth,' she said.

Süleyman leaned back in his chair. 'Is she?'

'Word is that it was Şukru Şekeroğlu who gave her her new face decoration.'

'Oh? Why would he do that, Sugar?'

There was a very slight pause, and then she said, 'Well, a gypsy I know who you know too is of the opinion that Şeftali was trying to blackmail Şukru over something to do with her son.'

'Do you know what, Hanım?'

'No, but my gypsy friend who is also yours might,' she said. 'For a consideration.'

Like a lot of poor areas, Tarlabaşı worked on several different levels that didn't always divide or join at the junctures one would logically expect. Sugar was a Kurd and yet here she was blagging cash for a gypsy.

'Oh, Sugar Hanım, my pockets are getting emptier by the day,' Süleyman said.

'What a shame.'

'What a shame indeed. However, I think I may be able to find the odd few kuruş if I look hard enough,' he said.

'I know that you can, Mehmet Bey.'

He smiled. She'd get her cut once the gypsy had been paid and had lied to her about how much Süleyman had given him.

'Tell Necati to come to me at the usual place; assure him that I will have money,' he said.

He heard her smile. 'You know he doesn't like to ask himself . . .'

'Mr Hallaç is such a sensitive soul.'

'And Şukru Şekeroğlu's eyes and ears are everywhere,' she said, and put the phone down.

Süleyman replaced his receiver and looked across the room at Ömer Mungan. 'Don't know if you caught all that,' he said. 'Necati Hallaç could have just called me himself, but he probably owes Sugar something and so she agreed to call me for a price that he can feel honourable about. It's not a debt, it's a payment. Do you see?'

'Well, yes, sort of . . .'

'In addition, if Şukru Şekeroğlu ever suspects that Necati is informing us about his movements, and beats him up to find out what he knows, Necati can lie to him with a clear conscience. Such is life amongst the poor and disenfranchised of İstanbul. Everyone must make a living.'

'So the gypsy has information for us.'

'About why the prostitute Şeftali has, it is said, taken a beating from Şukru Şerkeroğlu, yes.'

'Which is?'

'Blackmail,' he said. 'The subtext being that Şukru is concealing something from us.'

'Which we know already.'

'Yes.' He thought for a moment and then said, 'Let's save some money. Let's bring Şukru Şekeroğlu in.'

'Before you've spoken to your gypsy, sir?'

'Yes, I think so,' Süleyman said. He stood up, put his jacket on and began to walk towards his office door. 'To hell with convention. Let's do it now.'

The professor's office at Boğaziçi University was the kind of room that Çetin İkmen liked. Lined with books and full of strange and sometimes unfathomable artefacts, it was testimony to a mind that was wide-ranging in its pursuit of knowledge.

Cem Atay, who was almost as distinguished in the flesh as he was on television, sat behind a vast scarred desk covered with books and papers, in no easily discernible order, looking very comfortable. 'No historical phenomenon, be it the Ottoman Empire or early Anatolian civilisations, existed in a vacuum, and so one must sometimes refer to, and compare and contrast with, contemporary groups.'

'So your studies take you to other countries?' İkmen said.

'And continents, Inspector,' he said. 'For my series about Ottoman minorities, I went to Israel, Syria and Greece. I even visited gypsy communities in Macedonia and Bosnia. For the last few years I have been doing research for a book I have been commissioned to write about the relationship between the Ottoman Empire and the Spanish Empire. We engaged the Spaniards in a lot of sea battles in the Mediterranean and beyond, as I'm sure you know, in large part to try and get our hands on their prolific amounts of South American gold.' He smiled. 'But then we also relieved them of a lot of their unwanted Jewish citizens, as I am certain you also know.'

'That worked out rather better for us than it did for them,' İkmen said.

'It was an excellent PR exercise which also gave us some very clever scientists, mathematicians and doctors, yes. But I'm sure you didn't come here to talk about my work, Inspector.'

'No, sir.' İkmen took a sip of the excellent coffee the professor had given him and said, 'I'm afraid it is about your late sister, Professor Atay. Or rather it's about her husband.' He'd had to follow up on the interview he'd had with Suzy Greenwood. Cem Atay was Hande Genç's brother; he was involved.

He frowned. 'Faruk?' And then, seeming to remember

something, he said, 'Oh, about his, er, other woman, the one who . . . er . . .'

'Leyla Ablak,' İkmen said. 'Professor Atay, we're trying to find out who might have known about that affair before Mrs Ablak died. Did you know about it?'

'No,' he said. 'But – and here you may find me controversial, Inspector – had I known, I would have completely understood.'

'Understood?'

'Faruk is my brother-in-law. My sister was a very sick woman and had been for a couple of years,' he said. 'Her illness made her irascible and – if one can say this about a terminally ill person without sounding a beast – her self-pity, justifiable as it was, was constant and difficult to bear. Faruk was Hande's nurse, her uncomplaining companion; he funded her completely and he was also often her whipping boy too. She couldn't help it. I'm not saying she could. But if Faruk found any sort of happiness during those dark days, then I can only be glad for him. That it ended as it did is almost beyond imagining, and I feel sorry for him.'

Sympathy for Faruk Genç was not something İkmen had been expecting from Professor Atay, but he could see his point of view.

'Did any other member of your family know about the affair?' İkmen asked.

'Not that I know of,' he said. 'Had my mother or my other sister found out, I'm sure Faruk would have been made very aware of it.'

'Ah.'

'Yes, my mother is a vocal woman, to say the least. She has a very strong sense of what is right and what is not.'

'Infidelity is always wrong.'

'According to my mother, yes. When she did find out, when we all found out, she was furious.'

İkmen said, 'I understand, sir, that you attended Mr Genç's spa, where you had homeopathic treatment.'

'From Miss Greenwood, yes.'

'Did she ever say anything to you about Leyla Ablak and your brother-in-law?'

Cem Atay fingered the edge of a large brown book on his desk. 'I didn't even know that Leyla Ablak went to the spa, Inspector, much less that she was having an affair with Faruk. And anyway, why would Miss Greenwood have told me about her? As a non-Turkish-speaker, I'm pretty sure the whole Ergenekon aura that surrounded General Ablak would have passed her by.'

İkmen toyed with the idea of telling the professor that in his opinion, the Greenwood woman had been at least a little in love with Faruk Genç. He decided against it. 'Where were you on the night that Leyla Ablak died, Professor Atay?'

'Am I under suspicion, Inspector İkmen?'

'Inasmuch as everyone connected to a murder victim is, however tenuously.'

The professor opened the brown book, which was apparently his diary, and said, 'Well, that night I had dinner with a friend, a lady.' He looked up and smiled. 'I can give you her name, Inspector, if I must, but if I might ask you to be discreet . . .'

'Of course.' Now maybe the professor's take on Faruk Genç's situation became more understandable.

Cem Atay wrote a name and a phone number on a piece of paper and handed it to İkmen. 'This is her personal mobile number and I was with her all night.'

İkmen put the piece of paper into his pocket. He would be discreet. He had already decided to send Ayşe Farsakoğlu to

132

interview this lady rather than go himself. He said, 'Can you tell me why you consulted Miss Greenwood, Professor Atay?'

He smiled. 'Stage fright,' he said.

Suzy Greenwood had been right about that.

'Odd, isn't it?' he said. 'A colossal show-off like me. I've tried everything over the years: hypnotherapy, diazepam, meditation.'

'And did the homeopathy help you?' İkmen asked.

He said, 'Oh, sympathetic magic does work, Inspector; anyone who doubts that is, in my opinion, a fool.'

And İkmen, son of a witch with more than the odd bit of magic in his soul himself, said, 'Yes, sir.' Even though he did not, personally, include homeopathy in his own definition of sympathetic magic. But then he felt that the professor had just been touching the very tip of a large iceberg of examples he could have used, but had chosen not to.

'So you didn't tell us earlier about the fact that Hamid had seen the body of Levent Devrim because you wanted to protect the boy,' Süleyman said to the cowed figure of Şukru Şekeroğlu in the chair in front of him.

The gypsy looked him straight in the eyes. It hadn't taken a lot, oddly, to make him come clean. 'Yeah.'

'And then when it came out that the boy might have seen something he shouldn't, you got him out of Tarlabaşı and sent him to one of your friends.'

'I sent him to no one,' Şukru said. 'I just got him out.'

'Because you didn't want us to find out that you had been withholding information from us.'

'I didn't want the kid involved.'

Süleyman leaned back in his chair. 'Even if he had killed Levent Devrim?'

133

Şukru batted the suggestion away with a dirty hand. 'That kid couldn't kill a kitten!' he said. 'I was trying to protect him from an interrogation like this!'

'By concealing the truth and then compounding the problem by attempting to prevent us from finding out,' Süleyman said.

Şukru said, 'But it was all nonsense! Monsters and feathers and—'

'Maybe our murderer was in disguise,' Süleyman said. 'Maybe he, she or it really was a monster. Mr Şekeroğlu, your own Roma culture is rich in myth and legend . . .'

'Oh, so because I'm Roma, I'm fucking stupid!' Şukru stood up. He was a good deal taller than Süleyman and towered over Ömer Mungan, who also got to his feet.

Süleyman looked up casually at the gypsy and said, 'Oh do sit down, Mr Şekeroğlu.'

But the gypsy remained on his feet, as did Ömer Mungan.

'You don't understand our life, Inspector Süleyman, however much you might think you do,' Şukru said, alluding, albeit obliquely, to the time Süleyman had spent with his sister. 'There are things we believe in that you don't, just like there are things you believe to be true that we ignore. But monsters ain't a thing we tend to come across.'

Süleyman didn't ask him to sit again. For a moment he just stared at him with steady eyes, and then he said, 'All right, if we're playing the ethnic card, you can tell me all about your beliefs, Mr Şekeroğlu. And you can start by explaining what, if anything, the number twenty-one means to you.'

Chapter 12

He came awake fighting, as he so often did these days, for breath. But this was nothing to do with his heart or his asthma. Somebody had him by the throat; somebody was on top of him, holding him down. Rafik Efendi tried to shout, but he couldn't. All he could feel was fear and a rage he didn't even begin to understand. He was an old man and if somebody was killing him then they were probably doing him a favour. What did he do except sleep, try to get an erection and piss himself? Why shouldn't some kind soul put him out of his misery?

But this wasn't a mercy killing; it was far too painful to be that. Rafik looked up to see what his attacker looked like and found himself regarding a blankness filled with tiny silver stars. The oxygen to his brain was being cut off. He heard himself, an infantalised gurgling in his throat, and he was disgusted. Was this how it would end? With a sound like a baby newborn and choking for air?

It intensified. A pain in his chest that defied all description. Was this what a heart attack was like? he wondered. Like having his chest sliced open, and a smell of metal that reminded him of all those times he'd taken a boy who did it for money and then hurt him. Blood.

Blood bubbling up in his mouth where his teeth used to be and pouring out of his mouth on to his chin. Like a baby bringing up milk.

* * *

135

Çetin İkmen lay beside his sleeping wife and wondered what the city was doing. He thought about John Regan, Leyla Ablak and Levent Devrim, and he went through, again, those areas of their lives that seemed to intersect. They were few and slight and his heart began to pound as he considered the possibility that maybe their deaths were completely unconnected. Only the dates of their deaths provided any real consistency, and it was that that really kept him awake. It was the twenty-first again.

He'd heard of killers copying one another, or rather he was aware of it in crime fiction. Could such things happen in fact? Nothing beyond the most basic details of the victims' deaths had been released to the press, so how could a copycat know what to emulate?

He turned and looked at Fatma, who was just faintly smiling. The weather had improved considerably in the last week and there had been no need to light the soba for the past three days. In the scheme of things it was no great triumph, but then small victories pleased her and it made him envy her. She took joy where she found it, in what he arrogantly called the mundane. He knew there was nothing wrong with that, but he also knew that the mundane didn't please him. How was he going to deal with retirement without the necessary resources to take pleasure in an afternoon spent in a coffee house or a game of tavla with other 'old' men? He wasn't. The last time he'd gone to a coffee house just for pleasure was when his father had taken him as a young man, just before he'd married Fatma. Every subsequent visit to such places had been on business of one sort or another, and now that one wasn't allowed to smoke in public areas any more, that was as much of a chore as everything else had become.

İkmen wondered how it would be if he retracted his request for retirement. The soba aside, Fatma would probably welcome it if he continued on at work. At home he was going to get under her feet and irritate her, and with just the two of them in the apartment most of the time, they would certainly row. On the other hand, he was tired. His body felt like a particularly troublesome appendage most of the time and his last medical had thrown up a whole load of age-related irritations, some of which he had been given tablets for. Not that he took them. He didn't want to end up like Arto Sarkissian, taking tablets to counteract the side effects of other tablets. He just wanted to work and feel the way he had felt in the past. He wanted to get that tingle on the back of his neck and in the pit of his stomach as he closed in on his prey and knew that just his existence was making him or her sweat.

But then was that happening now? Was there someone in the city who was sweating as he lay there just at the thought of him? Was that real, a fantasy, or was he just too old and too cynical to see it? Çetin İkmen looked at the clock beside his bed and watched as midnight clicked over into the following day.

Going out was not something that Sezen Hanım often did. Since she'd been widowed, and particularly since her daughter's death at the beginning of the year, it had not felt right. But her friend Melek had really badgered her to go to what had turned out to be a very pleasant evening at the Swissotel in nearby Beşiktaş. So close it was almost walking distance from the house, she'd felt happy to leave her uncle for just a short time to have a couple of glasses of champagne with Melek.

She had also managed to convince herself that her time out had been improving. Melek worked as a curator at the Pera Museum, and the Swissotel event had featured a selection of the museum's new 'Contrasting Civilisations' exhibition. Through the prism of a carefully selected group of artefacts, Melek and her colleagues had presented a snapshot of the Ottoman Empire's relationships with other significant countries when it was at the height of its power in the 1520s. Süleyman the Lawgiver, or the Magnificent as he was known in the West, had been sultan then, and in 1529 he had extended the Empire to the gates of Vienna. Relationships with foreign powers had therefore been conducted from a position of strength, and people like the British and even the mighty Spanish Empire had quaked before Süleyman and his terrifying corps of Janissaries. After that high point, it had been downhill all the way until the early twentieth century, when the Empire had imploded.

Sezen walked up the creaking staircase that led to the upper storey of the house, trying not to make too much noise in case she woke her uncle. It was after midnight, and Rafik Efendi was brittle and easily woken now. The smallest sound could rouse him, and then it was always a fight to get him to go back to sleep again. But Sezen would check on him, even if it did wake him up. Having a very old person in the house was a bit like having a baby again: one was always looking and listening to make sure that they were still breathing.

She stepped on to the landing, the wooden house creaking and sighing around her. Light from the open door that led to her bedroom showed her that her uncle's door was open. This was unusual but fortuitous, because it meant that when she went in to see him, Sezen probably wouldn't disturb him.

She first realised that something was wrong when she noticed that the smell coming from Rafik's room was different. He'd been incontinent for some time and so she was accustomed to the sharp smell of ammonia, the occasional sick odour of faeces. But this was different; this was something she didn't know. Sezen peered through the darkness and for a moment she couldn't really tell what she was looking at. But then, as her eyes adjusted to the gloom, she realised that her uncle wasn't in his bed at all;

he was lying on the floor. Alarmed that he might have fallen out of bed and hit his head, she flicked on the light switch by the door and made as if to walk over to his bed. Then she stopped, frozen in horror, finding it hard to believe what she was seeing.

'You know, just for a few hours I clung on to the hope that we weren't going to have to leave our beds this time,' Çetin İkmen said as he smoked over the old man's washstand.

Commissioner Ardıç didn't even look at him. 'Put the cigarette out, İkmen,' he said.

The other officers in the room, including Süleyman, became still and silent. They were all in the presence of something unprecedentedly terrible, and Ardıç was telling İkmen to put his smoke out. They all waited for his reply. When it came, it was undramatic. 'No.'

Ardıç's response was muted too, to say the least. He just shrugged. Other people began to breathe again. Arto Sarkissian, who was the only person in the room who had been oblivious to what had just happened, stood up and looked down at the body he had just been examining. 'The heart is missing,' he said.

Ardıç switched his gaze from İkmen to the Armenian. 'You're sure?'

'The chest was cut open, again with a large-bladed knife, then the ribs were spread and the heart was removed with a smaller blade,' he said. 'A better job this time.'

'Than?'

'The Englishman,' the doctor said. 'That was a mess. This is not. He's obviously learning.'

Everyone in that room looked down at what remained of Rafik Efendi. A bloodied shell, its legs akimbo, it was not the image of the prince dignified in death that the woman whose crying they could all hear from downstairs had wanted for the old man.

İkmen looked over at Süleyman, whose distant relative the old man had been, and wondered what he was thinking. But his face was impassive.

'So the heart could be . . .'

'Having removed it, which must have taken some effort,' İkmen said, 'I doubt he'd just throw it away. He took it for a reason.'

'A trophy,' Süleyman said.

'A talisman.' İkmen shrugged. 'How can we even guess at what it might mean when we don't know his, or her, motives?'

Arto shook his head. 'From my point of view I'd say that the murderer was probably a man. To remove a heart from even an old chest is difficult . . .'

'Female surgeons,' İkmen offered.

'True, Inspector, but their patients are anaesthetised when they operate. This man was alive.'

İkmen saw Süleyman's face crease in disgust.

'Old as he was, he clung to life beyond the opening of his chest cavity,' Arto said. 'A terrible death; he must have been in agony.'

Again silence rolled in across the room until Ardıç looked across at İkmen, who had put out one cigarette and lit another. 'Why can't we catch this character?'

'Or characters,' İkmen replied. 'Not sure it's one person, sir.'

'But it could be?'

'Yes.'

Ardıç looked at his phone. 'And this date thing. Here we are again, the twenty-first. What about that?'

İkmen shook his head. 'Nothing,' he said. 'It doesn't mean anything. I mean, clearly it means something to the killer or killers, but it doesn't have any meaning that we have discovered so far . . .'

'Then you're obviously looking in the wrong places,' Ardıç said. His brows knitted above his dark eyes. 'Look again. Look again at every victim, every crime scene and every bloodied corpse this city has suffered since the beginning of the year. When this story hits the media, yet another killing on the twenty-first, we are going to have to answer some questions, quite rightly, about what the hell we think we've been doing for the last four months. This is now a serial killer, or so the media will say, and I for one won't have one of those fucking bastards in my city. Do I make myself clear?'

She didn't want to be with this woman, she wanted to be with Mehmet Bey. She'd seen him come in, go up to that terrible bedroom she would close up for ever as soon as she could, but he hadn't come down to see her.

Not for the first time, the policewoman, a Sergeant Farsakoğlu, said to her, 'Sezen Hanım, is there anyone I can call for you?'

Again she'd said, 'No.'

Of course there were people she could have called, a lot of them, but she wanted no one, except perhaps Mehmet Bey. With Rafık Efendi's death, her entire connection to her Ottoman past had dissolved and Sezen had never felt so exposed, mainly because she knew, deep as it was buried, what Rafık had done. What would she do, what would the family do, if damaged middle-aged men stepped out of the past with stories about anal rape and sex for money? When someone died like this, the papers and the TV stations were full of it; there was no way she could hide a death as violent as Rafık's. Maybe if she told Mehmet Bey the whole truth, she could persuade him to keep the details the police gave to the media to a minimum. But then Nur Süleyman, Mehmet's mother, was forever telling everyone how honest he was. Could an appeal to his blood persuade him to be

141

economical with the truth should anything bad emerge about her uncle?

The doorbell rang, which made Sezen immediately rise to her feet. But the policewoman told her to sit down. One of the constables upstairs would deal with it. Big male feet thundered down the stairs. The policewoman looked at her and said, 'Would you like some tea?'

'No.'

The front door opened with a creak – the police had told her, disapprovingly, that the back door had been unlocked; it always was. Sezen closed her eyes. Why had she done that? She'd done it because her uncle had told her to. How else could the boys he still occasionally rented come and go without anybody seeing them?

Then she heard a voice. 'I'm a neighbour. What has happened? Can I see Sezen Hanım?'

It was that interfering Elif Ceylan. She was one of those who thought that just living near those of standing invested her and her family with quality too. Sezen knew it did not.

The officer said something to the silly woman, then Elif Ceylan said, 'Oh, because when I saw the police cars, I wondered whether it had anything to do with the man who was in the garden.'

She'd seen something, or she'd claimed to! In the garden. With the ever-open back door. She'd never said anything before! Sezen, terrified, called out to her, 'Elif dear, I'm in here! Do come in.' She looked at Sergeant Farsakoğlu, who was frowning. 'She is my friend, I need to speak to her,' she said.

Elif Ceylan was a small, round, peasanty woman who dressed in clothes that had been designed in Milan. One did that when one's husband was rich. Because she was short and gossiped, Sezen was in the habit of giving her unpleasant nicknames, like 'poison dwarf' and 'short on style'. Now, however, she wanted to see her more urgently than anyone else she could imagine. Elif lumbered in. Sezen said to the policewoman, 'Can I have a moment alone with my friend, please?'

Farsakoğlu frowned. 'I heard the lady say that she saw someone in the garden . . .'

'Yes, a man,' Elif Ceylan said. Before Sezen could stop her, she was standing next to the policewoman. 'I was looking out of my bedroom window; I was just getting ready for bed. I always take one last look outside before I retire, because one never knows, does one, and Sezen Hanım's garden is so lovely. I can't imagine having a better image in one's head if one is about to die suddenly and in an untimely fashion in one's sleep. But—'

'Can I talk to Elif Hanım—'

'What did he look like, the man in the garden, and what time did you see him?' The wretched policewoman cut across her words and now put herself between the two women as well. As Elif opened her mouth, Sezen Hanım began to feel herself breaking out into a sweat.

'Oh, he was tall,' the neighbour said. 'Although beyond seeing that it was a man I couldn't make out any details. I suppose it had to be about two hours ago . . .'

'And you didn't think to call us or alert Sezen Hanım to the fact that a man was in her garden?' the policewoman said.

And then, oddly Sezen thought at first, Elif smiled. 'Oh, there are often men in the garden,' she said. 'I think they must have come to see the old prince. Young people are so interested in the Ottoman Empire these days, don't you think? It's nice. They often come when Sezen Hanım is out.' Sezen Hanım closed her eyes; she must have been watching the house for years. The bitch. 'Partial to young men, I always thought, old Rafık Efendi, but then I don't judge, and anyway, they're like that, aren't they, aristocrats? Eccentric.'

The policewoman looked at Sezen as if to say *Did you know about this?* But instead she said, 'You will need to talk to one of the inspectors, Sezen Hanım.'

Elif Ceylan took one of Sezen's hands in hers and said, 'I don't know what's happened here, dear, but judging by the police cars, I can only imagine that one of Rafık Efendi's liaisons must have ended in tears. Is that right?'

Mehmet Süleyman sat down in the chair opposite the crying woman. Although a distant relative, he hardly knew Sezen İpek. But the interview that Ayşe Farsakoğlu had tried to conduct with her after her neighbour left had just disintegrated into hysteria. It had also become unintelligible. Süleyman had been called, and as soon as she had realised that a relative was on his way, Sezen Hanım had calmed down. Now she just wept, gently.

'Sezen Hanım, I know that you have suffered a terrible shock and an almost unimaginable loss,' he said. 'And in truth there is nothing I can say that can make that any better for you. However, my colleague tells me that one of your neighbours claims to have seen a man in your garden this evening. I believe you were out.'

'At the Swissotel, yes.' She sniffed.

He nodded his head and just very briefly smiled. 'How nice.' He knew how to play the exquisitely mannered Ottoman game.

'So there was a man in your garden this evening around the time we believe your uncle was murdered,' he continued. 'My colleague tells me further that your neighbour asserts that young men were often to be seen coming and going from this house while you were out.'

'She's lying.'

'Your neighbour?'

144

She looked up at him. 'You know how they are, Mehmet Bey, the people . . .'

He looked into her eyes, afraid he might display how tired he was with all the Ottoman snobbery that dinosaurs like Sezen Hanım, like his own mother, enjoyed displaying. But he kept his gaze pleasant. In order to get out of her what he half knew had to be in her mind, he had to remain civil for a while.

'It's all jealousy with them,' she continued.

'The people?'

'Yes! They're not born to be anything special and so they crave proximity to greatness. I'm sure you know what I mean.'

He looked around what she no doubt called her 'salon' and wondered whether her common neighbour had mouse droppings on her soft furnishings, whether her Tiffany lampshades were cracked and filthy. He could so easily have been in his parents' home. He said, 'I accept that your neighbour may be . . . intrusive and maybe jealous too. I'm afraid I don't know her and so I cannot tell, but Sezen Hanım, I cannot see why she would make up a story about many clearly young men entering this house in your absence.'

'Well, they came to see Rafik Efendi, of course,' she said. All tears had now gone and suddenly she was smiling, if nervously. 'Young people are so interested in the Ottoman past these days; it's really rather heartening, don't you think?'

'So they were students? And all men?'

'It would hardly have been seemly for Rafik Efendi to see women or girls on his own, Mehmet Bey.'

'Oh come now, Sezen Hanım,' he said. 'A man of Rafik Efendi's age? I think a young lady would have been quite safe with him, don't you?'

She turned her head away.

Süleyman had only ever met Rafik Efendi twice in his life,

once as a child and once as a young man in his twenties. On both occasions his father had told him not to get too close to the old prince. He hadn't explained why, but Mehmet had understood. That was exactly why he had told his mother, when she'd asked about the İpeks in the wake of Leyla's death, that Rafik Efendi had given him the creeps.

'Because actually your uncle preferred the company of men, didn't he?' Süleyman said.

Her fury was instant. 'How dare you!'

'Oh come on, Sezen Hanım, it's common knowledge in the family,' he said. 'I admit I never imagined he was still active at his age. What did he do? Pay them?'

'Mehmet Bey, I thought that as a member of this family—'

'Who I am is irrelevant. The fact that your uncle has been murdered is,' he said. 'Now tell me what type of men came into this house, and why.'

She began to cry again. He lost patience. 'And please do not weep! Speak to me and tell me the truth! I can and will take you in for questioning if you attempt to lie to me.'

Oddly she did stop crying, which shocked him. Had he done such a thing to his own mother, she would probably have clawed his face in her fury. But then his mother was a peasant.

Sezen İpek pulled her spine rod-straight and looked down her nose, if not at Süleyman, then near him. She said, 'My uncle had a weakness for young men. He'd had it all his adult life. The men who came to this house in order to service Rafik Efendi were professional purveyors of sex. I know nothing about them except their profession.'

'And how old were—'

'They were adults,' she said. 'That I do know.'

'And when he was a younger man?' Süleyman asked. 'What then?'

'In what respect, Mehmet Bey?'

'In respect of the ages of the men, or boys, Rafik Efendi chose to love,' he said. 'Because I know that he liked young boys, Sezen Hanım. When I was eleven, my father told me to keep away from him.' He leaned forward in his chair so he could be closer to her. 'I remember how he looked at me.'

Their eyes met. She hadn't wanted them to but now she was caught by him. She said, 'Then I don't have to go into detail about what went on here, do I, Mehmet Bey.' Only then did she cry again. 'Oh Allah,' she said, 'what horrors are going to come out of the woodwork to pick over his poor corpse in a very public fashion now?'

Mehmet Süleyman said, 'Just those seeking justice, madam.'

Chapter 13

The Internet was, even Çetin İkmen had to admit, a marvellous thing to use when searching for a lot of facts about something very quickly. Even if some of the information online did represent the ramblings of lunatics.

It wasn't the first time he'd searched for facts related to the number twenty-one – in the past few months he'd discovered, amongst other things, that the twenty-first tarot card was the World, which represented the end of one life cycle and the beginning of a new one. But this was the first time he'd searched for significant twenty-ones in Turkish history. He looked at his computer screen and said, 'Did you know that the exact date upon which all Turks were obliged by law to have surnames was the twenty-first of June 1934?'

'I didn't.' İkmen could see that Mehmet Süleyman was looking down at his own fingers. This wasn't a good sign. Years before, when Süleyman's father Muhammed Efendi had been in charge of his own mind, he'd told İkmen that as a child his son had always bitten his nails when he was nervous. Now his teeth were only centimetres from his fingertips.

'On the twenty-first of November 1938,' İkmen continued, 'Atatürk's body was transferred to the Ethnographic Museum in Ankara prior to its interment in his mausoleum at Anıtkabir.'

'And why would either of those things make someone want to kill?' Süleyman said. 'Çetin, Rafık Efendi, my revolting paedophile uncle, paid for rent boys who visited him at his home. The Englishman was gay, too . . .'

'But Leyla Ablak wasn't gay and neither was Levent Devrim.'

'No, but then maybe we're connecting all these victims who are not in fact conjoined,' Süleyman said. 'After all, only John Regan and Rafık Efendi were killed in the same way.'

'The heart . . .'

'Levent Devrim was almost decapitated, while Leyla Ablak had her head smashed against the bottom of a therapy pool.'

'And yet each was murdered on the twenty-first of successive months,' İkmen said. 'And Mehmet, you know, I was thinking that in one way or another they were all outsiders, weren't they? Devrim was a sort of hippy/genius/lunatic, Leyla Ablak was an adulteress, John Regan, homosexual, and old Rafık Efendi . . .'

'I never knew that he was a paedophile before Sezen Hanım told me,' Süleyman cut in bitterly. 'He was my grandfather's youngest brother – creepy to me as a child, admittedly, and my father always told me to be wary of him – but in reality I hardly knew him at all.'

There was a pause, and then İkmen said, 'Do you feel—'

'Bad about it? Of course.' He bit the nail of his forefinger. Then he looked up. 'I know that all families have their secrets, but when you come from a family like mine, it's all bound up with what is deemed honourable, too. My family kept his paedophilia a secret. A crime as horrific as that! Imagine! Imagine how many boys might have been damaged by him!'

İkmen shook his head.

'And of course this Ottoman thing is made worse by these mad people who want my family to come back and rule them again. Rule what? The Empire is long dead and there's no place for monarchs in a republic. What are we supposed to do? Mount a *coup d'état*? And do any of these people realise just how

149

many of us there are? How twisted and awful some of us have become?'

Çetin İkmen nodded. The House of Osmanoğlu, the Ottoman royal family, was, and always had been, vast. In a system where the oldest male inherited and where sultans could have multiple wives and sometimes hundreds of children, those directly descended from a sultan were numerous.

'Oh, you can nod your head in sympathy,' Süleyman said, 'but such characters encourage people like my mother in their delusions of grandeur, and as for all the Islamists who'd like to see a modern caliphate, don't even get me started. Don't these people realise that my ancestors were some of the worst drinkers and fornicators in history?'

Contact with Sezen Hanım had clearly pressed all of Süleyman's anti-Ottoman buttons. İkmen had wanted to talk about the recent murders they had so far unsuccessfully investigated but was finding that his colleague was wanting to be far more specific. He gave up on his computer screen and said, 'So, Sezen Hanım . . .' In the end she'd refused to speak to anyone but Süleyman. 'Tell me everything.'

'She doesn't know who any of Rafık Efendi's rent boys were, only that they were adults,' he said. 'Or so she claims.'

'How did the old man meet them?'

'He got telephone numbers from the Internet,' Süleyman said.

'The Internet? How?'

He raised an eyebrow. 'Apparently Sezen Hanım went online and got them for him. Ömer is with her now so that she can talk him through all those she contacted. If she can remember, and if they're still online. But she says she hadn't done that for some weeks.'

'Maybe the old man had started to make arrangements without

her supervision. Asking boys to come back without booking,' İkmen said.

'Maybe. Maybe the ones he got for himself were children.' Süleyman frowned. 'If, for a moment, we assume that these four murders are connected, do you think that the perpetrator is punishing these people for immoral acts? Not that Rafik didn't deserve it.'

'You mean fundamentalists? Jihadis posing as rent boys? Putting on weird costumes? Going to spas? I don't know,' İkmen said. 'What does the number twenty-one mean in Islam?'

'I don't know.'

He sighed. 'Then maybe we ought to find out. The one person who doesn't fit in with the obvious sinner profile is John Regan.'

'But he was . . .'

'Gay, yes, but not actively so, not here,' İkmen said. 'As far as I know, that is. I got old Pomegranate to put the word out and he drew a blank. If John Regan was after some boy action in this city, he was being very discreet about it.' He shook his head. 'None of the connections we have so far extend across all four victims. We have two homosexuals, two members of your family; Levent Devrim and Leyla Ablak were both interested in alternative therapies, John Regan was an historian and a foreigner, and Rafık Efendi, well, what shall we say . . .'

'He liked little boys,' Süleyman said. 'After decades of turning a blind eye, now Sezen Hanım is having nightmares about it. She fears that old victims, upon hearing about his death, will come forward to, and I quote, "pick over his poor corpse in a very public fashion". It's truly difficult for me to count the ways in which I don't care, but I also fear the effect any fallout, should it come, will have upon my relatives, however much I may resent their previous inertia.'

151

'Of course.' İkmen leaned back in his chair. Then he said, 'I'm going outside. Thinking without a cigarette just isn't natural.'

They left his office and walked down to the station car park. It was packed with men and women smoking as if their lives depended upon it, and Ömer Mungan, who, oddly, didn't seem to need nicotine. He walked over to them.

'Şukru Şekeroğlu the gypsy has left Tarlabaşı,' he said. Ömer had been spending a lot of time in that district ever since Levent Devrim's death. As well as being able to speak several of the languages he heard on the streets, he also felt at home there.

'Do we know why?' Süleyman asked.

'No, sir. Word is he's travelling.'

'Gypsies often say that.'

'I know.'

'Do you think he's got out of town before Hıdırellez?' Süleyman asked.

'What, the spring festival? Why?' İkmen said. 'Gypsies love all that jumping over fires and dancing in the streets and they make a lot of money from telling fortunes. Why would Şukru go?' He shook his head. 'From what you've told me about his involvement with the boy Hamid when Levent Devrim died, I'm left with a distinct feeling of unease, I must say.'

'You think Şukru might be implicated in some way?'

'No,' İkmen said. 'But I think he might know more then he has told us even now. You've said that yourself, Mehmet Bey.'

He sighed.

'You should have continued the surveillance. With Şukru out of town, you only have his family to go to, and only one of them, as you know, will even entertain talking to you.'

He looked up at Süleyman, who knew exactly what İkmen wanted him to do. With his family up in arms about his dead

152

uncle, the last thing he needed was an ex-lover he still had feelings for.

There had been another killing. It had happened on the twenty-first, just like John's, but exactly one month after. Sitting alone in the Ada bookshop, Arthur Regan felt desolate. It didn't matter that the victim had been some ancient man with multiple health problems; he had been a human being and now he was just a corpse because of someone else. Some animal. It wasn't easy staying on in the city now that John's body had been taken back to the UK. He'd returned with it briefly for the funeral, but he'd said he'd stay in İstanbul until the police found his son's killer, and he was going to stick to it. Not that the police appeared to be making too much progress.

Arthur made his way laboriously through the pages of *Hürriyet*. Resurrecting his long-disregarded Turkish was tough going, although it did help to take his mind, at times, away from his troubles. Turkish politics had changed a lot since he'd last lived in the city. When he'd first met Betül in the mid 1960s, left-wing and religious political parties were banned. Then the government had still been dominated by the figure of İsmet İnönü, Atatürk's closest ally and a hero of the War of Independence. İstanbul had been a down-at-heel place back then, in stark contrast to the vibrant city it had become. Even the Communist Party was legal now – they had some really rather palatial offices on İstiklal Caddesi. But if they were free then so too were the religious parties who had over the years taken more and more control of people's lives. In some ways this was a positive move, promoting as it did a greater sense of moral responsibility for the poor and disadvantaged. But it had a down side as well, and things like censorship of literature and the press were becoming hard to ignore. And while İstanbul was the only large mainly Muslim city in the world to have a gay pride festival every year, Arthur was also aware of a brand of homophobia amongst some people that could have proved lethal to his son.

He drank his latte and turned back to the main story of the day, the murder of the old man out in what looked like one of those wooden yalıs in Ortaköy. He'd always liked those old Ottoman villas, even if he would forever associate them with Betül's ghastly family. They'd lived in a vast one back in the nineteenth century, or so they'd never tired of telling him when he had met them. Peering at the photograph on the front page, of a covered stretcher being carried from the ornate wooden house and into the street, he read that the victim had died an hour or two before midnight. His murderer, the report said, had been brutal and without mercy for such an elderly and esteemed member of the community. It was only then that Arthur found out exactly who the victim was. When he did, he picked up his mobile phone and called the police immediately.

'Hello, Gonca.'

She was pottering about in the small yard outside her studio, tending the few straggly flowers she grew in old olive oil drums. When she heard his voice, she looked up at him through a curtain of iron-grey hair. He hadn't seen her for years and she'd aged, but she was still amazingly beautiful.

'Mehmet Bey,' she smiled. 'What brings you to Balat? And don't say that you were just passing, because I know that will be a lie.'

In spite of the serious nature of his mission, he laughed. She had always made him laugh; that had been a large part of her appeal.

He looked towards the hill that swept down to the Golden Horn below and said, 'I need to ask you something.'

She stood up straight, one hand still massaging the side where she'd been shot by a deranged kid almost three years before. That was when their affair had ended, and he hadn't seen her since. 'Do you want to come in?' she asked.

'If it's not a problem.'

'It isn't.'

She led him into the large room at the side of her house that was her studio. With the exception of new works in progress, it was just as he remembered it, a chaos of paint, fabrics, floor cushions and ashtrays. Gonca made her living, very successfully, as a popular and collectable collage artist. Her work was exhibited and appreciated not only in Turkey but in Europe and America too. Her family, including her father, might try to fool themselves that they were independent operators in their own right, but everyone knew that, really, Gonca paid for everything.

'Would you like tea or something stronger?' she asked him as he lowered himself on to one of her larger cushions.

'Oh, tea. Thank you.' He switched his phone off. This was not going to be an easy conversation and he didn't want it to be disturbed.

She called through into the house and he saw a heavily pregnant girl briefly look around the doorpost and nod.

In spite of her injuries, Gonca was still as lithe as ever, and she sat down on a cushion opposite Süleyman in one smooth movement. 'How have you been?' she asked.

'Fine.'

'Your . . . parents?'

'My father is old now, but . . .' His voice trailed away. How did he even start to tell her that his father was senile, his mother still the same annoying snob? 'And you?'

'Oh, work is good and we have high hopes for a good Hıdırellez. A lot of people come from abroad now.'

'Yes, I know.'

The girl came in and gave them both tea. He recognised her, although he couldn't have repeated her name to save his own life. She looked at him resentfully; she obviously recognised him, and for a moment, Süleyman felt his face colour. When they had been together, Gonca had never protected her enormous tribe of twelve children from walking in on their lovemaking. Süleyman shuddered, his feelings a mixture of embarrassment and old erotic desire. No one before or since had ever made him feel the way that Gonca had done.

Gonca told the girl to go and then said, 'So what can I do for you, my friend?'

There was no virtue in not getting straight to the point. He said, 'Gonca, do you know where Şukru has gone?'

'My Şukru?'

'Your brother, yes.'

She shrugged. 'I don't. Why?'

He leaned forward. 'I'm assuming that you know your brother, in apparently trying to protect a boy called Hamid, withheld some information from us regarding a murder in Tarlabaşı.'

'We look after our own, Mehmet Bey,' she smiled.

'Yes, I know, but with what we think could be a serial killer in the city, we need to keep a tight rein on all our witnesses, and that includes Şukru. It's important.'

She shrugged.

'And with Hıdırellez coming up next month, I am somewhat confused as to why your brother has left the city.'

'You suspect him of something?'

'No. Not necessarily. But . . .' Nervous now, he took a cigarette out of his pocket, put it in his mouth and searched in vain for his lighter.

'Oh, let me.' She leaned over and lit his cigarette with a small

156

gold lighter. As she bent forward, he could see almost all of her breasts as they tumbled against the sweetheart neckline at the top of her dress. They were just as big and smooth as he remembered and he felt himself react to them immediately. Hopefully she was unaware of his discomfort, both psychological and now physical.

'We need to have access to your brother,' Süleyman said.

'You think he knows something he isn't telling?'

'Well, er . . .'

'If our people are involved, then he may do,' she said. He could feel her eyes on him and so he moved one of his legs slightly to impede her view. 'The man with the camera was not one of our own. So what do you want me to do for you, Mehmet Bey?'

'When you speak to Şukru,' because he knew that she could and would, 'tell him to come back to the city – or at least talk to me,' he said. 'As I'm sure you know, Gonca Hanım, another person has been murdered . . .'

'On the twenty-first, the day of endings and beginnings,' she said.

'What?' Then he remembered what İkmen had said about the tarot card. 'Oh, you mean the World.'

'That and more,' she said. 'Numbers have magical properties, Mehmet Bey, and twenty-one, the pairing of the singular with the plural, is a very powerful one. It has much destructive energy.'

'How so?'

'It's difficult for one and many to co-exist,' she said. 'The many will bring down the one, or vice versa. Also twenty-one is divisible by three seven times, the ultimate magic number, some believe.'

'With respect, that is—'

'Rubbish?' She smiled. 'You know that the Christian Messiah,

157

Jesus, was twenty-one years old when he was first presented at the Temple in Jerusalem? His mother, the Virgin Mary, lived for just twenty-one years after his death. He appeared twenty-one times to people all over Palestine after he was taken down from the Cross. Twenty-one is magic.'

'Yes, well, that is Christianity.'

'Ah, but not just Christianity,' she said. 'There are civilisations much older than Christianity that revere the number twenty-one. The ancient Mayans in South America, for instance. Now this year, 2012, is very special to them because of that.'

'What?'

'The twenty-first of December this year is significant to them.'

'Oh, surely you don't believe in that end-of-the-world rubbish . . .'

'How do we know? How do we know what it is and whether it's true?' she said. 'You may scoff at so-called primitives, but as a primitive myself, I know that sometimes we are more in touch with reality than you might like to think.'

He shook his head. 'So why didn't your brother tell me all this? I asked him about the number twenty-one and he just blanked me.'

She smiled. 'Ah, poor Şukru,' she said. 'It's difficult for him with you. How can he talk to a man who fucked his sister?'

The directness of her speech, which was something he had always loved about her, now made him blush.

She saw it and laughed. 'Oh, Mehmet Bey,' she said. 'It's true, why not say it?'

He looked down at the floor, bypassing that part of his body that was still relentlessly aroused.

'So is there a woman in your life now?' she asked.

For a moment he wondered whether he should tell her a lie. But then he knew she'd see through it, so he said, 'Yes.'

'That sergeant of İkmen's.' Her eyes glittered. 'She always had a thing for you, Mehmet Bey. But then you're a very easy man to have a thing about.'

It was then that he noticed that she was undoing the buttons down the front of her dress. He had about half a second to stop her. But he knew he didn't want to do that. He'd even daydreamed on his way to Balat about something like this happening. As he sat, mute with desire and anticipation, she threw her dress off and advanced, naked, towards him. Her fingers found his erection quickly, as they had always done, and soon he was inside her. The way she felt was the way she'd always felt. He closed his eyes and let her move on top of him.

Chapter 14

Halfway between Gonca's house and the Atatürk Bridge, Süleyman switched his phone back on. He still felt excited after his passionate lovemaking with the gypsy and he knew that he would be going back for more. Unlike with Ayşe, sex with Gonca was joyous and as focused on her own pleasure as it was on his. And he liked to give her pleasure. When she tore into his back with her nails as he made her climax, he felt like the powerful man he'd always been with her. This wasn't, however, something that would please İkmen, who, Süleyman knew to the very bottom of his soul, would know what he had done as soon as he saw him. And how was he going to explain the scratch marks on his back to Ayşe?

He only had one message on his phone. It was in English.

'Ah, Inspector Süleyman,' Arthur Regan said. 'Thought I should tell you something. I noticed in *Hürriyet* this morning that there has been another murder, and if I'm not mistaken, the victim was an old prince. If this is the case, then that is two members of the former royal family to be killed this year. Or rather, possibly, three. My late wife, Betül, was related too, you see, and so I'm wondering whether this could be some sort of pattern. Get back to me and I'll tell you all about it.'

Although Çetin İkmen knew that Mehmet Süleyman hadn't just brought Arthur Regan into the station to distract attention away from his own guilty countenance, he couldn't help but be angry.

The sex he'd had with Gonca was stamped on every pore of his skin, and İkmen's heart bled for Ayşe Farsakoğlu. He concentrated on the Englishman.

'My wife, Betül Şafak, was a direct descendant, through her father, of Sultan Abdülaziz,' he said. 'I know this because when I went to ask him for her hand in marriage, he banged on about it for about an hour. I was shown a family tree the size of this office . . .'

A relaxed Mehmet Süleyman said, 'I can imagine that. Where advancement to the sultanate was by eldest male and not father to son, we have had a lot of sultans who have each had their own harem, and from that very many children. The Osmanoğlu family is vast.'

İkmen wanted to say, *Then why do you behave as if you're so special?* But he didn't. Instead he said, 'So did Betül's father approve?'

'Oh no,' Arthur said. 'We married against his wishes and went to live in the UK in spite of him.'

'Good for you.'

'None of Betül's family ever wanted anything to do with John. As far as I am aware, they still live in the same apartment in Şişli.'

'We will check that out,' İkmen said. 'Did your son know where they lived, Mr Regan?'

'Oh yes, but I know he wasn't keen to meet them because of the way they had treated his mother and myself,' he said. 'Not one of them came to Betül's funeral or ever asked after John. And you know, I discovered that they were very minor members of the Osmanoğlu family. All the members who had any real power were exiled by Atatürk in the 1920s.'

That was true. Betül Şafak's family, just like the Süleyman family, were very small fish in the great Osmanoğlu pond.

'But John knew what his family were?'

161

'Yes,' Arthur said. 'Not that he cared.'

'Are you sure about that, Mr Regan?' İkmen asked.

He thought for a moment and then he said, 'Well I suppose I can't be positive. But I think it's unlikely.'

'Even though his book was to be about the Osmanoğlu family?'

'It was a romance,' Arthur said. 'They wouldn't have approved. He knew that. He came to İstanbul to be in the atmosphere, to explore the palaces where Abdülhamid and his Belgian mistress Flora lived. He was immersing himself in his mother's heritage, writing a book he'd gone on about for years and taking a break from the academic work he'd done all his life. I didn't think about the royal connection at all until I read the newspaper report about the murder of that old prince in Ortaköy. The victim before John, the woman, was the prince's great-niece, and I had to put this connection to you as a possibility.'

'You did the right thing, Mr Regan,' Süleyman said.

'There is a fourth victim,' Arthur Regan began. 'Is he . . .'

'We do not believe that that person is connected to the Osmanoğlu family, although we will of course check that out now, Mr Regan,' İkmen said. As far as anyone had been able to ascertain, Levent Devrim's family had been enriched by their connections with the military republican elite of Kemal Atatürk.

'I hope I'm wrong, but . . .'

Arthur Regan gave İkmen his in-laws' contact details and then left. As he shut the door behind the Englishman, Süleyman said, 'Odd that no member of the Şafak family came forward when Dr Regan's death was reported.'

İkmen, looking down at his desk, said, 'You heard him: they don't and didn't communicate.' Then he looked up and tried to catch his colleague's eye. 'Don't even try to deny that you had sex with the gypsy. I can see it on every jubilant centimetre of your skin. I feared it.'

162

Süleyman walked back to the chair opposite İkmen's and sat down.

'So does Gonca know where her brother has gone?' the older man asked.

'She says not.'

'And you believed her?'

'Not necessarily. She said she'd put us in contact.'

'Mmm.'

Süleyman's face had that look that often followed on from good sex – a cross between contentment and smugness. But suddenly his expression turned into something angry and he said, 'Well it's more than you would have got out of her, Çetin! She wouldn't have told you anything!'

'You think?' He shook his head. 'I had hoped, Mehmet, that maybe you had grown up a little in recent years and that, just possibly, a sexually voracious gypsy woman might be something you could resist, but clearly not.'

Süleyman leaned forward in his chair so that he could lower his voice. 'She seduced me!' he hissed.

'Oh, and that makes it all right, does it?' İkmen said.

'No.'

'Potentially you have compromised this investigation, to say nothing of what this might mean for your relationship with my sergeant. She gave up happiness with İzzet Melik for what appears to me to be misery with you!'

So he'd finally said it. When Süleyman's sergeant İzzet Melik had called off his engagement to Ayşe Farsakoğlu because she couldn't get over Süleyman, İkmen had said nothing. Even when İzzet had transferred back to his native Izmir he had held his tongue. But not any longer. This time his colleague had gone too far.

Süleyman said nothing.

After a pause, İkmen said, 'I will take Sergeant Farsakoğlu

with me out to Şişli to see these Şafak people now. You opened the first case, Levent Devrim; can you go and see his family today? Check out his connections?'

Süleyman took his phone out of his pocket and said, tightly, 'I'll call them.'

'Good,' İkmen said. He put his jacket on and had begun to move towards his office door when he stopped. 'I don't want to fall out with you over this, Mehmet.'

His friend looked up at him and smiled. 'Nor I with you.'

'You've had your fun this time, but it can't happen with Gonca again. If you compromise this investigation in any way and a murderer walks free . . .'

'I won't,' he said. But he looked down at the phone in his hands as he did so. 'I promise.'

The inspector had filled her in on the details about the Şafak family, but Ayşe Farsakoğlu couldn't get it out of her head that he was also concealing something from her. She couldn't imagine what it could be. They were both, after all, going about their business to the same end. Now here they were in the smart district of Şişli, the preferred area of those from wealthy minorities like Armenians and Jews and the home of the original İstanbul mansion apartment. Ayşe dismissed her feelings and watched İkmen press a buzzer in the entrance hall of a dark, particularly smart early-twentieth-century example.

Eventually a disembodied voice said, 'Yes?'

'Mr Abdurrahman Şafak?'

'Yes.'

'It is Inspector İkmen and Sergeant Farsakoğlu from the police,' İkmen said.

'Oh, right,' he said. 'Go to the lift on your right. We're on the second floor, apartment four.'

'Thank you, sir.'

İkmen had spoken to this Mr Şafak prior to leaving the station. Apparently he'd been agreeable to their visit, even if, now, his voice sounded somewhat hollow.

They got into one of those tiny metal lifts that, for Ayşe, characterised both these old apartment blocks in Şişli and her own building in Gümüşuyu. Travelling in them, especially with others, could make one feel claustrophobic and, with a stranger, even a little nervous at times. Neither of them said anything as the lift ascended, which, again, Ayşe felt was odd for İkmen. Usually on the way to an interview he couldn't stop talking. When the lift stopped, they got out to find a small, thin, suited man in his sixties waiting for them. His skin was grey and his eyes were overbright and alarmingly hollow. He was very obviously unwell.

İkmen extended a hand towards him. 'Abdurrahman Bey?'

'Yes.' He smiled, tilted his head and then led them both into a very large, art-nouveau-style apartment that, Ayşe noticed, smelt of cigarettes and spices. He showed them to two large armchairs either side of a photograph-heavy occasional table and then sat down himself on a long sofa opposite. Very briefly Ayşe looked at the photographs and then at the man, who said, 'Tea?'

Like her superior, Ayşe agreed that tea would be a very good idea. Abdurrahman Bey called a tiny servant girl to his side and told her to make tea for all them, adding that she should bring a tray of lokum with it. When the girl, who was not much more than a child, had left, he looked at İkmen and said, 'So. John Regan.'

'Who was the son of your sister, Betül,' İkmen said.

'Indeed.'

'Did you know that he had come to the city to research a book – a romance – based upon the life of one of your ancestors?' İkmen asked.

Abdurrahman Şafak took a cigarette from a wooden box beside

him on the sofa and lit up. He neither offered his guests a cigarette or gave them permission to smoke. 'The first I knew about his presence in the city was when he turned up dead,' he said.

'And yet you neither contacted the police or, I believe, spoke to Dr Regan's English father.'

'And why should I?' He shrugged. 'I met the man who became my sister's husband once; I never met their son.'

'And yet you are related.'

He shrugged again.

Ayşe watched İkmen, who, she could deduce, was becoming impatient with this man. In common, so it was said, with Mehmet Süleyman's mother, he was playing his role as a higher-order being to the hilt. The little servant girl came back in with their tea glasses and a small silver plate covered with traditional rose-flavoured lokum, then left with a bow to her master. Ayşe looked at the tea the child had so carefully put beside her and wondered whether she was happy.

Abdurrahman Şafak smoked. He said, 'So this book that Dr Regan was writing . . .'

'A romance set at the court of Sultan Abdülhamid II,' İkmen said. 'The subject of the piece is the relationship that existed between the sultan and a Belgian glove-seller called Flora—'

'Preposterous,' Abdurrahman Şafak said.

'Preposterous, sir?'

'Never happened,' he said.

'And yet,' İkmen said, 'the story is something I remember hearing as a child, and it features in the only in-depth biography of the sultan by—'

'I do not care where the notion comes from; it's a myth,' the other man said. 'Now, Inspector İkmen, do you actually have any questions you want to ask me, or are we simply going to argue about one of my ancestors?'

Ayşe saw İkmen perform one of those changes of mood designed to wrong-foot whoever he was talking to. 'Where were you on the night of the twenty-first of March 2012?' he said.

Abdurrahman Şafak's normally ashen cheeks flared red. 'Are you suggesting . . .'

'I'm not suggesting anything,' İkmen said. 'I'm asking where you were the night your nephew died.'

For a moment he didn't answer. When he did, his voice trembled. 'I was here,' he said. 'Ask the maid.'

'I will do,' İkmen said, and he paused and then smiled. 'Can you call the maid in, please, sir?'

Abdurrahman Şafak cleared his throat and called out, 'Girl! Come in here, please.'

Ayşe looked at İkmen, who didn't betray anything even though both knew what the other was thinking. *He doesn't even know the kid's name!*

Impatient, the man reiterated, 'Girl!'

From a far-distant corner of the apartment Ayşe heard a tiny voice say, 'I am coming, sir. I'm sorry.'

'Well make it quick!' He banged his hand down on the sofa beside him and then leaned towards İkmen and said, 'I don't mind people writing what they will about my family provided it is factual. I have helped film-makers, authors, theatre directors . . .'

'But you wouldn't have helped your own nephew,' İkmen said.

'No, I would not, sir,' he said. 'Because that story about Abdülhamid and the glove-seller is a lie. A sultan would never have had relations with a woman who was not a Muslim.'

The little maid came into the room and stood by her master, who said to her, 'Now, girl, these police officers want to know where I was on the night of the twenty-first of March – that is, last month. Can you tell them where I was, please?'

She only looked at her master when she answered, and Ayşe

noticed that she trembled as she spoke. 'You were here, sir,' she said. 'You are always here.'

'There you have it,' Abdurrahman Şafak said. Then he smiled, and Ayşe felt her skin crawl.

When they left, it was the little maid who saw them out. At the door, partly out of curiosity and partly out of revenge upon her careless master, Ayşe asked the girl her name.

In a small voice she said, 'It's Suzan, madam.'

'Şukru?'

There was a moment before he answered her as he put her voice and her face together in one place in his head.

'What do you want?' Gonca's brother asked her. Ever since she'd had that affair with Süleyman years before, there had been little love lost between them. She'd given her Mehmet up for Şukru, her father and her tribe. This time, however, things were going to be different.

'Where are you?'

'What's it to you?'

'The police have been asking,' she said. 'They want to know why with Hıdırellez almost upon us you are elsewhere. There's money to be made. What are you doing?'

'They don't care about my money or Hıdırellez. What are you talking about?'

'Şukru, like it or not, the police don't believe you have nothing more to say about the death of that madman,' she said.

She heard him click his tongue in irritation. 'I told them everything I know.'

'Eventually,' she said. 'You kept the boy secret.'

'To protect him! Kids like him get kicked around by them.'

'I know why you did it, Şukru, but . . .'

'But what?'

168

'But now you have disappeared, they are suspicious,' she said.

For a moment he didn't say anything, then he growled, 'Did they come to see you?'

She considered lying to him but thought better of it. Her daughter had seen her with Süleyman. She'd put her head around the studio door and, for a second, watched them make love. Other eyes had seen the policeman leave her place.

'Yes,' she said. 'They sent Süleyman.'

'Hah!'

'And yes, I did tell him that I would make contact with you somehow,' she said. 'Because until a solution is found to these deaths, then everyone who has come into contact with any of the victims will be under suspicion.'

'You think I killed a man whose life was cannabis and numbers? Who loved an old Kurdish whore?'

'No, of course not, but you have to prove to them that you know nothing.'

'The police?'

'You must be here,' she said.

'So that your boyfriend can beat me up and—'

'No!'

They both knew that whatever the police might want with him, she would not willingly allow them to hurt him, even though he'd made her howl in pain when he had insisted that she leave Mehmet Süleyman.

'Did you sleep with him?' he asked.

'Yes.'

She heard her brother clear his throat and spit in disgust.

'And if I hadn't, how much slack do you think the police would have cut you, eh?' she said.

'Oh, so you sacrificed yourself for me.'

'Yes!' she said. 'Yes, I did, Şukru. Süleyman can come after you whenever he wants, but he left you to me.'

'Because you opened your legs to him willingly.' His voice was bitter now, and Gonca began to feel just a little bit afraid. Şukru was capable of murder; he'd done it before. Even if she had given herself to Süleyman to protect him, he wouldn't forgive her.

'Şukru, come back,' she said. 'Come now and I will never have anything to do with Süleyman again.'

But he put the phone down on her, which was frustrating, but which at least meant that she didn't have to lie to him about Süleyman, not in the near future. Now that she had Mehmet Süleyman in her life again, she was never going to let him go.

It was late by the time Süleyman returned to the station. He'd sent Ömer Mungan home when they left the office of Selçuk Devrim, the late Levent Devrim's brother. Try as he might, Selçuk had not been able to make any sort of connection between his own family and that of the deposed Osmanoğlu dynasty. The Devrims had been high-ranking soldiers and faithful followers of Atatürk.

'Unlike poor John Regan's family,' İkmen said when his friend and colleague entered his office.

Süleyman sat down at Ayşe Farsakoğlu's desk. 'What happened?'

İkmen told him about Abdurrahman Şafak and his low opinion of his nephew's now defunct literary project.

'But of course they'd hate it,' Süleyman said. 'Especially now.'

'What do you mean?' İkmen asked. He put an unlit cigarette in his mouth for comfort. Soon he'd suggest that they both went down to the car park for a smoke.

'Because this government is the first one since Atatürk to pay

170

them any attention,' he said. 'The AKP like the Ottomans, provided they present themselves as good Muslims.'

'But half your ancestors were drunks!' İkmen said.

Süleyman laughed. 'Of course!' he said. 'But don't say it too loud, Çetin; some of these old efendis almost see themselves as constitutional monarchs these days.'

'That's ridiculous!'

'Tell that to my mother.'

Briefly they both laughed.

But then Süleyman's face dropped. 'It's like resurrecting a corpse,' he said. 'Our time has come and gone.'

'Ah, it's not a connection that works across all our victims anyway,' İkmen said. But there had been something particularly creepy about Abdurrahman Şafak . . . He said nothing.

Süleyman leaned his elbows on Ayşe Farsakoğlu's desk and said, 'You know, Çetin, when I was with Levent Devrim's brother, I began thinking about those equations we found scrawled across his apartment walls.'

'In what sense?'

'In the sense that although we know that the formulae are mathematically insignificant, we don't know if they have any other sort of meaning.'

'Didn't you check out occult meanings? Mr Devrim was a somewhat alternative man, wasn't he?'

'Yes, but nothing came up,' Süleyman said. 'Doesn't mean there's nothing there. Maybe the right person just hasn't seen them yet. What if we publish photographs of the equations from the apartment?'

'In the press?'

'Yes. Maybe they were just mad numbers in his head. If so, we've reached a dead end. But what if they have meaning for other people too? People we just haven't accessed yet?'

İkmen frowned. 'We've had enough trouble with the number twenty-one, if you remember, Mehmet. I've more unsolicited tarot cards than—'

'Yes, I am aware of the possibility that every lunatic in the city and beyond may very well contact us with the intimate details of their theories of life, death and everything in between, but if that means we find someone who can really unravel those numbers . . .'

'Mmm.'

The office door opened and Ayşe Farsakoğlu came in carrying a large sheet of paper. When she saw Süleyman she said, 'Oh, Mehmet Bey, I didn't know . . .'

'Ayşe,' İkmen said, 'you may as well finish for the day. Inspector Süleyman and myself are just discussing a few points.'

'Oh. Right.' She pulled a tight smile and put the document she was carrying on İkmen's desk. 'That's the photocopy of Mr Şafak's family tree,' she said.

'Thank you, Ayşe.'

'Sir.' Reaching behind Süleyman, she took her jacket off the back of her chair. Briefly their eyes met but neither of them said anything. Then she left.

İkmen, who had been looking at the document she had given him, said, 'And here we have John Regan's Osmanoğlu relatives. Endless, endless relatives.' He looked up. 'How, if our murderer is targeting this family – maybe Levent Devrim was a mistake – are we supposed to warn all these people without alarming them, and how can we possibly provide them, or rather you, with protection?'

'Me?'

'You're one of them, aren't you?' İkmen said. 'How extensive is the Süleyman side of the family?'

'It's big.'

'Precisely,' İkmen said.

For a moment they sat in silence, and then Süleyman said, 'We can only do what we can. We can't control everything. I'll be honest, Çetin, I feel as if I'm losing touch with some of the early details about these deaths, like the maths on Levent Devrim's walls, like the testimony the boy Hamid gave about having seen a monster leaning over Levent Bey's body.'

'Which takes us back to the gypsy Şukru Şekeroğlu,' İkmen said.

Süleyman looked uncomfortable. İkmen ignored it. 'Once he is back . . . But I leave that to you.' He looked down at the Şafak family tree again. 'I do agree with you about Levent Devrim's equations, though,' he said. 'Let's clear it with Ardıç and see what happens. How bad, after all, can a deluge of delusion actually be?'

İkmen left before Süleyman, who had to go back to his own office to collect his briefcase. When he went out to his car, İkmen had already gone. But Ayşe Farsakoğlu was waiting over by the entrance to the car park, smoking. 'Are you coming over tonight, or . . .'

He lifted up the briefcase and said, 'Sorry. Things to do.'

As he got into his car, he watched her face cave in on itself with disappointment. But he stuck to his guns and started the engine. Across the car park he saw her walk slowly towards her own car and get in, and he felt more than just a twinge of guilt. Once out of the car park and headed towards Balat and the waiting arms of Gonca, though, he soon started to feel better.

Chapter 15

Her daughter and her friends stayed in the house in spite of the good weather, but Gonca preferred to sit outside. The sun was warm, and with Hıdırellez only two days away, she wanted to make sure that her plants looked good for the festival. As a girl, before her first marriage, Gonca had always become very excited just before Hıdırellez. Not only was it a time of feasting and fun, it was also a small window of opportunity when young gypsy girls might meet young gypsy boys and fall in love. Back then she'd been in love with at least ten boys and had flirted with them all. Now she was in love with just one, a man whose name she was going to write on a ribbon and fix to the mulberry bush in the corner of the garden the night before the festival. Her need for him would be blessed by the prophets Hızır and İlyas, whose meeting on the earth thousands of years before was celebrated every spring at Hıdırellez.

But Gonca's thoughts were not just concerned with Mehmet Süleyman. She hadn't seen him for days. This was, he said, because he was very busy. She hoped he wasn't lying to her. But Gonca also thought about her brother. After the business with Şeftali the prostitute's son, he'd gone to stay with some relatives in Edirne. He hadn't told her himself, but when Gonca had called an old aunt of theirs in Edirne, she'd quacked with the pleasure of having 'our dear Şukru' in the town again. Gonca hadn't told her lover any of that, even though she had promised on her honour to do so. What was honour anyway? What use did she have for something non-gypsies had always denied her people? Her only fear was if Süleyman found out that she knew where her brother was. Would he leave her and go back to that insipid policewoman if that happened?

Her job was to keep Mehmet Süleyman in her arms for ever and to protect her brother at the same time. But she nevertheless had an anxiety about Şukru that just wouldn't go away. She couldn't reconcile what he had said about the discovery of Levent Devrim's body with what she knew to be the truth. He'd told the police that he'd been out collecting wood for the family's fire. But all the men had been out the day before collecting wood because everyone had known that snow had been forecast for that night. Şukru had had no reason to be out that early in the morning. Except that he clearly had.

Would she be able to protect Şukru while still holding on to her policeman lover? If the prophets Hızır and İlyas were with her, yes. She couldn't bear to lose him a second time. If that happened, she'd kill herself.

As Çetin İkmen had predicted, once the photographs of Levent Devrim's equations had been released to the press, and put on the Internet, every lunatic in the country came forward to offer his or her interpretation of them. And because the numbers were so arcane and apparently without meaning, it was difficult to sort the simply delusional from those whose theories could have a point. One woman even managed to 'prove' that some of the figures corresponded to the exact distance between the Great Pyramid of Giza and Sirius the Dog Star. It was quite an intellectual feat, which left Çetin İkmen, not the world's greatest number-cruncher at the best of times, exhausted.

Just occasionally a person of rather more substance would

either arrive at the station or call, and these would usually be directed to the office of Mehmet Süleyman. One of them was a man that Çetin İkmen had met before in connection with the death of Leyla Ablak. He was also someone that Süleyman was more accustomed to seeing on the television.

'Professor Atay,' he said as he stood to receive his guest in his office.

Cem Atay was as good-looking and as carefully groomed in the flesh as he was on the screen. In his mid fifties, he looked more like a well-preserved forty-five-year-old. He put his hand out to Süleyman, who shook it. 'Inspector Süleyman, I met your colleague Inspector İkmen some time ago in connection with the death of a lady . . .'

'Leyla Ablak.' His alibi for that evening, provided by a very attractive woman who lived with her aged parents, had been checked out by Ayşe Farsakoğlu, and Cem Atay had not been considered a person of interest since. Now, according to Ömer Mungan, who had met him when he'd booked in at the desk downstairs, he had come in to talk about Levent Devrim's numbers.

'Yes.'

Süleyman gestured towards the chair opposite his desk and said, 'Please do sit down, Professor.'

'Thank you.' He sat.

Ömer Mungan, who had ushered the professor into the office, now stood behind Süleyman at the back of the room.

Süleyman, smiling, began. 'Professor—'

'The calculations that you found on the dead man's walls relate to the Mayan Long Count calendar,' he said.

For a moment, Süleyman thought he had misheard him. He'd certainly heard about the Mayan Long Count calendar, from Gonca. A lot of end-of-the-world superstitious crazy stuff as far as he was concerned. Could this very eminent historian possibly believe such nonsense? And wasn't this Mesoamerican apocalypse meant to be happening in December? 'Professor Atay . . .'

'Just to be clear, Inspector Süleyman, I in no way believe that the world is going to end this year,' he said. 'But I have been engaged in a project aimed at comparing and contrasting the Ottoman Empire with that of the Imperial Spanish Empire – a project that has been picked up by a documentary film company and will eventually be televised – and during that time, of course, I have come across ideas that stem from the civilisations of ancient South America that were conquered by the Spaniards, including the Mayans.'

'You've studied this, er . . .'

'Long Count calendar, yes,' he said. 'Not in depth, but enough to know that what you describe as equations are in fact Mayan dates.'

'Right.' Süleyman looked down at his desk. This was either going to prove to be another complete waste of time, or Professor Atay had opened a door into Levent Devrim's world that might prove to be the key to his death. He looked up again. 'Professor,' he said, 'if you can explain this to me . . .'

'I can try.'

'Then I would like my colleague Inspector İkmen to be present too.'

'A very charming man,' the academic said. 'Yes, Inspector, I am happy to explain the Mayan Long Count calendar to him as well.'

'Thank you, sir,' Süleyman said. He turned to Ömer Mungan. 'Will you go and ask Inspector İkmen to come to my office, please, Sergeant.'

It had been Çetin İkmen's brother, Halil, who had become an accountant, who had been good with figures. Çetin had been, by

177

his own admission, useless all his life. Now, as he listened to Professor Atay talk about the Mayan Long Count calendar, he began to imagine that his brain had started to bleed.

'The Maya worked with a three-tier calendar system when it came to time,' the professor said. 'They had the three-hundred-and-sixty-five-day Haab calendar, which meshed with the two-hundred-and-sixty-day Tzok' in calendar, which they used to identify individual days in what amounted to a fifty-two-year cycle. This did not, however, allow them to look at larger spans of time or indeed to calculate years as we would recognise them. And so they developed the Long Count calendar.'

'This is the one some people say signals the end of the world?' İkmen asked.

'Yes,' the professor said. 'The Long Count allowed the Maya to look both backwards and forwards in time. It also allowed them to cut time up into epochs. This gave them history and a future. The current epoch, or Long Count Cycle, that will end on the twenty-first of December 2012 began on the thirteenth of August 3114 BC.'

'The twenty-first of December, you say?' İkmen said.

'Yes.'

İkmen looked at Süleyman.

'Whether the world will actually end when this current cycle finishes is not known,' the professor said. 'However, what I believe is important for you, gentlemen, is that your victim for some reason wrote Mayan Long Count dates on the walls of his apartment. Look at this . . .' He pointed to one of the original photographs of Levent Devrim's walls on Süleyman's desk. '12.19.19.17.19 = 12.19.19.17.19. Meaningless, yes? In our system, absolutely. But if we look at those numbers through Mayan eyes, they are enormously significant.'

'In what way?' İkmen asked. 'Aren't they the same?'

'No! That's just it. The first one refers to the beginning of this Long Count cycle, and, as you can see, when that cycle ends, those numbers come around again.'

İkmen couldn't really see, because his brain had shut down, but he nodded his head anyway.

'You see here.' The professor pointed at the photograph again. 'That date, 13.0.0.0.0, signifies the beginning date of the new cycle we will be in after the twenty-first of December 2012.'

'What about all the other figures?' Süleyman asked. 'What you've shown us is just a sample . . .'

'Oh, I'm no expert,' he said. 'I recognise only the Mayan dates that were pointed out to me when I was carrying out my research. I wrote a small amount about the Mayans in relation to 2012 – people like details like that. But just looking at what that man inscribed on his wall, I can see that his numbers are annotated in the way that a writer who uses standard numerals would do. The Mayans themselves used a system of dots and lines, which were read horizontally.'

'So Levent Devrim was not a Mayan purist,' İkmen said.

The professor smiled. 'I don't think so, but if you really want to know what all these dates mean, you will have to contact a Mayan civilisation expert. I met several when I was in Mexico, and there is a Mexican lecturer in Latin American civilisations at METU I can put you in contact with.'

Süleyman said, 'Thank you, Professor.'

İkmen was less enamoured of the professor and his Mayans. Whatever weird stuff Levent Devrim had been into, it hadn't been the Mayans who had killed him, although the fact that he, that all the victims, had died on the magic date of the twenty-first was not lost on İkmen. Could it possibly just be a coincidence?

But then the professor said something that did interest İkmen a lot.

'Of course where death and the Mayans are concerned, one has to be circumspect. I know that Leyla Ablak died violently and I get the impression – although I understand you've not released all the details to the public – that the other victims died violently too. I don't know how relevant this is, but the Maya did practise human sacrifice, which took many different forms, one of which was to cut out the hearts of their victims.'

Sezen İpek looked at the letter again and then screwed it up into a ball. If she received any more of that nature, she'd take it to the police. They knew everything anyway. This one crude, nasty little missive could just be a fluke. Sezen felt that it wasn't, though. She sat down on the chair by her front door, uncreased the letter and looked at it again. It was full of disgusting bile about her uncle Rafık and about what this person claimed he had done to him many years ago. Her fears made real.

The letter, menacingly put together from newspaper type, alleged child abuse, rape and some acts that Sezen couldn't even fathom. He – if it was a man – wanted money or he'd tell all to the media and to the police. Didn't he know that she didn't have any money? Even if she'd wanted to meet him in the gardens of Yıldız Palace to hand over a bag full of cash, she wasn't able to do that. And yet just the thought of how her family would be vilified and discredited if Rafik Efendi's crimes ever came out in the press made Sezen sweat. In recent years their position in the country as national role models and assets had begun to be recognised. Some people, even in high places, had started to talk about a 'reappraisal' of the Ottoman Empire, which was most encouraging. But Rafık Efendi had represented the worst that the Empire had been, that louche, selfish, soft thing that Atatürk's republic had almost wiped off the face of the planet. And now, from beyond the grave, he was still undermining his family.

Although she had genuinely loved her uncle, there was a part of Sezen İpek that wished she'd had the courage to confront him and maybe even stop him years ago. She'd known for decades what he had been, what he'd done, and she'd turned a blind eye to it. Leyla had warned her. Just weeks before her death she'd told her mother, 'You have to stop allowing rent boys into the house.' But she hadn't listened. If she remembered correctly, she'd turned Leyla's argument against her and complained about her discredited husband. Now they were all dead. All except for Sezen.

It had been a long day for everyone, and Ayşe Farsakoğlu was very grateful to Ömer Mungan for inviting her to go for a drink with him once work was over. She'd put no pressure on him to do so; he'd done it out of the goodness of his heart. He was a thoughtful young man, and had she been ten years younger, she might have made a romantic play for him. But he was like the younger brother she'd never had and, further, the younger brother who knew she needed taking care of because her heart was broken. Everyone knew that because everyone knew where Mehmet Süleyman was going whenever he wasn't going back to his own little apartment in Cihangir after work.

Ömer, who was hungry, had gone inside the little restaurant they had chosen to sit down outside in Nevezade Sokak, to look at the fish and meat on offer that evening. Ayşe, who wasn't hungry, sat with her untouched beer and smoked. When he returned, the young man said, 'Fish is a ridiculous price.'

'So what are you having?' Ayşe asked.

'Chicken şiş.' He sat down. 'Are you sure you don't want anything to eat, Ayşe Hanım?'

'No thank you, Ömer.' She smiled. He still referred to her either

181

as Sergeant Farsakoğlu or Ayşe Hanım even when they were on their own. Acknowledging her seniority and her experience in the job they both loved.

Ömer, who was drinking red wine, said, 'I don't know about you, Sergeant, but I'm still reeling from today.'

'I think we all need time to take it in,' she said. Briefly Ayşe thought, spitefully, *Except for you, Mehmet Süleyman, who are being given all the occult help you need by that whore Gonca the gypsy!*

'What do you think about this idea that the killer has some sort of fixation on the Mayans?' Ömer said.

After Professor Atay had given İkmen and Süleyman the names of his academic contacts in Turkey and Mexico, he had left. İkmen had immediately called the expert at the Middle Eastern Technical University in Ankara, a Dr Maria Santa Ana. All four of them had been in İkmen's office when he'd put the Mexican on speaker phone.

'I don't know,' Ayşe said. She put one cigarette out and lit another. Unhappiness was turning her into her superior.

Çetin İkmen had told Dr Santa Ana, who had communicated with him in English, the relevant facts about the four murder cases and had emailed – or rather, instructed Ömer to email – photographs of Levent Devrim's equations over to her. It had been Dr Santa Ana's opinion that if one added in the fact that three of the victims had 'royal' blood, the case for some sort of Mayan-influenced fixation became still stronger. 'The Maya liked to sacrifice high-status victims to their gods,' she'd said. 'Better blood meant a better offering, which they believed would produce better crops in the year to come.' She'd also told them that there had been more than one method of dispatch. 'Everyone knows about the heart-cutting, but sometimes the Maya decapitated their victims, and there was another method too, which was to throw people into a sink hole called a cenote. This was usually done in order to propitiate the rain gods.'

All their thoughts had gone back to the image of Leyla Ablak floating, dead, in that therapy pool. But it was what Dr Santa Ana had said just before she'd had to go to give a seminar to her students that had really chilled the four police officers. 'The Maya believed that the blood they spilled, when collected and smeared on to idols or significant buildings, ensouled those items, giving them power to enter the world of men and influence their lives. High-status blood would have a particular power especially at a time like this when a Great Cycle is coming to an end. According to how Mayan belief is interpreted, we are in a dangerous place in time where the cycle may end successfully and peacefully or everything may just explode.'

İkmen had said, 'The end of the world?'

'The coming of Ah Puch, the god of death,' she'd said.

Ayşe sipped her beer. 'But why here, Ömer? This is Turkey; nobody believes in gods of death here.'

'No, but have you heard about the village of Şirince?' he said.

'No. Where's that?'

'Somewhere near Efes. There's a movement building amongst New Age people to put it forward as a place where the Mayan apocalypse won't reach.'

'How can a global apocalypse not reach everywhere?'

'I don't know.' His chicken şiş with bulgar wheat and salad arrived and Ömer began eating.

'How do you know that?'

He chewed on a nugget of chicken, swallowed and said, 'Oh, my sister works as a nurse in the German Hospital and they get all sorts of people through. She found this magazine about astrology and fortune-telling and there was an article about Şirince in there. The local people are going to open up more pansiyon rooms to cope with the demand they are expecting.'

Ayşe shook her head. When she'd been a child in the 1970s, such superstitions had been frowned upon. Now that religion was having a resurgence, so, apparently, were a lot of other beliefs and practices that until very recently had been discouraged by the state. She couldn't find it in herself to approve.

'A lot of people do believe in the Mayan Long Count calendar and they are frightened that the world will end on the twenty-first of December this year,' Ömer said.

'And our victims have died on the twenty-first of each month since January.'

'Yes.'

'So, as Inspector İkmen said, we have to take that into account, but without jumping to conclusions.' When İkmen had put the phone down on Dr Santa Ana, he'd told his colleagues that although he felt that the Mayan connection could be significant, he believed that something else had to be present as a motive to kill too.

Ömer finished his şiş and said, 'Maybe he just dislikes aristocrats, Levent Devrim excepted, of course.'

'Or maybe he fears them,' Ayşe said.

'Fears them? Why?'

She frowned. She knew why *she* feared them, or rather one of them. But for other people the issue was not personal.

'Those who admire and maybe always have admired the Ottomans feel free to talk about them positively now,' she said. 'For some people the Empire was a golden age. Our new bogeymen are our military, like General Ablak. Republicans . . .'

'You don't approve, Ayşe Hanım.'

But she said nothing. In light of the sensitive Ergenekon investigation, Ayşe didn't want to lay her cards on the table even with Ömer.

'Well, whatever the rights and wrongs may be, it must be nice for someone like Inspector Süleyman to feel that he and his kind are valued again,' Ömer said. He said it thoughtlessly and without malice, but as soon as the words were out of his mouth he knew he had done wrong.

Ayşe drank her beer quickly to try and cover the fact that just the mention of his name had made tears spring to her eyes. But Ömer saw.

Chapter 16

Even though he didn't tell the police where he was going, Arthur Regan had copied his son's work on to a disk, which he left at his apartment in Beyoğlu. The computer John had used to write his book on had been given back to him by İkmen the previous week. He took only a paper copy of his son's novel with him to Şişli. Just in case.

He hadn't seen the man who had once been his reluctant brother-in-law for over forty years. As he remembered him, Abdurrahman had been a good-looking, vigorous man who spoke flawless English and enjoyed tennis, swimming and horse-riding. But the shrunken creature that met him at the door of the Şafak apartment, which hadn't itself changed a bit in four decades, was a very frail copy of the man that Arthur remembered.

'You look well,' Abdurrahman said as he offered Arthur the very same seat his father had offered him when he had come to Şişli to ask for Betül's hand in marriage.

Stumped as to what he could possibly say in return, Arthur just smiled.

Abdurrahman said, 'I have cancer and so I look appalling.' He smiled, and Arthur noticed that his lips were yellow. 'I know it and you know it. It's made me even more cruel than I was before, too, which is something maybe you don't know. Would you like tea?'

Arthur muttered a 'yes' and wondered what the hell he was

doing in that mausoleum of an apartment again. Betül had run away from it with a glad heart and he hadn't given the place or anyone he'd met in it any thought until John's murder. But then his brother-in-law had tracked him down. İstanbul, for the natives, could be a very small village indeed.

After an awkward silence, a girl not much more than a child brought tea and lokum in vessels made from precious metals. Arthur worked hard at not looking impressed. Last time he'd been in that place he'd done quite the opposite. He'd been sneered at by the whole family, including Abdurrahman.

'So this book your son was working on,' Abdurrahman said. 'Did you bring me a copy?'

Arthur took fifty pages of A4 out of a carrier bag and put them on the table in front of his host.

Abdurrahman looked up at him. 'Is that all?'

'He had only been writing for just over a month,' Arthur said. 'There's a lot of research material, but—'

'Lies written by liars.' Abdurrahman picked the manuscript up and glanced at it, then put it back down on the table again.

On one level Arthur wanted to scream at him, challenge him about calling his son a liar, but he didn't. What was a sick man like this going to do about it? When he did speak, it was gently, even if the message he delivered was barbed. 'Your opinion is noted by me, Abdurrahman. But I'm irrelevant.'

'What do you mean?'

'I mean that the publisher who expressed an interest in my son's book when he sent them a synopsis is far more relevant than either of us.'

For a moment Abdurrahman didn't seem to understand.

Arthur clarified. 'John had a UK publisher,' he said. 'I'll need to talk to them about whether they want to give the project to another writer. Personally I'd like to see my son's work finished.'

187

He watched, without any compassion, as Abdurrahman's breath shortened. 'I wouldn't,' he said. 'It brings dishonour to my family.'

'By telling the truth about a particularly notorious relative of yours who had a child with a non-Muslim woman? What about all the Turks Abdülhamid killed because he feared they were plotting against him? Not worried about those?'

'He had a . . . he was not a well man . . .' Arthur knew that Abdülhamid II was widely acknowledged to have been suffering from extreme paranoia for much of his life, but that didn't excuse his actions in the eyes of those who came after him.

But there was something else that John's book alleged about Abdülhamid. It was contained in just a few lines at the end of his synopsis, but they were lines Arthur knew would upset his brother-in-law, and they were the reason he had come.

'My son was keen to prove that Abdülhamid fathered a child on Flora Cordier,' he said. 'And although I haven't been through all his research material yet, I think that John came up with some evidence to prove his thesis.' He could see that the other man was speechless with fury, but he carried on regardless. 'The tragic climax to the book is where Abdülhamid had Flora's daughter tied into a sack and thrown into the Bosphorus. Taught her a lesson for seducing his son, didn't he?' It felt so good, so refreshingly spiteful to say it!

Abdurrahman shook. 'Your son had no evidence for any of that!'

Arthur shrugged. 'Even if he didn't, what does it matter?' he said. 'Abdurrahman, the book is a romance, a fiction.'

'It is defamatory!'

'Is it? So was that why you had my son killed?' He said it without thought, not even knowing whether he believed it on any level himself.

Abdurrahman made a noise in his throat.

'Because I don't believe you didn't know that John was in town,' Arthur continued. Now that he had started the cruelty, he had to finish. 'You soon tracked me down via your contacts here, there and everywhere. And anyway, who else would have killed him, eh? My son was the best of men, he was . . .' He broke down and sobbed, while Abdurrahman watched him.

When Arthur's tears finally subsided enough for conversation to be possible, Abdurrahman said, 'I didn't kill your son. I didn't know he was here. Ask the maid, she will tell you how often I leave this place. It is never.'

Arthur shook his head as he wiped his eyes.

'Only since the police came do I know of this terrible book,' Abdurrahman said. 'But even if I had known, what would I have been able to do about it?'

'You? Nothing. But you could have paid someone.'

Abdurrahman waved a hand in front of his face. 'This is ridiculous,' he said. 'I didn't kill your son! I invite you to come here and be honest about this book your son was writing, and you—'

'Yes, I came here to confront you and humiliate you,' Arthur said. 'Frightening you is a bonus.'

'You don't frighten me!'

'And you didn't frighten me when I came to this apartment the first time,' Arthur said. 'Standing next to your father, trying to look both regal and hard at the same time! I wasn't frightened then and I'm not frightened now. Betül chose me, remember. Whatever you do or say, however many lies you tell, you can't change that.' He looked down at the tea the little maid had brought him and said, 'I don't fancy this tea any more.'

Abdurrahman glared at him through yellowing eyes.

Arthur rose to his feet. 'You can keep that manuscript,' he

said. 'I've got copies, John's publisher has copies, everyone has copies.'

The Turk continued to stare at him.

'I only came to piss you off and I've done that now and so I'm going,' Arthur said. 'Just a pity your father isn't still alive so I could have pissed him off too.' He began to walk towards the door, then stopped and turned. 'You know, I could have forgiven you lot much, but when none of you came when she died, I knew I'd never get over my hatred for you.'

Watching as he went, Abdurrahman was seized by a coughing fit. Once he'd managed to recover, he shouted out, 'Publish that book anywhere in the world and I will kill you!'

But Arthur just kept on walking. As he reached the front door, his eyes briefly met those of Abdurrahman's little maid, who with a shaking hand let him out. He muttered his thanks to her and left.

Çetin İkmen didn't usually make house calls on demand, but on this occasion, for Sezen İpek, he made an exception. Driving along the coast road out to Ortaköy, he saw a group of brightly dressed gypsies practising their Hıdırellez songs and dances, and he fancied he saw a bear amongst their number. But he must have been mistaken. Bears hadn't danced in İstanbul since the late 1990s, when people like Şukru Şekeroğlu had been finally forced to give up tormenting the poor creatures for money. İkmen had approved. As a child he'd always found the sight of the dancing bears almost unsupportably sad. But he also knew that the demise of the bears had in turn heralded the later crackdown on traditional gypsy lifestyles in places like Sulukule. And that he couldn't condone. Gypsies settled for hundreds of years in communities that worked were now scattered all over the city in groups that he knew found life at times almost impossible.

One of the excuses given for the breaking up of the gypsy clans had been to reduce crime. Many of the old families had made their living from alcohol and prostitution and the government had wanted to curtail those practices. But closing the brothels and trying to move the clans out of the city to 'nice' new tower blocks had largely failed. Unable to make a living outside the city, the gypsies had moved back in to neighbourhoods like Tarlabaşı, where they had either gone back to their old ways of making money or had found new and often even less savoury methods of putting food in their children's mouths. And sore though he was at Gonca Şekeroğlu for bewitching his Mehmet yet again, İkmen hoped that the gypsies had a good Hıdırellez and made lots of money for the summer to come.

He pulled up outside Sezen İpek's listing wooden house and found her waiting in her doorway for him. When he got close, he could see that she had been crying. But then her phone call had been hysterical.

When Ayşe Farsakoğlu had interviewed her, a process that had been interrupted by one of her neighbours, Elif Ceylan, it had become very apparent that Sezen Hanım had things to hide. Elif had said she'd seen a man in the garden earlier in the evening, and Sezen had tried to silence her. But Elif had just carried on anyway, revealing to boot that old Rafık Efendi had been homosexual and rather fond of the visits young men made to his home when his niece was away. Later Sezen Hanım had confessed all to her relative, Mehmet Süleyman. In addition to having a liking for men, Rafık Efendi had also been a predatory and sometimes violent paedophile. But İkmen didn't want to talk to her about that until he knew exactly why she was so keen to speak to him now.

She ushered him into her salon. The first time he'd been there it had been full of her relatives and she had behaved like some sort of thwarted empress. Now it was just her, and she was frightened. She offered him a seat and he sat down.

'You told me on the phone that you're being threatened, Mrs İpek,' İkmen said. She'd asked for Süleyman but he hadn't been available.

'Yes.' She shook her head and then ran a hand through her hair. 'Blackmailed.'

She handed him a piece of paper on which were stuck words and letters cut from newspapers. He took a moment to read what he recognised as pretty standard extortion fare. When he'd finished, he looked up at her and said, 'If it's any consolation, Sezen Hanım, murder victims' families are sometimes targeted by mischief-makers. And this is a very amateurish attempt . . .'

'No, no, no, no, no!' Her other hand flew up to her head as she massaged her temples. 'No, Inspector, what this person alleges . . . it's true,' she said.

'About Rafik Efendi. Yes,' he said. 'I know. Inspector Süleyman told me.'

'If it had all been lies then I would just have thrown it away,' she said. She picked up another piece of paper from the chair beside her and handed it to him. 'And this.'

İkmen began to read the second letter.

'That one has dates, places, including this house, and there is a suggestion that the blackmailer and my uncle were not alone.'

İkmen read a catalogue of buggery and other sex acts carried out on the old man's bed as well as in other parts of the house. The letter didn't just go on to ask for a large sum of money; it also accused Sezen of knowing all about her uncle's proclivities – which was entirely true.

He said, as a statement of fact, 'You knew what your uncle did and in his later years you helped him do it.'

192

She sat in silence for a moment and then she said, 'I never brought him children.'

He looked down at the letters again. 'It's alleged that Rafik Efendi abused this man, whoever he is, when he was a child.'

She looked away and said, 'I don't know about that. I told you I never brought him children.'

He said nothing.

'I don't have the kind of money this man is asking for and I don't want my family's name blackened,' she said. 'What am I to do, Inspector?'

What indeed. If she had no money, then she couldn't possibly give the blackmailer the 500,000 Turkish lira that he demanded. As İkmen knew, a proportion of blackmail plots didn't ever actually come to anything. But where such an obviously jealously guarded reputation was concerned, there was far more at stake than just money. Well, there was for her. İkmen silently wondered whether the blackmailer knew that most of Sezen's Hanım's family were already aware of what the old man had been.

'You probably think I'm a terrible woman for not handing my uncle over to the police for his crimes, but what could I do?' she said. 'When I was young, my family was despised. If my uncle's proclivities had become known in the 1970s, who knows where we would have ended up. In jail?' She shook her head. 'And now? Now the people and the government are learning to love us again. How can I disappoint them? How can I ruin their dreams?'

And your own, İkmen thought.

She wrung her hands. 'Leyla told me I should have gone to the police years ago!'

'Your daughter was right,' İkmen said. 'Some things, Sezen Hanım, are just wrong, and what your uncle did was one of them.'

Her face flushed. 'You think I'm a terrible person, don't you? Well you live my life. Come from where I came from, suffer the ignominy of your daughter first ruining herself and then marrying a traitor. I don't know how much more I can stand!'

İkmen had a limit for absorption of self-pity and he'd reached it, but he controlled himself. 'We don't know whether General Ablak, your son-in-law, was a traitor or not,' he said. 'But by your own admission, Sezen Hanım, your uncle was a predatory paedophile who you knew about – for years.'

She gazed at him through glassy, tear-washed eyes, but this time she didn't speak.

He looked at her, and for a while he was silent too. Then he said, 'Whatever happens now must be practical. I can't do anything about what your uncle did or what you didn't do. Not right now. But blackmail is a crime, and in addition, until we catch this man, we can't be sure that he isn't also your uncle's murderer.' He doubted this but he didn't tell her that. This blackmail just looked opportunistic to İkmen.

'So what do we do?' she asked.

İkmen looked down at the second letter again and said, 'Well, Sezen Hanım, you keep this appointment with this man in the gardens of Yıldız Palace this afternoon at four.'

Her eyes bulged in horror. 'But I told you I don't have any—'

'You won't need any money,' İkmen said. 'All you will need is a bag that looks as if it is full of money, and a strong nerve. I assure you, Sezen Hanım, we will do the rest.'

Şukru Şekeroğlu had come into İstanbul with a group of Edirne gypsies. Given the fact that he didn't want to attract too much attention, particularly from the police, he felt more secure in the company of others. They'd taken a ferry across the Bosphorus from Kadıköy to Karaköy and then he'd joined them, dancing and begging, as they made their way along the coastal road to the village of Ortaköy. There, they'd danced through streets lined with coffee shops and chichi restaurants, playing the whole Hıdırellez thing for the rich people who found such activities authentic enough to give money to.

Ortaköy wasn't Şukru's usual stomping ground, but it was near to where he needed to be in order to do a bit of business he should have done some time ago. In spite of everything, Tarlabaşı wasn't going to last long and soon they'd have to be on the move again. And despite his various business interests that had over the years made him quite a bit of money, Şukru knew that he could always do with more. The business with the kid Hamid had caused him a lot of grief, and that needed to be recompensed. Şukru took off the hot bear costume he'd put on in Edirne and which had so entranced the people of Ortaköy, and put on the suit he'd folded up into his rucksack. Looking at himself in the window of an art shop near the old synagogue, he was pleased with what he saw. Being in Edirne with three doting aunts had given him a chance to clean himself up. He almost looked respectable, which, given where he was going, was a good thing.

He put the fedora one of the other dancers had given him on his head and rang his sister from his mobile phone.

'I'm coming home and then I'm moving the family on,' he told her. 'Soon as I can.'

'Moving on? Where to?' Gonca asked. 'Some smart Bosphorus village?'

'I'll find somewhere,' he said.

'How? They want everyone to go outside the city.'

'Maybe I'll have money,' he said.

He heard her gasp. He knew what she was thinking. 'Oh Şukru, nothing dangerous!'

'You think I'd put myself at risk while you're fucking a policeman? No,' he said. 'Not dangerous, Gonca.'

He said nothing about illegal – she knew that was a given – or immoral, but then he was aware that that wasn't the way her mind would move. Like him, Gonca's morality was a thing that shifted with the time, the place and the person.

'Well come and see me before you take my father who knows where,' she said.

'And your policeman?' he said.

She snorted. 'Oh Şukru, don't you know me? I will tell Süleyman you've been to see me when you've gone.'

He smiled. 'OK. But I have some business to attend to first.' He finished the call and began to make his way north out of Ortaköy towards the village of Arnavutköy.

There was a time when Çetin İkmen would have joined his colleagues secreted in the trees and flower beds around the Malta Kiosk. But the afternoon was overly warm and he found that as long as he could see Sezen Hanım from his vantage point in the lee of the baroque kiosk, that was good enough for him. Unless whoever she was meeting knew him somehow, he, or she, wouldn't give a slightly scruffy man in sunglasses, smoking furiously, a second look. But then how likely was that anyway? In his heart of hearts, İkmen knew that no one was coming.

Someone clearly knew about Sezen İpek's uncle's crimes and was trying to frighten her, but İkmen didn't think that he or she was about to make good on those threats. For a start, the location for the 'drop' didn't make sense. The Malta Kiosk, which was a very smart café in the centre of the Ottoman palace of Yıldız, was a very public place. It had CCTV cameras and, while busy, was not busy enough to provide cover for any nefarious activities that might be taking place on its premises.

But from İkmen's point of view it was a pleasant enough place to be. Sitting at the back of the palace's outside terrace, he had a fine view of the Bosphorus and he was drinking very nice coffee, which was on expenses. The woman he was watching was tense, as were the officers who had positioned themselves around the kiosk, but İkmen himself, although a little hot, was perfectly calm. In the scheme of what he'd had to face over the past few months, a little blackmail was a very small crime. And anyway, the real 'victim', if the odious Rafık Efendi could be called such a thing, was already dead.

İkmen concentrated on the back of Sezen İpek's neck. Although he didn't like her, he had to admit that she was an attractive woman. She had that air about her that a lot of the old nobility had. It led to good posture and a certain attitude towards grooming that was very far in advance of his own. The Osmanoğlu clan had a sheen. And yet it was something their most prominent representatives in the past had not always had. Sultan Abdülhamid II, whose palace Yıldız had been, had looked like a thwarted crow in the ill-fitting greatcoat he had always seemed to wear when he'd been photographed. His predecessor, his brother Murad V, had looked like the lush he had been, and their father, Abdülmecid II, had been a tiny sliver of a man who had lived his life in the shadow of tuberculosis. İkmen wondered what John Regan's creation Tirimujgan had looked like. If, as he had contested, her mother had been a blonde Belgian, had the girl been a blonde too? Her imperial father had been very dark indeed, so dark in fact that rumours had circulated about the possibility of his mother having been from an Armenian family. Had the girl had that sheen İkmen always saw in the modern Osmanoğlus?

A young man passed in front of Sezen Hanım's table, looked at her briefly and then moved on. It was four fifteen already and so the blackmailer was late. Had he or she worked out that some of the people on the pathways and in the arbours around the kiosk were police officers? It was unlikely, as the team had assembled only slowly across the course of the day, with İkmen appearing last, at three thirty. There was no way of knowing until and unless he or she contacted the press with the story Sezen İpek did not want told. But İkmen, for his part, found it impossible to be worried about that eventuality. However back in vogue the old Imperial family might be, they, just like the republican generals who had followed them, couldn't escape their past. The old generals had mounted coups designed to consolidate their power in the 1960s and the 1980s, for which soldiers like General Ablak had been rightly brought to book, even if his involvement in the alleged modern version, Ergenekon, was open to question. But the Osmanoğlu still had cases to answer, not least of which was the terrible sense of entitlement that people like Rafık Efendi still believed they had. However, even that did not give whoever had taken Rafık's heart from his chest the right to behave with such barbarity.

In the days since he'd talked to Professor Atay and Dr Santa Ana from METU, İkmen had read bits and pieces about the ancient Mayans on the Internet. They had undoubtedly been brutal to their enemies. They had also practised some extreme forms of self-mutilation. But these acts had been performed for practical reasons, in order to propitiate the gods that they believed in, to encourage them to bless the Mayans with healthy crops or rain or whatever it was that they needed. But this modern Mayan he was trying to apprehend, if indeed such a person actually existed, had another agenda. It had been the academics' contention that the individual who could be killing all these people in İstanbul was doing so in order to affect the end of the current Mayan time cycle in some way. And that might indeed be the case. But İkmen also felt that there was something more personal in the horrors that had been inflicted upon these people. As he imagined someone he didn't know smearing Rafik Efendi's blood on some fat-tongued idol, he felt a hatred there too that made him shiver. In time with his spasm, he saw Sezen İpek shudder just a little also, and he wondered what she'd either seen or what had just passed through her mind.

Time ticked and the hour of four became five and then six, and then darkness began to fall over Yıldız Park and eventually İkmen took Sezen İpek home. The rest of the team stood down.

Chapter 17

Her daughter gave birth on the night of Hıdırellez, and so Gonca didn't think about Şukru until the festival was over. As soon as the child, Hızır, had been born, Gonca had taken him into the garden and danced with her daughters around the mulberry bush to which they had all tied their wishes. The baby's mother, her unmarried daughter Hürrem, had stayed in the house drinking mint tea. Her mother had shown the child her one wish, a red ribbon with the name Mehmet Süleyman written on it.

But once the festival was over and little Hızır was feeding contentedly from his mother, Gonca began to look around at her world, and when her father telephoned to ask after her brother, she realised that Şukru was missing. To begin with she consulted the cards, but they were unclear. The reading was confused, and although she wouldn't always interpret an unclear reading with misfortune, this made her feel uneasy. She told Hürrem she was going to call Mehmet Süleyman.

Her daughter was contemptuous. 'Why? Uncle Şukru is always going here and there. Why are you worried now? If you want Süleyman to come and have sex with you, then why not just ask him? He'll come.'

Hürrem, like the rest of Gonca's family, didn't like Süleyman or any other kind of police officer. But Gonca ignored her. She called Süleyman, who said that he'd be with her as soon as he was able. Gonca went out into her garden and looked at his name written on the ribbon tied to her mulberry bush, and she hoped that the sick feeling she was experiencing was just a little bit of food poisoning.

'I'll need to take photocopies or scans,' Çetin İkmen said as he waded through the stack of papers that constituted the Osmanoğlu family trees in the possession of Boğaziçi University.

'Of course.' Professor Atay smiled. 'Anything the university can do to assist you, Inspector. However, given the size of the problem . . .'

İkmen looked up. 'Oh, I can't hope to protect all these people, Professor,' he said. 'I will have to think carefully before I even warn them. Those closest to the victims we already have are only too aware that a pattern could be emerging. Do those relatives oblivious of a connection to the deceased need to know? I'm not sure. But I need to know who they are.'

Professor Atay picked up his phone. 'I'll ask one of our students to scan them for you.'

'Thank you, sir. I appreciate your seeing me like this. To be honest, given the size of this family, coupled with your noted expertise, I didn't know where else to go.'

'It's no problem.'

While the academic organised the scanning of the family trees, İkmen sat down and considered the professor's office. Boğaziçi University, formally the American-run Robert College, was housed in a group of elegant turn-of-the-twentieth-century buildings in the fashionable Bosphorus village of Bebek. A highly respected institution, it had produced a slew of famous alumni, including government ministers, artists, writers and of course some celebrity academics such as Cem Atay.

While the professor was on the phone, İkmen let his eyes wander around what was a very diverting room. There were some fantastic terracotta pots which looked as if they probably came from Italy, a framed print of one of the bulbous mother goddess idols from the ancient Anatolian site of Çatalhöyük and a large wooden panel that, to İkmen, looked like something the Mayans or the Aztecs might have produced. When Atay had finished his call, he said to İkmen, 'It's a copy of a sarcophagus lid from Palenque in southern Mexico. It shows King Pakal the Great descending through fleshless jaws into the Underworld. Above him is a bird god or monster, I'm not sure which. But he is passing from this life and into another, which to my way of thinking doesn't look too comfortable.'

'The Mayan way of life doesn't seem to me to be comfortable full stop,' İkmen said.

The professor sat down behind his desk. 'Do I detect that you've been doing some reading around the subject, Inspector?'

'A little.' İkmen smiled. 'A catalogue of anxiety over crops and weather conditions and some really most spectacular self-harm.'

'Ah, yes, the thorn through the penis ritual.'

'Made my skin crawl.'

'And yet,' the professor said, 'is that any better or worse than the self-flagellation practices that the Spaniards brought with them when they let their Catholic clerics loose on the Maya? We tend to think that anything that is not a monotheistic religion is by definition barbaric. But think about what the "civilised" Spaniards did in the New World. Plundered its gold and forcibly converted its people to Christianity.'

İkmen shrugged.

'I'm not excusing the Maya,' Atay said. 'They were undoubtedly cruel and barbaric, but if you speak to their descendants, you get a sense of a whole lost perspective on the world. We

– as in the monotheistic empires of Europe – just cut them out like a malignant growth. And who were we to do that?'

'They had gold.'

'Absolutely!' he said. 'That's the thesis of my book and what will be my television programme.'

'Gold?'

'When the Ottomans fought the Spaniards for supremacy in the Mediterranean, it wasn't just about Muslims versus Christians or one empire against another; it was ourselves and the Spaniards fighting over South American gold. Civilisations that for all we know held the key to curing some of the world's most virulent bodily ills were sacrificed so that greedy Western empires could have more jewellery.'

'When you put it like that . . .'

Atay smiled. 'Ah, you have to go there to appreciate it,' he said. 'And of course the outfall from empire-building can be seen all over the world, can't it? I don't know what you think about the Middle East situation, but as an historian, I can't help but lay the blame for the current mess firmly at the feet of the Ottomans who once controlled it and the British and the French who wrested it from them and then attempted to take it over. But I'm going on, I'm sorry.'

'No,' İkmen said, 'it's very interesting, sir.'

'But you have crimes to solve. Real events in a real present. Academia doesn't bother itself with too much of that.'

'It doesn't matter,' İkmen said. 'If what you've told me or pointed me towards with regard to the Mayan Long Count calendar turns out to be irrelevant to these offences, then that is something that I will accept with no ill will towards you, Professor. Exploring theories that might explain a crime is all part of our process, and even if such theories are wrong, we can at the very least discount them.'

'True. And have you discounted the Mayan connection yet, Inspector?'

'No,' he said. Then he smiled. 'I'm just having some trouble putting what is happening in a modern context. Maybe it's easier if one is religious or believes in things like astrology or homeopathy.'

'You don't have a faith or . . .'

'No, sir,' İkmen said. The fact that he had always believed in magic as practised by his mother – and, via the tingling in his spine that sometimes told him when a significant event was happening in his life, his own magic too – wasn't something he discussed with those he didn't know well.

The professor stood up. 'Well, Inspector,' he said, 'I imagine that by the time you get back to your desk, my student will have emailed those family trees to you.'

İkmen stood too. Of course this very busy man had things to do.

They shook hands.

'And if you need my help again, for any reason, please do ask,' Atay said. 'Although this has not had a direct effect upon my family, I am in daily contact with my brother-in-law Faruk, who continues to suffer.'

'I am sorry about that, sir, truly,' İkmen said. 'I will work as hard as I can to bring this offender to justice and I will study the family trees you have so kindly given me, minutely.' And then he left.

Sezen İpek was aware of the fact as she scanned through all the online editions of the national dailies that her breathing was ragged. What if her blackmailer had realised that she had been surrounded by police up at the Malta Kiosk and had decided just to go ahead and smear Rafik Efendi anyway? And what kind of proof, if any, did he have? He'd never said.

204

But the newspapers were devoid of references to elderly paedophiles and so Sezen felt herself begin to relax again. She made herself some tea and even had a croissant once she felt her stomach muscles unknot. Then, after a pause, she made a phone call. It was to someone she should have contacted a long time ago, someone she had known many years before. She waited for him to answer and then she said, 'Abdurrahman Efendi?'

'Yes?'

'It's Sezen İpek. I heard about your loss . . .'

'What loss?' He sounded old. But then he was old, as was she.

'Your nephew? The—'

'I never knew him. What would he have been to me?' he said. 'He was a foreigner.'

'I understand, but I call you out of courtesy, as one from the same background and a . . . a friend, long ago.'

There was a pause then, and she wondered what he was going to say next. His first utterances had been aggressive. How was he going to take her reference to the short liaison they'd had many years ago, before Leyla had been born?

When he did speak, he sounded deflated. 'Oh, Sezen Hanım, you must not mind me,' he said. 'I'm an old, sick man and my life is more of a burden than a pleasure to me these days. It is I who should have called you, when Leyla . . .'

'Oh, Abdurrahman, you don't need to . . .'

'And then your uncle. What can I say, Sezen? Such terrible things! What have any of us done to deserve such evil in our lives?'

She didn't even let herself think about her uncle and what he had done. Or Leyla. But what had Abdurrahman's nephew done to deserve the death that had come to him on 21 March? Was it just because he was who and what he was in the same way

205

that Rafik and Leyla had been? 'It's who we are,' she said. 'That's why we're dying. People don't like us really, Abdurrahman Efendi, it's all just lies.'

She heard him sigh. 'Do you really believe that?' he said. 'You know, Sezen, in the last few days I have come to realise that maybe what we are doesn't matter any more.'

'Yes, but—'

'Hear me out,' he said. 'We hear about these people nowadays, don't we, people who want us to be caliphs, heads of Islam, figureheads to lead their jihad. But how can we do that and why would we want to? Most of the principal members of the family live abroad, and those of us who don't, well, we don't fit with these new Ottomans, do we? We drink and we smoke and we wear collars and ties on our shirts. It's just an illusion.'

For a moment she was speechless. As a young man, Abdurrahman had been an almost dangerously vocal advocate for a return to Ottoman rule. What had changed his mind? What had made him so cynical? Suddenly she wanted and needed to see him, and she told him so immediately.

His response was unexpected and harsh. 'But I don't want to see you, Sezen Hanım,' he said. 'All I want in life is to be left alone.' And he put the phone down on her.

Sezen Hanım cried. In spite of all those female cousins and nieces, distant relatives and hangers-on, she had no one. She was alone in a city that contained someone who was killing people like her, and she was afraid.

'Do you know where he was going?' Süleyman asked.

Gonca shook her head. 'No. He travelled from Edirne with a group of gypsies.'

'Do you know who?'

'Some of the Edirne people come up to İstanbul for Hıdırellez because they think they can make more money here.'

'What was Şukru doing in Edirne?' Süleyman asked.

'Our father's sisters live there,' she said. 'He'd gone to visit them.'

He sat back in his chair and drew on his cigarette. All the time he looked her in the eyes. 'You didn't tell me,' he said.

'I was going to.'

'That's easy to say.' He leaned towards her. 'I won't be used just when it suits you, Gonca,' he said. 'Don't manipulate my love for you, because I can cut that off in a heartbeat.'

Suddenly she felt sicker than she had done when she'd realised that Şukru was missing. Having only just reconnected with the love of her life, was she going to lose him again? She said, 'I was wrong not to tell you, and yes, I do need you now, but Mehmet, I am so afraid for Şukru. He phoned and told me that as soon as he'd finished some business he'd come and see me. But he didn't.'

'Do you know where he was when he phoned you?'

'My father has spoken to my aunts. They asked the people he travelled with from Edirne where they last saw him. It was in Ortaköy.'

'Do you know anyone in Ortaköy? Does your brother?'

'Not that I know of,' she said. 'You know, Mehmet, Şukru does go missing sometimes for long periods, but both my father and I have a bad feeling about this time. I tried to read the cards, but they were confused and I don't know what to think.'

'What else did Şukru talk to you about when he called you from Ortaköy?'

'Oh, he was still mad that I was seeing you,' she said. She watched his face for any sort of reaction, but there was nothing. She looked away so that she could concentrate on her memories

207

of her last conversation with Şukru. 'He said that he was going to move his family and my father away from Tarlabaşı.'

'To where?'

'He didn't say. Somewhere in the city. He'd talked to my father about somewhere on the Bosphorus,' she said. 'Şukru has money, but not lots. If he was going to move the family on to somewhere in the city, especially by the Bosphorus, then he'd need to get more business.'

'Business? What do you mean?'

She looked away from him. 'You know what Şukru does, Mehmet.'

There was no need for her to say any more. Mehmet knew that Şukru provided kids to pickpocketing rings, that he distilled illegal liquor and ran questionable cigarettes into Turkey from Eastern Europe. He was an unemployed bear man who had lost the home his family had owned for hundreds of years; what else was he supposed to do?

She watched him think, and then he said, 'I'll need to speak to your family in Tarlabaşı; they'll have to give me access to Şukru's friends and associates.'

She was about to say that that would be impossible, but he silenced her. 'No ifs or buts,' he said. 'I won't arrest anyone for pocket-diving, prostitution or even illegal brewing. All I want to know is where your brother is.'

And then Gonca said the unspoken thing that had been in her mind ever since her brother had failed to visit her. 'Because people are being murdered in the city?'

'Yes,' he said simply. 'Nothing but that matters now.'

Chapter 18

Fires happened on waste ground for all sorts of reasons. Discarded cigarette ends, kids messing around with magnifying glasses; sometimes in the summer everything was just so dry a spark from a passing car could set one off, but sometimes it was arson. Bedrettin Balbay hadn't been a gardener up at Yıldız Park for long, but he knew that this fire, which stank like something he half recognised but didn't dare give a name to, was a bad one. This fire however was not in the park, but across from his two-roomed apartment in Aksaray.

Once, long ago, the place where the smoke was coming from had been an office block. But that had been torn down at least ten years before, and now the area was just a tangle of thick bushes, old clumps of barbed wire and junkies' needles. Sometimes the Eastern European prostitutes who plied their trade all over Aksaray took their customers there to have sex. But they didn't, or so Bedrettin thought, usually light fires.

His wife, as she generally did whenever there was any sort of local trouble, told him to ignore it and just go to work. But he couldn't. Working in the park had taught him that fire, if not quickly brought under control, could spread rapidly. Bedrettin called the fire brigade and then made his way out of his apartment block and over the road to where he could see both smoke and flames.

The seat of the blaze appeared to be behind some bushes at

the back of the site. And although he knew that he should really wait for the fire appliances to arrive before he attempted to do any sort of investigating himself, Bedrettin began to pick his way through the wire, the needles and eventually the bushes. At first the fire was wreathed in too much smoke for him to be able to really make it out. But when the smoke began to clear and he could see the source of the smell that had offended him so much, everything he'd eaten that morning made a bid for freedom. What Bedrettin found himself looking at was a funeral pyre.

'There's nothing like getting your work done early,' Çetin İkmen said to Ayşe Farsakoğlu as they watched the fire officers check what remained of the pyre for flames. It was seven thirty in the morning and both İkmen and his sergeant had been asleep when they'd got the call out to Aksaray.

'But then that's a salutary lesson to us, Ayşe,' he continued as, in the face of the human-flesh-scented smoke all around him, he lit a cigarette, 'not to underestimate our offender. Usually he strikes at night on the twenty-first of the month, but today it's in the morning. Who knew?'

Ayşe, who was caffeine-deprived and nauseous, murmured, 'Yes, sir.'

Once the fire chief gave him the signal that the pyre was safe, İkmen walked over to it and looked at the blackened body that lay half consumed on what remained of a considerable wood pile. Beyond the fact that it was tall and therefore probably male, there was not a lot that could be deduced just by looking at it. İkmen frowned. 'Didn't think the Mayans went in for cremation,' he said.

'Maybe the killer burned the body after death,' Ayşe said.

'Good point.'

Heavy feet moving slowly through the surrounding bushes

210

signalled the arrival of Arto Sarkissian, who stopped in front of the pyre. 'Burning. Not quite as bad as drowning, but . . .' He put his bag down on the ground and began to walk slowly around the body.

İkmen moved out of his way and went back to stand with Ayşe Farsakoğlu. 'I wonder which scion of the imperial family he was,' he said.

'The body?'

'Yes. If this runs true to form, then he'll've had his heart cut out—'

'Ah well, that's where you're wrong, Çetin,' Arto Sarkissian interrupted. 'I can see the heart, such as it is, through the ribs. He's not had his head cut off either. But I am fairly certain that he – and yes, it is definitely a man – was put on this pyre post-mortem.'

'So dead before he was burned, but not killed in the traditional way?' İkmen said.

'No, I don't think so. No signs of a struggle.' Surgical gloves on, Arto began to gently tease at clothing fibres with a pair of tweezers. 'I'm going to have to unwrap him very carefully when I get him back to the lab,' he said. 'Time of death? Who knows. Hopefully he's got a relatively undamaged ATM card on him or something. If not . . .'

'A job for DNA?'

'And just pray for a match. Oh, and by the way,' the doctor said as he looked down at his watch, 'life is extinct, eight oh five.'

He shouldn't have taken the day off. It was, after all, the twenty-first of the month. But he'd been tired, worn out from weeks of looking at endless family trees, trying to work out how, apart from by blood, their royal victims were connected. Aside from the fact that they all had secrets connected to their sex lives, they were not. And even that was tenuous, because John Regan's homosexuality had not been concealed. Then there was the almost total lack of evidence across all four murders. They'd eventually managed to get their hands on two Bulgarian gypsy men who, it was fairly certain, ran groups of pickpockets across the city. But the old Jewish man who claimed to have seen a person like that outside John Regan's flat just before he died hadn't recognised either of them. Whoever was killing these people, his people, was cleaning up after himself most efficiently.

Mehmet Süleyman turned over and looked at the sleeping figure of Gonca beside him. It still struck him as odd that of all the women he'd known in his life, he should finally fall hopelessly in love with this one. She was a gypsy and an artist, who had colour and fury and a little madness in her soul, and he – well, he wasn't any of those things. She was as different as she was unsuitable, and he found himself intoxicated by whatever it was they had together every time they met. Because contrary to what he knew İkmen thought, it wasn't just sex, although that was a strong bond between them. Gonca gave herself to the sex act in a way that Ayşe Farsakoğlu never could, even though he knew she had tried.

Gonca turned towards him and opened her eyes. He felt her hand reach for his penis. When she found it, she smiled.

'I think someone wants my body,' she said as she first straddled and then mounted him. He lasted as long as he could, which was difficult. She so rarely gave him the opportunity to demonstrate his sexual control. With her he had so little.

But then as quickly as her passion had arrived, it left with the same alacrity, and after she'd made him tea and given him cigarettes, she got on with her day, which, since Şukru had gone missing, always started in the same way. She consulted the cards.

Süleyman didn't know what she consulted the cards for – whether it was to find out if Şukru was still alive, where he might be or who he might be with. All he knew was that the last time he'd seen her do it she'd cried, and when he'd asked her what she'd seen that had so upset her, she'd said, 'Nothing.'

On this occasion she didn't cry, but she did look sad. He thought about not asking what was wrong, but then he decided that if he did that, he wasn't being true to his own character. He said, 'What now?'

Oddly, she smiled. 'There's nothing to be done,' she said. 'It's written.'

'What is?'

She looked confused. 'You're a Muslim,' she said. 'Everything.'

He didn't actually believe that life was predetermined, but he knew that she did, even though she was about as far away from a practising Muslim as it was possible to get.

'What about Şukru?' he asked.

'What about him?'

'I know you look at the cards to find out if he—'

'Ah, I have a day to get on with, don't talk to me!' she said. Then she looked at him still laying naked on her bed and said, 'Now what am I to do?'

He frowned. 'What do you mean?'

'Well, I have a grandson to help wash and dress, breakfast to make for my daughter, work to do, or . . .'

'Or what?' he said.

She sat down on the edge of the bed and then lay down beside him. 'Or you tell me,' she said. 'It is your day off, after all, and you have chosen to share it with me.'

He smiled. She was no longer young. He didn't know exactly

how old she was, but then he got the feeling she didn't know the answer to that question herself. But whatever her age, it hadn't affected her sex drive and had only minimally compromised her beauty. He leaned over and took one of her breasts in his mouth. Gonca began breathing hard, and when he put a hand between her thighs, she groaned.

And then his mobile phone rang.

Arthur Regan looked up at the front window of Abdurrahman Şafak's second-floor apartment and wondered what his reluctant brother-in-law was doing. Ever since the wretched man had asked him to come and visit with what existed of John's book, and in spite of the angry words they had exchanged, he'd plagued him with phone calls about it. Arthur didn't know how many times the old fool had read through it, but whenever he did, he just seemed to find more in it to complain about. And then there were the threats. If Arthur or anyone else published what he called 'this trashy book', he'd sue, and he already had a lawyer standing by, waiting to go. Arthur wished he'd just blanked the old idiot, but he had honestly thought that by engaging with him he might be able to help them both to come to terms with their pasts. What a moron he'd been! And now he'd been summoned again.

He went into the building and pressed the apartment's intercom. Almost immediately the old aristocrat answered. 'Who is it?'

'It's Arthur Regan. You called me, remember? You said we needed to talk, and so we do.'

'Well I've changed my mind. Go away!' the old man said as he switched seamlessly into English. 'I have nothing to say to you, sir!'

'Well I have something to say to you. The threats have to stop,' Arthur said. 'My son's UK publishers are going to give

214

the book to another writer to finish, with or without my help, so you'd better get used to the idea.'

'I've told you, I will sue!'

'Sue away,' Arthur said. 'I've lost the only thing in life that meant anything to me. You're welcome to what little money I have, I really don't care.'

'Do not worry, I will.'

Arthur Regan lost it. 'Well fuck you!' he yelled into the intercom. 'Fuck you and all your fucking kind to fucking hell, you miserable, snobbish, soulless old bastard! And by the way, I'm glad you're dying! I'm so happy you've got cancer and I hope to God that it fucking hurts!'

A man who passed him in the hall and who clearly spoke at least some English looked shocked. But from the other end of the intercom there was only silence. Arthur, red-faced and frankly exhausted after an outburst he had, in retrospect, being waiting over forty years to have, leaned against the wall and tried to get his heart rate down. He'd said some bloody awful things to Abdurrahman but he'd deserved every one of them. Like his father, he'd only ever cared about Betül as an object in which his own blood ran, and they had both abandoned her when she'd died. It was entirely because of them that her body didn't lie in Turkish soil, as Arthur knew she had wanted. At the time he'd been too poor to repatriate her body himself, but they'd had money.

He wiped the sweat that had gathered on his forehead with the back of his hand and then stood up straight. He was just about to leave when suddenly the intercom crackled into life again.

'If you come up now, we can talk,' Abdurrahman said. 'The girl is out so we won't be disturbed.'

Arthur thought about it for a moment. After that outburst,

Abdurrahman was the last person he wanted to see. But then he decided, *Well, why not do what I came to do?*

He leaned in towards the intercom and said, 'I'll be up.'

Süleyman, whose day off had come to a shuddering halt, looked at Arto Sarkissian across something that came straight out of a horror movie. He'd seen burned corpses before, but it was not something that got any easier over time. He kept his eyes firmly on the Armenian's face. 'Are you sure?' he said.

'Not in the least, but it is a possibility,' Arto said. 'Şukru Şekeroğlu is an unusually tall man. He's the only missing person of this height that I have any information on. It could be him, but then again, it could be someone who is entirely new to us.'

'I thought our killer only went for those of us with royal blood,' Süleyman said.

İkmen, who was standing behind his colleague and who wanted to move the investigation forward, said, 'Dr Sarkissian has been able to remove samples that are suitable for DNA testing, but we will need Şekeroğlu family DNA with which to compare it.'

Süleyman turned to look at him. 'Gonca.'

'Or any other of Şukru's siblings or children,' İkmen said.

Süleyman shook his head. 'She's convinced herself that he's dead,' he said. 'With the cards and . . .'

'You know her,' Arto Sarkissian said. 'You know how she'll take it. You'll know whether she is open to providing a DNA sample.'

Süleyman moved away from the corpse and leaned against one of the white-tiled walls. İkmen and the doctor followed him.

'Do you want blood?' Süleyman asked.

'Ideally. But I know that sometimes people like gypsies can be superstitious about giving their blood away,' Arto said. 'I'd be grateful for saliva.' He stopped and put a finger in the air as a thought struck him. 'Even better would be a hair – with an intact follicle.'

İkmen looked at Süleyman. 'A hairbrush?'

'You want me to pull hair out of her hairbrush,' Süleyman said.

'With her permission, of course.'

'After telling her that the burning man here just might be her brother?'

İkmen said, 'We need to do this because of the height of this corpse, but it might not be Şukru. Whoever talks to Gonca or any other member of her family will have to emphasise that. Do you think she'll do it?'

Süleyman thought, and then gave the only answer he could. 'I don't know,' he said. He looked at İkmen. 'In a way, I think she might take such a request more negatively from me than from . . .'

'Me?' İkmen raised an eyebrow.

'You've known her a lot longer than I have.' Even saying the words made him hate himself. How could he be so cowardly? He was Gonca's lover; why couldn't he tell her that a hideously burned body found in Aksaray might be her brother? Because if it wasn't, she'd be angry with him?

But İkmen, as was his wont, acquiesced. He had known Gonca Şekeroğlu for many decades. His mother had told fortunes with the gypsies of İstanbul all her life, and so when he'd joined the police they had already known and trusted him. 'I'll do it,' he said. 'Do you know if she's in Balat today?'

'She's out at present, back this evening,' Süleyman said. He didn't even try to put distance between himself and Gonca's life now. Everyone knew. It was pointless.

'Then I will visit her this evening,' İkmen said. 'Phoning her now would be insensitive, and a few hours won't make a difference, will they, Doctor?'

'No,' the Armenian said. 'I can give you swabs to take saliva from her and bags for hair samples. If she does want to give blood, then she'll have to come and see me tomorrow. Nothing can go off for testing until then.'

'Then that's settled,' İkmen said.

Süleyman smiled back when the older man smiled at him, but he felt a scintilla of disapproval too. He should have just said he'd go and see Gonca himself and taken whatever her grief and fear meted out to him. He could always change his mind . . . Instead he said, 'So do you think that this . . . the dead man is our twenty-first of the month victim?'

'I think so,' Çetin İkmen replied. Then he added, 'I certainly hope so.'

Chapter 19

The girl Suzan entered the building in what neighbours would later report was her usual state of trepidation. Everyone knew and had always known how the old man treated her, even though nobody had ever so much as thought about intervening.

Suzan entered the lift with shaking hands and knees. By the time she got to the second floor, she was sweating, and when she reached the door of the apartment, she began to feel sick. As she always did, she called out to the old man when she turned the key in the lock, 'Abdurrahman Efendi! It's me, Suzan!' Then she waited for an answer, which was usually quite a long time in coming. On this occasion there was just silence.

Suzan took her shoes off and walked slowly forwards. She felt her skin go from hot to cold in less than a second. The icy silence that seemed to fill that apartment made her feel as if she was being compressed against its walls. Just like every time she returned to the apartment, she wanted to run but she couldn't. There was nowhere to go. She had to carry on.

At the end of the entrance hall was the lounge where her employer spent most of his time. Abdurrahman rarely went to bed at night any more. He claimed that sitting up was more comfortable for him these days. As she drew closer, Suzan found herself cringing at every sound that her feet made, every creak of the apartment's walls. She expected to hear his voice at any moment and her ears ached with an anticipation she could barely endure. And then she was in the lounge and he was there.

Suzan looked at Abdurrahman Efendi for some time and with a sense of detachment she didn't know she had. It – he – was ghastly. What had been done to him was almost beyond belief, and just on the level of pity for a fellow creature, she should have felt some sympathy for him. But she didn't. She regarded his drained, vampire-ravaged-looking body as one might view a piece of meat. Because he'd always shown such contempt for her, because he'd used her, shamed her, she couldn't find it in herself to feel anything but contempt for him. And now that he was dead, she could do that with impunity.

And so in the half-hour before she called the police, Suzan mocked Abdurrahman Efendi, called him rude names and told him that nothing in her whole life had made her so happy as his death.

Çetin İkmen watched the news with Gonca the gypsy on her ancient television set. In spite of the fact that a body had been found in Aksaray, TRT was still appealing for help in finding Şukru Şekeroğlu. They showed a tiny piece of film of him taken back in Sulukule some years before.

Gonca put one cigarette out and then immediately lit another. Both she and İkmen were chain-smoking, but neither of them cared. 'I've felt Şukru to be dead almost from the start,' she said. 'My cards have been . . . indistinct.'

'We don't know the body *is* Şukru,' İkmen said.

'Because it's too badly burned?'

'Yes. There's no ID on the body we found up at Aksaray. The only connection to your brother is the height, and that is why I'm here now.'

Şukru's scowling face disappeared from the screen. Gonca shook her head. 'He was such a life force.'

'He may still be a life force,' İkmen said.

She looked him in the eyes and said, 'Don't try to make me feel better, İkmen. I know what I know.'

He shrugged. He'd known Gonca ever since he was a young constable, and he was well aware of what he could and couldn't say to her. He knew he couldn't kid her.

'So you need some of my hair, do you?' she said. She walked over to the TV and switched it off.

'Dr Sarkissian would be very grateful,' İkmen said. He put his hand in his jacket pocket and pulled out a roll of small plastic bags. 'He's trusting me to transport it to him, but I expect I can manage that. You've got the hard job.'

'You want a hair pulled from my head?'

'Complete with follicle, yes,' he said. 'You have to pull it out.'

She put a hand up to her head and gripped her hair. 'If it's for Şukru . . .'

'Whoa! Whoa! Whoa!'

He tried to stop her pulling out a great lump, but it was too late. Without a murmur she tugged out a hank of hair and put it into İkmen's hands. While he looked down at it in a rather horrified way, she said, 'Is that enough for him? It comes out easily now that I am old.'

She sat down again while İkmen bagged up far more strands of hair than even Arto Sarkissian could possibly need. 'This is, er, it's . . .' He sealed the bag. 'So what's this about being old? You're not old.'

For the first time since he'd entered her house, Gonca laughed. She usually laughed a lot. 'I remember you when you were young, and now you're retiring,' she said. 'We're both old, İkmen, although it doesn't matter so much for you because you're a man. Men can look like shit and women will still love them.'

221

He put the hair-filled bag into his pocket. 'Ah come on now, Gonca,' he said. 'You don't have any trouble attracting men. You never have had and now . . .' But his voice faded out. He both did and didn't want to talk to her about Mehmet Süleyman.

'Is there any reason why Mehmet Bey didn't come to ask me for my hair tonight?' she asked.

'Beyond his rather squeamish desire not to hurt you, no,' İkmen said.

'So you came instead.'

'You and I are not . . . involved,' İkmen said. 'We never have been and so, much as I like you, Gonca, I am a disinterested outsider in your life.'

She sat down on the cushion beside his and put an arm across his shoulder. 'Maybe my life would have been better if we had been involved,' she said.

He looked into her eyes and shook his head. 'Oh no, Gonca. What would you do with me, eh? You don't do ugly men, do you?'

'You're not—'

'I'm short, I'm skinny, I'm ugly, and really only Fatma has ever had the courage to love me, which makes her a remarkable woman.'

Gonca curled her fingers around his neck. 'But had I had a good man, a reliable man . . .'

He gently disengaged her fingers. 'But you never have and you never will,' he said. 'Gonca, you do beautiful, crazy men who let you down. Your first husband . . .'

'Enver.' She smiled. 'He could make love all night long and then get up, chop wood and . . . well . . .' She looked down at her lap. Her first marriage, just like her second and all her other relationships with men, had ended badly.

'Enver liked a drink,' İkmen said, 'to put it mildly. And you

222

know that although Mehmet Süleyman doesn't like a drink more than he should, or run about all over the city on amphetamines like, er, your second husband . . .'

'Demir.'

'Like Demir did . . . still, that boy has a weakness and you and I both know what it is.'

Her face fell. 'Women.' She took her arm off his shoulder and laid both hands in her lap.

'I don't want you to get hurt and I don't want him to get hurt either,' İkmen said. 'I care about both of you.'

She looked up at him and he saw that her eyes were wet.

'Gonca Hanım, even if you married Mehmet Süleyman, you couldn't have the life of a normal policeman's wife with him. How would that work? What would you do? Read all the other police wives' cards and then hand out the rakı?'

'There's been no talk of marriage,' she said.

'And yet you love him,' İkmen said. 'Against everything your family said to you last time you two were together, you have got back with him and you've – both of you – broken my sergeant's heart in the process.'

She looked into his eyes. 'I had to have him,' she said.

'I know,' İkmen replied. 'And don't think that I'm advocating on behalf of my sergeant, because I'm not. That was a desperate, unhappy relationship, and I know he is and always has been besotted with you. But think about where this relationship is going. Think about the future and ask yourself honestly whether the life of a—'

'You don't want me to carry on seeing him, do you, Çetin Bey?' she cut in.

İkmen had to think about what she'd said for a moment before he answered, because much as he did like them both and want what was best for the pair of them, he realised he had another agenda too. And he was honest about it. 'You'll end up destroying each other, you know it and I know it,' he said. 'A long time ago I said to you that proximity to princes was dangerous, and that still holds. Mehmet Süleyman Efendi may be a prince without a country, but those who support the return of such people are being listened to and regarded, and that's quite apart from his family themselves, who I think would oppose any sort of permanent union between you with every force at their disposal.'

She didn't attempt to contradict or argue with him. But she looked sad when he left her, even though she kissed him on the cheek, as she usually did, with affection. Tough love was a bastard.

Ömer Mungan took the call. Süleyman, deep in both paperwork and thought, hardly noticed. All he could think about was Gonca, and what Çetin İkmen had gone to tell her. He'd seen the Aksaray body, and although he hadn't been able to recognise it, he felt that it was Şukru, and not just because of the height. Like the gypsy's sister, Süleyman knew that Şukru Şekeroğlu had always been involved in things that were either only just inside the law or completely outside it.

'Sir?'

He looked up into Ömer's slanted brown eyes.

'A call from Şişli, sir,' Ömer said. 'The maid of a man called Abdurrahman Şafak has found him dead. She thinks he's been stabbed.'

Süleyman looked at his watch. It was still well and truly 21 May, in spite of the fact that it felt as if he'd been working for over twenty-four hours.

'So we have a second death?'

Ömer shrugged. 'Who knew we'd get to be so lucky?' Slowly but surely he was developing a slick, sick city sense of humour

224

as well as a rather harder shell than he'd had in Mardin. But then Süleyman knew that the young man's introduction to İstanbul had been more bloody and shocking than any other time he could remember.

He stood up and put his jacket on. 'Abdurrahman Şafak,' he said. 'That sounds familiar.'

Ömer was way ahead of him. 'He is or was the uncle of the Englishman John Regan.' Süleyman clicked his fingers. 'Of course. Well done, Ömer, that's good.'

'Thank you, sir.'

Süleyman drove to Şişli, where they found Abdurrahman Şafak's apartment building ringed by uniforms. Up on the second floor, where the old man had lived, they heard the familiar sound of Arto Sarkissian's voice, and as they entered the apartment, he walked towards them.

'Doctor.'

'Inspector.' He smiled at Ömer. 'Sergeant.' He took off blood-stained gloves and placed them in a rubbish disposal bag. 'This declaring life extinct job is becoming tedious.'

'Twice in one day.'

'Yes, it's bordering on the excessive. But life, whether I like it or not, *is* extinct in the case of Abdurrahman Şafak Efendi, and again we have been able to do nothing to prevent it.'

Süleyman lowered his gaze. What the doctor had said was not a criticism of him; rather a more generalised expression of the frustration they all felt. But Süleyman felt bad anyway.

Arto Sarkissian, aware that he had caused some distress, cleared his throat. 'Well, cause of death I have yet to determine, but if I tell you that the victim is lacking a heart, I'm sure you'll get the picture. Time of death, again I will have to do some more tests, because the man's apartment was heated like a sauna.'

Süleyman shook his head.

'However, you do have, if not a witness, the man's maid. She found the body, and of course, as you can imagine, she is not exactly jumping for joy. She's in the kitchen.'

'Thank you, Doctor, I'll speak to her,' Süleyman said. He turned to Ömer. 'Take a couple of uniformed officers and see what, if anything, the neighbours witnessed.'

'Yes, sir.'

Süleyman walked past the doctor and into an apartment that reminded him all too vividly of his parents' house in Arnavutköy. Although the Bosphorus village where his family lived had recently become chic in the extreme, the Süleyman family home was like the shabby abode of some sort of imperial Ottoman hoarder. This apartment was the same. Every centimetre of wall was covered with portrait photographs of men in fezzes and women looking extremely uncomfortable in tight European dresses of Victorian vintage. Any occasional tables not covered in silver cigarette boxes and ornamental nargiles were used to prop up piles of books about Ottoman regimental insignia and accounts of the reign of every sultan who had ever lived, all topped off with endless maps of the city that were eighty years out of date.

He walked past the butchered corpse – a dead man without a heart was sadly something he had become accustomed to – and went into the kitchen. He saw the uniformed female officer first. A very overweight woman, she was in stark contrast to the tiny, almost anorexic-looking girl who sat at the kitchen table with her head down, weeping. He asked the officer the girl's name and then sat down beside her.

'Suzan,' he said, 'my name is Inspector Süleyman. I'm afraid I need to ask you some questions about what has happened here. I know it will be distressing, but there really isn't anything else I can do.'

226

She just sobbed.

The overweight officer said, 'She hasn't said a word beyond her name, sir.'

'OK.' He looked at the girl again. 'Suzan,' he said, 'do you want to see a doctor? Would you rather talk to a doctor? We can arrange that. You've experienced a terrible thing, you—'

'They took his heart,' she whispered between her trembling frightened fingers.

'They?'

'Someone.' Her entire body shook as she raised her head from the table.

'Did you see anyone, Suzan?'

Now that her head was up, she looked at him with frightened if slightly curious eyes. 'He is dead, isn't he, Abdurrahman Efendi?'

'I'm afraid he is, yes,' Süleyman said. And then he smiled. He knew that because he was good-looking, he appealed to almost everyone he interviewed in virtually every type of scenario.

Suzan duly looked at him, through her tears, with wonder. She said, 'What am I going to do?'

Where maids went when their masters died he really did not know; besides, that was not his concern. 'Suzan, I need you to tell me how and when you found Abdurrahman Efendi.'

For a moment she looked at him as if she hadn't understood. He was just about to reiterate his question when she said, 'I was due back at six.'

'And were you on time?' Süleyman asked.

'Oh, I'm always on time, sir,' she said. 'Especially when I've had the afternoon off.'

'You had the afternoon off today?'

'Yes, sir.'

'And what did you do with your afternoon off, Suzan?'

'I went to look at the shops in Nişantaşı,' she said.

'Which shops?'

'I like the big stores, Beyman and Vakko,' she said, naming two of İstanbul's most famous department stores.

'And you spent all afternoon in Beyman and Vakko?'

'Yes, sir. Efendi had a visitor due to come at four. He said he didn't want me back before six.'

Süleyman briefly looked at the uniformed policewoman, and then said, 'Who? Do you know who Abdurrahman Efendi received here this afternoon?'

'It was a man he'd seen before,' she said. 'A foreigner. He didn't like him and he said he didn't want to talk to him for long. They spoke some Turkish but mostly English.'

'Do you know the name or the nationality of this foreigner?' Süleyman asked.

'I don't know his name, but I think he might be English,' the girl said. And then she began to cry again. 'I'm so sorry, sir, that I didn't call the police as soon as I found Efendi. I was so frightened I just couldn't move.'

After dropping off Gonca's hair samples at the pathology laboratory, Çetin İkmen was almost home when his phone rang. Although he couldn't fathom his hands-free mobile phone kit, he answered it anyway and spoke to Süleyman for some time before turning the car around and heading for the station. It was already dark, and after the difficult time he'd had with Gonca, he'd just wanted to go home as soon as he was able. But he couldn't, because for the first time a twenty-first-of-the-month murder had been committed and they actually had a lead.

Süleyman had already arrived with Arthur Regan when İkmen entered Interview Room 2. It was very strange to see the elderly

Englishman in this particular context, but it did make some sort of sense.

'Mr Regan,' Süleyman began. 'You know by now that your brother-in-law Abdurrahman Şafak was found dead at his apartment earlier this evening.'

'Yes,' he said. 'You told me yourself, Inspector Süleyman. I am, if not sad, shocked and distressed. Abdurrahman Şafak was my wife's brother.'

'You were not sad . . .'

'It's no secret that I didn't get on with Abdurrahman. He didn't get on with me.'

'Why was that, please?'

'You know why.'

'We are recording this interview, Mr Regan,' Süleyman said. 'Please, you must repeat what you have told us of your family before.'

The interview was conducted in English, and for the duration of Arthur Regan's story about his marriage and his son John, he spoke rapidly so that only İkmen could understand him with anything approaching ease. When he'd finished, Süleyman asked him, 'Mr Regan, did you go to visit Abdurrahman Şafak this afternoon?'

'Yes,' he said, 'at four or thereabouts.'

'Why did you go to see him?'

'He asked me to visit,' the Englishman said. 'He wanted me to somehow stop my son John's British publisher from going ahead with reassigning his book to another author. I told him I couldn't do that, just as I'd told him over the phone about a hundred times before.'

'Abdurrahman Şafak, he, er, he was, er . . .'

'He was bothering you with calls?' İkmen cut in.

'Yes, he was, and threatening me with court action too. It had to stop,' Arthur said. 'Apart from anything else, there was nothing I could do about preventing the book from being published.'

Süleyman looked at İkmen, who motioned for him to continue. Sometimes the younger man's language skills would let him down, and İkmen would pick up for him, as he'd just done, but it was still Süleyman's interview.

'One witness at Mr Şafak's apartment block tells us that you had an argument with Mr Şafak before you got to the apartment, on the intercom . . .'

'Yes,' he said. 'The stupid old fool told me he didn't want to see me. But the only reason I was there in the first place was because he'd wanted me to visit him.' He shook his head. 'He wouldn't let me in and it made me angry. I said some awful things to him. You know he was dying?'

'I did not,' Süleyman said.

'Well I told him I was glad,' Arthur said. 'I swore and shouted and made a real fool of myself.' He shook his head again. 'But then he let me in and we talked in quite a civilised fashion. Still with no resolution, but I think I left him with at least some understanding of my point of view. When I took my leave, he was most certainly alive, that I can tell you.'

'Which was at what time?'

He thought for a moment and then said, 'It must have been about four forty-five. I didn't stay long. I can't remember exactly.'

'And what did you do after you left Mr Şafak's apartment in Şişli?'

'I went back to the apartment I'm renting in Beyoğlu and had a drink,' he said. 'I needed it. Then I watched television, BBC World.'

'Er, Abdurrahman Şafak's maid, Suzan Arslan, can you tell me . . .'

'Oh, she wasn't there,' he said. 'The poor little thing had the afternoon off. She must've been delighted.'

'Why is that?'

'Didn't she tell you? Probably too scared. He treated her like rubbish.'

'In what way?'

'You mean apart from shouting at her, ignoring the fact that she had a name and generally behaving like some sort of autocrat? I don't know, but I saw her shake every time she had to come close to him. Abdurrahman when young was an arrogant prig; in old age it seemed he'd become a spiteful one. As I say, I don't know what he did to that girl, but whatever it was she didn't like it.'

Arthur Regan submitted willingly to DNA and forensic testing, but it was hard for either Süleyman or İkmen to entirely discount him as a suspect. Until Dr Sarkissian had completed his examination and testing of Abdurrahman Şafak's corpse, a time of death as well as a definitive cause could not be clearly established. Also neighbours in the Şişli apartment block reported hearing raised voices speaking English on several occasions over the past weeks since Arthur Regan had been in İstanbul. Obviously the men had been very much at odds with each other, but had this turned to violence? Specifically had it turned to the kind of twisted violence that allowed one person to cut out another's heart? Had Arthur Regan killed his hated brother-in-law in almost exactly the same way as his own son had been murdered?

'It's highly unlikely,' İkmen said.

'But that means that someone else must have come into Şafak's apartment after Arthur Regan.'

'Yes.'

'But none of our witnesses saw anyone apart from the Englishman and the maid.'

'Not on that day, no,' İkmen said.

'What, you mean . . .'

231

'Mehmet, my dear boy, we're clearly dealing with an offender who is very clever,' İkmen said. 'He or she comes and goes from these people's lives apparently at will and with a level of invisibility that conceals him from us. But I am beginning to wonder whether we're asking those witnesses that we have the right questions. For instance, do we have any idea about who might have visited John Regan the day before he died?'

'No.'

'Then maybe we should find out,' İkmen said.

Süleyman narrowed his eyes. 'You think that he could have secreted himself in the building?'

'Why not?'

'For over twenty-four hours?'

'Why not? With the exception of Levent Devrim, all of our victims lived in either considerable apartment blocks or, in Rafik Efendi's case, a big house.'

'Leyla Ablak was murdered at the spa.'

'Yes, and how difficult would it be to hide out at a spa, especially one attached to a hotel?'

'We interviewed all the staff and the guests at the hotel.'

'We also interviewed the manager of the spa, Faruk Genç, who was Leyla Ablak's lover. We know he wasn't there when she died. But do we know whether he let someone else in before he left to return home?'

'Why would he do that?'

'I don't know,' İkmen said.

'You're implying that Faruk Genç orchestrated Leyla Ablak's murder via a third party. You're also implying that Genç wanted his lover dead. Why would that be?'

'I don't know,' İkmen said. 'I'm just speculating. But I think I'm speculating constructively. We now have five unsolved murders; six if you include what may or may not be Şukru Şekeroğlu. Why haven't we made an arrest?'

'Who would we have arrested? No one has seen anything or anyone when these people have been killed, and so far the common factors between our victims have only worked up to a point.'

'But there is the Mayan connection,' İkmen said. 'In terms of the dates of the murders, that is holding firm. Also, we do seem to be in a pattern now of heart removal . . .'

'With the exception of the Aksaray body.'

'If indeed that is connected to these killings at all,' İkmen said. He paused and shook his head. 'Four of our victims come from the former Imperial family, and if Professor Atay and Dr Santa Ana are correct, then their royal blood would be interesting to a person who is obsessed with the Mayan 2012 belief system. The fact that Levent Devrim's death doesn't conform to that pattern says to me that either it was just a fluke, or he is connected in ways that we don't yet understand. Did he know people who knew the others? Did he perhaps have acquaintances he met at the Ada bookshop, other people interested in the occult who in turn knew Leyla Ablak, John Regan, Rafik Efendi and Abdurrahman Şafak?'

'Levent Devrim kept himself to himself,' Süleyman said. 'With the exception of the old Kurdish prostitute, Sugar.'

'Maybe. But the more I think about it, the more I wonder whether Levent Devrim is the key. Of all our victims, he was the only one where the killer was, possibly, seen.'

'Disguised.'

'Maybe,' İkmen said. 'But a figure was seen, and however outlandish it was, we need to know more about it.'

'The gypsy boy Hamid saw it, and possibly Şukru Şekeroğlu.'

'Which may explain why Şukru, if that body is his, is now

no more,' İkmen said. 'You've questioned that boy before, haven't you?'

'Yes.'

'So question him again,' İkmen said. 'And while you're doing that, I think I might have a look at our victims' address books, get the sad techies to do whatever one does to access their Facebook pages. This offender got to these people too easily for me to think that he doesn't know them personally.'

Chapter 20

Predictably, the old man had only used paper records. There wasn't even a computer in the apartment. But the small diary he had kept in an old roll-top desk was neat and appeared to be up to date. What didn't help was the fact that when Abdurrahman Şafak had made a note of an appointment with a person, he had always omitted, after the old Ottoman custom, to record their surnames. So Arthur Regan was recorded as 'Arthur Bey', and even his doctor was expressed as 'Cemal Bey'.

İkmen, bleary-eyed from the frantic activities of the previous day, looked up from the diary at the girl, Suzan, who had brought him a very welcome morning glass of tea. He smiled at her and she looked a little shocked by it. Her own face was still covered with tears. He said, 'Suzan, your master's diary is blank with regard to appointments for the two days before his death. Did he perhaps receive an unexpected visitor in that time, do you remember?'

She thought for a moment, sniffed, and then said, 'No, sir. Not that I know of.'

'Were you in the apartment the whole time during the course of those two days?'

'No. I went shopping for maybe two hours for Efendi, the day before he died.'

'Shopping for what?' İkmen asked.

'Groceries,' she said. 'And also I had to go and have his

prescription made up at the pharmacy on Ihlamur Yolu. I had to wait, which was why it took me so long.'

'What time was this?'

She thought for a moment. Then she said, 'About midday. When I went out.'

'So you returned at approximately two,' İkmen said.

'Yes.'

'Suzan,' he said, 'I have to ask, but . . .'

'Yes, sir.'

'Your staying on in this apartment. Are you all right with that? I mean, after . . .'

'I have nowhere else to go, sir,' she said. 'I came to this city to work for Efendi, I know no one. I am grateful that his family have said I can stay here. And the room where Efendi . . . where he died, it's locked.'

The forensic team had taken everything they needed from the old man's living room, which nevertheless still left a very large apartment.

He smiled at her and said, 'Yes, yes it is. Thank you, Suzan.' When he turned back to the desk again, he heard her sob.

'Enjoy your tea, sir,' she said, and then she left to go about her business.

İkmen had thought it was odd that the only other bed in the apartment apart from Abdurrahman Şafak's was an ornate, clearly unused gilded confection that had apparently once belonged to the Efendi's parents. He hadn't known where Suzan slept until she'd told him that her 'bed' was in fact a large wooden chest outside the kitchen. İkmen had been disgusted, but he had also been intrigued. People who retained servants had generally moved on from such barbaric practices. But then the old man had been locked in the kind of past that did not permit the modern world. He hadn't even had a television.

And yet Suzan had cried for the old man. A lot. Was she just putting that on because she thought she had to? Or had the old man in fact possessed a softer side to his nature that she had come to appreciate in some way?

'It was a monster!' the boy reiterated.

His mother, Şeftali the prostitute, looked up at Süleyman and said, 'That's all he knows, now leave him alone!'

But to Süleyman it was all just so much superstition. That these people believed in such, to him, patent nonsense was infuriating. He said, 'Hanım, there are no monsters. There's no such thing. There are just people and things that evolve in people's minds to look like the supernatural.' He looked at the boy again. 'Hamid, I need to know exactly what you saw on the morning of the twenty-first of January and what, if any, involvement Şukru Şekeroğlu had in what you saw.'

'He told me to run away,' the boy said.

Late the previous evening Süleyman had been to see Gonca, who had told him that Şukru could not have been collecting wood on the morning of Levent Devrim's death. She'd had no idea what he'd been doing, but it hadn't been that.

'Şukru Bey is missing,' Süleyman said now to Hamid.

'Yeah, I saw it on the TV.'

'So he isn't here to tell you what to say.'

The boy looked around at his mother and Süleyman felt his heart sink. Was she now going to control what he said?

But it was Şeftali who spoke next. 'Şukru spent the night with me,' she said.

'When?'

'The night that Levent Devrim died,' she said. She tipped her head at her son. 'He went out. He always went out when Şukru visited.'

Süleyman looked at the boy. 'Where did you go, Hamid?' he asked. 'It was snowing.' Then he looked at Şeftali again. 'Why did you let him leave in the snow? What were you thinking?'

But it was the boy who answered. 'When Şukru Bey visits, I always go to the old houses where people say the Armenians used to live.'

Süleyman thought he knew where the boy meant, but he asked, 'Where the demolition has just started?'

'Where I found Levent Bey, yes.'

'How soon after leaving your mother's apartment did you find Levent Bey's body?'

He shrugged. 'Some hours.'

'Some hours.'

'Two or three. It was cold. I made a fire in the house with the Elvis Presley picture on the wall. I was tired. I went to sleep.'

Süleyman knew where the boy meant; it was three derelict piles down from what remained of the house where Levent Devrim's body had been found.

'What woke you up?' Süleyman asked.

'I don't know. Nothing I remember,' the boy said.

'So what made you move from your fire?'

'It'd gone out and I needed a piss. Where Levent Bey . . . where he was, that house has a bit more shelter than the others and the wind was blowing. I didn't want to get piss all over my clothes.'

'So then you saw your monster and you saw Levent Bey,' Süleyman said.

'Yes.'

'Did you see anyone else?'

'Until Şukru Bey came? No,' he said.

'Şukru Bey arrived after your monster had gone?'

'Yeah.'

'How long after?'

'I dunno. Five minutes. I was looking to see whether Levent Bey was still alive . . .'

'Poking him with a stick,' Süleyman said. He turned to the boy's mother. 'And what about Şukru Şekeroğlu?' he asked her.

'What about him?'

'When, in relation to your son's departure, did he leave your apartment? Was it one hour later? Two? More?'

Although she was a prostitute by trade, Şeftali still experienced what looked to Süleyman like a level of shame. She lowered her eyes. 'It was probably an hour,' she said.

'Only that?'

'He usually stayed longer,' she said. 'But he said he had to meet someone.'

'In the early hours of the morning?'

She shrugged.

'Did he say who?'

'I didn't ask.'

He understood this and he believed her. Şukru Şekeroğlu was a powerful force amongst Tarlabaşı's gypsies. Süleyman himself knew only too well that Gonca's brother could have power over life and death in the quarter.

Süleyman steepled his fingers underneath his chin. 'So Şukru Şekeroğlu went out after Hamid. Assuming that the boy found Levent Bey two hours after he left the apartment, then Şukru was out and about at the same time that the murder was being committed.' He looked at Şeftali. 'You know that Şukru told us that he was collecting wood that morning?'

'He wasn't.'

'I know, but why didn't you tell us that he was with you and then at some meeting?'

Şeftali shook her head. 'He is Şukru Şekeroğlu,' she said.

'And he told you not to tell us?'

'He didn't have to.' She looked up at him. 'You're the police.'

This time he shook his head in frustration. With the city authorities in open conflict with the gypsies, it was, of course, the police who took the blame and paid the price.

'Şukru looked out for my son when that sergeant of yours came scratching around about his pocket-diving – supposedly. I knew that someone had blabbed about my Hamid finding Levent Bey's body and Şukru got him out of Tarlabaşı for me.'

'Yes, to Beyoğlu to work stealing tourists' cash for a Bulgarian called Marko,' said Süleyman. He looked at the boy. 'Tell me about it, Hamid.'

But the boy turned away from him and looked at the wall. Even with Şukru Şekeroğlu possibly dead, he still wouldn't say anything. It was amazing that Süleyman had got as much out of Şeftali as he had, and it was significant. Because if Şukru Şekeroğlu had gone to meet someone in the early hours of the morning when Levent Devrim had died, that meant that he could have been involved in his death. Maybe Şukru had met Levent and then left him to go on his way, but what if he hadn't? What if he'd either killed Devrim himself – which was unlikely given the description the boy had supplied of the probable killer – or assisted Hamid's 'monster' in some way?

Süleyman asked the boy one more time, 'Hamid, did you really see a monster with Levent Devrim's body?'

'Yes.'

'It definitely wasn't Şukru Bey?'

'No, it wasn't,' he said. 'Şukru Bey came later, I swear it.'

They all met up at midnight in a bar that İkmen knew well. Because it was in the back streets of Sultanahmet, it was a little squalid, in Süleyman's opinion, while Arto Sarkissian just found it odd.

'I thought that Fatih council wanted to close down all the bars in Sultanahmet,' he said as he drank deeply from his glass of gin and tonic.

'They want to,' İkmen said, 'but as we both know, Arto, the human spirit has a way of surviving religion, just as it can often get through war.'

The waiter brought him his second brandy of the evening, while Süleyman sipped at a glass of red wine. When the waiter had gone, İkmen said, 'So what have we learned today?'

'Not a lot,' Arto said. 'My DNA results will take a few days, if not a week, to come back from the lab, although I can tell you that I now know that Abdurrahman Şafak – mercifully for him – died of a cardiac arrest prior to the removal of his heart. When I got to him I estimate he'd been dead for about two hours – the heat in that place notwithstanding.'

'Mmm. But it's spiteful, isn't it?' İkmen said.

'What is?'

'I feel spite in these crimes. Contrary to what Professor Atay and his academic colleagues have told us about the Mayans, and the notion that our offender may well be emulating their methods of execution in line with some sort of disordered belief in the imminent end of the world, I feel very strongly that our victims have been selected for reasons we don't yet fully understand.'

'Beyond the fact that, with the exception of Levent Devrim, they were all members of my extended family,' Süleyman said.

İkmen frowned. 'I think so,' he said. One of the barmen put some quirky music on the DVD player. It was 'This Charming Man' by the 1980s British band The Smiths. For a moment it caught İkmen unawares and he said, 'Morrissey? How odd. Like it, but . . . Anyway, yes, for example all of our victims, in one way or another, have transgressed in some way.'

'Who has not?'

'I know what you mean, Arto,' İkmen said, 'but I sense a moral judgement at play here.'

'In what way?'

'Well think about it like this: Levent Devrim was an eccentric who didn't work, who smoked cannabis and who sponged off first his father and then his brother. Not a bad person, but lazy and possibly indulged. Then we have Leyla Ablak, a spoilt adulteress; John Regan, homosexual – apparently harmless, but homosexual nonetheless and so repellent to some religious people and those of an intolerant nature. Rafik Efendi was, as we now know, a monstrous paedophile, and even poor dying Abdurrahman Şafak was an unpleasant man who had disowned his own sister and was unkind to his maid. With the exception of Dr Regan, I would not have liked to have been friends with any of them.'

'What about our burning man in Aksaray?' Süleyman asked.

'I have found signs of decay on him, underneath the carbonisation,' Arto Sarkissian said. 'This tells me that he died some time before he was cremated.'

'So someone kept his body somewhere?' Süleyman said.

'Must've done.'

'But until we know who he is, we can't make any sort of judgement about him,' İkmen said. 'However, if we look at all our twenty-first of the month victims, then . . .'

'You think they weren't so much killed because of the end of the world but rather that whoever murdered them did so for his own reasons of dislike, outrage or hatred,' Arto said. 'So why can't we find him, Çetin? Someone so full of spite that he can steel himself to cut out another person's heart is a most unique individual.'

'I agree. And the fact that he or she is such an unusual person is exactly the reason why we can't catch them,' İkmen said. He turned to Süleyman. 'Mehmet, you remember we discussed the possibility of our offender hiding out in his victims' properties before he struck?'

'Yes. I think it's a little—'

'It's a theory, only,' İkmen said. 'But what I don't think is a theory so much as a fact is that our offender is hiding in plain sight. He or she enters these people's lives, enters their properties, is seen by others, up to and beyond gypsy children who may or may not be deluded, and then moves along, again in full view, as if nothing has happened.'

Arto sipped his gin. 'Wasn't there something about a gypsy lurking outside John Regan's apartment in Karaköy?' he said.

'Yes, a very obvious one,' İkmen said. 'I mean, ask yourself, who wouldn't suspect a heavily set foreign Roma man in a leather jacket? Even if we found that man, it's my contention that his hands would be clean. Now he may or may not have been asked or paid to be in that place at that time . . .'

'Then surely if we found that man . . .'

'Our patrols in Karaköy have reported a strange lack of gypsy activity in the area ever since Dr Regan died,' İkmen said. 'And remember, the only person we know who has any connection with foreign gypsies is himself missing.'

'Şukru Şekeroğlu.'

'Yes.'

The barman switched the CD player off and put the television on. Some nonsense about a reality TV star was followed by a shot of Şukru Şekeroğlu's face and a plea for information. İkmen looked at it. 'He's under our noses.' He turned back to his colleagues. 'And what's more, he's getting help with this.'

'From whom?'

'I don't know,' İkmen said. 'But all these victims had people in their lives who disapproved of what they were doing, disliked who they were or knew things about them that made them anxious or uncomfortable. Of course because of who I am, a man of a secular bent, I have to be careful not to ascribe some sort of fanatically religious motive to these crimes against homosexuals, adulteresses and drug fiends. And I must remember that some of the religious people like the Osmanoğlus these days. Why kill them if you want them to rule you? But then it's more personal than that.'

'So how do we, or you, move forward with this?' Arto said.

'We find the common denominator,' İkmen said. 'All our victims are known to one person or a group of people. We have to find out who that one person or group might be. And although whoever it is is right underneath our noses, he is also not someone we are going to be able to easily connect to these people, and that is because he is clever. Above everything else we are dealing with a cunning and brilliant mind, and that is why we are going to re-evaluate every piece of evidence we have collected on these five murders so far.'

Süleyman shook his head. 'That's a vast task, especially if one includes electronic data.'

'Absolutely,' İkmen said. 'Which is why Ardıç is going to pull uniforms off the streets, thin out Organised Crime Investigation for a bit and give our postgrads in Security Services some mental stimulation.'

'When did all this happen?' Süleyman asked.

'I went to see the old man as soon as I got back from Abdurrahman Şafak's apartment in Şişli this afternoon,' İkmen said. 'All the time I was in that place something was niggling away at me that I just couldn't place. Then I realised it was the old prince's maid, Suzan.'

'What about her?'

'All that sobbing.' He shrugged. 'And yes, I know that she will lose her job now, but the old man treated her like dirt. He didn't even know her name, and by the girl's own admission he had her sleep not in a bed but in a wooden box outside the kitchen.'

'Painful though it is to admit it, I can remember my grandfather's servants sleeping in his stables,' Süleyman said.

'Back in the old days, yes,' İkmen replied. 'But now? These days, Mehmet, even little country girls can vote with their feet. No, he had something on that kid that kept her there and I want to know what it was. I also want to know where that girl goes, who she sees and who she calls on the telephone from now on.'

'You think this child killed her own employer?'

'No,' İkmen said. 'I don't think she's up to cutting out a heart. But I do think she might know someone who is.' He smiled. 'You know, with all these extra officers under our command, Mehmet, you and I are rather like Ottoman pashas ourselves.'

'Then we had better not let it go to our heads, Çetin,' Süleyman said. 'I know I don't have to tell you how dangerous proximity to princes and princely things can be.'

'Sulukule is the oldest Roma settlement in all of Europe,' Şukru said. 'We belong here! Not people always in the mosque praying, not businessmen doing deals with Russians or Americans. Us! So we're Roma? So we drink and dance and we live with our bears and with our horses? These are our traditions. What are you going to do to us, eh? Kill us?'

Gonca put her fingers up to the television screen and touched his face just before it faded out and some smart anchorwoman appealed for information. She knew that she was wasting her time, and she cried.

Even though she hadn't been in it herself, she remembered that documentary well. Şukru had really thought it would save the district and he had been the principal mover in getting the producers of the film to come to Sulukule. Of course greater interests than just the opinions of one loud-mouthed gypsy had had to be in place before the production company had even agreed to look at the place. But once they'd got their celebrity presenter, as well as the selection of eccentrics and cuddly oddities that Şukru had chosen for them to interview, the whole lot of them had been born-again believers.

Not that the documentary, or anything else for that matter, had or could have saved Sulukule, just like nothing was going to save Tarlabaşı. Gonca switched off the television and sat down to wait for her lover to return to her.

Chapter 21

Now that the efendi was dead, his apartment was going to pass into the hands of some cousin. She didn't know who he was. All she knew was that she had a week to leave and that the cousin would pay her up until the end of the month. Not that it mattered.

The intercom buzzed and Suzan answered. 'Hello?'

'Hello, Suzan?' The voice was slow and the accent foreign. 'It's Arthur Regan. You know, Efendi's brother-in-law?'

'Oh, yes.' She felt her nerve go a little, but she said, 'Do you want to come up, Arthur Bey?'

'I'd like to see how you are, Suzan, yes,' he said. 'Do you feel up to visitors?'

'Yes.' He had been a nice man, nicer than Abdurrahman Efendi, but then the old prince had upset Arthur Regan too and threatened him – right up to the end. As she walked towards the front door of the apartment, she remembered the story about how her employer had disowned his own sister because she'd married this foreigner, and how cold he had been towards the Englishman when his son had been found killed. Somehow that made her feel better. She opened the door and smiled at the elderly man as he got out of the lift.

'I am sorry my Turkish is slow and not so good,' he said.

'It doesn't matter,' she said. 'You are welcome.'

She made him apple tea, fresh, not out of a packet, and he

gave her a large box of biscuits he told her were called shortbread.

'They come from Scotland, where it's very cold, and so they're full of butter to keep you warm,' he said as he opened the box and offered her a biscuit. 'Unfortunately they make you fat too, not that that is a problem for you, Suzan Hanım.'

Embarrassed at what amounted to a compliment from a man, Suzan pulled her headscarf down a little on her forehead and smiled.

'What will you do now, Suzan? Will you look for another job or will Efendi's family look after you?'

She told him about the cousin, who he didn't know, and then she said, 'At the end of the week I will go home for a while.'

'Where's home?'

'We, that is my father, works on a farm in a village.'

The Englishman drank his tea. 'And will you stay there?' he said. 'Permanently?'

'Maybe.'

'You've had enough of İstanbul?'

She laughed. 'Oh, it's such a wonderful place, Arthur Bey, what can I say?' But then she let her features drop. 'But a bad place too. Look at what happened to Abdurrahman Efendi.'

'People are not murdered every day or even every week here.'

'No, but the police don't seem to be able to find who is doing these things, do they? I mean, your poor son . . .'

'John is why I stay,' he said. 'You may find it strange, Suzan, but I have faith that the police will find out who killed my son and the other people who have been murdered too, including your master.'

'But they haven't made any arrests,' she said. 'Everybody in the street thinks they are many, many kilometres away from a solution.'

Arthur Regan frowned. 'Oh, I don't know about that,' he said. 'I've spent a lot of time around Inspector İkmen, Inspector Süleyman and their team, and I must say that the impression I have is that they're getting close.'

In spite of the fact that she knew that what Arthur Bey had been told by the police was absurd, Suzan felt her heart beat a little faster. 'I think the police tell lies to foreigners sometimes to make them feel better,' she said. 'You know, Arthur Bey, that Turkish police are not like English police. Sometimes they are not good people.'

But he just smiled, and so she changed the subject and they talked of other things until he left about half an hour later. When they parted, at the apartment front door, they shook hands and he wished her luck for the future. 'And remember, the police, whatever you may think about them, will catch Efendi's murderer in the end,' he said, and she felt her face change colour from pink to white. She wondered, as she eventually closed the door on the Englishman, whether he had noticed it. But then she heard him get into the lift and she made a decision to forget about what Arthur Bey had said and just get on with her packing. One thing that was for sure was that Arthur Bey had not seen her on the day that Abdurrahman Efendi had died, and that was a good thing. By the end of the week she would be back home to a very grateful and happy family.

The 'Incident', as the series of five murders that had occurred in İstanbul since the beginning of the year was now known, was dominating the station to an unprecedented degree. Technical officers looking at how frequently, if at all, the victims used social media sites worked alongside Security Sciences postgraduate officers who were searching for similar patterns in the daily lives and activities of the deceased. İkmen, out of his

249

office and so instantly available to them, responded to every query and request for attention that came his way.

He knew what some people thought: that his intense dedication to this case was because it was not only his biggest but also, probably, his last. But he didn't care, and anyway, in part at least, they were right. He wanted to solve this one, not just because whoever was committing these crimes had to be locked up for the safety of the public, but also because of course he wanted to go out on a high. If necessary he'd sleep at the station – he hadn't been home the previous night as it was, and he'd even told Fatma to get a quotation for central heating to keep her quiet and stop her moaning about being lonely without him. Because it was all about the case now, and those officers who were not working on it in the station were out and about their business with the friends, relatives and neighbours of the victims.

Eventually he went outside for a cigarette. It was a pain to have to go into the car park every time he wanted to smoke, but it was unavoidable. As soon as he got out and lit up, he saw that his sergeant, Ayşe Farsakoğlu, was smoking over the other side of the compound too.

'Ayşe!' he called.

It took her a few seconds to locate him, but when she did, she came over.

'Sir.'

He smiled at her. 'Come out to get away from all that intensity?' he asked.

'Some of those graduates . . .'

'Yes,' he said, 'a terrifying intelligence combined with a lack of street knowledge that may or may not be useful to us.'

'They are the future, sir,' she said.

İkmen chose not to respond. As far as he had always been concerned, it wasn't possible for people to have too much academic learning, but then the same could also be said of street smarts. Not that he could always understand what the young graduates said to him or to each other. But then a lot of it was 'Internet speak', which was a whole other matter and which seemed to afflict everyone, however bright or dim, under the age of thirty. Against the pressure from a cringe he felt start in the pit of his stomach and reach the top of his head he said to Ayşe, 'John Regan and Leyla Ablak had Facebook pages, you know.'

She looked at him as if he was a little bit mad, although in a way she probably expected, and said, 'Most people do have them, sir.'

'Levent Devrim didn't, nor did Rafik Efendi or Abdurrahman Efendi.'

'With respect, sir, the two efendis were old men, and Levent Devrim, well, he was I think too taken up with his numbers.'

'He would have found out a lot more about his Mayans if he'd gone "online", as they say,' İkmen said. 'Not that I do it myself, but I have children who seem to live there almost exclusively now.' He took a final drag on his cigarette and threw it to the ground. Then he lit up another one. 'But it does have its uses in terms of space-saving,' he continued.

'Mmm?'

'Yes, when I went to see Professor Atay, the historian, he had all the Osmanoğlu family trees on paper and so he had to get a student to scan them into the computer before he could email them to me. It was very time-consuming and means we're now drowning in printouts.'

'Yes, sir, I remember,' she said.

He saw a small glint of humour in her eyes and realised that he was behaving like a terrible old man who thought that the entire modern world was magic. He changed the subject. 'So are you going somewhere, or . . .'

'Levent Devrim's brother Selçuk has just returned from a short trip abroad,' she said. 'Sergeant Mungan called him because he's now got all of his brother's effects, the ones that we don't have, over at his house in Bebek. There are a lot of items and so I said I'd go with Sergeant Mungan to help him. I know I should have cleared it with you . . .'

'But you'll be doing my job in less than a year's time,' İkmen said.

'Oh, sir, I . . .' She felt her cheeks go red.

He ignored the colour change. 'I'm serious, Ayşe,' he said. 'Go for promotion. I will recommend you with all my heart. You can do this job.' He wanted to say *Concentrate on your career and forget about Süleyman!* But he didn't, and then his phone rang, and when he answered it, the caller had some very interesting information for him which made him forget about Ayşe Farsakoğlu almost entirely.

Gonca knelt down beside the old man and took one of his hands in hers. 'Baba,' she said.

He kissed her. 'You have come to tell me that my oldest child, my Şukru, is dead.'

'Yes,' she said.

Hadı Şekeroğlu looked at her through ancient, bloodshot eyes that, in spite of the topic of their conversation, did not weep. He said, 'Their scientific tests . . .'

'I don't care about their tests,' Gonca said. 'Şukru is dead, Baba. Every coffee ground looks like a skull, every card is Death, every glass is empty.'

The old man sat in silence.

'Baba, do you know exactly what Şukru was going to do when he came back from Edirne?'

He shrugged. 'He said that we could move.'

'I know.'

He looked around at the scarred and battered walls of his house and said, 'What is here for us? There is nothing except misery and filth. They take us from Sulukule and put us somewhere we can't work, and so we move and we end up here.' He shook his head. His eyes were fixed on the floor now; he looked as if he was staring into a nightmare.

'Baba, where was Şukru going to take you?' Gonca asked.

'He said we would move to one of the villages on the Bosphorus.'

'Yes, I know, but which one?'

'I don't know.'

Gonca had thought about this. 'It's not possible,' she said. 'Şukru must have been having a joke. How could he get enough money to live in such a place?'

'I don't know.' The old man looked up. 'But he wasn't joking, Gonca, he was serious. I know when your brother was joking and when he wasn't, and this was too serious for him to make fun of. We had to go, he had to go.'

Gonca frowned.

'He may have thought that he could hide things from me, but he couldn't,' the old man said. 'Your brother was in trouble.'

'Was it to do with the man who died? Levent Devrim? The boy Hamid? Did Şukru kill that crazy man?'

'No, no, no, no, no. Why would your brother kill a thing like that, a mad innocent?'

'Then . . .'

'I think he knew who did, though,' he said. 'He wanted the boy Hamid – whose filthy mother he sleeps with and thinks I do not know – out of the way, and for what reason? Because the boy saw a "monster"? I think that the boy, although he didn't

253

know it, saw a person, and that your brother knew who that person was.'

'So if Levent Devrim was an innocent who did not threaten Şukru in any way and he knew who killed him, why didn't he tell the police?'

'Maybe to spite you . . .'

'Oh, Baba!' She stood up, exasperated.

'I know you open your legs to Prince Süleyman again,' he said.

'But I didn't until he came to me,' she said. She lit a cigarette and paced her father's small bedroom. 'When Levent Devrim died, I hadn't seen Mehmet for years.'

'Then I don't know,' he said. 'Maybe Şukru decided that blackmailing the murderer was a more profitable way forward. As you say, Gonca, where would your brother have got enough money to move to a Bosphorus village, eh?'

She sat down. 'For all of you to move to such a village would take a huge amount of money.'

'Well, then maybe whoever Şukru had in his sights had a very great deal of money,' her father said. 'There are such people in the world. They are usually not Roma.'

She paused for a moment, and then she said, 'Baba, what are we going to do?'

'About your brother?' He shook his head. 'Whatever he was doing was dangerous and he has paid the price. We can do nothing for him. The police?' He shrugged. 'All they care about are the deaths of princes.' He leaned forward in his chair and took one of her hands and laid it on his knee. 'The thing I want, and all I can have now, is the image of my child. You know this piece of film of Şukru that they run on the news programmes, asking for help? Back home I had a copy of that, but when we moved I lost it. I should like to have that again, so that I can see my child alive on the television.'

'Oh, Baba!' She began to cry.

He stroked her hand. 'Ah, you live in the Turks' world; you can talk to the television people and they will listen to you,' he said. 'Gonca, get that for me. It has your brother and our old Sulukule on it, and I want to see them both again before I die.'

The house where Selçuk Devrim lived was small but very beautiful. By Bebek standards it was modest, being only two-storeyed, in a back street next to a derelict church. It possessed a tiny back garden and Ömer Mungan had to park his car on the street directly in front of the door. But both he and Ayşe Farsakoğlu were impressed. Of late Ottoman vintage, the house was made of honey-coloured wood, and every door and window frame was decorated with the most delicate metal filigree.

As Ayşe got out of the car, Ömer said to her, 'How would you like to live here, Ayşe Hanım?'

Ayşe shook her head. 'Only in my dreams,' she said.

He smiled. Colleagues had told him that his boss Inspector Süleyman's parents lived in what had to be a very expensive house in nearby Arnavutköy. Had things gone well between them, Ayşe Farsakoğlu could have lived in a house like the Devrims'. But the word was that he was still with his gypsy, with the sergeant well and truly out in the cold.

He said to her, 'You know, these Bosphorus villages are so pretty, they almost make me like İstanbul.'

Ayşe smiled. 'You'll get used to it,' she said.

They walked up to the front door together and Ömer rang the bell. It took quite a long time for anyone to come and answer it, and for a moment Ayşe wondered whether the Devrims were in. But then the sound of unlocking bolts was heard and both officers breathed more easily.

The door opened to reveal a woman of about forty. Slim,

blonde and attractive, there was something familiar about her that made Ayşe Farsakoğlu frown. Looking at Ömer Mungan only, the woman said, 'You must be Sergeant Mungan.'

And then Ayşe knew who she was.

'Yes,' he said as he took her hand and shook it.

'I'm Hatice Devrim, Selçuk's wife.' She turned to look at Ayşe Farsakoğlu, and as their eyes met, Hatice Devrim's face turned white.

Chapter 22

Suzan felt her heart pound. She was panicking. Suddenly the money she'd got for them wasn't enough. Paying for her mother's surgery with no aftercare was pointless. And the aftercare cost yet more. Suzan's father had been furious on the phone. He'd called her 'thick' and 'cheap' and had completely ignored her few protestations that her conscience, inasmuch as it was troubled at all, was like that because of him and her mother. But he didn't listen. All he did was tell her to get hold of some more money before she came home. But how was she supposed to do that?

The money she'd been given had been a one-off that had come with threats. If she ever told anyone about what she'd done for it, she knew she would be killed. Similarly if she attempted blackmail, it would end badly for her. Abdurrahman Efendi, that mean, cruel creature who had taken her honour from her and then just put her away in a box, had been killed and, just for leaving a door open, she'd been given more money than she had ever dreamed of. She hadn't killed the old man, and in truth, she didn't know who had. All she knew was that a woman who had been the old man's friend had given her money to leave the front door to the apartment unlocked the day that Abdurrahman Efendi was found dead. Had she ever said that someone wanted to come in and kill the old man? No, but she had said that when Suzan came home, the prince would give her no more trouble. Who had she been? And why had she wanted him dead?

Suzan didn't read that well, and so the Efendi's diary, where he might have written down the woman's name, was a mystery to her. She didn't know who she was or where she lived, and she hadn't seen her since the woman had given her the money. So she couldn't blackmail her. She couldn't steal from the apartment either. The cousin's people had already taken an inventory. All she could do was what she'd done before, when Efendi had found all those new clothes with the labels still on them in her bag and then made her do sex with him as a punishment. Now he was dead, she wouldn't have to do that this time. But she would still have to go shoplifting.

While Selçuk Devrim showed Ömer Mungan the boxes that contained his brother Levent's effects, Ayşe Farsakoğlu joined his wife in the kitchen. Hatice Devrim, still white-faced from her earlier encounter with the policewoman, was making coffee.

'I thought your surname was Öz,' Ayşe said as she watched the woman fill a large cafetière with water.

'It is.' She put the lid on the coffee pot and tried not to look at Ayşe's face.

'But you're married to . . .'

'I kept my surname.' She looked up. 'I was a nurse when I married Selçuk, we often do. All right?'

She was quite aggressive and Ayşe could understand why, but she ignored it.

'I appreciate that a person can have multiple roles, Miss Öz,' she said. 'But do you live here, or with your parents in Fatih? And does your husband know about—'

'No!' She walked over to the kitchen door and shut it. She was a statuesque woman with large, slanting emerald-green eyes. Ayşe, uncharitably, assumed their colour had to be due to green contact lenses.

'I met you as Professor Cem Atay's mistress at your parents' house in Fatih,' Ayşe said. 'You told me you spent the night that Leyla Ablak died with Professor Atay. Now I find that you are in fact married to Mr Selçuk Devrim. So, through your husband and Professor Atay's brother-in-law, Faruk Genç, you are, loosely, connected to two of the murder victims we are investigating.'

'You mean the woman that Professor Atay's brother-in-law was having an affair with? I didn't know her!' She sat down at her kitchen table and lit a cigarette. 'Of course I knew Selçuk's brother, but . . .'

'Tell me about your affair with Professor Atay,' Ayşe said as she sat down opposite the woman, who was now looking actively resentful.

'Why?'

'I've just told you why,' Ayşe said. 'You exist on the fringes of two murders. And you concealed your true marital state from me. You can tell me why, when I interviewed you before, you gave me the impression you lived with your parents, or we can go to police headquarters together.'

Hatice Öz sat in silence for a moment, then pushed the plunger down on the cafetière. 'Let me pour the coffee and I'll tell you,' she said.

She gave the men their drinks first and then served Ayşe and herself.

'Selçuk works away for at least half the year, on and off,' she said once she'd sat down again and begun to drink her coffee. 'He works in telecommunications, in Russia. When Levent died he was away and I think I saw another officer, at police headquarters. A tall, rather elegant man . . .'

Süleyman.

'There was nothing I could do. Selçuk dealt with it when

259

he came back,' she continued. 'When my husband is away, I spend a lot of time at my parents' house. I don't like being alone here.'

'Does your husband know that?' Ayşe asked.

'Of course.'

'But he doesn't know about . . .'

'Cem and I met at Boğaziçi University,' she said. 'Many years ago.'

Although Ayşe hadn't yet met the professor in the flesh, she knew what he looked like from his TV programmes. He was considerably older than Hatice Öz.

'You were his student?'

'Yes. I studied Ottoman history,' she said. 'He was my tutor. Things . . .' She looked down at her hands. 'Things happened. We fell in love.'

'And still are?'

She looked up. 'Yes.'

Ayşe sipped her coffee. 'If that is the case, why are you with Mr Devrim?'

'Cem, Professor Atay, was married when we met. He didn't love her.' Her rush to declare that her lover hadn't cared for his wife when the affair had begun struck Ayşe as typical of the things 'other' women told those around them and themselves. She'd done it herself when she'd helped Mehmet Süleyman commit adultery.

'If I remember correctly, though,' Ayşe said, 'I believe that Professor Atay is single now, isn't he?'

'Yes.'

'So why . . .'

'I care about Selçuk,' she said. 'And anyway, Cem wouldn't want to be married again, not after last time.'

As a single man with a married mistress, Professor Atay was

both having his cake and eating it. But Ayşe asked anyway. 'Why not?'

'Because she disappeared,' Hatice Öz said. 'I'd been married to Selçuk for almost two years. I hadn't heard from Cem for a long time. When I left university we ended our affair, and although I never forgot him, I moved on and married Selçuk. Then one day Cem called me and told me that his wife, Merve, had disappeared.'

'Disappeared?'

'It was in the papers,' she said. 'The police . . . you looked for her, but she has never been found.'

'When was this?'

'Ten years ago.'

Ayşe didn't remember it. But then she'd been working for Çetin İkmen for over ten years, so a simple missing person case would not have come her way unless there was some reason to suspect murder. Clearly in this case no one had believed that Mrs Merve Atay had been killed. But with a patently adulterous husband in the woman's life, Ayşe wondered why that question had apparently never been asked.

'Cem was very upset about it.'

'Even though he didn't love his wife?' Ayşe countered. If Cem Atay had really not loved Merve he would have divorced her and married Hatice. There had to be a reason why he had stayed with her until she disappeared. Ayşe suspected it was probably because Merve on some level tolerated his 'messing around' with his students and with the media types he must have met since he had become a television academic.

'Her disappearance has scarred his life,' Hatice said. 'When he called me to tell me about Merve that first time, I just dropped everything and went to him.'

'Did your husband know?'

'Of course not! He was abroad, Azerbaijan. Poor Cem was devastated. He'd gone to bed one night, and when he woke up in the morning his wife had gone.'

'And so you picked up where you'd left off.'

'I comforted Cem.'

'And then . . .'

She turned her face away. 'Cem Atay is a remarkable man, Sergeant. Whatever you may think about me, us, you have to understand that.'

Ayşe, who knew all about 'remarkable' men, raised an eyebrow. Being cynical about Mehmet Süleyman since his latest defection to his gypsy was getting easier every day. Maybe, she thought, İkmen was right about how she should just concentrate on her career.

'What we have suits us both,' Hatice Öz said. 'I care for Selçuk and I would never want to hurt him; he's had enough trouble in his life one way or another. But I love Cem and the excitement of his world and I couldn't give it up again. When I was a student, my life was full of interest and incident. But since then . . .' She shrugged. 'Some people would say that I haven't grown up.'

Ayşe looked at her. She *was* rather childlike. Not to look at, but in her enthusiastic reactions to things and to people, like her lover, Cem Atay.

'Does anyone know about your affair?' Ayşe said.

'We're very discreet.'

'You've not answered my question,' Ayşe said.

Hatice Öz looked at her. 'I don't think so,' she said.

Ayşe thought for a few moments. 'Not maybe your brother-in-law, Levent . . .'

'Levent?'

'Yes, Levent who died in Tarlabaşı. Levent Devrim.'

'I hardly knew him,' she said. 'Selçuk wouldn't let me near that terrible flat he had. He came here once, just after we got married, but . . . While he was alive, after my in-laws died, Selçuk paid him an allowance, but we never went to see him.'

'And the allowance . . .'

'Oh, that was up to my husband,' she said. 'But he got no opposition from me. Ask him! The poor man was mad and he had a heart condition; who wouldn't want to help him?'

She hadn't been expecting him. When he'd arrived, she had just finished on the phone to the production company who had made the documentary that her brother had been in. They hadn't been helpful and she'd been furious, but she'd put that aside to make love to him. Now he was fucking her and all she could think about was how hot he felt inside her. Just the thought of him made her grind her hips still harder against his. In spite of Şukru, in spite of everything, when Mehmet Süleyman wanted her, Gonca gave herself to him without a thought. Only afterwards, as he lay half asleep beside her, did her thoughts go back to Şukru once again.

The TV production company who had made the Ottoman minorities documentary had been called Hittite, as in the ancient Anatolian civilisation. The man she'd finally managed to speak to there had been arrogant and terse, and when she'd told him who she was, he'd become even worse.

'Oh that was years ago,' he'd told her. 'If we have got it, it'll only be on old videotape.'

'But they've played bits of it on the news,' she'd said.

He'd gone away to apparently find out about that, but when he'd returned, he'd just said, 'That was a clip from an old videotape.'

'Oh, so can I have a copy?'

'Of videotape? What will you play it on?' he'd said. 'Anyway, it wasn't the whole programme; it was just a tape of clips that we had.'

'Where can I get a copy if you don't have one?' she'd asked.

He'd said he didn't know, and so she'd told him to fuck off, put the phone down and then cursed him and his wretched company. Afterwards she'd thought that maybe she should have been a bit nicer, because perhaps he would, given time, have agreed to give her the clip. But then she could record that off the television herself. No. What her father wanted was the whole programme. Not just for Şukru, but for all the shots of Sulukule that were in it too.

She looked over at Mehmet Süleyman. He'd be on his way soon, back to his work and the life that he had without her. There had been no news about the DNA test, and as soon as he'd told her that, she'd taken him to her bedroom. Now he was catching some rest after his exertions and it made Gonca smile. But only for a moment. Recalling her conversation with her father, she wondered whether she should tell Süleyman about the old man's suspicions regarding Şukru. After all, if the body that the police had found burning in Aksaray *was* Şukru, then whoever had done that had to be punished. Not that her father would want the police to do it. But if the police could find the bastard for them, the community could think of a way to deal with him. Anyway, Gonca had a question for her lover.

She tapped Süleyman on the shoulder.

'What?' He raised his head. His hair was, Gonca noticed, uncharacteristically awry.

She rolled over and put an arm on his naked side. 'I went to see my father,' she said. 'He thinks Şukru was blackmailing someone.'

264

'Blackmailing who?' He lit two cigarettes and gave her one. She put an ashtray on the bed between them.

'He doesn't know. But he has a theory.'

'What?'

'Baba thinks that Şukru saw whoever killed that crazy man in Tarlabaşı back in January. Before he left to go to Edirne, Şukru told him that he was going to move the family out to a Bosphorus village when Hıdırellez was over. That takes money.'

'Do you think that he may just have been boasting?' Süleyman asked.

Gonca stroked his face. 'Gypsy men don't boast unless they can follow through, darling,' she said. 'We are not like you. We don't boast about our big penises unless we can show them.'

'I've never—' he began.

'You have to prove nothing,' she said. 'But Mehmet, what if my Şukru went to see someone to blackmail him that day when he returned to İstanbul?'

'But who? Does your father have any idea?'

'No. My father doesn't leave the house. What does he know?' She puffed on her cigarette. 'Şukru was in Ortaköy with the Edirne gypsies when he called me just before Hıdırellez,' she said. 'And his body was found in Aksaray.'

'Hıdırellez is the sixth of May, and Şukru's body – if it is Şukru's body – was found on the twenty-first,' Süleyman said. 'Dr Sarkissian is of the opinion that the Aksaray man was killed some days before he was cremated.'

'But if Şukru disappeared on Hıdırellez, which he did,' she said, 'then whoever had him must have kept him prisoner.' She frowned. 'But who could keep a man like Şukru as a prisoner? He wouldn't allow it. And why Aksaray?'

'There were no security cameras where the body was found,' Süleyman said.

She changed the subject. 'Mehmet,' she said, 'many years ago my brother took part in a documentary about Sulukule. My father wants a copy, so I spoke to the production company who made it to try and find one. But they didn't have one. They were offhand with me and I lost my temper with them.'

'Gonca . . .'

'I know! I know I should be a better woman! But look, Mehmet, do you remember that documentary?'

'No,' he said. 'I don't.'

'It was made when all the trouble first started with the council threatening to demolish Sulukule,' she said. 'I didn't really pay attention at the time, and the piece they showed on the news programmes just shows Şukru being a loudmouth. But I want it, for my father. Will you ask people you know about it? If I knew who the director was . . .'

'So ask the production company,' he said.

She said nothing and lowered her eyes.

'You really abused them, didn't you, Gonca?' He shook his head. 'I will ask everyone I think might know.'

Çetin İkmen motioned for Ayşe Farsakoğlu to sit down in front of his desk while he finished his telephone call. Once the call had ended, he wrote some notes on one of the scrap pieces of paper that littered his desk and then he said, 'Ayşe?'

She told him what she'd found out at Selçuk Devrim's house and how his wife had turned out to be someone she had met before. 'Hatice Öz provided an alibi for her lover Professor Atay for the night that Leyla Ablak was murdered,' she said. 'In addition, because Miss Öz is Levent Devrim's sister-in-law, that creates a link between those two crimes.'

'Did Miss Öz know Leyla Ablak?' İkmen asked.

'She says not, sir.'

'What about the spa, any connection there?'

'Again she says not, but I have yet to check that out.'

'OK.'

'What she did tell me was that Professor Atay was at the centre of a missing person case some years ago,' Ayşe said. 'His wife, Merve Atay, apparently walked out of their house in Arnavutköy in 2002 and never returned. I don't remember it myself.'

'Nor I,' İkmen said. 'But I'll look it up. The woman's still missing, you say?'

'Yes, sir.'

'Mmm.' He shook his head. 'Professor Atay has been helpful to us with regard to sharing his knowledge of the vast Osmanoğlu family. I don't know whether the Mayan connection really has any validity, but . . .' He looked up at her and smiled. 'Have you ever watched his television programmes?'

'I saw one he did about Süleyman the Lawgiver,' she said. 'That was good, if a bit depressing. I mean, he really explored the whole notion of the Ottoman Empire going into decline from then on.'

'It did,' İkmen said.

'At the end of the narrative it sort of went into the inevitability of Kemalism and the Republic,' she said. 'But that has to be over ten years ago now, before all this re-evaluation of the Ottoman period came into vogue. I think Professor Atay has made a lot of documentaries since then.'

'Oh yes.' İkmen put his hand in his desk drawer and pulled out a large sheaf of paper. 'Told me he's just written a book about the relationship and rivalry between the Ottoman and the Spanish Empires. Hence some fascinating trips to South America and his interest in the Mayans. That will I believe become a documentary at some point too. But then the professor is a very personable man with a rather lovely speaking voice.' He smiled again. 'Sexy academics. Very in demand. Have you seen that British physicist? Professor something or other from Manchester University? My daughters make very strange noises when he comes on the television. I don't think they understand a word he says. I know I don't.' He frowned. 'I presume that Levent Devrim's brother doesn't know that his wife is having an affair with . . . Did you say that Hatice Öz had been a student of Professor Atay?'

'Years ago, yes,' she said. 'And no, according to his wife, Selçuk Devrim does not know.'

İkmen put the sheaf of paper he'd taken out of his drawer on his desk. 'The Osmanoğlu family trees given to me by Professor Atay,' he said. 'I've read and read them. They're just names . . .' He looked up. 'If Selçuk Devrim doesn't know about his wife's affair, that doesn't mean that other people are as clueless as he is – if he *is* clueless. And if other people know and maybe take advantage of that knowledge in some way . . . But how does any of this relate to the death of either Levent Devrim or Leyla Ablak?'

'It doesn't,' Ayşe said. 'At least it doesn't given what we know about these people at the moment. Hatice Öz hardly knew her brother-in-law Levent. The money his brother gave him every month was clearly not stretching the couple financially and she seemed to have actually had a sneaking affection for the man. Whether Professor Atay knew Leyla Ablak from the spa is open to question, but he has an alibi for the night she died . . .'

'From Hatice Öz.'

'And what would have been his motive for killing Leyla anyway?'

'Because she was having an affair with his brother-in-law, Faruk Genç, the husband of his dying sister?'

'And yet you said that Professor Atay exhibited some understanding of Faruk Genç's situation.'

He shrugged. 'Yes. But you've raised an interesting connection,

268

Ayşe,' he said, 'and it does mean that the professor's alibi for Leyla Ablak's death may be unsafe. Not because he has a mistress – we knew that – but because he concealed, as did she, her connection to a previous crime. Why do that? We could have cleared them both with little trouble had we known the truth. But they didn't tell us the truth.' He rubbed his eyes, which were bloodshot. 'I'll look into his missing wife; we have to have historical data on that, especially if the woman is still officially alive.'

They sat in silence for a few moments as they both absorbed what had just been discussed. Then İkmen said, 'When you came in, I was on the phone to the father of victim number three.'

'John Regan.'

'Arthur Regan had been to see the maid, Suzan, at Abdurrahman Efendi's apartment in Şişli. Not at my request, I should say.'

Ayşe knew that İkmen was having the little maid watched, although she couldn't really understand why. It came down, as far as she knew, to a feeling İkmen had about how the young girl had cried too much when the old man had died. One of his hunches, apparently, but it was also backed up by her own and Arthur Regan's observation that the old man had treated the girl badly. If that was the case, why was she so cut up about his death?

'Did Mr Regan find anything out?' Ayşe asked.

'Only that Suzan intends to go back to her home village at the end of the week,' he said. 'Oh, and she has very little faith in our ever finding her master's killer.'

'That's not unusual, sir,' Ayşe said. 'The public—'

'Understand neither our problems nor our methods,' he said. 'But you know, the girl was very calm with Mr Regan. And how she can stay in that apartment, given that she is choking with sobs every time I see her, I don't know. She says she knows nobody in the city . . .'

'Then that explains it,' Ayşe said.

269

'Yes, but we could have moved her into a hostel,' İkmen said. 'I asked Inspector Süleyman if he'd offered her alternative accommodation, and he said that he had but she turned it down.'

'Do you think she wants to maybe take something from the apartment before she goes?' Ayşe asked.

'I believe an inventory has been produced; it would be stupid of her. But maybe,' he added. 'She's a little country girl; she may be that . . . what do you call it, unworldly?'

She smiled. 'You'll find out. You're having her watched.'

'Yes, I am, Ayşe,' he said. 'At the moment I'm having a lot of people watched. In that sense, if in no other, I do feel Ottoman.' Then, realising that she didn't know what he meant, he added, 'In the latter stages of the Empire, from the nineteenth century, successive sultans continually increased their spy network until, under Abdülhamid II, it was reckoned that half the country was spying on the other half.'

'Oh.'

He shook his head. 'And the sort of people, I am told, who want to rebuild Tarlabaşı want people like that to rule over us again. I despair.'

Hatice got as far away from Selçuk as she could to make her phone call. She went to the spare bedroom overlooking the now darkened back garden. But it wasn't far enough.

'Don't call him.'

She pressed the end call button on her phone and turned around to confront her husband. 'Who?'

'You know,' Selçuk Devrim said. 'Don't make me have to say his hated name, Hatice.'

'Whose hated name? I don't know what you mean.' But she felt her face go red as she spoke, and she knew that he knew with every centimetre of her flesh. But how?

'Cem Atay,' he said. 'That was who the policewoman was talking to you about in the kitchen, wasn't it? Cem Atay. Your lover.'

'No!'

'I heard you,' he said. 'I left the young man in the living room with Levent's effects and came to get more coffee. But I heard what you were talking about and so I just listened outside until I couldn't take it any more.'

She looked into his eyes and saw that they were wet.

'I was so touched to hear that you don't want to hurt me,' he said bitterly.

She moved towards him. 'Selçuk . . .'

He retreated from her. 'Don't come near me! While you were just screwing your hot, famous old tutor I could just about cope with it. But when I had to stand there and listen to you talk about how you loved him . . .'

She realised the import of what he'd just said. 'You knew? Before today?'

'Of course I did.'

'But . . .'

'How?' He shook his head. 'Well even if I could have persuaded myself to ignore the stolen phone calls that you habitually made, even if I could forgive your lack of interest in our sex life, when I was told, it all became a bit unavoidable for me.'

'Told! Who told you?'

'Who do you think?' he said.

She sat down on the spare bed and with a shaking hand put her phone into the pocket of her jeans.

He leaned towards her and said, 'Levent. My brother.'

Chapter 23

Suzan was sweating. She had to keep focused. What she took had to be small enough for her to carry and able to be resold easily. She looked around the shining metallic halls dotted with chandeliers that made up the Vakko department store and made her decision. She'd have to take jewellery. Anything else would be too bulky and wouldn't make her enough money. Good jewellery on the other hand was something she could give to her father to sell. There were always men who wanted to buy gold and diamonds for their wives or their daughters or their mistresses.

The problem that Suzan had was that the really expensive items were displayed in large glass cases that couldn't be opened from in front of the counter. It meant that if she was to have any chance of stealing anything, she had to ask the shop assistant to get the items out of the cases for her to look at. Only then could she try to take something. And as well as shop assistants and security guards, there were cameras everywhere. Suzan looked at herself in a small mirror over by the costume jewellery earrings. She wasn't the only woman in the store who was wearing a headscarf, but she was the only one who was not wearing make-up and whose clothes had been darned. Even women who looked as if they too could be domestic servants were smarter than her. And people were looking at her. She was about to give up and go back to the apartment empty-handed when something caught her eye.

A woman, probably somewhere in late middle age, all powdered face and fake blonde hair, had just bought something from the jewellery counter and had put it in her handbag. So casual was she about a purchase that Suzan couldn't imagine would have cost her anything less than a thousand lira that she didn't even bother to zip up her handbag after she'd put the jewellery box inside it. Suzan could see the little box even from where she stood, which was five or six metres away. To say that it was too easy was overstating the case, but it was easy enough that for a moment Suzan wondered whether the woman was some sort of security operative tasked with flushing out shoplifters. But there was only one day left before she had to leave the city and go home, and this was probably her last chance to make her father proud of her. She just had to do it.

She walked towards the counter just as the woman began to talk to another middle-aged lady who had come up beside her, distracting her completely. Suzan couldn't help but feel that her luck was in. Passing slowly in front of the woman's handbag, she looked over at some strings of multicoloured pearls on a tall, slim display stand. At the same time, her hand slid into the bag and, without disturbing anything but the jewellery box, she began to draw it out towards her own tattered handbag.

When she first felt the weight of something heavy on her arm, she did think that maybe the tension involved in bag-diving had caused her to wrench an already stiffened shoulder. But then she saw that a man had come alongside her, and when he said, 'Can I see what you've just put in your handbag, please, miss?' Suzan felt her heart sink through Vakko's highly polished marble floor.

Çetin İkmen knocked on Mehmet Süleyman's office door. When the younger man said, 'Come,' he let himself in. Both men had tired very quickly of being in the investigative operation room and had retreated back to their respective offices. As he entered, İkmen said, 'I've got news.'

'Oh?'

The older man carried a sheaf of papers underneath one arm and Süleyman thought this was what he had come to show him. He held out his hand. 'Let me see,' he said.

But İkmen shook his head. 'Not these. No. I've just heard from Dr Sarkissian about the DNA test on the burning man of Aksaray.'

'Ah.' Süleyman nodded. 'And?'

'It is indeed Şukru Şekeroğlu,' İkmen said.

'Oh.' Süleyman looked down, probably, İkmen thought, wondering how he was going to tell the man's sister.

'And there's something else,' İkmen said. 'The doctor found large quantities of a benzodiazepine tranquilliser in the body.'

'Enough to kill him?'

'He's not sure,' İkmen said. 'He's not entirely sure that it *can* kill. The body, as you saw, is very badly degraded. But Dr Sarkissian is of the opinion that the actual cause of death was strangulation. My guess is that he was somehow disabled by the tranquilliser first and then murdered.'

'Unless he was already taking benzodiazepine, although I find that notion bizarre to say the least.'

'Because he was such a confident man? Mehmet, if our super-smooth Professor Atay has dabbled in diazepam, then anyone can.'

'I don't know whether confident is the right word,' Süleyman said. 'Şukru was afraid of no one and nothing. But whether he possessed actual confidence I don't know. He was a wrestler until he put his back out, then a dancing bear man until dancing bears became illegal. Then I think he lost his way.'

'Do you want me to tell the family?' İkmen asked.

'No,' Süleyman said. 'Gonca knows anyway. Via the cards, the coffee grounds . . .'

'Ah, ancient wisdom,' İkmen said. 'It worked for Mother and it's worked for me, as you know. But then I'm not alone in believing that ancient systems can be useful.'

'And yet you don't believe in homeopathy?'

İkmen shook his head. 'That's a relatively modern construct,' he said. 'No, I'm talking about things like herbalism, which is the precursor to modern medicine.'

'But you're also talking about what some would call magic.'

'Yes, because we don't yet understand how our brains work,' İkmen said. 'When we do, maybe things like precognition won't seem magical to us any more. But don't take my word for it, Mehmet. Greater minds than mine believe that you can't discount the beliefs and technologies of the ancients. Professor Atay is of the opinion that many of the South American civilisations he studied for his latest book, including the Maya, possessed knowledge the rest of us have discounted to our cost. Have you ever watched any of Professor Atay's television programmes?'

'No.'

'I thought you'd find that sort of thing interesting.'

'No,' he said. 'If I want relics of the Ottoman Empire, all I have to do is go home. But the subject of television reminds me: Gonca's brother was in a documentary about Sulukule about ten years ago. Her father would like a copy of it. She called the production company but they weren't very helpful and she lost her temper . . .' He raised his eyebrows. 'If we could find out who directed it, or if anyone remembers it . . .'

İkmen shook his head. 'Those sorts of social justice shows tend to be on in the middle of the night,' he said. 'I don't recall it at all. Why don't you phone up the production company and ask them; they should talk to you.'

'True.'

İkmen frowned and opened his mouth to speak, but was interrupted by his telephone.

The girl shook. When she looked at the bag they'd put on the table in front of her, her bag, she cried.

Where Mehmet Süleyman looked at her with contempt in his eyes, Çetin İkmen viewed her with kindness. He even smiled. 'Well, Suzan,' he said, 'I can understand the diamond earrings. I've got that you tried to steal them from a Mrs Günel. It's the five thousand lira that puzzles me. Where did you get it and why were you carrying it about with you in your handbag?'

Suzan didn't say anything.

İkmen reached across to Süleyman, who gave him a large transparent evidence bag full of banknotes. 'And all nice crisp new notes too,' İkmen said. 'Tell me, Suzan, had you just been to the bank?'

She began crying again and Süleyman rolled his eyes in frustration.

'Now, now, Inspector,' İkmen said to him, 'the young lady is upset. We must exercise patience.'

'She's a thief,' Süleyman said. 'Why should we? She tried to steal those earrings. We know that. The money's probably stolen too. She deserves no special treatment.'

'Even though she's just lost her beloved master?' İkmen said. 'Oh, Inspector, I think you're being a little harsh.'

Ayşe Farsakoğlu, who had seen the good cop/bad cop routine many times before and employed by many different officers, watched the girl as she sobbed. She noticed that every time Süleyman spoke, Suzan tensed.

'I don't see what you hope to achieve here, Inspector,' Süleyman said to İkmen. 'We can get where she purloined this money out of her very easily.' He turned to Suzan. 'I was kind to you when Abdurrahman Efendi died, but not any more! Tell us where you got the money!'

İkmen shook his head impatiently, then said softly, 'Suzan, tell me, do you have a bank account?'

She looked up, and for a moment Ayşe Farsakoğlu thought the girl was about to speak, but then she just burst into tears again.

Apparently exasperated, Süleyman threw his hands in the air and stood up. 'I'm sick of this!' he said. 'Do what you like, Inspector İkmen, I need some fresh air and a cigarette before I can even think about continuing with this thief!' And attracting the attention of the constable outside the interview room door, he left.

İkmen leaned across the table. 'Now listen, Suzan,' he said. 'You need to talk to me before he comes back. Inspector Süleyman can be a very nice man, but he lacks patience and he can sometimes override my decisions. Now please tell me where this money came from.'

For a moment neither Ayşe Farsakoğlu nor Çetin İkmen thought the girl was going to speak, then she raised her head and said, 'The money's mine.'

'Good.' İkmen smiled. 'So did you take it out of your bank account?'

'No.'

'Where did you get it?'

'I earned it.'

'What, your wages from Abdurrahman Efendi?'

She paused for a long time before she replied. 'Yes.'

İkmen looked across at his sergeant, who said nothing. He leaned towards the girl. 'Ah, but that isn't true, is it, Suzan?'

She turned her face away. 'It is.'

'No it isn't,' İkmen said.

'Why not?' This time she faced him. 'Why isn't it true?'

'Apart from the fact that I doubt that was even your annual salary? Are you telling me that you saved five thousand lira, Suzan?'

She didn't say anything.

'And why, if indeed those were your savings, were you carrying them around with you in your handbag?'

This time she answered immediately. 'Because if I left it in the apartment then someone might break in and steal it,' she said.

'So no worries about being mugged on the street, then?' İkmen said.

'Nobody knew I had it with me.'

'Nobody knew it was in the apartment,' İkmen said. Then he leaned back in his chair and added, 'Or did they?'

And for the first time since Süleyman had left the room, Ayşe Farsakoğlu saw real fear in the girl's eyes.

'Levent had already told him,' Hatice Devrim said.

Cem Atay sat down beside her and said, 'So why didn't Selçuk say anything to you before? Why wait until now?'

He was so calm, it was infuriating. 'Because of the police!' she said. 'That policewoman had been to see me before, when I told her you were with me the night that Leyla Ablak was killed. Then when she turned up at the house, what could I do? I couldn't suddenly lie about our relationship.'

'Yes, but what has that got to do with Selçuk?'

'He overheard me speaking to the policewoman,' she said.

He dipped his perfectly groomed head for a moment. 'Did you see him?'

'No.'

'So why did . . .'

'Why did he tell me he knew now?' she said. 'Because hearing me telling that policewoman was too much for him. Knowing that someone else knew damaged his pride.'

'So does he want a divorce?'

'No.' But she said it tetchily, as if she had wanted him to. 'He wants it, us, to stop.'

'You want him to divorce you?' Cem said.

'No, yes, I don't know.' She leaned her head against his shoulder and sighed. 'I just want to be with you, that's all.'

He looked down at her and smiled. 'But you've always said you didn't want to hurt Selçuk. You and I have done a lot to avoid hurting him. He is, after all, one of the good guys, isn't he?'

'I know.' She kissed the side of his face. 'But Cem, the night Leyla Ablak died . . .'

'When we were together, yes.'

'Now that the police know that I am Selçuk's wife as well as your lover, they might not believe that,' she said.

'Why not? There is no connection, beyond the loose association that existed through my brother-in-law, between Leyla Ablak and ourselves.'

'Yes,' she said, 'but if they start digging around, if they talk to my parents, they'll realise that we weren't at their house the night the Ablak woman died.'

'You told this policewoman we spent that night at your parents' house?'

'I told her they were away, yes. But they weren't.'

He thought for a moment, and then he said, 'Well then, you'll have to tell this policewoman you were wrong and that we spent the night at your marital home.'

'Oh, Cem, what—'

'What? What do you mean, "what"?' he said. 'What are we going to do? Nothing, Hatice. You'll tell your policewoman you were mistaken about that night and then we will do nothing. And do you know why that is?'

She looked up at him.

'Because we've done nothing wrong,' he continued. 'Nothing!'

'No, no,' she said. She took one of his hands and put it between her legs. 'Cem . . .'

He pulled his hand away. She put her hand on the front of his trousers. He looked into her eyes.

'I'm frightened,' she said. 'I need you.'

'There's no need to be frightened,' he said. He watched as she unzipped his fly and moved her hand up and down the shaft of his penis, which hardened. 'You'll hold your nerve, Hatice.'

'Cem . . .'

'Hold your nerve and I'll let you,' he said.

'I need a lollipop,' she said in a little girl's voice. 'That'll make me feel better, Cem. I'll do whatever you say, I promise.'

She watched him make her wait. He always made her wait. It was so exciting.

Eventually he said, 'All right, you've been a good girl, you can have it, Hatice.'

'Thank you, Professor,' she said. And she took him gratefully into her mouth.

'Why did you mourn the death of Abdurrahman Efendi so very effusively, Suzan?' İkmen asked.

The girl looked confused.

He said, 'All right, why were you so upset when Abdurrahman Efendi died?'

'Because he was my master,' she said. 'He gave me shelter, he was kind to me and—'

'You told me yourself that he made you sleep in a wooden box outside the kitchen!' İkmen said. 'In what way is that kind?'

'Lots of people don't want their servants sleeping in their beds,' she said.

'Really?' He shrugged. 'Well, even if I, as a person without servants, accept that that is true, what I can't get around are my own observations, plus independent verification that Abdurrahman Efendi treated you with utter contempt.'

'Who said that?' she said. She looked afraid.

'It's not important,' İkmen replied. 'I know, that's all. Where'd you get the money, Suzan? Did someone pay you to let them into the apartment the day Abdurrahman Efendi died?'

Someone had let the killer into the Efendi's apartment, and that someone came down to either the old man or his servant.

'I never let anyone in,' the girl said.

'Then maybe you just left the door open,' İkmen said. 'I can understand it. The life of some awful old man who treats you like rubbish, or five thousand lira in cash for you to spend on whatever you like.' He frowned. 'Talking of which, why didn't you just buy yourself some earrings if you had all that cash on you?'

The girl said nothing.

'I mean, had you spent, say, a thousand lira on a pair of Vakko earrings, you wouldn't be here now, would you? Strikes me that you took a somewhat silly risk.'

'You had to know that if you got caught you'd be handed over to us,' Ayşe Farsakoğlu said, 'and that we'd find your money.'

'No spending sprees for you until we find out where it came from,' İkmen said. 'No designer handbags, no jewellery, no clothes . . .'

'I never wanted to use it for that!' Suzan said. 'Why'd you think I wanted to use it for rubbish like that?'

'Well I think that a clue may be found in the fact that you tried to steal a very pretty pair of diamond earrings from a customer in Vakko,' İkmen said.

'Only for what they were worth!'

'For what they were worth? You mean you intended to sell them?' İkmen said.

'Yes.'

'Why?'

'To get money,' she said.

'You had money, Suzan.'

'Well I needed, I need more,' she said.

'What for?'

She looked down at the floor. 'My mother's sick.'

İkmen, who had heard more than a few sob stories concerning sick mothers in his time, said, 'Sick with what?'

'She has lung cancer,' the girl said. 'She needs an operation to take one of her lungs away. I got this money for her operation and then my father, he tells me that she needs more. That's why I stole the earrings.'

'To top up the money you'd got?'

'Yes.'

'Not that you'd saved?'

'Yes, saved, got. Money I had.'

'Suzan, where did you get the money from?' İkmen re-iterated.

'I told you . . .'

'Yes, and I told you that I didn't believe you,' İkmen said. 'Because I don't.' He leaned forward. 'Suzan, we are staying here until you tell me the truth. Your employer, Abdurrahman Şafak, was murdered, and it seems to me that the coming together of his death, your need for money and an unaccounted-for five thousand lira has to be more than mere coincidence.'

282

'I didn't kill him!' the girl said. 'I didn't!'

'I'm not saying you did,' İkmen replied. 'But I think you may have a good idea who might have done.'

Still the girl said nothing.

Selçuk Devrim put his phone down on his desk and sank his head into his hands. Why Hatice suddenly wanted to talk right now wasn't clear to him. Had she spent the day with the Atay man, and was she going to ask him for a divorce? Selçuk had told her that he didn't want one, but what did that matter? She was besotted.

He raised his head and said to his assistant, 'I have to go home early.'

He'd planned, as he so often did, to work late into the night.

The assistant, a small man in his fifties, said, 'I hope nothing is amiss, Selçuk Bey?'

'No, nothing is amiss.' He stood up and put his jacket on. Hatice's obsession with her old tutor was, in a way, understandable. When she'd been at an impressionable age, he'd been her academic hero, and he had also been her first lover. But what he saw in her was rather more difficult to fathom. Yes, she was attractive, and she was good in bed, but she was hardly ideal consort material for a celebrity academic. And Cem Atay was still, officially, married.

Selçuk shut his computer down and locked his papers in his desk drawer. He didn't like working in the office. Being out in the field in places like Siberia was more his style. But those absences had done him no favours. Selçuk began to walk. He'd known right from the start that Hatice had had an affair with Cem Atay when she'd been a student. But he hadn't known that they'd resumed their liaison until he'd gone to Tarlabaşı one day to make sure that his brother was still alive.

283

'I know a man round here who knows the professor,' Levent had told him. 'He said he's seen him with your wife.'

Selçuk had asked, 'How does he know me? How does he know my wife?' He'd thought that Levent was just making trouble, because that was what druggies did.

But then Levent had said, 'He said the woman was called Hatice Öz. He said she was blonde and he told me, this man, that she had mentioned that she lived in Bebek. I can still put two and two together, you know.'

Even taking into account the obvious coincidences inherent in Levent's story, Selçuk couldn't believe him, not until Hatice went out one day and he decided to follow her. She went to a house in Arnavutköy, where she kissed the male owner, the professor, on the doorstep. Selçuk had cried.

He left his office and got into his car. He'd said nothing to Hatice after he'd discovered the affair because he hadn't known what to say. Although he had been hurt in a way he'd never been hurt before, he'd known right from the off that he didn't want a divorce. And then Levent had been murdered and his mind had gone elsewhere for a time. What he hadn't been able to bear had been Hatice telling other people, namely that police-woman. Why, he didn't know, but something inside him had just given way. Had it been because when she'd spoken about it, Hatice had appeared to be so unashamed?

He put the car in gear and drove it up the ramp that led from his office car park and on to İnönü Caddesi. It was nearly five o'clock and so the roads were packed. He thought about calling Hatice to tell her that it would take him some time to get home, but decided against it. She would know that anyway.

Ayşe Farsakoğlu sat down opposite the girl and offered her some börek. Neither İkmen nor Süleyman were anywhere to be found and she wanted to eat her pastry before it got cold. And why not give Suzan Arslan one too? Ayşe had bought far too many for just the two men and herself, especially in view of the fact that İkmen hardly ate anything anyway.

'Have some börek, Suzan,' she said as she pushed one of the cheese and spinach pastries across the table towards the girl.

'No.'

'Go on, it'll do you good.'

'I can't, I'm too nervous,' she said.

Ayşe, who had been ravenous, finished her börek before she spoke. 'Listen, Suzan, if you just tell us the truth, then everything will be all right.'

'But it won't be!' the girl said.

'Why not?'

'Because I . . .'

'Because you what?' Ayşe asked. 'What did you do, Suzan? Did you kill Abdurrahman Efendi?'

'No!'

'Did you steal the money you had in your bag when you were arrested?'

'No!'

'Well then, what can be so terrible?' she said.

'I have to get that money to my mother or she'll die,' Suzan said. 'You have to let me go home, Hanım.'

'I can't do that,' Ayşe said. 'Suzan, you have to understand that you will be charged with theft whatever happens. Of the earrings. In order to make bail you'd have to go to court, but we could, possibly, transfer your money to your parents, if you can prove to us that it is in fact yours.'

'It is mine!'

'So you keep saying, but look at if from our point of view. You didn't earn enough money from your employer to allow

285

you to save five thousand lira. All the notes are sequential, so they came from a bank. But you don't have a bank account. Can you see how this looks?'

She looked down at the table in front of her and said nothing.

'Suzan, if you're being threatened by anyone . . .'

The girl looked up sharply. And then Ayşe knew. 'That's it, isn't it?' she said. 'You're being threatened to say nothing.'

Still the girl didn't speak.

'What are they saying will happen to you if you talk? Because you know that we can and will protect you,' Ayşe said. 'If you know who killed Abdurrahman Efendi and you're being threatened to keep quiet about it, what makes you think that those people who paid for your silence will let you get all the way home with their money? Eh?'

Suzan put her head so far down she looked as if she was trying to tuck it under her arm.

'If you know something, you have to tell us,' Ayşe said. 'Suzan, if you've come by this money from criminals, then they're not going to let you leave this city alive – and they'll take back their money. Your mum will never get it. Do you understand?'

The girl looked up at her. 'Mum won't get it now anyway,' she said.

'Well if that's the case, then you've nothing to lose, have you?' Ayşe said.

Suzan Arslan looked back down at the table once again.

Chapter 24

Time became odd. It extended so that it seemed as if he'd been in that room for ever, but also contracted to make that second he touched her face almost disappear. She was red from the neck downwards, the colour uneven as if she'd been splashed with paint. At her throat the redness was black. When Selçuk Devrim managed to have a thought, it was *How could she have done this to herself?* But he wasn't sure that she had.

Had *he* done it? He took one of her hands, which was still slightly warm, in his and tried to reconstruct his route from the front door to the kitchen, where he was now. But his mind wouldn't obey him. And what was he supposed to do now? Hatice was dead; what did you do when you found somebody dead?

Or *was* she dead? He looked up into her green-white face and found that he couldn't marry that image to the warmth that was in her hand. Did she still live in spite of the slash to her throat? If she did, he had to get a doctor! Sobbing now, he put one of his hands into his jacket pocket and took out his phone. Somehow, and in spite of the blood he was smearing over the screen every time he touched it, he found his contacts, but then he failed at the final hurdle when he couldn't locate or even remember the name of his doctor. But if he didn't find his doctor then Hatice would die! Unable to find what he needed or even think straight, Selçuk threw his phone to the floor, where it smashed.

Panic set in and he began to feel as if he couldn't breathe. He'd come at her request, to talk about their relationship. What had happened between that request and whenever it was he had found her? And then there was the smell. So much blood gave the air a ferrous tang. Selçuk attempted to breathe normally, but with his heart banging around in his chest like a beach ball, that was impossible. Was she still alive? He put a hand on one of her shoulders and pushed it. Her head flopped backwards, exposing still more of her vast, liverish wound.

Horrified, he ran from her and blundered his way back to the front door, covered in her blood; some of it had even found its way on to his tongue. He opened the door and said weakly, 'Help me!'

Someone's hand took his and a voice said, 'What has happened, Selçuk Bey?'

Süleyman looked up as İkmen entered his office. 'Finished?' he asked.

The older man had been interviewing the girl Suzan Arslan for several hours and he looked exhausted.

'I left her with Sergeant Farsakoğlu,' İkmen said. 'Then I went for a very protracted smoke.'

Süleyman smiled.

'I may need you to come back and terrorise that child for me,' İkmen continued as he sat down at Ömer Mungan's desk. 'I feel quite weak. What have you been doing?'

'Well, I have called Gonca,' he said.

'And?'

'She was prepared. She cried, of course, but she quickly calmed herself and she's with her father now.'

'Good.'

'Then I called that film company, Hittite, to ask for a copy of the documentary Şukru appeared in some years ago. I don't know what kind of difficulty Gonca had with them, but they agreed to make a DVD for me and get it over here tomorrow.'

İkmen smiled. 'Ah, the power of authority,' he said.

'And what of Suzan Arslan? And her money?'

'What of them?' İkmen said. 'She worked for Abdurrahman Şafak for eighteen months; there is no way she could have managed to save five thousand lira out of her wages in that time. By her own admission she was sending money home to the back of beyond via Western Union every week and the old man made her buy her own food!' He shook his head. 'And yet she insists that the money constitutes her savings.'

'The notes are new and sequential; we can check them with the banks.'

'Ultimately. But I want her to tell me first,' İkmen said. 'That girl knows something she shouldn't and I think it's about her master's death.'

'You don't think she killed him, do you?'

'No. But I think she may know who did.' Then he said, 'I need more cigarettes.'

Süleyman took his packet out of his pocket and put it on his desk.

İkmen rose to his feet. 'All this ridiculous al fresco non-sense . . .'

'Passive smoking, Çetin,' Süleyman said. 'It's a worry.'

'Not for me.'

'Well, clearly. But you know what a chain-smoker my ex wife Zelfa was? Well, she doesn't smoke in her house any more and certainly not around our son under any circumstances. The world's changing.'

But İkmen wasn't really listening. Looking over Süleyman's shoulder, he saw what the younger man had been looking at before he came in. He said to him, 'Checking your family tree – again?'

Süleyman stood up. 'Ah, you've caught me – again. Yes, those genealogies Professor Atay gave you proved just too intriguing.'

'Really? I didn't think you were interested in your Ottoman past,' İkmen said acidly. 'I thought it bored you.'

Süleyman smiled. 'That's what we tell people, yes. But if you are, albeit indirectly, related to a family like the Osmanoğlu, then you are almost compelled to give in to a certain level of curiosity. And especially now . . .'

'Because you're related to Leyla Ablak?'

'Absolutely. I've also discovered too that . . .' He shuffled the large sheets of paper in front of him. 'Just a minute . . .'

But then his phone rang and he answered it. 'Süleyman.'

Çetin İkmen, a cigarette already between his lips, watched as his colleague, in response to what he was being told on the phone, allowed his usually very proper mouth to drop open like a fish's.

Selçuk Devrim sat on the floor of his hall with a blanket around his shoulders. His face, his hands and his clothes were all smeared in his wife's blood. Above him, leaning against the wall, was the man who had called the police, Professor Cem Atay. When Süleyman and Dr Sarkissian first saw the professor, he had been crying. Now, however, he was quiet and the doctor had gone to attend to the body of the woman who had been his lover.

Süleyman looked down at the husband, who just gazed ahead without blinking. He was clearly in shock and a medic was on the way to attend to him. The inspector turned his attention to Cem Atay.

'Sir, I will have to interview you formally later . . .'

'Of course.'

'But can you tell me, in brief, what happened when you arrived at this house?'

He shook his head, then said, 'I arrived, parked outside and then Selçuk Bey opened the door looking like . . . covered in blood.' He shook his head again. 'He said "Help me" and at first I thought he was hurt, so I asked him if he was OK and then he showed me . . . her . . .'

'Mrs Devrim.'

'He took me into the kitchen and he showed her to me.' His eyes filled with tears. He looked up at Süleyman. 'We were all meeting to discuss something. Hatice, Selçuk Bey and me.'

'To discuss what?' Süleyman asked.

He put his head down and lowered his voice. 'Hatice, Mrs Devrim, and myself, we had been having an affair for some years. Selçuk knew.' He glanced at the man on the floor.

'For how long?' Süleyman asked.

'How long?'

'How long had Mr Devrim known about your affair with his wife?'

'I don't know. Some time. But Hatice and I didn't know he knew until recently.'

A small man carrying a large black bag appeared in the doorway and said, 'Inspector Süleyman?'

Süleyman excused himself to Professor Atay and approached the man, who put his hand out for Süleyman to shake. But the latter had plastic gloves on and so he just said, 'You are?'

'Dr Emre. I'm told there's someone here in need of medical attention.'

'Yes.' Süleyman indicated the man on the floor. The doctor put his bag down and got on to his haunches to talk to Selçuk Devrim. Süleyman meanwhile escorted Cem Atay into the Devrims' living room.

'How did you find out that Mr Devrim knew about your affair?' he asked.

'May I sit down?'

'Oh, yes, of course,' Süleyman said. 'You must be feeling . . .'

'Yes,' the older man said. When they were both seated on yellow leather lounging chairs, the professor said, 'Hatice told me that a couple of your officers came to this house, about Selçuk Bey's brother who was murdered . . .'

'Levent Devrim, yes. That was my Sergeant Mungan and a Sergeant Farsakoğlu.'

'Yes, it was the woman . . .'

'Farsakoğlu.'

'Whatever her name was, she was talking to Hatice and she knew that she'd met her before because I had given the police Hatice's contact details after the Ablak woman was found dead at my brother-in-law Faruk's spa in Sultanahmet. Well, Selçuk overheard their conversation and confronted Hatice about it after the police had gone. Apparently he said that hearing her tell someone else about it upset him enormously.'

'Did he say anything else to her?'

'Not that I know of,' the professor said. 'But from that moment, things got bad. Selçuk didn't want a divorce and he wanted our affair to stop.'

'And you weren't . . .'

'Hatice and I were in love,' he said. 'It was nightmarish. Hatice didn't want to hurt either of us. She asked us both to come and meet with her today so that we could maybe sort out what we were going to do like adults. I didn't for a moment believe that she'd do something like this . . .'

'You think Mrs Devrim killed herself?'

'Well I can't believe that her husband would have killed her, and he was the only other person here when I arrived.'

'Mr Devrim definitely arrived before you?'

'Definitely.'

'Inspector Süleyman, may I have a moment, please?' The voice that came from the doorway belonged to Arto Sarkissian.

Once again Süleyman excused himself to the professor and went to join the doctor in the kitchen. The body of Hatice Devrim, sitting on its chair, existed between them like a sin.

Süleyman looked at it and said, 'Doctor?'

'Well, I can tell you that she didn't kill herself,' the Armenian said.

'Why's that?'

'Because the pressure on the weapon that killed her was the same at the end of the cut as it was at the beginning. Had she slit her own throat she would have lost purchase after she started to bleed out. Look at this.' He took Süleyman behind the body and pointed to the back of the neck. 'The cut starts almost behind the left ear and carries on until it reaches the lobe of the right ear. That's massive. Whoever killed her was standing behind her; he or she was right-handed and I imagine that he probably held the victim to the chair with his left hand just prior to cutting. That's how I would have done it.'

'But he or she would have to have been strong.'

'Oh undoubtedly, yes.'

'Do we have a weapon, Doctor?'

'As a matter of fact we do,' he said. He took Süleyman to the kitchen sink. A sheet of blue plastic had been laid over the draining board. On it was a small knife with an ornate mother-of-pearl handle.

'If I were to make a guess, I'd say Ottoman,' Arto Sarkissian said.

Süleyman frowned. 'And I'd concur.' He looked up into the doctor's wide face. 'I think I might even know what it is.'

'What is it?'

'My father has one,' he said. 'It belonged to his aunt Gözde. She lived in Nişantaşı, in a terrible old mansion that eventually burnt down. She was a princess.'

'And she had a knife like this?'

'They all had knives like that,' Süleyman said. 'All the princesses.'

Arto, smiling in spite of his colleague's solemnity, said, 'Odd thing for a lady of quality to carry, wasn't it?'

Süleyman sighed. 'It was so that they could kill their husbands if they stepped out of line,' he said. 'The sultan himself would present the knives to the princesses when they got married. They were a constant reminder to their consorts about what royal blood really meant. For this to be used on a woman is bizarre to say the least; well, it is to me.'

'Ah, but not many people have your background . . .'

'True. Well either our killer knows exactly what this knife means, or he or she just grabbed something suitable for the job. But it's an odd thing to just grab . . .'

'The husband was first on the scene, wasn't he?' the doctor asked.

Süleyman looked through the kitchen door to where Selçuk Devrim sat on the hall floor being attended by Dr Emre. He said, 'Yes. And he was a cuckold.'

'Was he?'

'Courtesy of the other man, Professor Cem Atay,' Süleyman said.

'Who arrived afterwards?'

'So he says.' Süleyman lowered his voice. 'You know, Doctor, it was Hatice Devrim, or Öz as she preferred to refer to herself back then, who provided an alibi for Professor Atay for the night when the spa murder victim, Leyla Ablak, was killed. Leyla

Ablak, you may or may not recall, was the lover of Faruk Genç, Professor Atay's brother-in-law.'

'Yes, his sister's husband.'

'His dying sister's husband, yes,' he said.

'What are you thinking, Inspector?' the doctor asked.

Süleyman paused for a moment and then said, 'I'm thinking that Selçuk Devrim had a very obvious reason to kill his wife. I'm also thinking that under certain circumstances so did Professor Atay.'

Arto Sarkissian frowned. 'Depends whether Mrs Devrim's alibi was sound, and if it wasn't, whether she was using that fact to her advantage,' he said. 'No doubt in the fullness of time we will see.'

Chapter 25

The girl had to crack in the end. İkmen knew she wouldn't sleep in that cell and so he stayed close at hand. At ten o'clock a neighbour's boy arrived with the bread his wife had got for him and the chicken she had cooked for him. He was, as ever, grateful but he only really picked at the food. With instructions to the custody officers to call him if the girl so much as sneezed, he sequestered himself out in the car park so that he could smoke. Looking out over a city that boasted far more light than had been seen in the whole country when he'd been a child, İkmen wondered how he'd manage to survive in an increasingly expensive megacity on a pension. Of course if necessary he could sell his Sultanahmet apartment to some rich media type who would no doubt give him a laughable amount of money for it. But if he didn't live there, then where could he live? And anyway, he didn't want to live anywhere else.

It didn't help that he knew Mehmet Süleyman was up too. Or more to the point, it didn't help that he knew *why* his colleague was still up. Another murder had occurred and he'd been interrogating Professor Cem Atay, who had been found at the house of the brother of Levent Devrim, their first twenty-first of the month victim. Apparently the professor had discovered Selçuk Devrim with the body of the latter's wife, Hatice, who had had her throat cut. And it wasn't even close to the twenty-first of any month.

İkmen knew little more than just the bald details of the events that had taken place in Bebek. He hadn't had a chance to talk to Süleyman or Arto Sarkissian, who had also attended the scene. But then the girl Suzan was still preoccupying him. Had it really been just her excessive mourning for her master that had alerted him to the idea that she might have done something wrong? Or had he picked up something else from her? And was his position on that even tenable? He'd given the banks the serial numbers of the notes the girl had had on her and was waiting to hear from them. What if they had come from the old man's own account? What if he had given her the money for some reason? But if that was the case, why hadn't the girl just told him? Unless she'd taken money from him in exchange for something shameful, like sex. This was not the first time Çetin İkmen had asked himself these questions, and it probably wouldn't be the last.

Although he was quite happy being alone with his thoughts, he wasn't able to stay that way for very long. Although he could ignore the odd nicotine-starved constable, he couldn't cut his deputy, Ayşe Farsakoğlu, who walked towards him from her car.

'I couldn't sleep,' she said, 'so I thought I might as well come back and find out what was going on here.'

She didn't have anything much to go to her apartment for now that her brother had moved out and since all romantic contact with Mehmet Süleyman had ceased. But then İkmen had held out hopes for a long time that she would devote most of her time, if not her life, to her job. She was a good officer, and if he could, he wanted to make sure that she at least expressed an interest in taking over from him when he retired. Retired. Just the sound of the word depressed him.

'Ayşe,' he said, 'I am always glad of your company.'

'Suzan needs to weigh up whether she's more afraid of us or of whoever I'm pretty sure is threatening her,' she said.

'Yes.'

She lit a cigarette. 'Do you know anything about the death of Mrs Devrim?' she asked.

'I know that Inspector Süleyman is interviewing Professor Atay right now,' İkmen said.

'He was her lover. Did he kill her?'

'I don't know,' İkmen said. 'I've not had a chance to speak to the inspector or to Dr Sarkissian about it. For all I know the woman killed herself.'

'Mmm.'

And then the sound of a furious alcoholic who had just been brought in to dry out in the cells ripped into the night and silenced them both.

In spite of the screams from the drunk in the next cell, Suzan could hear the custody officers talking and sometimes laughing. Mainly young men, they all had homes to go to at the end of their shifts and families to take care of them. Why should they worry too much about whoever they had in their cells?

Suzan thought about her father and how he and her sick mother had to be feeling. The police had called them to confirm Suzan's story about her mother's illness and to try to discover what they knew about the five thousand lira. But beyond the existence of the money she hadn't told them anything, and they had never asked. They'd told the police nothing because they knew nothing.

Her mother was in pain all the time now. Her father and her brothers had told her that Suzan had been arrested. Her cancer was bad and that was why she would need aftercare and why those earrings would have been such a good idea if Suzan hadn't got caught. Being locked in a police cell was not something she had anticipated, although she had to admit, if only to herself, that where she was now was appropriate, even if she hadn't sought out the evil that she had done. Everything that had led her to this place was vile and wrong and even though she'd done it primarily to make money for her mother, it had been an act of vengeance too. Not that any of that mattered now.

Now her priority had to be to get that money to her parents, and if that meant dying herself, then that was how it was going to have to be. The threats that had been attached to the money could only, after all, be put into practice outside the confines of a police station or a prison, and she was going to go to one of those for certain. But if she did come clean, would the police give the money to her parents? They hadn't said and she didn't know. And if she didn't test it out, she never would know.

As soon as the drunk in the next cell had quietened down, she walked over to her cell door and stood for a moment in front of it, breathing hard. It was a big step. Her life had been threatened. But it was the middle of the night, her mother was in pain; what choice did she have? Suzan banged on the door with the heel of her hand and yelled, 'Hey! You out there! I want to speak to Inspector Çetin İkmen! Now!'

Süleyman held up the small knife, which was enclosed in a plastic evidence bag, for the professor to see. 'I don't suppose I have to tell you what this is, do I?' he asked.

Cem Atay nodded his head gravely. 'I imagine we both know what it is, Inspector Süleyman.'

'Yes, sir, but if you would just tell me . . .'

'It's an Ottoman knife, nineteenth century, given to an Imperial princess by her father, the sultan. I can't tell you which one; these artefacts were somewhat similar in character across the Ottoman centuries. I am sure, being an Osmanoğlu yourself, you are well aware of that fact!'

'Well this knife was used to kill Mrs Devrim,' Süleyman said.

'Professor, in your capacity as an Ottoman historian, and as, by your own admission, Mrs Devrim's lover, do you know whether she or her husband possessed such an item?'

He said nothing and so Süleyman said, 'Do you perhaps own such an item yourself? I understand you are a collector of artefacts both Ottoman and—'

'I don't own such a thing myself, Inspector,' he said. 'And I don't know if either Hatice or Selçuk owned one. But I think it more likely that it was Hatice's.'

'Why?'

'Well because, albeit distantly, through her mother, Hatice was related to the Osmanoğlu family.'

'Hatice Öz?'

'Her mother is a Şafak,' he said. 'A cousin, I understand, of the old man who was recently murdered in Şişli.'

'I see.'

'Have you told Hatice's parents? About her death?'

'My sergeant has been to see them, yes.'

'Unfortunately, Inspector, the extended Osmanoğlu family is so vast it is almost impossible to trace every last relative. Over the years I have compiled family trees . . .'

'Yes.' Either the professor had forgotten about the copies he had given to Çetin İkmen or he had chosen not to allude to them. 'Professor, what are your feelings about the fact that Hatice Devrim was killed with this knife?'

'I'm horrified.' He looked drawn and exhausted and there was the familiar dullness of shock in his eyes. 'For something so personal to be used . . .' He shook his head. 'Hatice wasn't open about her background, Inspector. In spite of the fact that the Ottoman world is currently under some reappraisal, she didn't like what it represented and neither did her husband.'

'Did Selçuk Devrim know about his wife's ancestry?'

'I don't know,' the professor answered. 'Hatice never told me very much about him. All I can tell you, all that Hatice told me, is that Selçuk came from a military family. All very Atatürkist . . .'

'I see.'

'So if he did kill her with that knife, I doubt very much whether he would have fully appreciated the affront that represented.'

'To her family.'

'Of course! Those knives were given to the princesses by the sultan as a way of keeping their husbands in line. A princess could kill a damat, a royal son-in-law, if she so wished, if he cheated on or displeased her.'

Had Selçuk Devrim come home, apparently at his wife's request, to talk, and then killed her with a family heirloom? If the professor was right and Hatice Devrim kept her background quiet, then how had her husband lighted apparently so easily upon that object? Whatever he had or hadn't done, he was now in hospital in a state of fugue from which, so far, he had not emerged, and so asking him wasn't as yet an option. Material for forensic analysis had been taken from both Selçuk and the professor, and so in time, other elements might come to light pointing towards one or other of the men. What was indisputable was that Selçuk Devrim had been covered in his wife's blood and Professor Atay had not. Selçuk Devrim's mobile phone had been broken somehow, while the academic's had remained intact. But then Süleyman also had to take into account what Arto Sarkissian had told him about the murder. The killer had cut Hatice Devrim's throat from behind, which meant that he wouldn't have come into contact with her blood except, possibly, as it sprayed over his hand. The woman's husband, on finding her, could have attempted to revive her by applying CPR or just hugging her body to his. Until Devrim could be spoken to, there was no way of knowing.

'Professor, what were you doing prior to your arrival at the Devrim house in Bebek?' Süleyman asked.

'I was at home,' he said.

'Can anyone verify that?'

'No. I live alone.'

'Did Mrs Devrim call you from her home in the same way that she summoned her husband?'

'No,' he said. He leaned forward on the table between them. 'Inspector, Hatice was at my house this morning. This sudden knowledge she'd come upon that her husband had known about her infidelity for some time was a shock to her. She'd always wanted to protect him against that knowledge.'

'She loved him?'

'As one might love a brother, yes, but any more than that . . .' He shrugged. 'Hatice wanted to tell Selçuk, in my presence, that their relationship was over. She asked me to meet her and Selçuk at their home in Bebek at six. I was a few minutes late because of the traffic.'

'When did she ask you to do this?'

'This morning.'

'And yet from looking at Mrs Devrim's mobile phone records, we can see that she didn't call her husband today until just gone four thirty this afternoon.'

He shrugged. 'I don't know how to explain that,' he said. 'She asked me to meet her at her house at six. She said she'd make sure Selçuk got home in time. Maybe she couldn't get through to him until four thirty?'

'Maybe. So what did you do when Mrs Devrim's visit to your house in Arnavutköy came to an end? Did you take her home?'

'Yes. I drove her to Bebek at about one.'

'You didn't stay with her?'

'No, I had some book proofs to read. I've a new book coming out in the autumn; I mentioned it to Inspector İkmen.'

'This is about the Ottoman Empire's rivalry with the Spanish Empire.'

'Indeed.'

'Yes, of course, your very interesting theories regarding the Mayan Long Count calendar that so fascinated the brother-in-law of your lover Mrs Devrim,' said Süleyman. 'Professor Atay, did you know Levent Devrim?'

'No.'

'Mmm. Just as you didn't know Leyla Ablak, your brother-in-law Faruk Genç's lover.'

'No.' He frowned. 'What are you driving at, Inspector?'

'I am driving, sir, at the fact that you appear to be indirectly connected to two of our victims and directly connected to a third.'

'No. I didn't know Levent Devrim or Leyla Ablak myself, and surely, if you look at just the date connections that exist, so I understand, across many of the other deaths that this city has sadly experienced in the last few months, you will see that Hatice's murder doesn't fit that pattern.'

'If we take it as read that some sort of Mayan conspiracy lunatic is amongst us, yes,' he said. 'But Professor, that is your theory, which may or may not reflect reality. The fact remains that Mrs Hatice Devrim, your lover, a member of the Osmanoğlu extended family by your own testimony, is dead, and so at the moment we have no choice but to add her name to our list of victims of a possible serial killer.' He looked down at his notes. 'You see, if she called her husband at four thirty and he arrived in Bebek in his car, according to a witness, at six, then someone could have killed her between that phone call and Selçuk Devrim's arrival.'

'Yes.'

He looked down at his notes again. 'So if you went home after you took Mrs Devrim to Bebek at one, what time did you leave Arnavutköy to get to the Devrim house at six?'

Atay thought for a few moments. 'I was late. It must have been about ten to six. I became engrossed.'

'In spite of the seriousness of the meeting you were going to?'

'I'm an academic; we—'

'I see. And can you please tell me, sir, what was to be the outcome of this meeting between Mrs Devrim, her husband and yourself?'

'What do you mean?'

'I mean, was Mrs Devrim going to ask her husband for a divorce?'

'Yes, she was,' he said. 'That was why she wanted me to be there.'

'For support, or was she afraid of her husband?' Süleyman asked.

'For support, of course. As to whether she was afraid?' he sighed. 'I don't know, Inspector. Hatice never said she feared him. But maybe she didn't always tell me everything.'

'And when that marriage was over, were you going to marry Mrs Devrim?'

'Yes,' he said. 'İnşallah.'

'I didn't know what he was doing at first,' Suzan said. The light in the interview room was inadequate and gave her slim face a yellowing tinge. 'I knew what animals did because my parents keep sheep and goats. No one had ever spoken to me properly about anything like that; I just saw it,' she continued. 'But I do have brothers and they'd told me some things I didn't know if I believed, whether I'd wanted to hear them or not.'

'About sex?' Ayşe Farsakoğlu asked.

'Yes.' She looked down and then quickly looked up again. 'He just did it to me, the old man.'

'Abdurrahman Şafak.'

'How could I stop him? He'd caught me with clothes I'd taken from Vakko and he was my employer; he could get rid of me if he wanted to.'

'Do you shoplift often, Suzan?' İkmen asked.

She shook her head. 'No. Only that once.'

'So why did you do it on that occasion?' Ayşe asked.

She shrugged. 'Just two pretty dresses and a little bolero. The rich shop could afford it. I looked down at myself and the holes in my clothes, and knowing I had no choice but to spend all my money on food and on my family, I wanted something for myself. I wanted to look, if not pretty, then normal for this city. People stare down their noses when you look like me.'

'How did Abdurrahman Efendi know you'd shoplifted?'

'He found the clothes in my bag ,' Suzan said. 'He asked me where I'd got them. He accused me of taking a lover who was paying for sex with me. I couldn't have him thinking that, I just couldn't!'

'And so you told him.'

'The truth! I know it was stupid, but it just came out. I couldn't have him thinking I'd been with men. What if he'd told my family?'

'What if he'd told your family you were a thief?' İkmen asked.

The girl put her head down.

'Not that I think in light of later events your father would have bothered too much about that,' İkmen said.

'My father . . . My mother is . . .'

'Ill, I know. How many times did the old man make you have sex with him, Suzan?' İkmen asked her.

305

'He made me do things to him a lot,' she said. 'But he only put it in me once.'

'You had intercourse one time?'

'Yes. But it made me pregnant,' Suzan said.

The room went silent then, until she spoke again. 'I didn't know what was going on at first. I thought I was just getting fat, but then he noticed it too and he asked me about my monthlies and I told him I wasn't having any. He got really angry then. One day this woman came and she took me to a clinic. They took the baby away.'

'Who was this woman?' Ayşe asked. 'Had you seen her before?'

'Yes. She came to see Efendi sometimes. At first she was very nice.'

'When you had the abortion?'

'Yes. She was very sympathetic. She said I should call her "Abla" and she came two times after I had my operation to make sure that I was all right.'

'Do you know who paid for the surgery you had?' İkmen asked.

'Efendi,' she said. 'That's why he was so angry with me. He kept saying "I'm dying. So why am I spending money on other people? It should all be for me." The woman, Abla—'

'What did she look like?'

'Blonde and pretty,' she said. 'I couldn't believe it when she said that if I ever told anyone about leaving the door unlocked, she'd kill me. She didn't look like that sort of person at all. But I believed her.'

'Suzan,' İkmen said, 'we're getting ahead of ourselves here. Please go back to what happened after the abortion. When that was all over with, when did you see the woman you called Abla again?'

'She came maybe once or twice to see Efendi. She was a lot younger than him, but when they were together they talked very intensely.'

'What about?'

'I don't know. When I went in to serve them tea or something they always went quiet. Anyway I wasn't interested. My mum became ill at that time and so that was all I could think about.'

'Did you tell your employer that your mother was ill?'

'Yes, he said I could go home if I wanted to but he might have to replace me if I did that. But I couldn't because I needed to send money home. I was worried, though, and then that woman, Abla, saw me crying in the kitchen. She asked me about my mum and I told her that I just wanted to go home to see her. I said she had cancer and needed an operation.'

'And then?'

'And then I didn't see her for a while,' she said. 'Not until the end of April. She came, as she did from time to time, and they had tea. But he was sicker now and so he went to sleep after he had his tea and she left him and came into the kitchen. She asked me about Mum and I told her that she was still sick and she still needed an operation. She asked me why Mum wasn't having the operation and I said it was because Dad couldn't afford it. Then she asked me how much the operation would cost and I told her.'

'Five thousand lira?' It seemed such a small amount of money, but then İkmen imagined it was probably to be performed at a country hospital in the middle of nowhere.

'Yes.'

'What happened then?'

'Then? Nothing. She went back to Efendi. It was a few days later that she offered me the money.'

'What exactly did she offer you the money for, Suzan?' Ayşe asked.

'To leave the front door unlocked when I left to go for my afternoon off the following Saturday,' she said.

'The twenty-first of May?'

'If that was the date, yes.'

'Did she say why she wanted you to leave the front door unlocked on that day?' İkmen asked.

'No.' She lowered her head as if she were ashamed. 'But she did say that when I got back, Efendi would give me no more trouble.'

'Did you think that she meant he'd be dead?'

Suzan thought for a few moments. 'I thought I didn't, but I think now maybe I did.'

'Why was that?'

She began to cry. 'Because when I came in and found him, I felt nothing for him. I even called him bad names and laughed at his poor old body. What kind of person am I?'

She wept and wept and İkmen and Ayşe Farsakoğlu just let her do it. She'd held this guilt, as well as the fears she had for her mother, inside her ever since the old man had been murdered.

When she finally got her tears under control, İkmen said, 'Did Abla give you the money before or after you left the door unlocked, Suzan?'

'Before. She came on the Friday before he . . . he died,' she said.

'His diary for that day was blank,' İkmen said.

'She just arrived. Which was just as well.'

'Why?'

'Because by that time, I knew that Efendi was meeting the Englishman on the Saturday afternoon.'

'Arthur Regan.'

'Yes. It threw me into a panic. Should I leave the door open for the Englishman or wait for him to leave? I didn't know!'

'What did Abla say about that?' İkmen asked.

'She told me I'd have to pretend I was going out for my afternoon off and hide somewhere instead. Then when the Englishman left, I could go too, and leave the front door unlocked. I could have the money there and then as long as I did what she told me and then never told anyone what I'd done or who I'd done it for. If I did tell, she said she'd kill me.'

'Did you believe her?'

'Yes.'

'Why?'

'Because she was one of them.'

'One of whom?'

'Like Efendi,' she said. 'You know, the sort who can order other people around as if they have some right from Allah.'

İkmen looked across at Ayşe, who said, 'Relative?'

He shrugged. 'Maybe.' He turned back to the girl again. 'So, Suzan,' he said, 'what did you do next?'

'I called my dad when I was able, when Efendi was asleep, and I told him to book Mum into the hospital.'

'Why didn't you send him the money then?'

'Because he said he didn't need it then. He'd only have to pay after Mum had had her treatment. Dad doesn't like having a lot of money in the house; he isn't used to it.'

İkmen said, 'So the plan was for you to send your father the money, what, via Western Union?'

'Yes.'

'When the hospital asked for it?'

'Yes.' She frowned. 'She is booked in for tomorrow. I want to be with her.'

Çetin İkmen felt for the girl, but it was clear that she'd had at least some notion of what had been about to happen to her employer when he was murdered. And the money the woman had given her had been earned, if that was even the right word, in almost the worst way imaginable.

'I can't let you go, Suzan,' he said. 'I'm sorry.'

'Oh no!' She began to cry again.

'By your own admission, you had some idea about what was going to happen to Abdurrahman Efendi, and because it is illegal to benefit financially from crime, that money isn't yours. However, if you tell me everything you know, I will see what I can do to try and help your mother get to hospital.'

Ayşe Farsakoğlu looked at him and wondered what he meant.

'It's all I can do,' İkmen said. 'Now, Suzan, you must tell me everything you can remember about the day that Abdurrahman Efendi died. Where did you hide when he thought you'd gone out?'

Suzan sniffed. 'In the cupboard where the vacuum cleaner is kept by the front door,' she said.

'And how long were you in there before the Englishman arrived?'

'I don't know. Ages!'

'What happened when he arrived?'

'They argued,' she said. 'I don't know what it was about because they spoke in English. But he didn't stay long, the Englishman, and I know that Efendi was still alive when he left because my master let him out. The foreigner didn't kill him.'

'So you then left the apartment with the door unlocked,' İkmen said. 'Did you notice anything unusual about the apartment before you left?'

Crying again now, she shook her head.

'Are you sure?'

She looked agonised. 'I don't know!'

310

'Did you see anyone as you left the apartment to go . . . where did you go?'

'To the local shops.'

'To the shops. Did you see anyone lurking outside the apartments in the street or maybe in the hallway or by the lift?'

Suzan Arslan made a supreme effort to stop crying, which was only partially successful, and then she said, 'No.'

'I see. Sure?'

'Yes.' She paused, and through her tears her brow wrinkled. 'But if you don't think it's mad, I did feel as if someone was watching me as I left the apartment. I don't know why.'

Chapter 26

The old man wept, as did all the other people in that dark, smoke-filled room. Only Gonca's eyes were dry, and that was because she'd known of her brother's death for a long time.

At intervals people came in from the community to pay their respects. They brought food, drink and cigarettes for the family, who they hugged to their chests and wished long lives. Şukru had been a man of power in Tarlabaşı.

Şukru's wife, Bulbul, sat opposite Gonca with her dead husband's nine children clustered around her. He'd never been faithful to her for a moment but still she mourned him as her lover, the father of her children and her breadwinner. But she was a woman whose beauty and temper had disintegrated many years ago, and this had left her bitter. When there was a lull in the visits from neighbours she looked at Gonca. 'What is the policeman you open your legs to going to do about my Şukru's death?'

The old man waved a hand, hoping that he could calm the situation and silence his daughter-in-law, but Bulbul persisted. 'Well?'

'He's doing everything he can,' Gonca said, not rising to the bait that only a few years before would have had her out of her seat and at the woman's throat.

'Even though my Şukru is just a gypsy to him?'

'Mehmet Bey isn't like that,' Gonca said. 'He—'

'Oh, I suppose he isn't, no,' Bulbul said. 'If he fucks you.'

'Enough!'

The old man, aware that his daughter was preparing to get her claws out, eyed both women sternly. 'We gather here to mourn my son, not to turn on each other like savages!'

And although the two women still shot glances like daggers at each other from time to time, the room eventually returned to its previous dark, smoking soft-sob-racked state.

Eventually other neighbours arrived, including the boy Hamid, son of the prostitute Şeftali. He carried a tray of halva which he said his mother had made and which he offered respectfully to the family of Şukru Bey. Şukru's father took it with grace and patted the boy on the head. But Gonca saw Bulbul figuratively hiss. She'd known about her husband and his birthmarked mistress, and the sight of her son clearly made her want to do or say something that she nevertheless wouldn't.

Gonca knew something of the part Hamid had played in the affair between her brother and his mistress, how tense it had made him feel, and she felt sorry for him. So when he came to respectfully kiss her hand, she took him in her arms and gave him a hug. His small body clung to hers for some moments before he began to move away. Before he left her, he said, 'Gonca Hanım, do you think my monster killed Şukru Bey?'

'Your monster?' And then she remembered. 'Oh, the man or creature or whatever it was that you saw the night Levent Bey was killed?'

'That boy just makes up lies!' Bulbul snapped. Some of her children, too, looked at the boy as if they wanted to bite him. 'Like his mother!'

Again the old man waved a hand to try and calm the situation.

313

Gonca was intrigued by what the child had said. 'Hamid, why do you think your monster might have killed Şukru Bey?'

'Because when the monster saw Şukru Bey that night, he growled at him.'

'But I thought,' Gonca said, 'that the monster had gone by the time my brother arrived.'

'Oh no,' the boy said, 'I only told the police that because Şukru Bey told me to.'

It was after three a.m. by the time İkmen had finished with Suzan Arslan and taken a description of the woman who may have killed Abdurrahman Şafak. Not only did he consider the hour too late for him to go home to bed, he also felt too agitated to sleep. The money the girl had been found with presented him with a moral dilemma. Although it had to be said that the five thousand lira had been obtained via illegal means, could it also be said that Suzan Arslan, if she kept the money, was benefiting from the proceeds of crime? Strictly that had to be true, but although Suzan had been cruelly pleased when she'd come home and found her elderly employer dead, she had not killed him herself and had never, as far as İkmen could tell, been told explicitly that he was going to be murdered.

Sitting outside the little all-night restaurant on Ordu Caddesi, İkmen lit yet another in a long line of cigarettes and took a swig from his beer glass.

'Early-morning drinking. Oh dear.'

He looked up and saw Mehmet Süleyman standing over him with a cigarette between his lips. İkmen stood and embraced him.

'I trust you will join me in sin?' the older man asked.

'Of course.' Süleyman called one of the waiters, a lad they both knew very well from other late-night eating and drinking

314

sessions. 'Hüsnü! One more Efes over here, please. Oh, and some pide too, cheese and egg.'

The boy turned quickly. 'Right away, Mehmet Bey!'

Süleyman sat down. 'So what have you been up to, Çetin?' he asked.

İkmen told him about Suzan Arslan and the problem of the five thousand lira.

'Well you can't let her have that money,' Süleyman said as he took the glass of beer from the boy. 'That's benefiting from if not the proceeds of crime, then an innocent person's death.'

'According to the girl, the old man raped her, made her pregnant,' İkmen said.

'Still didn't deserve to die.'

'No.' He looked across the road at the baroque exterior of the Laleli mosque, lit by harsh street lamps and even harsher light from the neon that flashed on and off even above businesses that were closed for the night. He found that his moral compass was, as ever, a movable object. 'But without that money, her mother, who is entirely innocent, will almost certainly die.'

Süleyman put a hand on İkmen's shoulder. 'It isn't your problem,' he said. 'We implement the law. That's it. We do not provide social relief.' He changed the subject. 'So no idea what this mysterious woman's real name is?'

'No,' İkmen said. 'I've a description I'll pass on to our artist . . .' He shrugged. 'What about you? I understand the wife of our first victim's brother died earlier today.'

'Yes.' He relayed the story, including his recent interview with Professor Cem Atay.

İkmen nodded his head. 'You're right, the professor does seem to be involved in several of our victims' lives, not to mention our own. But with regard to Hatice Devrim in particular, what would be his motive?'

315

'He wouldn't be the first man to want to get out of a relationship with a woman who has become too clingy,' Süleyman said. 'Such women can be a liability, and let's face it, Çetin, someone like Cem Atay can have any woman he wants.'

'Because he's on TV.'

'Because he's a celebrity academic and he's well off and handsome,' Süleyman said. 'On the other hand, Mrs Devrim, like every victim so far with the exception of Levent Devrim, is someone Professor Atay, in part, relies upon for his living.'

'She's an Osmanoğlu?'

'A distant one, yes. I'm quite amazed Atay has never turned up at my parents' house, to be honest. He made it clear in his interview that he knows exactly who I am. What's wrong with us?'

İkmen smiled.

'But seriously, why destroy the main thing that defines your life? And why all the Mayan stuff? It can hold up, as a theory, but it doesn't . . . if you see what I mean . . .' He bit into his pide and then closed his eyes for a moment. After a whole day of no food, the cheese and the egg mixed with the soft, fresh bread was blissful. 'Oh, Çetin, you should try this.'

İkmen wrinkled his nose and lit a cigarette. 'No thank you, Mehmet, I'll stick to what I know. If I start making contact with healthy things, who knows where it will end? Anyway, what about Hatice Devrim's husband? He was at the scene . . .'

'Under sedation at the Taksim Hospital. He went into shock, there was nothing I could do with him,' Süleyman said. 'As I told you, Atay's story is that he found Selçuk Devrim with his wife's body when he arrived. Selçuk was covered in blood, I observed that myself. However, the knife that Dr Sarkissian identified as the murder weapon was oddly free of fingerprints.'

'Implying that it was not a crime committed spontaneously.'

'Given the circumstances, a crime of passion could be expected, but that detail mitigates against it.'

'Mmm, so it would seem.' İkmen watched a dustcart lumber down Ordu Caddesi. 'Did the professor mention his Mayans at all?'

'Yes, he did,' Süleyman said. 'He was at pains to make it clear to me that Hatice Devrim's death, in spite of her background, did not conform to the pattern so far established for Osmanoğlu slayings.'

'Oh. I suppose he would,' İkmen said.

'What do you mean? If he'd done it? Killed her?'

'Whether he had or not,' İkmen said. 'You won't get an academic to accept that anything outside of their own pet theory has any validity. But we should keep him in mind. I should, I will keep an eye . . .'

'Absolutely,' Süleyman said. 'Not that we haven't got enough to do . . .' He took his mobile phone out of his pocket and waved his fingers across its technologically advanced screen until his text messages came into view. 'Gonca wants to speak in the morning,' he said. 'Can't speak now because she's at her father's house, but it's important, blah, blah, blah . . .'

'I take it she told her father about her brother.'

'Yes,' he said. 'Something else to do.'

İkmen drank his beer, draining his glass. 'What happens if and when Selçuk Devrim wakes up from shock or fugue or whatever state he is in?'

'Ömer is at the Taksim,' Süleyman said. 'His sister works as a nurse at the German Hospital opposite. He volunteered.'

'He's a good lad,' İkmen said. 'Fortunate for you that yet again you attract talent from the east. But I do think he may be a little homesick.'

'You think?'

317

'Yes. I'd put some praise his way if I were you, Mehmet, from time to time. It would be a shame to lose him.'

'Yes.' Süleyman smiled. His first sergeant had been from the east, a Kurd called Isak Çöktin, who he remembered with affection.

'So what now, my friend?' İkmen asked as he looked at his empty beer glass and lit a cigarette. 'Do we order more beer and see the forty-eight hours round, or do we attempt to go home and catch an hour's sleep?'

Süleyman shook his head. 'I think we both know the answer to that, Çetin,' he said. He called the waiter over again. 'Hüsnü! Two more Efes over here when you're ready.'

Suzan didn't sleep. But when the custody officer came in with tea and bread she did manage to eat and drink. Inspector İkmen had told her that now she had admitted to the offence of being an, albeit unwitting, accessory to murder as well as withholding information from the police, and had been formally arrested, what would happen to her next was out of his hands. She had asked to see a lawyer and İkmen had said that he would arrange that for her. But nobody had come. She had thought that lawyers, particularly criminal lawyers, worked at night as well as in the day, but maybe she was wrong about that.

Shortly after breakfast, though, she did have a visitor.

'Suzan, a gentleman called Murad Hasanzade is going to meet with you soon,' Ayşe Farsakoğlu told her.

'Is he my lawyer?' Suzan asked.

'Mr Hasanzade is a lawyer, yes,' the policewoman said. She sat down next to Suzan on the side of her tiny cell bed with its scratchy grey blankets.

'Have you managed to eat something?' Ayşe asked. She had a newspaper in her hands which she seemed to be half reading, so it wasn't easy for Suzan to really talk to her.

'I had some bread and tea,' she said. 'Sergeant Farsakoğlu, what is going to happen to me? Will I be able to go home soon?'

She knew she'd been arrested, which probably meant prison, but she hadn't deliberately hurt anyone, so perhaps it would only be for a few weeks. She didn't know how it worked. None of her family had ever been to prison. She said, 'Will you wait with me until the lawyer comes?'

'I can,' Sergeant Farsakoğlu said. 'But Suzan, you will have to speak to him on your own. That's how it is. He'll tell me to go away.'

'Oh.'

The policewoman unfolded her newspaper so that the front cover was showing.

'You mustn't be scared, Suzan, Mr Hasanzade is coming to help you. And you must tell him everything, just like you told us.'

Although Suzan was looking right at the image on the front of the paper, it didn't register immediately. To begin with she just thought it was a nice photo. Only when she really began to study it did she realise who it might be.

Ayşe Farsakoğlu must have seen the look of shock on her face because she said, 'Suzan, are you all right?'

Chapter 27

He didn't bother to call Gonca before nine. Even when she wasn't at her father's place, surrounded by her extended family and exhausted by grief, she rarely rose before ten. But when Süleyman did call, her phone was off and so he left a message on her voicemail. Ömer Mungan hadn't yet contacted him to say whether Selçuk Devrim was ready to talk or not, and so he busied himself with paperwork until a knock at his office door got him to his feet. A constable gave him a small package labelled 'Hittite'. This was the film that he had ordered for Gonca, of her brother. Once alone in his office, Süleyman opened it. He'd just slipped the disc into his laptop when his phone rang. He picked it up.

'Mehmet,' İkmen said.

'Çetin.'

As far as he was aware, his colleague was either on his way to or had arrived at the Great Palace Hotel's Wellness Spa. He had decided very early on that morning that he wanted to quiz the manager, Faruk Genç, about his brother-in-law, Cem Atay.

'Mehmet, dear boy, I'm at the spa now but I've just had a call from Ayşe about Suzan Arslan.'

'Abdurrahman Efendi's servant.'

'Yes,' he said. 'It seems she has finally identified the woman who gave her the five thousand lira.'

'Oh?'

'From a picture on the front of today's edition of *Cumhuriyet*.'

Süleyman couldn't get the disc to play for some reason that he couldn't fathom, so he ejected it. 'Of?'

'Hatice Devrim,' İkmen said.

Süleyman felt a jolt through his chest. 'Hatice Devrim is "Abla".'

'It would seem so, yes,' İkmen said.

'Abdurrahman Şafak was her mother's cousin,' Süleyman said, 'according to Professor Atay.'

'Whose somewhat florid profile on the Boğaziçi University's website I'm just about to check out with Faruk Genç,' İkmen said.

'OK. Although I still don't really get what motive the professor would have for killing either his mistress or any of our twenty-first of the month victims,' Süleyman said.

'Neither do I. But in the absence of anything else at the moment . . .'

'Maybe Hatice Devrim killed them all,' Süleyman said.

'Maybe she did.'

'Maybe whoever killed her knew.'

'Possibly. Is her husband ready to be questioned yet?'

'Not that I know . . .' He was interrupted by the sound of another incoming call. 'Just a minute.' He moved the phone so that he could see its screen. 'That's Ömer now. Have to go.'

İkmen said, 'I'll speak to you later.' Then he cut the call.

'Ömer?' Süleyman said.

'Sir,' the young man replied. 'Mr Devrim is awake and he says that he wants to confess to his wife's murder.'

'My late wife's mother comes originally from Adana, her father was a railway worker from Afyon,' Faruk Genç said. 'I don't know when they came to the city, but it was before Cem was born.'

'Cem Atay is the eldest sibling?' İkmen asked.

'Yes. There was Cem, my wife Hande and then the youngest, Nilüfer. The parents were typically working class. The father worked at Sirkeci Station, the mother cleaned rich people's houses until her darling son became famous. Hande and Nilüfer were clever too and they both finished high school, but Cem was always the star of the show.'

'He studied at the university where he now teaches?'

'Yes. He just lectured for years, attracting little or no attention from anyone, until some female film director consulted him on something to do with the Ottomans for a documentary she was making. Then suddenly he was in it, the documentary.' He leaned across his desk conspiratorially. 'He has a way with women, if you know what I mean.'

İkmen did. He said, 'When was this, and can you remember what the documentary was about?'

Faruk Genç sighed. 'It has to be over ten years ago,' he said. 'I don't know exactly when. But the documentary was about Süleyman the Lawgiver. Not Cem's strongest suit, if I remember rightly, but his enthusiastic accounts of Süleyman's various military campaigns, as well as his colourful personal life, made him a TV star. Have you not seen any of his programmes, Inspector?'

'I'm afraid the TV just tends to be on in my apartment; we rarely actually watch anything,' İkmen said. 'Although I did read your brother-in-law's excellent book about the end of the Empire.' He paused, marshalling his thoughts. 'He had a wife, I understand . . .'

'Yes, Merve. She disappeared around the same time that Cem became famous.'

İkmen had read a summary of Merve Atay's file, and although her husband had been a suspect early on in the investigation into her disappearance, no evidence had ever been

322

discovered that might have led the police to believe he could have murdered her.

'In fact,' Faruk Genç continued, 'it was his involvement with that film that got him through all that, I think. He loved Merve, even though he probably cheated on her right from the start of their marriage, not that I can take the moral high ground there.' He lowered his head for a moment and then looked up again. 'There have always been girls and women around Cem.'

'Do you know any of them?' İkmen asked.

'Not wittingly, and I certainly didn't know the poor woman who has just died.'

'Hatice Devrim.'

'Yes. My late wife wasn't close to her brother. I think there was some jealousy there. He went to university, she got a job in the Sultanahmet tourist office. Sibling rivalry, you know. But putting that aside, Hande was sort of pleased for him too, in his career. And of course it all ramped up enormously for Cem after the death of that Ottoman prince in 2009 – you know, the one who had the massive state funeral at the Sultanahmet mosque.'

'Yes, I do,' İkmen said. How could he forget? The funeral of Osman, Ertuğrul Osmanoğlu Efendi, had attracted thousands of mourners as well as a smattering of high-profile cabinet ministers. The prime minister himself had even sent his condolences. İkmen recalled it particularly clearly because Mehmet Süleyman's mother had phoned her son from the funeral every five minutes. Such public as well as political approval for the ancient regime had given people like her hope.

'It all went Ottoman mad,' Faruk Genç said. 'Cem seemed to be lecturing about it either somewhere abroad or on TV at home all the time. People started talking about the "New Ottomans", as if somehow they were coming back to lead us all into some sort of powerful Imperial future. Leaders of the Middle East and all that rubbish.'

'You don't approve?' İkmen asked.

'Of neo-imperialism? No, I don't,' he said. 'Turkey as some sort of leader of the Muslim world?' He shook his head. 'I think the Arabs had enough of us the last time, don't you? Five hundred years or whatever it was under the Ottoman yoke. They wouldn't want that again, and quite honestly, why would we bother? The Middle East is a nightmare. One thing I do know about Cem is that he was perturbed about that too.'

'About neo-Ottomanism?'

'Yes. He thought it was nonsense. Ask him. The Empire may be his subject and everything, but he recognises that it's had its time, as most right-thinking people do.' He frowned. 'You know, come to think of it, that name, Hatice Devrim . . .'

'Levent Devrim was found murdered in Tarlabaşı in January,' İkmen said. 'He was Hatice Devrim's brother-in-law.'

'Oh, but that's awful!' Faruk Genç said. 'Two victims in the same family.' His eyes became wet. Not only had he lost his wife, he'd lost his mistress too. He remained raw. 'How did my brother-in-law know this woman?'

'She was, I believe, a one-time student of his.'

'In the papers it said she was married,' he said. 'What about her husband?'

'That investigation is ongoing, sir,' İkmen said, neatly sidestepping any reference to who might or might not have killed Hatice Devrim.

'You don't think that Cem . . .'

'I don't think anything at the moment, Mr Genç,' İkmen said. 'I am merely checking out everyone who was in the vicinity when this crime occurred.'

'Cem would never kill a woman, Inspector, he loves them too much.'

Çetin İkmen smiled.

'You know, Hande once told me that when Cem was a student, he got knocked back by some girl who was out of his league. But he still went around to her house and put flowers on her doorstep for her birthday.'

It was difficult for İkmen to decide whether that was sweet or creepy.

The call from Gonca came just before Mehmet Süleyman went back in to Selçuk Devrim's hospital room for a second time. Both he and Ömer Mungan had given the distraught man some space to think before they took any more information from him.

Gonca said, 'My brother told the boy Hamid to lie to you.'

'But he told you the truth?'

'He swears on his mother's life,' she said. 'The creature he saw, Hamid's monster, not only saw Şukru, it growled at him.'

'Did it run after him? Did he run after it?'

'No, and clearly it didn't kill him – then,' she said.

'Then?'

'The kid thinks that it was the monster that burned my brother. He thinks it came after him later to silence him.'

'Because of what he had seen?'

'Yes.'

'Does the boy have any evidence for this?'

'No.'

Ömer Mungan tapped him on the shoulder. 'Sir, we'd better . . .'

'I have to go,' he said to Gonca. 'But I'll need to speak to the boy. Can you secure him for me?'

'I can bribe him,' Gonca said, and cut the connection.

Süleyman put his phone in his pocket. 'All right,' he said to Ömer, 'we go in there with the aim of shooting his story down.'

'Yes, sir.'

'Because even if Mr Devrim did kill his wife, he still needs to prove it to us. Just crying and claiming that he did it doesn't do that.'

'No, sir.'

They walked past the constable stationed outside Selçuk Devrim's room and approached the bed in which the pale figure of the bereaved husband lay. He had a drip in his left arm and a monitor attached to his chest. Süleyman stood on one side of the bed while Ömer Mungan stood on the other.

'So, Mr Devrim . . .'

'I wanted to kill my wife, Hatice,' he said. 'I even tried to keep it from myself, but when I drove from my office to Bebek I knew that she was going to ask me for a divorce and I knew that I couldn't bear it. She could have carried on with Atay and I would have allowed it, but I knew she didn't want that. I'd known it ever since I'd told her I didn't want a divorce and I saw the look of disappointment on her face.' He turned his dark eyes up to Süleyman. 'I went home to kill her.'

'Yes, Mr Devrim,' Süleyman said, 'you told us about your motives last time. What we are interested in is *how* you killed her.'

'I stabbed her.'

'What with?'

For several seconds it almost seemed as if he was confused by the question.

'What with?' Süleyman reiterated. This had been the sticking point the first time they had spoken. He hadn't known what he had stabbed her with.

326

'You see, we know what was used to kill your wife,' Süleyman began, 'and—'

'It was that knife,' Devrim said. He looked up at them. 'The one she thought I didn't know she always carried.'

'What knife?'

'She was ashamed of it because it was so at odds with her politics,' he said. 'But one is what one is even if one doesn't like it. She was an Ottoman, she had "Imperial" relatives, not that I ever met any of them, apart from her mother. But I knew she had one of those knives the sultans gave to their daughters to use on their husbands.' His face fell into a sour grimace. 'I wonder if he knew she had it. I wonder if she ever showed it to him.'

'Who?'

'The good professor,' he said. 'He collects things, doesn't he? That's what he says on his TV programmes.'

'Mr Devrim, are you telling us that you killed your wife with a small-bladed Ottoman dagger?' Ömer asked.

'Yes.'

This represented progress on the last time they had spoken. But then Süleyman said, '*How* did you kill your wife, Mr Devrim?'

'With the knife.'

'Yes, I know that, however—'

'I don't remember,' he said. 'I just . . .' He put a hand up to his head. 'I was covered in her blood!' he sobbed. 'Covered!'

'Yes, we know, Mr Devrim, but we need to know how that blood got there.'

'I don't remember!' Tears were falling down his face like thick dew. 'I just walked into the house and the next thing I knew . . .' He shook his head. 'There was the knife . . . She just sat there, like a rag doll.'

'Because she was dead when you got there?'

'I don't know! How do I know? I wanted her dead. Now she is dead!'

'But that doesn't mean you killed her,' Ömer said.

'But if I didn't, who did? The great professor arrived after me, I do remember that.'

Süleyman asked, 'Are you sure there was no one else in the house when you arrived?'

'No. Yes. No. I don't know! I killed my wife, why won't you believe me? Charge me with murder and have done with it!'

One of the monitors above his head started beeping. Süleyman said, 'What's that?'

'I don't know!'

It beeped still harder. Ömer looked at it and said, 'I'd better get a nurse.'

'OK.'

His sister was a nurse. Süleyman had seen her briefly earlier; she was one of those handsome, bony eastern women. She'd brought her little brother a chicken sandwich.

Ömer left the room, and in spite of the alarming beeping from the monitor, Süleyman bent down and said to Selçuk Devrim, 'You may want to end your life now that your wife is dead, but you're not going to do that at the expense of the truth, Mr Devrim. You can believe what you like, but I don't believe you killed your wife.'

Selçuk Devrim stared at Süleyman with what looked like hatred in his eyes until a nurse arrived and told both of the policemen to leave.

Once outside the hospital, Süleyman lit up a cigarette. 'That's either the best double bluff I've ever seen in my life, or he's on a crazy mission to punish himself.'

'His prints were not on the knife, sir,' Ömer reminded him. 'I know he could have wiped them . . .'

'Somebody else was there,' Süleyman said.

'Who?'

He shrugged his shoulders. 'I don't know. The Devrims' neighbours only saw her go in at one o'clock with the professor. Two people saw him leave ten minutes later, and then – nothing until her husband.'

'And then the professor.'

'Yes, and then the professor,' Süleyman said, 'afterwards . . .'

Chapter 28

There was nothing more that İkmen could do for Suzan Arslan, even though her predicament, and that of her mother, bothered him enormously, so he went home to get some sleep. But in spite of the soothing light tea that Fatma had brewed for him, he couldn't rest. After less than an hour he left his bed and walked into the living room, where his wife was dusting.

'What are you doing up?' she asked as he flopped down into a chair and lit a cigarette.

'Things on my mind,' he said.

Fatma İkmen knew of old that 'things on my mind' could cover a multitude of sins. 'What things? Work?'

'In part,' he said.

She carried on rubbing a copper coffee pot she had inherited from her mother. 'Can you tell me about them?'

He looked up at her. She'd hated his job for over forty years and had said she couldn't wait for him to retire, but she was also always willing to listen to him. And she was discreet. Fatma never gossiped. He launched straight into it. 'I've got this kid,' he said, 'in custody. She's done something bad but she did it unwittingly . . .'

'She from the country?' Fatma put her duster on the sideboard and sat down beside her husband.

'What do you think?' He smiled. 'The fact is that she obtained some money via a crime that she didn't commit but colluded in.'

'So that's gone.'

'Yes, and so has any chance of her mother getting the surgery she needs for cancer. That's why the girl did what she did. Five thousand lira.'

'And you know that this is genuine?'

'Yes. We've spoken to the family and the local cops and the woman will die unless she gets to hospital as soon as possible. I asked Ardıç if I could maybe collect money from members of the department, but he said that under the circumstances that wouldn't be appropriate, which I can see.' He shook his head. 'I just feel so sorry for them: the girl, her mother. And it isn't even a large amount of money. Five thousand lira . . .'

'There's nowhere else the family could get it?' Fatma asked.

'They were relying on the kid to get the cash, so I can't imagine they have bank accounts,' her husband replied. 'The old man is some dirt farmer in the east.'

Fatma squeezed his arm and then kissed him on the cheek. 'I know you want to help, but I can't see there's anything else you can do,' she said. 'Five thousand lira is a lot of money for ordinary people.'

'Yes, but if a lot of people contributed . . .'

'I know, but Ardıç has said no,' Fatma said. 'I'm sorry, Çetin. You're a good man and I know that you care about this girl, but you're going to have to let it go.' She pushed herself up off the sofa and changed the subject. 'I've had a think about the central heating and I've worked out that we can probably get away with five radiators for the whole apartment . . .'

It didn't matter how many times he was asked or in how many ways, the boy Hamid didn't have a clue as to the identity of his monster.

'Hamid, Şukru Bey is dead, he can't tell you what to say any more,' Süleyman said to the child. 'So if you know the identity of the monster . . .'

'I don't! I just seen him from the first house, where I had the fire; he never saw me. Şukru Bey never saw me neither. I never told him nothing. Then I started having dreams about my monster and I told people and then it come out what I'd seen. Şukru Bey got angry.'

The child's mother was off her head in some far-flung corner of Tarlabaşı and so Hamid was being supported by Gonca and old Sugar Barışık.

'You said that when the monster was standing over Levent Bey's body and he saw Şukru Bey, he growled at him,' Ömer Mungan said. 'What did Şukru Bey do when that happened, Hamid? Was he frightened? Did he run away?'

The boy shook his head. 'He didn't do anything,' he said.

'So he . . .'

'He just looked at him and then he walked away.'

'Did he look at Levent Bey at all?' Süleyman asked.

'No, only when he came back later, when he saw me.'

'And what were you doing when he saw you?'

The boy shook his head. 'I don't know why I done it but I was . . . I wanted to know if he was really dead. I pushed a stick where he'd been cut . . .'

In spite of their past differences, usually involving Hamid picking her pocket, Sugar pulled the boy in close and hugged him. Gonca shook her head. 'What was my brother doing?' she muttered.

Hamid looked at Süleyman. 'Mehmet Bey, if I knew who the monster was, I would tell you. Honest!'

'Ever since Levent died, the developers have been using his death to promote their view of this place as a den of vice and danger,' Sugar said. 'We are stigmatised! Nobody wants to find out who did this terrible thing more than the people of Tarlabaşı.'

Süleyman sat back in his chair and looked at the boy. 'True. But we are under pressure with all these murders . . .'

'And we only know what we know, Mehmet Bey,' Sugar said. 'And that includes the boy. I know you want to solve this, but you, like us, have only what you have.'

Süleyman left Sugar's apartment with Gonca and Ömer and went briefly to pay his respects to the Şekeroğlu family. Gonca's father greeted him with bemusement but also with some gratitude, but neither of the policemen stayed. When they left the Şekeroğlus', they walked through the dust-choked streets of Tarlabaşı, watched, Süleyman knew, by at least three separate drug dealers.

Süleyman looked at his text messages. 'Ömer, can you please go and visit Dr Sarkissian for me? He wants to talk about his autopsy on Hatice Devrim's body.'

'Yes, sir, of course,' Ömer said. 'But you usually go.'

Süleyman sighed. 'In spite of Mr Devrim's insistence that he must, albeit without remembering it, have killed his wife, I feel I need to speak to Professor Atay again. He was the only other person who was there, and maybe he can recall something that will back Devrim's story up.'

'I thought you had suspicions about the professor, sir?'

'I do,' he said. 'And in part I also want to see just how far, if at all, Atay will push his story in order to implicate Devrim. No one saw him at his home in Arnavutköy that afternoon; maybe he went back to Bebek. From where he lives he could have walked and still been back in time to pick his car up at ten to six. You go off to the lab now and I'll get an appointment to see the professor. I'll meet you back at the station in a few hours.'

'Yes, sir.' Ömer walked to his car and drove off.

Süleyman called the professor's office at Boğaziçi University but was told that it was his day off. So he called him on his mobile phone. The professor was at home in Arnavutköy and said that of course Inspector Süleyman could come and see him in his lovely garden. It was, after all, a very beautiful day.

It was only a theory and in truth he was thinking and fretting about several things. It wasn't even a theory that could really be tested scientifically, because he had no other murder weapon to compare with the small Ottoman knife. But Arto Sarkissian had been of the opinion ever since Leyla Ablak's death that more than one blade had been used on the twenty-first of the month victims. Now he wondered whether the Ottoman knife used to kill Hatice Devrim was that second, smaller blade.

Forensics had produced a series of photographs across four of the victims, including Hatice Devrim, of throat and chest wounds. In the victims prior to Hatice Devrim, the smaller knife appeared to have been used within the chest cavity in order to remove or attempt to remove the heart. And of course that made sense, because a large-bladed weapon would not have been suitable for the finer work of cutting veins and arteries within the restrictions of a chest cavity.

Arto Sarkissian shook his head. And then there had been Çetin.

Apparently trying to get some sleep at home after a sleepless night at the station, the inspector was nevertheless fretting about Abdurrahman Şafak's servant girl, Suzan. Arto was glad to hear that his friend had discovered that Hatice Devrim was implicated in the old man's death. She herself was dead, but it was still a lead. Although all Çetin seemed able to do was go on about how Suzan had needed the money that had been found on her for her mother's operation, and what were they going to do about it? An almost classic sob story to Arto's way of thinking; he'd told Çetin that they didn't have to do anything about it, which had not gone down well. But he'd heard it all before, from everyone from shoe-shine boys to deeply indebted colleagues at smart dinner parties. He didn't care what Çetin said: he just couldn't believe it.

But of course İkmen's need to help Suzan Arslan was not just about her or her situation. This was Çetin attempting, in some small way, to impose control over a situation that was running out of control. Including Hatice Devrim and Şukru Şekeroğlu, İkmen and Süleyman had been confronted with six unsolved murders since the beginning of the year, and so far there had been no breakthrough. It was a beautiful İstanbul May and İkmen was due to retire at the end of the year. Arto knew that he would hate to leave on what he would consider a failure.

A knock on the laboratory door roused the pathologist from his gloom and he said, 'Come in.'

The professor's home was on the other side of the Greek Orthodox church of the Taksiyarhis from where Süleyman's parents lived. So he knew the area well, even if the smart as well as stunning facade of the academic's house was not one he recalled having taken notice of before. Unlike his parents' home, this wooden building was freshly painted and its delicate fretwork had either been well preserved or very expertly restored.

When he'd found out where Atay lived, he'd parked his car in the bay that he usually used outside his parents' house and walked the two short streets to his destination. In spite of its almost semi-rural atmosphere, Arnavutköy was fashionable and popular and so parking was always difficult. He pulled on an old-fashioned bell cord and waited in the hot afternoon sun, sweating. After what seemed like a long time, but was only seconds, the professor opened the door.

'Inspector,' he said, 'come in.'

The hall was cool with marble and there was a small, silent Greek fountain in one corner. And although Süleyman instantly felt cooler once he was inside, he did also feel compelled to ask his host whether he could freshen up a bit before he followed him out into his garden.

'Of course,' Atay said. 'My bathroom is up on the second floor, first door on the right.'

'Thank you.'

Old Ottoman summer houses like this one had few rooms on each floor, and Süleyman noticed that there was only a hall and a kitchen on the ground floor. As he ascended, he passed a very pleasant living room, plus a shut door that concealed either another living room or a bedroom. On the second floor he found the bathroom. Opposite that was a room he could see was lined with books.

'I've made a small meze,' the professor called up from the kitchen below. 'I do hope you'll join me.'

Süleyman didn't really feel like eating; he hadn't been to sleep for well over twenty-four hours and couldn't really contemplate anything beyond tea and cigarettes, but he said, 'Thank you, that would be nice.' Then he went into the bathroom.

His sleepless image in the mirror was even more horrible than his imagined notion of it. Not only were his eyes shadowed with skin that was almost purple, but his face was both white and blotched with red patches. Once he'd been to the toilet, he splashed his face with cold water and then washed his hands with the fine pistachio soap the professor had laid out on the sink. He finished off by dragging some lemon cologne that he always kept in his jacket pocket through his hair. He looked at himself again, decided that he didn't look quite as bad as he had, and left the room.

For a moment he stood quite still on the landing, looking into what was clearly a study and listening to the sound of the academic moving around in his garden. However suspicious or otherwise of this man he might be, he knew that he had no right to enter the study without his permission, but that was what he did.

As well as books and what looked like the sprawling first draft of a manuscript, complete with red-penned edits, on a large wooden desk, the main thing he noticed about the room was the preponderance of statues and pictures it contained. And while the statues were mainly classical or what he imagined were probably Mesoamerican in character, the pictures were almost exclusively late Ottoman oil paintings of the Bosphorus and the Old City. One of them he thought represented the nineteenth-century waterfront at Arnavutköy when it had been a mainly Greek village. He was advancing to look more closely at it when his jacket caught the edge of the door to a full-length cupboard or wardrobe that stood next to the painting. Embarrassed by his own clumsiness, Süleyman stopped to close the door, but he couldn't help but have a look inside.

Adrenalin spiked up from his gut to his head in a jagged, hot rush. He touched the cloak and the ghastly mask that sat on top of it with shaking hands. It was monstrous. And when he felt the feathers framing the face that looked so much like the idols of the Americas that sat on every surface around the room, he began to feel sick.

'Inspector, can I help you?'

The cupboard door wasn't quite shut and his hand had moved out of it, he thought, just in time when the professor's voice interrupted him. He looked round and felt his face drain.

'I was just looking at this picture,' he said.

'Ah, Arnavutköy in 1900,' the professor said with a smile.

337

'Yes, its style is after the Ottoman court painter Fausto Zonaro, as I am sure you recognise.' He stood to one side so that Süleyman could pass out of the study and into the hall. 'Shall we take tea? Then I shall gladly answer your questions.'

Chapter 29

It was late afternoon when Ayşe Farsakoğlu knocked on Mehmet Süleyman's office door. İkmen was at home resting and she wanted to see whether, in his absence, Süleyman would check the notes she had taken pertaining to the transfer of Suzan Arslan to prison where she would await trial. But it was Ömer Mungan who answered the door.

'Oh,' she said, 'is . . .'

'Still out,' Ömer said. 'Can I help you, Ayşe Hanım?'

'No, not really, but . . . Why aren't you with him?'

He let her into the office. 'Oh, it's this Hatice Devrim thing. I don't have to tell you, it's stretching us all to the limit. The inspector is out interviewing and I went over to see Dr Sarkissian. Sit down.'

He motioned towards Süleyman's chair.

'What, in . . .'

'He's not here, is he?' Ömer said.

Ayşe sat down. 'So what did the doctor have to say?' she asked.

'He's got a theory, which he can't as yet prove or disprove, that the knife that killed Hatice Devrim may also have been used on some of our twenty-first of the month victims. Don't get me wrong, Ayşe Hanım, I can see his point, but when he was showing me photograph after photograph of cuts to neck veins and internal organs, I didn't really know what I was looking at.'

She smiled. Dr Sarkissian was a very clever man, but sometimes his absorption in the minutiae of forensic work did leave others at a loss as to just what he was seeing that they were not.

'He's as desperate to make sense of all this as we are,' she said. 'If somehow all these deaths are connected to or were perpetrated by Hatice Devrim . . .'

'But Dr Sarkissian is certain she couldn't have killed herself.'

Ayşe, distracted slightly by a disc on Süleyman's desk, said, 'Maybe whoever killed her wanted to put a stop to her activities.'

'The old Şafak man was her relative.'

'Yes, but . . .' She picked the disc up. 'What's this?'

'That? Oh, it's a film of the gypsy Şukru Şekeroğlu,' Ömer said. 'I don't know how he features in it. The inspector tracked it down for the family.'

He had been very careful not to say Gonca's name and Ayşe was grateful for that.

'We saw the family earlier on and the inspector was annoyed with himself because he forgot to take it with him,' Ömer continued. 'Those poor people.'

'The family . . .'

'The gypsies in general,' he said. His face suddenly became red. 'Nobody should be marginalised like that. Nobody!'

Taken aback by Ömer's sudden flight into passion, Ayşe looked down at the disc again and said, 'Have you watched it? The film?'

He took a moment to calm himself. 'No.'

She shrugged. 'You can play it on your laptop, can't you? Why don't we have a look at it?'

'Well, because the inspector—'

'He isn't here.'

340

'No.' But he still paused for a moment before he took the disc from her. 'Well I suppose if it was on TRT . . .' he said.

Although he could drink, eating was impossible. There was too much adrenalin in his system. If the man he was with was what that costume in his office seemed to indicate, then he was highly dangerous. And if he knew that Süleyman had seen it . . .

'I do accept, Inspector,' Cem Atay said, 'that physically I could have left this house and gone back to Bebek and killed Hatice. Arnavutköy is quite an isolating place these days, what with all the new rich incomers, not to mention the foreigners, so I don't know my neighbours and they don't know me. But why would I do that? I loved Hatice; her death has left me shattered.' Noticing that Süleyman's glass was empty he said, 'Would you like more tea?'

It was a little bit stewed, but since he hadn't been able to eat anything, Süleyman felt obliged to say, 'Yes.'

The professor poured tea from the pot on top of the samovar for the policeman while Süleyman said, 'Professor, I am not saying that I believe you killed Hatice Devrim, but I do have to cover every eventuality.'

'Well I can't add anything else to what I've already said. I found Selçuk with the body as I described it to you, Inspector. I'm not prepared to make any sort of judgement about him based on that.'

'No . . .' Oddly the feeling of raw fear that had overcome him in the study had left him now. In its place was a slightly disconcerting calm.

'It has to be possible that someone else entered the premises before Selçuk and killed Hatice. But that person wasn't me.'

He was rather matter-of-fact about his lover's death now that the initial shock had passed. But then if he had killed her . . .

341

'Who could it have been?' Süleyman asked. 'You knew Mrs Devrim. Did she have any enemies?'

She'd killed or been instrumental in arranging the murder of Abdurrahman Şafak, and so she had clearly had an issue with him. Had those around him, albeit distant relatives, had an issue with her? Süleyman wondered why he was even thinking about such things. This was the man he had reason to fear, this academic he was sitting with now. But his mind didn't seem to be processing anything as quickly as it normally did. He thought, *I must be sick.* And that thought made him anxious.

'Everybody loved Hatice,' Atay said, 'because she was such a loving person herself. She'd do anything to help people, and the lengths she would go to to save someone's feelings were quite extraordinary.'

'Oh?' A thought crept into Süleyman's brain. It was something to do with a notion he'd just developed that Levent Devrim had possibly known about Hatice and Atay's affair. But he couldn't put it into words for some reason. His eyes began to close.

He heard the professor say, 'Are you all right, Inspector?'

He mumbled something that might have been *No, not really.* But he didn't know.

'Inspector?'

He felt something. A slight pain in his shoulders maybe? And then there was nothing.

It started off being all about Jews. An elderly Turkish Jewish academic who they both recognised, told the story of how his people had escaped from Spain and Portugal to the Ottoman Empire in 1492 at the invitation of Sultan Beyazıt II. It was a familiar tale of Sephardic Jewish survival, known to most Turks. The academic wandered around synagogues in places like Balat, Karaköy and Ortaköy talking to people. Next there was a bit on the Greeks and then the documentary moved to Sulukule, the old gypsy quarter as it had been before the demolition. And there was Şukru Şekeroğlu, a cigarette in one hand and a halter attached to the muzzle of a dancing bear in the other.

'Whoa!' Ömer Mungan said. 'Wasn't bear dancing outlawed decades ago?' Officially the practice had ceased in 1988, but unofficially it had carried on well into the twenty-first century.

'It was their livelihood,' Ayşe Farsakoğlu said. Watching Şukru on the laptop screen brought old Sulukule flooding back to her. Ömer of course didn't remember it. Whatever the ethics of things like bear dancing and drinking dens, when the gypsies had been allowed to ply their traditional trades they had been happy. They'd had some pride, too, which was written all over Şukru Şekeroğlu's thin, arrogant face. Looking at him made Ayşe smile in spite of herself. She'd never had anything against the Şekeroğlu family; in fact she'd always had a sneaking regard for them as lovable rogues. It was only Gonca that she took issue with, and that was only because she loved the man that Ayşe loved. That men like Şukru had been reduced to recruiting kids for pickpocketing rings run by foreigners was tragic.

A voice behind the pictures on the screen said, 'This is Şukru Şekeroğlu, gypsy, bear man and ex-professional grease wrestler.' And then a figure came into shot, and it was one that, though younger in the film, was still instantly recognisable. 'Şukru, tell us about Sulukule,' Professor Cem Atay asked. 'How long have your people lived here?'

Ayşe looked at Ömer. They both heard Şukru say, 'A thousand years.'

'You were in this city before the Turks?' the professor said.

'We've always been here,' the gypsy replied. 'Our blood runs in these waterways, along the walls of these houses the Turks want to demolish.'

The camera panned – a shot of the houses, cafés and drinking dens of Sulukule.

Ayşe said, 'Did we know that Professor Atay knew Şukru Şekeroğlu?'

'I don't know that we ever asked,' Ömer said. 'But just because he's interviewing him . . .'

'Professor Atay was Hatice Devrim's lover. She was connected to Levent Devrim, our first victim, by marriage, and to our fourth victim, Abdurrahman Şafak – who she may have killed – by blood. He was in turn related to our third victim, John Regan.'

They looked at each other while the younger professor on the screen said, 'The Roma or gypsy community of İstanbul are one of the most fascinating and mysterious minorities we have. In Ottoman times their women were welcomed into harems, including the Imperial harem, as purveyors of perfumes and aphrodisiacs and as fortune-tellers par excellence.'

'But what about Leyla Ablak?' Ömer said. 'He didn't know her.'

'She was his brother-in-law's mistress,' Ayşe said. 'Remember?'

Frowning, she paused the documentary and said, 'We should tell Inspector Süleyman. Where is he?'

'Oh, he's with Professor Atay,' Ömer said.

He felt a vibration against his leg, and it occurred to him that it was probably his phone, which was on silent, but it was very far away. He felt heavy and a little sick and he had to lean on the professor, who he knew was dangerous even if he couldn't care about that now, in order to get inside the house and walk down the stairs.

Down the stairs to where? Why inside the house?

He didn't know. All he wanted to do was lie down.

He heard a voice say, 'I expect you just need a rest. How did you get here, Inspector? I didn't see your car.'

He heard himself say, 'No.' But he couldn't say any more. He'd left the car at home . . .

'Where is your car? Did you leave it at Arnavutköy police station?'

But he just said, 'Home.'

'Home?' The word echoed through his brain as if his head was inside a kettle. 'Where is home?' And then it was as if he was under water, in a full kettle, fighting for his breath. He fell backwards on to something that was softer than a floor, and then he didn't know anything else.

Professor Atay wasn't at the university. Apparently someone had phoned from the police earlier and the professor's secretary had told him that the academic was at home in Arnavutköy. Again Ömer Mungan called Süleyman's mobile, but to no avail. But then sometimes he did turn it to silent when he was interviewing someone.

'We'll have to call Professor Atay,' Ömer said, looking up the professor's home phone number on Süleyman's computer.

But Ayşe put her hand on his. 'Do you think we should?'

'Why not?'

'Well, if we call him and he is implicated in some way . . .'

'If he's dangerous, we need to warn the inspector,' Ömer said.

'Yes, but we can't warn him through the professor, and what if—'

'Atay won't know that we've seen this film,' Ömer said. 'What he does know is that we have our suspicions about him with regard to Hatice Devrim, and of course Inspector İkmen did question him about Leyla Ablak. But what else he may have deduced . . .' He shrugged. 'Ayşe Hanım, we have to call or go to Arnavutköy.

345

Even allowing for terrible traffic, the Inspector should have been back by now. He would have phoned me anyway.'

The office phone began to ring.

'Maybe that's him,' Ayşe said.

Ömer picked it up. 'Hello, Inspector Süleyman's office.'

The voice, when it came, was old and female and tetchy, and Ömer Mungan recognised it. 'Where is my son?' Mrs Nur Süleyman asked.

'Ah, Mrs Süleyman.'

Ömer looked at Ayşe Farsakoğlu, who rolled her eyes. He'd been told she knew the inspector's mother and didn't like her. Now he knew it.

'Do you know why my son's car is parked outside my house?' the old woman continued. 'We haven't seen him and yet it sits there.'

'Well, Mrs Süleyman, could it be that the inspector has maybe gone shopping, or perhaps he's visiting a friend.'

'For hours at a stretch?' she snorted disgustedly. 'He comes here to visit us, whoever you are. His father saw the car draw up hours ago. I asked the girl to put on the tea and then – nothing. Now we have a guest and I don't know what to do. Do I wait for him or don't I? Where is he?'

'I will find him, Mrs Süleyman,' Ömer said.

'You'd better,' she said. 'We have a guest, a princess, and his father, having seen his car, is now expecting him for tea. His father is a prince. He isn't accustomed to people letting him down.' She rang off.

Ömer looked at the telephone receiver and then replaced it on its cradle. 'She seems to think that the inspector's father was expecting him for tea,' he said.

Ayşe shook her head. 'Ömer, the inspector's father has dementia.'

'Oh.'

'Didn't you know?'

'No. Still, his mother says that his car is outside their house.'

'Which is in Arnavutköy.'

'Of course! Maybe he left it there when he went to the professor's? This is mad, we need to find out if he's still there.'

He dialled the number on Süleyman's screen and waited for an answer. It took some time to come, but when it did, that smooth, rather soothing voice that Atay had cultivated over the years almost made Ömer smile.

'Professor Atay,' he said, 'it's Sergeant Mungan from the police, Inspector Süleyman's deputy. I've been trying to get hold of the inspector but I don't seem to be able to do so. I know that he was planning to see you this afternoon. Is he still with you?'

'No, Sergeant, he isn't,' the professor said.

'When did he leave?'

'Oh, it must be about an hour and a half ago,' he said.

'Do you know where he was going, sir? Did he say?'

'No, he didn't. I presume you've tried his mobile phone.'

'It's switched to silent,' Ömer said.

'He must be driving, then.'

'Yes, that is a possibility. Thank you,' Ömer said.

'Sorry I can't be more helpful,' the professor said. 'I do hope that everything is all right.'

'Thank you, sir,' Ömer said and put the phone down.

'He's not there,' Ayşe said.

'No. Left an hour and a half ago.'

'So where is he now?'

Ömer shrugged. 'Do we carry on ringing his mobile? What do we do?'

Ayşe shook her head and looked back at the frozen image of

347

Şukru Şekeroğlu and Professor Cem Atay on the laptop screen. 'I've a bad feeling,' she said.

'Should we call Ardıç?' Ömer asked.

'No,' Ayşe said. 'But we should call my boss.'

'Isn't he at home?'

'Yes. But if we don't call him and this does turn out to be something bad, he will kill us both. Mehmet Bey is like the younger brother Inspector İkmen never had. He loves him.'

Chapter 30

Gonca looked grotesque. With that hideous mask on her face, she was leaping around naked except for a cloak that wasn't hers. At her feet the boy Hamid laughed and Mehmet heard him say that soon they'd all have to leave here too. Whatever it meant, which he couldn't fathom, was frightening and made him feel as if he should be doing something. But he didn't know what. For some reason he couldn't locate his body, and so for the moment he was just a free-floating mind, which was useless. And when he did feel again, and had some notion of his physicality, something pierced the skin on his arm. Mehmet Süleyman briefly roused from his nightmare and screamed.

Whenever Çetin İkmen was particularly worried about something, he broke rules. He walked into Süleyman's office with a lit cigarette hanging out of his mouth and nobody dared tell him to put it out.

Throwing himself down in Süleyman's chair, he turned to Ayşe and Ömer and said, 'Tell me everything you know.'

They told him, they showed him Şukru Şekeroğlu and Professor Atay on film, and then he said, 'Have you called his apartment?'

'No. But he would have told us if he was going home,' Ömer said.

Since the previous December, Süleyman had rented a small

apartment in Cihangir. İkmen brought the number up on his phone and called it. 'I don't know, maybe he's had a nervous breakdown,' he said. 'Nothing would surprise me.' He put his cigarette out in an old saucer that Ömer had hastily found for him and then lit up another. He got no response from Süleyman's home phone and so he cut the connection.

He looked at the two sergeants again. 'So what do we think?'

'About?'

'About what may have happened to Inspector Süleyman,' he said. 'What are our theories or fantasies about that?'

'Well, he's missing,' Ömer said.

'Yes, and why is that?' İkmen asked.

'Er . . .'

'We don't know,' he continued. 'Do we? No. His car is at his parents' house, he can't be reached on his mobile and the last person he was known to be with, we think, is Professor Cem Atay.'

'Yes.'

'So,' İkmen said, 'with my straightforward, entirely practical face on, it seems logical to me that we go and talk to Professor Atay.' Before either of the others could speak, he raised a hand to silence them. 'Minus a warrant, I would suggest at this stage. But let's get in there if we can and see what we can find.'

'Sir, the inspector had his suspicions about Atay,' Ömer said.

'As do I,' İkmen answered. 'But we do not, as yet, have any actual physical evidence to connect this man to any crime in this city or anywhere else. Cem Atay has a high profile; we must be careful.'

They all looked at each other. Even potential high-profile arrests could be problematic. They were normally the preserve of those who worked in state security and counter-terrorism; ordinary cops didn't like them.

'I'll go and speak to Ardıç,' İkmen said, 'and then we'll pick up a clutch of uniforms and get over to Arnavutköy.'

Visiting her cousin Muhammed was always a trial. He had started to dement a few years ago; sometimes he would talk as if he were still at home in his father's house, while other times it was just nonsense. But he was generally calm and quiet about it, which was in stark contrast to the real problem that existed in the Süleyman household: Muhammed's wife, Nur. Sezen İpek had never liked her. Right from the start she had come across as a common social climber and she hadn't changed in the fifty-plus years since Sezen had first met her. She was cruel, too. When Leyla had had her bit of trouble when she was a student, Nur Süleyman had whispered whatever details she came across into ears that she shouldn't have. Now suddenly Nur was in trouble, and Sezen felt a small glow of something like pleasure. A routine social visit had turned into a drama because the favoured, handsome Süleyman son, Mehmet Bey, appeared to be missing.

'I always said that job was beneath him,' Nur said as she walked backwards and forwards across the living room. 'If you mix with criminals they will hurt you.'

'I'd really like to take tea now,' Muhammed Süleyman said. He sat in a corner beside the television, a shattered stick of a man in too large flannel trousers and a green home-knit jumper. 'My father will be very angry if you don't serve it soon.'

Nur heard him, but she didn't respond. Instead she said to Sezen, 'I can't apologise enough for all this. What must you think of us?'

Sezen nodded her head graciously. 'I know only too well the worry of having a child,' she said. 'Don't worry at all, Nur dear. We can wait for tea if that is what you want.'

She was parched. But to say so would have seemed like insensitivity, and, like her or loathe her, Nur had been there for Sezen when Leyla had been found dead. Of course she hoped that Mehmet Bey would be found alive and well, although she did also hope that Nur would be made to wait a little longer.

What Nur Süleyman had said about Leyla when she'd been, after all, just a silly student had got back to Sezen via her cousin Muhammed's older sister, Esma. Nur had apparently told Esma that in her opinion Leyla needed a firmer hand than Sezen was giving her. She had also said that the boy involved needed a damn good thrashing. But then that had been true. Sadly, Sezen mused upon where he was at that moment and where her daughter now resided. Had he not ruined her all those years ago, Leyla would never have had to marry a man she didn't love, she wouldn't have had that affair with that spa man and she wouldn't be dead.

'I'm going to take you to the hospital.'

Süleyman's head felt as if it had been smashed repeatedly against a wall, while his eyes trembled at the small amount of light from the bulb that swung over his head. Occasionally this was obscured by Professor Atay's face, which always seemed to be smiling at him. He wanted, and yet at the same time didn't want, to say something to the academic about what he'd seen in his wardrobe. But if he spoke and the man was in fact a killer, then he'd kill him; and if he wasn't, he'd be offended and maybe complain to Ardıç. But there was fear at the back of all that and so he knew what he really believed, even though he didn't like it. And now he was ill, and as such, he was at this man's mercy.

'Call the station,' he said. His tongue felt too big for his mouth and he was disgusted to realise that he was dribbling.

'I'll call them once I've got you to hospital,' the professor said. 'But you'll have to help me.'

'Help you?'

'The car's in the back garden. I just need to get you up a few steps, but I can't carry you, you'll have to help me.'

He felt himself being lifted by his shoulders into a sitting position.

'We need to find out what's wrong with you,' Atay said. He slipped an arm around his waist, and Süleyman felt himself rise to his feet on distinctly shaky legs.

'What *is* wrong with me?'

'You collapsed,' the academic puffed. 'Started raving.'

Süleyman put one foot in front of the other, watching fascinated when one of his ankles collapsed. The professor took his weight. Süleyman turned his attention to Atay's face, which was contorted with effort, and wondered whether he should ask him if he was going to kill him. He decided against it. Another half-step, and then a knock at the door caused all movement to stop. Süleyman began to feel the professor's legs tremble as he strained to keep them both upright.

Another knock followed the first one, and then a voice that was almost as familiar as Süleyman's own shouted, 'Professor Atay, it's Inspector İkmen. I need to speak to you.'

'You can let Çetin take it from here,' Süleyman said.

But the professor didn't move, and when İkmen knocked on the front door again, he put a hand over Süleyman's mouth. Any doubts the policeman might have had about this man's intentions evaporated now, and even though his brain and his movements were almost impossibly difficult and slow, he did manage to get one of the professor's fingers into his mouth and bit it as hard as he could.

He could see that Atay had to use every bit of self-control

he possessed to stop himself yelping in pain, but he also felt the full force of his wrath when he took his other arm away from Süleyman's back, let him drop to the hard, cold floor and then punched him in the face until he felt his nose crack. The professor's bitten finger, which was bleeding now, was, Süleyman thought, quite wrong.

'Can't see anyone,' Ömer Mungan said. 'But there is a car in the back garden.'

Çetin İkmen stopped trying to ring the professor's mobile phone and moved away from the front door. 'A car?' he said. 'How did that get there?' The house backed on to a Greek church and there was no side entrance.

'There's a gate in the wall at the back of the church,' Ömer said. 'He must have some sort of access arrangement whereby he drives through the church property. Back door's shut.'

'But there was a table with a samovar and tea glasses under a tree,' a young uniformed officer said.

İkmen shrugged. 'The professor never denied that Inspector Süleyman had been to see him. So if he offered him tea, that is perfectly understandable.'

'What do we do now?'

'You mean apart from carrying on calling his mobile every five minutes?'

'I think he's turned it to silent, like the inspector,' Ömer said.

'Has he?' İkmen sighed. 'Well then, if Professor Atay has gone out on foot, which seems likely, there's a chance he's only gone out for a short while. Ömer, see if you can raise the church caretaker or find a priest or someone who might know about the arrangement between themselves and the professor regarding the car.'

'Yes, sir.'

İkmen looked at Ayşe Farsakoğlu, who said, 'You don't think we should just . . .'

'I think, Sergeant, that we should move away from this house now,' İkmen said. Arnavutköy was a smart suburb, but groups of street kids had started to gather, albeit at a distance from the police cars. 'I think we should pay a call on Mr and Mrs Süleyman.'

Ayşe winced.

İkmen walked over to the first of the two squad cars and said to the driver, 'We're moving into the next street, other side of the church. I'm going to visit Inspector Süleyman's parents. You park up at the local station and ask about Professor Atay.'

'Yes, sir.'

He went to the second car and said, 'Follow me.'

As he walked past the professor's house, İkmen looked in every one of its windows very carefully, but he couldn't see anything. And yet something had happened and it wasn't something good. Even when he was sneaking off to see Gonca, Mehmet Süleyman did not disappear; he just didn't.

He was about to turn into the street on the other side of the church when Ömer Mungan ran up beside him and said, 'Caretaker says that the professor has been paying them to let him bring the car through their garden for years. It's nothing new. But what he did say that was interesting was that the car was outside the church until about an hour ago.'

'So an hour ago the professor brought his car into his garden and then went out,' İkmen said.

'So it would seem, sir.'

İkmen frowned. 'I wonder why he did that?' he said.

'Caretaker didn't say, sir,' Ömer said. 'But he didn't think there was anything odd about it. Professor Atay's in and out with his car all the time, it seems.'

They walked up to the front of the Süleyman house, where they were joined by Ayşe Farsakoğlu. The second squad car pulled up behind Süleyman's white BMW and İkmen called over to the uniforms inside to wait where they were. They all lit up cigarettes almost in unison.

İkmen turned to the two sergeants, 'Now, Ömer, I'd like you to go back and watch the professor's house from the front. There's a café almost opposite.' He put his hand in his pocket and took out a twenty-lira note, which he gave to Mungan. 'Buy yourself a drink and keep your eyes on the house and the exit from the church. And call the professor's mobile phone – just in case.' He looked at the car full of uniformed officers again and shook his head. 'If this is going to be some sort of long game, then I need them like a bullet wound to the leg.'

'Why don't I watch the house from the back?' Ayşe Farsakoğlu said. 'I mean, sir, you don't need me to be with you when you speak to Mr and Mrs Süleyman, do you?'

He shrugged. 'No, I suppose not.' Then he said, 'Actually, a woman lurking in a church garden on her own could attract unwanted attention. Ayşe, you go for coffee.' He took the twenty-lira note out of Ömer Mungan's hand and gave it to his sergeant. 'Ömer, sorry, boy, you'll have to do without.'

When he came round, all he could see was the professor's face looking at his and all he could smell was blood. Breathing was difficult.

'They've gone away now, your colleagues,' the professor said. 'And so I am left with the problem that you are on a time limit I have no real knowledge about.'

There was nothing to say. His body was quite inert, and although his face hurt, it didn't hurt enough to rouse him from his stupor.

356

'When it's dark, I'll take you to the car,' the academic said.

Time was no longer fixed. When he closed his eyes, Süleyman couldn't tell whether an hour had passed or a minute. The only thing he could liken it to was when once, years ago, he'd had a general anaesthetic when he'd broken his collarbone.

The next time he opened his eyes, he looked down at his body but saw something that looked like a grey sack. He couldn't relate to it in any way. The professor looked into his eyes, then pulled one of his eyelids up and shook his head. 'I've so little knowledge about this stuff.'

What stuff?

Süleyman felt a sharp pain in his left bicep, and after that he really didn't care. After that, for some reason, he was in a moving version of a woodcut of Hell he'd seen as a teenager when he'd been studying Dante. He'd never believed in the existence of Hell – then. Now he wasn't so sure.

Chapter 31

She'd dialled his number a hundred times and still he didn't answer! It just rang out. Infuriated, Gonca threw her phone across the room, where it hit the wall and smashed to pieces across her father's sofa. The old man shook his head. 'Is that any way to behave?' he said. 'What were you thinking?'

She put her head in her hands. At least ten pairs of eyes watched her from around the room and none of them were impressed. 'Mehmet Bey said he'd come tonight,' she said. 'Now he doesn't answer his phone!'

'Well he's a policeman, these people get busy,' her father said.

Gonca, crying now, felt hands on her shoulders and looked up to see her eldest son, Erdem. He took her in his arms and hugged her. Just over forty and entirely integrated into mainstream Turkish life, Erdem was nevertheless still her little boy who loved his mother unconditionally.

'And I've broken my phone!' Gonca said.

'I'll get you another one,' Erdem said.

'Well someone needs to clear my sofa,' the old man said. 'How can I lie down now and not get glass in my backside!'

Two of Gonca's sisters, tutting with irritation as they did so, took the covers off their father's sofa and brushed what remained of the mobile phone on to the floor. Calmer and chastened now, Gonca allowed her son to lead her to the chair next to her father's pile of cushions by the fire and she sat down. After a moment she took the old man's hand in hers. 'I'm so sorry, Baba.'

'Oh, it's a harsh time,' the old man said. He squeezed her hand back. 'Tomorrow I bury my son and you bury your brother.'

'When I saw Mehmet, he said he'd come and bring halva and pay his respects,' his daughter said.

'He's paid his respects already.'

She looked at him.

'You want the support of the man you love,' the old man said. 'But Gonca, you know maybe he is catching whoever killed Şukru now. You want him to do that, don't you?'

'More than anything!'

'Well then, give him a chance. I no longer object to this love you have that I don't understand. It has endured over the years for reasons I . . .' He shrugged. 'Şukru and I, we wanted to kill him and we would have done. But that's in the past. Now I accept this man, but you must be realistic about him.'

Erdem, who had been listening to what his grandfather had been saying, said, 'He has his life and you have yours. They're different. Unless you want to become a policeman's wife . . .'

'No!'

'Well then you must accept that he will not always be available to you.'

'Why are we talking about that policeman again?'

They turned to look at the furious face of Şukru's widow, Bulbul Şekeroğlu. 'Tonight is about my husband,' she said. 'Tomorrow we will bury him and my children will be fatherless.' She pointed at Gonca and spat. 'Everyone always takes care to make sure that she is all right! The world itself revolves around her!'

Erdem stood up and placed himself between his aunt and his

mother. 'Auntie Bulbul,' he said. 'We are all upset, including my mother. She meant no—'

'The man is younger than you are!' Bulbul screeched. 'She's a whore and a witch and she—'

'Hold your tongue, Bulbul Hanım,' the old man said. 'We are all grieving and we should not say things that make each other hurt more than we do. You will be cared for and so will your children, because this family does not reject its own.'

For a moment, Bulbul looked as if she might start shouting at Gonca again. She'd never liked her, had always been jealous of her success both as an artist and with men. But instead she burst into tears, and when Erdem took her into his arms she let him hug her while her own youngest children clustered around her legs.

The old man looked at Gonca. 'We will have no more division in this family, do you hear me?'

When he used that tone, it made her feel like a child again. 'Yes, Baba.'

'Because you know the old Kurdish whore, Sugar, who came here today to pay her respects, she told me that they have taken down the fences around the latest group of old buildings that are due to be demolished and the wrecking balls have moved into place. We will need to be strong now and fight this together, as a community. If we don't, we will be forced to leave the city, and I for one will die.'

İkmen had heard such sentiments before; they usually came out of the mouths of elderly people with either an Ottoman or a military background. Although very much at odds in terms of politics and beliefs, the old Atatürkist military elites and the Ottomans had a lot in common.

'Nobody is still here who was here when we bought this house in the 1960s,' Nur Süleyman said.

İkmen knew the story well. His friend and colleague Mehmet had been born in a terrible, half-ruined palace on the Bosphorus, which the family had hung on to until the place finally collapsed. Then they'd moved to Arnavutköy, disappearing into what they must have felt then was something very much akin to Trotsky's 'dustbin of history'.

'Now everyone is nouveau riche,' Nur continued. She called over to her husband's cousin for support. 'Is that not so, Sezen?'

'Oh yes,' Sezen İpek said. 'All the Bosphorus villages are full of either terrible footballers, men with silly haircuts or girls who flout their parents' wishes by wearing headscarves.'

He hadn't expected to see Sezen İpek, but then she was Muhammed Efendi's cousin and so her presence could have been predicted. The old man himself, a bib at his throat to catch drips from both his tea glass and his mouth, said, 'My stomach hurts. Call Dr Savva.'

Nur Süleyman's distress and impatience with her husband were evident from the pain in her eyes, coupled with the way she shook her head when he spoke to İkmen. 'Of course Mehmet knows no one here. We don't know anyone! There is a man who has been here for I think a decade who lives over the other side of the church, but . . .' He saw her look at Sezen İpek and then away. 'We don't speak to him or about him.'

'Oh?' It could only be Professor Atay. There was no one else on the other side of the church. 'The historian? Professor Atay?' İkmen asked.

Again the two woman looked at each other, but neither of them said anything.

Muhammed Süleyman Efendi said, 'Dr Savva and his kaolin and morphine solution will put me right. It always works for my grandfather and he's a very old man.'

361

Nur Süleyman looked at İkmen. 'Do you have an interest in . . . in the man . . .'

'Inspector İkmen, I am sorry, but I'm afraid that we don't discuss the person who lives on the other side of the church,' Sezen İpek said.

If it were possible for Nur Süleyman to look cowed or even ashamed, she did so now. İkmen turned his attention to Sezen Hanım. 'Oh,' he said. 'Is that so? Well, I'm afraid I'm going to have to ask one of you to talk to me about him.'

'And why would that be?' Sezen stood up, her hands clasped in front of her chest in what İkmen felt was a very dramatic pose.

'Because the man in the house on the other side of the church was the last person to see Mehmet Bey before he apparently evaporated,' İkmen said. 'I only have that man's word for the fact that Mehmet Bey isn't still in his house, so I need to know as much about him as I can.'

'Professor Atay is a public figure,' Sezen said. 'I'm sure you can find out anything of interest about him on the Internet.'

'Oh, I've met him, several times.'

'Well then you know him.'

'A little,' İkmen said. 'What I don't know, Sezen Hanım, is why you and Nur Hanım seem to have an issue with him.'

'It's not up for discussion,' Sezen said.

'Well it should be,' İkmen said. 'With respect. After all, if this family has some sort of feud with Professor Atay, and Mehmet Bey is missing . . .'

Not that he knew of any such feud, which surely Süleyman would have told him about.

'Ladies, you know from sad personal experience that there is someone in this city who kills people like you. Now I'm not saying that Professor Atay—'

362

'The Atay man and little Leyla İpek.'

The voice was old and cracked but its words were unmistakable. İkmen went over to Muhammed Süleyman Efendi with the man's wife and cousin at his heels.

'Efendi . . .'

'Made her pregnant.'

For a moment the room fell silent, and then Nur Süleyman said, 'My husband, he isn't well . . .'

İkmen just looked at her, watching her shrink before his eyes. Then he turned to the old man again. 'Go on, Efendi.'

The old man frowned. 'You know, I really could do with kaolin and morphine . . .' He touched his stomach. Çetin İkmen sighed.

'My cousin doesn't know what he's saying,' Sezen İpek said. 'Ignore him.'

And then something that might have been anger or hatred or even just rebelliousness came into the old man's eyes.

'Efendi . . .'

'Sezen had to sort Leyla out. But it was my brother Beyazıt who beat the dirty pig. Beat him with the whip our father used on his horses.'

'He beat Professor Atay? Your brother Beyazıt Efendi?' İkmen said.

Now hunkered down beside the old man, he saw the light of recognition switch off in his eyes, and he felt his heart sink a second time. Muhammed Süleyman Efendi said, 'Pardon, monsieur, pardon.' He'd clearly disappeared back into a past that no one else could understand.

Sezen İpek said, 'We all had to learn French.'

'Yes,' İkmen said. 'Your ancestors spoke it at court. I don't care. Now look, ladies, is what Muhammed Efendi said true or not? Did Leyla Ablak, your daughter—'

His phone rang; he took it out of his pocket and said, 'Sorry.' Then he put it to his ear.

'Sir.'

'Ömer.'

İkmen moved towards the back of the Süleymans' dark, heavily furnished living room.

'Sir, I can see a light in the basement of Professor Atay's house,' Ömer Mungan said.

'Have you just noticed it now because it's getting dark?'

'No, I saw it come on. Just now. I mean, I suppose it could be one of those that switches on automatically . . .'

'Or maybe it isn't,' İkmen said. 'Stay where you are. I'll be with you.'

'Might be as well to bring the guys in the car, sir,' Ömer said.

'OK.' He cut the connection and looked at the women again. He was about to give them a last chance, but Sezen İpek pre-empted him.

'It's all true,' she said.

'Sezen!'

She put a hand on Nur Süleyman's arm to silence her. 'No, my dear, this is your son who could be at stake here.' She looked up at İkmen. 'Professor Atay, Cem Atay, made my daughter Leyla pregnant when they were students at Boğaziçi University together. She had an abortion and he, as Muhammed Efendi says, was beaten by my cousin Beyazıt Efendi. That man ruined my daughter. That man was the whole reason she married first a foreigner and then an awful Atatürkist traitor.' Her eyes filled with tears. 'And she could never have children.'

İkmen put a cigarette into his mouth, then stepped forward and took her hands in his. 'Thank you, Hanım,' he said.

Then he lit his cigarette and left the house.

* * *

364

There was no consciousness now. Mehmet Süleyman was vulnerable. Unconscious, he couldn't defend himself, and so he could be shot or stabbed or suffocated at will.

Was he dreaming? There were no physical signs beyond shallow breathing, and so there was no way of knowing what his experience might or might not have been. When he was hefted up on to shoulders that were not really up to the job, he did make a small noise, and for a minute or more the man who carried him stood as still as a tree, his ears trying to close themselves against the sound of his own breathing.

The street in front of the professor's house was rowdy with evening drinkers. To Ayşe it looked as if some of the more fashionable corners of Beyoğlu were on a group excursion that was doubling as a competition in who could pose the most effectively. She found it tiresome and the young people on display made her feel old, but that didn't matter. Ömer had just called to say that there was a light at the back of the house, and only a minute later three of the uniformed guys had positioned themselves near her, across the road from the property. Having them around, as opposed to plain-clothed detectives, wasn't ideal, and they were clearly making some of the more nervous media and digital types anxious, because quite a few had moved away when the cops arrived. But then in a way that was a good thing. Thronging streets and dangerous situations rarely mixed well.

Ayşe's phone rang again. It was İkmen. 'Ayşe, this light in the basement. Can you see it from the front of the building yet?'

She squinted at the place where the wooden house seemed to join the cracked pavement, where she'd looked the first time he'd asked some minutes before. 'No.'

'OK,' he said. 'That's it for now.' He rang off.

Ayşe took a sip from her long glass of lemonade and grenadine and lit a cigarette. An ageing media type three tables away had been looking at her almost non-stop for half an hour and she wondered when he was going to make his move. If ever. She hoped it was never. She looked at the professor's dark and silent house. Was Mehmet Süleyman in there? Oddly, at first, she wondered why her musings were just thoughts, devoid of any emotional content. The man she had loved for years and years was missing and yet she could still drink her drink, think her thoughts and throw the occasional unpleasant glare at her unwelcome admirer. What was happening?

And then a feeling of such terrible loss overwhelmed her that Ayşe almost cried out. Her heart raced, her head swam and for just a moment she wondered whether she was actually going to faint. Was she still so much in love that not even what she had thought was a very firm state of denial had managed to keep the demons of passion out of her head?

She drank a little shakily from her glass and then smoked her cigarette and lit another one. Her admirer attempted a smile and she looked away. Not only was she shaken by what had just happened, she was resentful of it too. How had she come to invest Süleyman with so much power? How had she given herself so completely to him that even when he was with another woman he could still exert total control over her emotions? She looked at the front of that house and she experienced a bitterness that she could barely contain. Then there was resolve. She'd go for İkmen's job and become the best police officer she could be, and to hell with Mehmet Süleyman!

Her phone rang. She picked it up. İkmen said, 'If and when I tell you, break the front door down. Get the guys to move people away from the house now.'

'Yes, sir.' She beckoned one of the uniformed officers over to her table. 'What—'

'Just do it!' İkmen whispered.

Çetin İkmen put his phone in his pocket and watched as a figure came out into the professor's garden and opened up the boot of the car.

Ömer whispered, 'He must have been in there all the time.'

Atay – İkmen could see that it was him by the light coming out of the cellar – went inside again, and for a while, a long while, the police officers thought that maybe he wasn't going to re-emerge. Eventually, panting and grunting, he came out backwards on to the sparse brown and green grass, dragging something that was clearly giving him problems.

Ömer looked at İkmen, who took out the gun he almost never drew. The younger man followed suit.

'What now?' he whispered.

As İkmen looked into the garden again, the professor stopped to rest. Once he was on the move again, the inspector spoke. 'Let's go.'

Chapter 32

The academic smiled. Then he frowned. 'What an extraordinary way to enter a person's property,' he said to the two men who'd just pushed open the gate from the church and let themselves in. One, he knew, was Inspector Çetin İkmen.

'We tried to call you and we knocked at your door,' İkmen said. 'But there was no reply.'

'Well my phone has been switched to silent and I've only just got home.'

He looked pale by the thin light from the cellar door, and exhausted too. But then Cem Atay was not a young man. He and Leyla İpek, as she had been then, had been students together back in the 1970s.

'Ah, but you haven't, have you, Professor?' İkmen said.

'How do you know what I've been doing?' Atay looked and sounded offended. But then he could be as offended as he liked. He was entitled to do that.

'We know because we've been watching this house,' İkmen said. 'You haven't just got home, and I need to search these premises on the basis that this is the last place my colleague Inspector Süleyman was seen, by you.'

'I told you,' he said. 'I had tea with the inspector, we talked and then he left. Anyway, if you want to search my house you'll have to get a warrant.'

Ömer Mungan, who had been silent up until that point, said, 'Let's see in that sack, then.'

The professor looked down at his burden and then up again. 'I said, you'll need a warrant.'

'But if I have reason to believe that you could have illegal drugs in that bag . . .'

'Don't be absurd!'

'Which I do,' İkmen said.

All three men looked at each other. Çetin İkmen didn't usually make things up to get his way, but both he and Ömer Mungan wanted very badly to see what the professor had in his heavy sack.

'It won't take a moment,' İkmen said. 'Just let Sergeant Mungan—'

'No. No, you've no right,' the academic said. 'I've never been convicted of drug offences in my life; you have no reason to search me or my property. Go and get a warrant. Go away.'

He was standing his ground, which İkmen had expected. He said, 'Sir, for all I know my colleague Inspector Süleyman may never have left this house after his appointment with you this afternoon . . .'

'He did.'

'I need to verify that.'

'Then get a warrant. Go away, get a warrant and then come back and I will gladly show you my home.'

He was trying to get them to leave. But if they went, they would be giving him time to do who knew what both inside the house and with the sack that Ömer Mungan was gradually moving closer to.

'And I mean all of you,' the professor said. 'If you think I'll tolerate people staking out my home . . .'

'Who we leave on the public highway is up to us,' İkmen said. 'The grounds of the church are not your property . . .'

'You have no reason to watch me! You've no reason to follow me!'

'Follow you? Who said anything about following you?' İkmen said. Ömer was almost in a position where he might be able to see inside the sack. 'Are you planning to go somewhere, Professor?'

'Well, clearly, because I am preparing my car.'

'Where are you going?'

'That's none of your business!' he said. In his anger he shook his head, and it was then that he saw what Ömer was trying to do. 'Get away from that!' he screeched.

'If you'll just let me look inside . . .' Ömer reached down.

'No!' In a movement that was both very rapid and amazingly smooth, Cem Atay took a gun out of his jacket pocket and fired it.

They all heard the shot. It sounded as if it had come from behind the property. Ayşe Farsakoğlu, outside the professor's front door, told the uniformed constables to kick it in. It was one of those ornate, heavy Greek doors and so it took some doing, but eventually it gave.

Ayşe went in first and ran through the marble front hall and into the kitchen. By a light that seemed to come from somewhere underneath the house she could see three figures standing by a car. İkmen was instantly recognisable, and she thought the taller man could be Ömer Mungan. What she could see easily, however, was that the other figure had a gun. She said to the constable at her back, 'No one down as far as I can see.'

'That's good.'

'But I'm going to get closer.'

'Ma'am, don't you want us to—'

370

'No.' She held up a hand to stop the men behind her. Then she moved from the back of the kitchen to the front and tucked herself down behind what she could now see was the partially open back door. In that position she could hear what was going on outside.

İkmen said, 'You have to see that you were always too close. And that in part was your own fault. You came to us and told us about the connection to the Mayan Long Count calendar.'

'I came to you in response to a request for ideas and information you made in the press,' Atay said.

'You still put yourself on our radar,' İkmen continued. 'Both Inspector Süleyman and myself had doubts about you, but it wasn't until I managed to speak to Leyla İpek's mother this afternoon that the possibility of a deeply personal motive emerged.'

Ayşe opened the door a little wider so that she could see the garden more easily.

'The İpeks humiliated you when you were little more than a child,' she heard İkmen say. 'You and the girl had sex, she got pregnant and you were treated like a peasant. I understand. And now, in recent years, the parasites appear to be moving back into public life . . .'

'And you know what, exactly? Nothing!' Cem Atay's body appeared to stiffen. 'I've studied these people all my life. They're still the same morally redundant, greedy, stupid, vicious family they have always been. And people want them back?'

'Some people.'

'Some people in the government, yes! I've spent my life studying and teaching the history of empire as a catalogue of failure and inequality that we have grown out of!' His voice became shriller and shriller as his agitation increased. 'But then in 2009 we, this country, gave one of them what amounted to a state funeral! One of those people who kept the rest of us enslaved

371

for centuries in the mistaken belief that they were divinely appointed by a God whose every commandment they abused!'

'We can talk about this,' İkmen said. 'We can talk about all this, just—'

'This gun is all I have,' Atay said. 'I'm not putting it down and you are going to let me get into my car or I will kill you.'

'You can't kill both of us.'

'You know, I really don't care.'

'Where is Inspector Süleyman?'

Ayşe felt her heart jolt in her chest.

'What do you care where another one of them is or isn't?'

'He's my friend.'

'He's one of them! Do you have no consciousness of your own class at all?' He waved his gun. 'Now move to the back of the garden and let me get in my car and go.'

There was a pause. No one moved, then İkmen said, 'No.'

Another pause followed, after which Cem Atay said, 'I have your weapons. You're unarmed. What are you going to do?'

He must have taken their guns. Ayşe began to sweat. She looked at the men lined up behind her and then back into the garden again. What she needed to do was to deploy them around the property, effectively cutting off all escape routes.

'If you're not with me, you're against me,' Cem Atay said. İkmen moved towards him and the professor clicked the safety catch off.

'Give me the gun,' İkmen said.

Ayşe knew that this was her moment, the one where she unequivocally proved her worth and İkmen's job became hers by right. As she got to her feet, she saw İkmen push Ömer Mungan away from him, and then she was outside the kitchen door with her own weapon raised.

'Put the gun down now, Professor,' she said.

They all looked at her, and for just a moment Ayşe felt a glow of triumph. With her gun trained on the professor's head, she'd brought this stand-off to a close. İkmen and Ömer Mungan behaved as if they believed that too, because they both took one step towards Cem Atay. But what none of them had noticed was that even when the others had stopped looking at Ayşe, the professor hadn't.

He shot her in the stomach, and she fell to the ground before the men at her back could reach her.

Ömer kicked the weapon out of the professor's hand and pulled him into a headlock while he took his own and İkmen's guns out of Atay's trouser waistband.

Completely oblivious to anything else, İkmen ran to where Ayşe lay on the ground in the arms of a uniformed constable. Another cop was calling an ambulance and a third officer had gone back into the house to secure the front door. He heard the snap of handcuffs as Ömer disabled the professor. Before he even squatted down beside her, İkmen knew that Ayşe was dead. Not just because shots to the stomach were difficult to survive but because she looked at peace. There was no fight for survival, no struggle to take breath or attempt last, significant words.

The constable holding her said, 'She's gone.'

And although he knew that was a fact, İkmen took one of her wrists between his fingers and felt for a pulse that was never going to be there. Only then did he say, 'Yes.'

He heard Ömer call for backup and he felt entirely impotent to either help or advise the young man.

The constable holding Ayşe said, 'What do you want me to do, sir?'

İkmen put his arms out. 'Give her to me.'

The constable moved out of the way and a gentle exchange

of the dead body of Ayşe Farsakoğlu took place. As soon as he had her, İkmen smiled and held her to his chest as he would have done one of his own children. Because in many ways she was one of his daughters, and he had loved her.

'Sir?'

Ömer had put the professor into the custody of the constable who had called the ambulance. Its siren could just now be heard in the far distance, towards the centre of the city.

'Sir?'

İkmen looked up. 'She's dead.'

Ömer sank to his knees and looked at her with eyes imbued not so much with horror as with the light of having seen some sort of miracle. Because she was still smiling. 'She saved us,' he said. He went to touch her hand, but İkmen gathered her still closer to himself. He put his head in her hair and he curled himself into her terrible blood-soaked wound, and Ömer Mungan knew that for the moment there was only him, and so he took charge. He had liked Ayşe Hanım a lot, but to İkmen she was almost family. Now it was his time: Ömer Mungan, the boy from the back of beyond who still had to find his boss, the man who'd chosen him above all the slick city boys in İstanbul to be his deputy. Now he had to prove whether he was prepared to fight to stay in İstanbul or not.

Once again he checked the sack the professor had been dragging towards his car. Just like the first time he'd looked in it, it contained only a very old mattress and some bedding.

He went over to the academic, who was now sitting on the ground in a stress position with the constable looming over him. Ömer knelt down beside him and said, 'What have you done with Inspector Süleyman?'

There was no answer. Whether he was in shock or just noncompliant Ömer didn't know. He took Atay's chin between his fingers. 'Listen to me. Where I come from, revenge is a way of life. Tell me where Süleyman is and it will go easier for you. Don't, and I will reach inside your cell and I will increase your torment.'

Still Cem Atay said nothing. Ömer Mungan toyed with the idea of kicking him in the head as he rose to his feet, but then decided that he had better things to do. As İkmen continued to cradle Ayşe Farsakoğlu in his arms, Ömer ordered the other constables into the house and told them to search every corner of it. He had been so convinced that Süleyman was in that sack, he couldn't imagine where else his boss might be.

When he did eventually find Süleyman, on the cellar floor, covered in a thin grey blanket, he was sure that he too was dead. But although his breathing was so shallow as to make it almost invisible, it was there, and when the ambulance arrived it was Süleyman who was loaded into it and taken to hospital.

Ömer tried to tell İkmen the good news, but he didn't appear to be able to hear anything.

Chapter 33

Proximity to the death of a loved one put those who experienced it under a sort of a spell. Çetin İkmen had seen it a hundred times in his work and had experienced it himself when his father and his son had died. It involved an increasing appreciation of the irrelevance of time, a conviction that one was dying from the pain one was experiencing, as well as a terrible fear about where and what the dead person was about to be subjected to next. Even when Forensics arrived to investigate the scene, still he wouldn't give Ayşe up. They were a team. In the real world she was meant to be his successor when he retired, and until she left him, how could he leave her?

For a good hour nobody came near them. He told her how much he appreciated everything she did for him and what a brilliant career she had ahead of her as he desperately tried to cling on to the real world that had existed just that morning, just that afternoon. But far away inside the depths of his mind, he knew it couldn't last. He just didn't know how to end it. Because if he left her then he'd know she was dead and she was never coming back.

'Çetin?'

The voice was soft and familiar and it washed against his strained nerves like water, because it was a sound that came right from the roots of his childhood. He looked up into Arto Sarkissian's face.

'You need to give Ayşe to me now, Çetin,' the doctor said. 'You know I will take good care of her.'

It was true. Arto always took care of the dead; it was what he did. And impervious to the spell they cast, he could find out exactly why and how they had died, which sometimes helped to bring them justice.

Arto put an arm between the body and his friend. 'It's OK to let go now, Çetin,' he said.

And it was. Arto took her, and together with two of his orderlies he put her on a stretcher, then he covered her face and her body with a sheet.

İkmen looked down at himself for the first time since he'd taken Ayşe in his arms and suddenly her blood disgusted him. It wasn't where it was meant to be. While the orderlies took the body away, Arto helped him to rise to his feet. As Ayşe receded into the distance, everything about her faded: the smell of her perfume, the feel of her skin, the spell that she had put on him. Did he imagine it as a mist that followed her corpse into the plain green transport that would carry her to the Armenian's laboratory, or was there really a mist that had come up from the Bosphorus, giving the pretty Arnavutköy garden an eerie feel?

'You must go home and rest,' Arto said.

Suddenly everything he had to know and do came crashing in upon him. 'Yes, but we must find Süleyman,' he began, as adrenalin burst out of his glands and flooded his bloodstream.

'He's been found,' Arto said. Recognising the signs of mounting panic, he added, 'He's fine.'

'You're not lying to me, are you? You're not . . .'

'I'm telling you the truth, as I always have,' Arto said. He put a hand in his pocket and took out a small bottle of pills. He shook one out into his palm. 'Now I want you to take this.'

İkmen looked at the pill as if it were a live hand grenade. 'What is it?'

'It's a mild tranquilliser.'

'What? Diazepam?'

'Yes.'

'I don't want that! What do I want that for?' He pulled away from his friend, stuck a hand in his jacket pocket, took out his cigarettes and lit up. His legs buckled and he fell to the ground.

Arto helped him to his feet again. 'A sudden rush of nicotine, oddly, isn't always a panacea for all your ills, Çetin,' he said. Then he pushed the tablet between İkmen's lips and made him swallow. 'And no spitting it out.'

İkmen did as he was told. 'But what about the man who lives in this house?' he said. 'Professor Atay?'

'Your colleagues have taken him to the station,' Arto said.

'I'll have to interview him!'

Arto put one of his arms through İkmen's and led him into the professor's house. 'No,' he said. 'You can't.'

'Why not?'

'Because you have to go home and rest,' the doctor said.

They passed into the marble hall with the silent Greek fountain. In front of them, the wreckage of the academic's door lay splintered across the threshold.

'But who will interview Professor Atay?' İkmen said. 'Who?'

When Gonca arrived at the hospital, she found Nur Süleyman beside her son's bed talking to a doctor.

'We've given your son a drug called flumazenil, which is the antidote to a benzodiazepine overdose,' he was saying. 'If his respiratory function had been better we could have just left him to wake up. But there is an outside risk of coma in some of these cases, which I now think we've averted.'

'He will live, won't he?' the old woman asked.

Gonca looked at the long, pale figure of her lover and began to cry.

'Benzodiazepine overdose is rarely fatal,' she heard the doctor say. Then she saw him look at her. 'Can I help you?' he asked.

She looked a mess. She'd been trying to get some sleep, more for her father's sake than for her own, when the constable had called. Sergeant Mungan had sent him; such a nice boy, that boy from the east. He'd told her that Mehmet Bey was in the Taksim. So she'd come.

'Madam?' The doctor looked at her as if he had a bad smell under his nose. But then she was dishevelled. Her hair was uncombed and knotted and she wore a dirty shift, with no bra, over which she had just flung a skirt that wasn't even hers. On her feet she wore her father's slippers. Who was she going to say she was? What relation could she possibly be to a high-ranking police officer?

But then an old, cultured voice said, 'Oh, Doctor, this is a friend of my son's.'

And although Nur Süleyman wasn't exactly smiling at her, Gonca did not get the impression that she wanted to bite her.

Nur urged her forward. 'Come along,' she said. 'The doctor has said that he can be sat with.'

Gonca, tentatively at first, moved past the doctor and joined the old woman at the bedside. At first she stood, but then Nur told her to go and get a chair. She found one in a corridor and returned to see what she hoped was a little more colour in her lover's cheeks. It turned out to be just a smudge of blood from his nose, which was swollen and pushed to one side.

After what seemed like an eternity of silence, the old woman said, 'You know, I hate my son doing this job. Again a madman tries to kill him. You must hate it too.'

Gonca, taken aback by this tacit acknowledgement of her position in Mehmet's life, took a few moments to gather her thoughts. 'It's what he does,' she said.

'You are very accepting.'

'As you know, Hanım, I am a gypsy. We have no choice but to accept.'

The old woman – who had once, Gonca could see, been very beautiful – said, 'And yet you are a very successful artist. I don't think you always have to accept what fate hands out to you.'

'My father lives in Tarlabaşı and today they began to pull it down around him,' Gonca said. 'That I have to accept. And my brother Şukru, some terrible person murdered him and then burnt his body. What remains of him we have to bury in the morning. These are things I can do nothing about, Hanım.'

'I am sorry for your loss, ' Nur Süleyman said, following up with the more traditional exhortation to the bereaved to 'live long'.

'Thank you.'

'As for Tarlabaşı . . .' The old woman shook her head. 'You know, my husband's Armenian wet nurse came from there. It makes me sad to see it disappear. Some people talk in terms of what they call "new Ottoman" projects. But what connection that has to my husband's family is anybody's guess. The old Ottomans want things to be left as they are. Who these new Ottomans are I do not know.'

Gonca said nothing. She didn't really care who was tearing down Tarlabaşı or why, she just wanted it to stop. 'They moved us on from Sulukule,' she said. 'Where I was born and my brother and all of us.'

'And that too was a disgrace,' Nur said. 'Our city is famous for many things, and one of those is the fact that we used to have one of the most colourful and happy gypsy communities in Europe.'

'A thousand years.'

'As you say, a thousand years of living side by side in peace.' She turned to look at Gonca. 'You know, Hanım, I will not pretend to be happy about my son being with a woman like you. You do not conform to the norms of life as my family understand them and you are far too old for him, but I will never try to dissuade him from you again. On that you have my word. I can see that you love him, and that is worth something. There has been too much interference with love in the past.'

It was hard to know how to respond to what was hardly a compliment; more a declaration of peace. But Gonca was gracious and she was truthful. She said, 'I expect nothing, Hanım, except the right to love your son. Loving him is something I cannot help and I will not apologise for it.'

'You're charged with the murder of one police officer and the imprisonment and assault of another,' Commissioner Ardıç said.

He didn't often get his hands dirty by interviewing suspects, but this one was a TV star, and Çetin İkmen, who would normally have performed this function, had been sent home. His sergeant was dead and he was in shock. Had he come in with the offender, he would either have had nothing to say to him or he would have beaten him up. The former would have been useless, while the latter, in view of the massed ranks of the press who had suddenly appeared outside the station, would have been unwise to say the least.

Ardıç looked at the young eastern boy who had taken over from İzzet Melik. He was a good officer and had handled the entire crime scene most efficiently.

'So tell me, Sergeant . . .'

'Mungan,' he cut in quickly.

'Apart from those facts we are sure about – the death of Sergeant

Ayşe Farsakoğlu at this man's hands – what else do we know about our professor? I don't mean age, education and all that rubbish.'

'No, sir.'

The subject of their conversation, Cem Atay, sat in front of them, silently, with his lawyer.

'I want to know why a man such as you, Professor Atay, would kill one of my officers and wound a second,' Ardıç said. 'You have everything a man could want – money, fame, the respect of your peers.' He leaned, with some difficulty, towards the professor, denting his large stomach uncomfortably as he did so. 'How did we get here, Professor Atay? Eh?'

Still the famous man didn't speak.

Ömer Mungan cleared his throat. 'Sir, when Inspector İkmen and myself were trying to apprehend Professor Atay, the inspector put it to him that his behaviour had something to do with an incident that had happened a long time ago.'

'What incident?'

Ömer looked down at the few notes he had made prior to joining Ardıç in the interview room. 'Inspector İkmen had learned from murder victim Leyla Ablak's mother, Sezen İpek, that Professor Atay and Leyla had had a relationship back in the 1970s when they were both students. Leyla İpek, as she was then, became pregnant and her family organised an abortion. However, the father, Professor Atay, was humiliated by the İpeks and was never allowed to see Leyla again.'

The professor's face coloured.

'This incident, and I think the professor's political views too, developed in him a hatred not just for Leyla İpek's family but for all members of the former Imperial Ottoman family, of which they were one small part.'

'And given that we've had so many unnatural deaths in that family this year . . .'

'Professor Atay volunteered what he hoped we would find to be useful information about our increasing caseload,' Ömer said. 'By pointing us in the direction of something called the Mayan Long Count calendar.'

Ardıç, who was accustomed after so many years to be unsurprised by every esoteric lead that Çetin İkmen and those around him chose to follow, said, 'I see.'

'It's South American . . .'

'It's all mixed up with the end of the world; yes, I know, Sergeant,' Ardıç said. 'Contrary to appearances, I do keep up.'

Ömer looked down, to smother a smile – Ardıç was a wry bastard – then said, 'We believe it's very possible that the deaths of Leyla Ablak, John Regan, Rafik İpek Efendi and Abdurrahman Şafak Efendi were committed not as some sort of blood sacrifice to a South American god but as an act of vengeance. You see, sir, Professor Atay has connections to all those victims, albeit loosely in some cases. He remains the only suspect who does.'

'And the first victim? In Tarlabaşı?'

'Levent Devrim. He was the brother-in-law of the professor's now deceased mistress, Hatice Devrim.'

'Royal?'

'Not at all,' Ömer said. 'But Inspector Süleyman thought it possible that he knew the professor was having an affair with his sister-in-law. And for the record, sir, Levent Devrim was a believer in the Mayan Long Count calendar. It's my personal belief that Professor Atay could just as easily have come up with the idea of pinning these killings on some mythical crazy conspiracy theorist by observing Levent Devrim as he could have done by studying the Maya on a trip to Mexico in 2011.'

'Mmm.' Ardıç looked down at a sheaf of papers in front of him on the table and took a few moments to read something.

'Says here that Hatice Devrim's husband has confessed to her murder.'

'Yes, sir.'

'So not the professor?'

'A connection also exists between the professor and a gypsy called Şukru Şekeroğlu, whose burned body, you will recall, sir, was found on some waste ground . . .'

'Know him too, did he? Mmm,' Ardıç said. He looked at Cem Atay. 'Well you can sit there in silence beside your very expensive legal adviser, but eventually you will have to answer questions relating to yourself and these unfortunate members of the Osmanoğlu family, plus the madman and the gypsy too, lest we forget. Silence can be interpreted as guilt, especially if we ally it to forensic evidence. Do you see?'

For a moment Cem Atay didn't speak. Then he said, 'I'll talk to İkmen, and only İkmen.'

He was cold, and he feared that Fatma would use the unseasonal weather to talk about the soba and the central heating again. But she didn't, and when he looked at her properly, he could see that she was actually quite warm.

'Get into bed and I'll bring you some tea,' she said as she helped him into his pyjamas and pulled the bedclothes up to his chin.

Still confused by the temperature, he said, 'But don't you want me to light the soba?'

'The soba? It's . . .' She gave him an ashtray and then she briefly hugged him. 'It's not cold, Çetin, you're just very upset,' she said. 'And it's not surprising.' Her eyes filled up. 'That poor girl!'

He kissed her on the cheek and let her go.

'I'll make tea and then I might cook some börek,' she said as she walked towards the bedroom door.

It had to be past one o'clock in the morning, but İkmen didn't say anything. When times were hard, or she was upset, Fatma cooked. It was her therapy, and if cooking all night meant that she kept her sanity, then it was time and ingredients well spent. She'd always liked Ayşe Farsakoğlu. As a religious woman, she hadn't always approved of the sergeant's lifestyle, but she'd never told her that. Ayşe had been welcomed into the İkmen household time and time again, and had she lived, she always would have been.

İkmen pulled the covers around his body so that they warmed his sides. He was like a man caught in the snow, shaking with chills and aching from head to foot. Did Mehmet Süleyman know about Ayşe? Was he even awake? Last time İkmen had spoken to Ömer Mungan, the sergeant had only known that Süleyman had been given an overdose of benzodiazepine and that the hospital were going to administer an antidote. Had that drug come from the same bottle as the stuff that had been given to Şukru Şekeroğlu? Serial murderers were rare, very rare, especially in Turkey. But had they suddenly found one? In plain sight? On their televisions?

People could become fixated on anything. In the past İkmen had been obliged to arrest obsessed people. It might be money they got hooked on, or sex, or all sorts of oddities including the dead, the occult, power and religion. And although he had met people who found the ex-Imperial family fascinating, and had even known those who resented them, he'd never before come across someone who wanted to kill them. There were vast numbers of them and so it was a fool's errand anyway, and also they were so benign. All the calls that various politicians and other interested parties made to bring back the monarchy in truth fell on deaf ears. The Osmanoğlus would never run the country again, not even as constitutional monarchs. It was absurd. But maybe because he'd been rejected by them as a youth, though possibly for other, more complicated reasons yet to be discovered, Cem Atay, a brilliant man with absolutely everything, had decided to kill them. Or so it seemed.

He had certainly killed Ayşe. She had bled out into every centimetre of İkmen's clothes, which Fatma had taken away from him as soon as she could and put into a plastic bag like a good policeman's wife. Then she had washed him in the shower, his skinny body trembling with cold and with the sobs that had only just left him, exhausted and alone in his bed. Ayşe had been his successor, and now that she was gone, there was no one. Ardıç would say that they'd find someone from another force to take over after he left, but that wasn't good enough. İstanbul had to be policed, where it could be, by İstanbullus. Officers like Ömer Mungan were good, but it took them years just to understand the city: its byways, its quirks and its intense frustrations. There had been no one else; there was no one else.

He wanted to sleep, but he knew that he wouldn't, and so he lit a cigarette and stared at the ceiling. A few minutes later, Fatma, smelling of flour and butter, came in with his tea.

'What will you do?' she asked.

He sipped the hot liquid. 'About what?'

'About when Ayşe's funeral is over and you are alone in that office.'

He shrugged. 'I don't know. We have to get through tomorrow, today or whatever it is first.'

She frowned. 'This won't affect what you're going to do, will it?'

She meant his retirement. Çetin İkmen didn't answer.

Chapter 34

'You know,' Çetin İkmen said as he looked at the man in front of him through sore red eyes, 'I have other things I could be doing. Later on today I have to go to a funeral for a friend and colleague you killed in front of my eyes.' He leaned forward on to the table in front of him. 'Now my boss, Commissioner Ardıç, told me that you won't speak to anyone but me, so if that is the case, then speak. Stop fucking me around and confess or whatever it is you want to do. Just get it over with.'

The smart, very young lawyer who sat at Cem Atay's side whispered something in his ear.

İkmen, irritated by this, said, 'Don't you tell him to carry on the silent act, for fuck's sake!'

Ömer Mungan, who was conducting the interrogation alongside İkmen, had never heard him swear quite so much before and was a little taken aback.

'If he stays silent it won't do him any fucking good and you know it,' İkmen said to the lawyer. He looked at Cem Atay again. 'Well? We know you killed my sergeant, you wounded Inspector Süleyman. You'll be happy, maybe, to know that he is still alive, is now better than he was and is talking.' He looked at Ömer Mungan, who had not long returned from Süleyman's bedside. 'What did he tell you, Sergeant Mungan?'

'We know that the inspector was drugged, with a

benzodiazepine. He thinks it was, initially, in the tea that you served him. You didn't drink it, Professor?'

'No.'

'Ah, he speaks!' İkmen said.

Ömer continued. 'After a visit to your bathroom, Inspector Süleyman went into your study and in there, in a cupboard, he found a cloak, a feathered headdress and a mask that could be described as frightening, especially by a child. He thought, as you must have realised, that it looked very like the description we were given of the creature that murdered Levent Devrim in Tarlabaşı back in January. Because if you didn't think he thought that, then why did you try to kill Inspector Süleyman?'

Even when Ömer spoke directly to him, Professor Atay only ever addressed his answers to İkmen. 'I didn't know until later that anyone except Şukru Şekeroğlu had seen me that morning,' he said. 'Much less a child. I wouldn't have planned for a child to see such a thing. As for Süleyman, I knew he'd seen it and so I had to think quickly. Yes, I put diazepam in his tea. I needed him quiet while I thought what to do next.'

'Why did you kill Levent Devrim?' İkmen asked. 'Was it just because he knew about your affair with his sister-in-law?'

The young lawyer put a hand on his client's arm and said, 'You don't have—'

'It's all right,' Cem Atay said. He smiled at İkmen. 'It's all publicity, isn't it?'

That a man who had been a serious academic could have been so seduced by fame that even talking about how he had killed people was making him smile caused Çetin İkmen to shudder.

'Şukru Şekeroğlu had seen Hatice and myself together. He recognised her as Levent's sister-in-law and so he let him know. Maybe he thought there was some money to be made out of it. Şukru was all about money. Levent told Hatice that she had to tell her husband the truth about us,' he said. 'He didn't want money, it wasn't blackmail; he just thought it was the right thing to do. But Hatice wouldn't tell Selçuk and so Levent said that *he* would.'

'So you killed him on the twenty-first of January 2012.'

'I did.'

'To silence him.'

'I didn't want Selçuk to know about us either.'

İkmen narrowed his eyes. 'Because you didn't want your lover to get ideas about leaving her husband?'

'To be honest, yes. Hatice was a lovely woman who adored me and would do anything I asked, but that can be tiresome sometimes, you know? I also wanted to see what I could do, whether I could kill. It was by way of a dry run.'

'Did you tell Hatice?'

'Eventually.'

'I think you also killed Levent Devrim to confound us,' İkmen said. 'Is that true?'

The professor smiled. 'It did, didn't it?'

'Four victims with Imperial blood, one without: yes, it did. For a while. One way or another, you were and always had been the common denominator, Professor Atay,' İkmen said. 'Did Şukru Şekeroğlu help you to kill Levent Devrim? I know that you knew each other.'

'He was in one of my documentaries. I liked him. But he didn't help me, no.'

'Did he know that it was you behind the ridiculous "Mayan" costume?'

He laughed. 'I knew I had to get into and out of Tarlabaşı without being seen, and knowing how superstitious gypsies and Kurds are . . .'

'That's something of a generalisation.'

389

'The Maya gave me the headdress as a gift and I purchased the mask, in Mexico City, because it appealed to me,' he said. 'The snow and the ruinous nature of Tarlabaşı gave me excellent cover, or so I thought, but the theatrics meant that I could feel more secure than I would have done just creeping about as myself. I had planned to break into Levent's apartment and kill him there, but when I arrived, he was out. I was going to give up and leave when I saw him sharing some rakı with a man who I later learned had come to meet Şukru Şekeroğlu: a Bulgarian gypsy he often did business with that could not be done in the light of day.'

'Stolen bags or drugs?'

He shrugged. 'I don't know. Once Levent had parted from the foreigner, he started collecting wood for his fire. I followed him, let him collect fuel for a while and then I killed him.'

'Did you think that anyone had seen you?'

'I obviously knew that Şukru had seen my "character", for want of a better word,' the professor said. 'But I didn't think he had realised it was me, and when I hissed at him, he left, which implied that maybe I had frightened his superstitious gypsy soul. However, like most gypsies, Şukru was a very observant man. That was how he came to blackmail me. He recognised me from my hands.'

'What do you mean?' Ömer asked.

Cem Atay held up his left hand, and they all saw that he had six fingers. None of them had noticed it before with the unwitting exception of Süleyman who had bitten it when he'd tried to escape from the academic. 'There you are, deformity as well as poverty. Can you imagine what Sezen İpek said when she saw that? When she realised that the child Leyla was carrying might inherit it?'

'So, just to be clear, when you killed Levent Devrim, did you have your subsequent Osmanoğlu killing spree in mind?'

'Of course.'

'And what about your lover, Hatice Devrim? Did she know what you had lined up for members of her own family?'

'Yes.'

'Think carefully before you implicate a dead person who cannot defend herself,' İkmen said.

The professor leaned across the table so that he was closer to the policeman. 'Inspector,' he said, 'in order to understand what Hatice did, you have to know about the nature of our relationship.'

'Do I?'

'Yes.'

'Then tell me about it,' İkmen said.

'Hatice Öz was one of my students in the late 1990s. She was very pretty, very left-wing, and she enjoyed my classes because she liked to learn more about what I eventually discovered was her ancestry, mainly so that she could debunk all the romance that existed around it. We were attracted to each other and she offered herself to me. She'd never been with a man before and that was significant. You never really get over your first love, especially women.

'She knew I was married to Merve then and that it was not advisable career-wise for a senior academic to be mired in any sort of sexual controversy, especially where students were concerned. Hatice knew there was no future in it but she couldn't stop herself loving me. When she left Boğaziçi she got on with her life and I got on with mine; media work came in for me and Hatice made a career for herself and married Selçuk Devrim.

'It was when Merve disappeared – and before you start to speculate that maybe I killed my wife too, I didn't. I didn't know where she went then and I don't know now. When Merve disappeared, Hatice got in contact again. She loved her husband but there was no passion in her life, and she was a woman who needed passion. We started seeing each other, but although she was in love with me, I wasn't in love with her. I never have been. I don't believe I've ever been in love with anyone – except my Leyla, of course. It was sex. She was good at it.

'I became famous, and if anything, that was what really engaged me, if I'm honest. But then in 2009, the then head of the Osmanoğlu family, Prince Osman Ertuğrul, died, and because I am an Ottoman historian, I chose to go and watch his funeral. Hatice came with me. We were horrified. Tens of thousands were there, weeping and calling for the family to come back. It shook me to my core. I'd had no idea so many Turks felt like that! Then I started to notice a trend towards recognition in the newspapers and on television. People began to talk about a new Ottoman age, and I realised that what I'd been doing for years on end was not just informing people about their history; inadvertently I'd been promoting that anachronistic form of government, those useless people and their pointless lives. For months I was in a state of despair. In 2010 I made a documentary about the Ottoman occupation of Bosnia and I nearly had a breakdown. The İpeks, my first love's family, had been high and mighty on their golden Ottoman past, and Hatice told me that there were relatives in her family too who were like that. Awful old autocrats and perverts who believed that the world owed them a living. It was also at this time that Hatice started to tell me stories about her brother-in-law Levent and his obsession with the end of the world, 2012 and the Mayans.

'Last year I went to Mexico. I spent time with what remains of the Mayan people on the Yucatan peninsula. I liked them. They told me stories about their ancestors: how the Spaniards had forcibly converted them to Christianity, how they'd tortured and brutalised them and stolen everything they had, including their gold. I told them how our Ottoman masters had fought the Spaniards for the Mayan gold and used it to oppress their own people and build an unjust empire that enslaved millions. As I've said, the Maya made me the headdress I wore when I killed Levent Devrim. To be honest, part of me hoped that the sight of me would give him a heart attack; he was always complaining of chest pains. But it didn't, and so I had to cut his throat, with him squirming to get away from me. I didn't want to do it like that – he wasn't a bad man – but if I was going to use a mythical Mayan conspiracy theorist as my supposed murderer, I had to kill in the way of the Maya. If I hadn't, any connections I could build between the Long Count calendar and the killings would take too long to lose their obscurity. Your request for information about Levent Devrim's calculations just speeded things up.'

'So you were on a mission to justify your career, were you?' İkmen said. He shook his head. 'But it was also deeply personal, wasn't it? Let's talk about the İpeks. About Leyla.'

He shrugged. 'Why not start with her? The first time I saw her at the Great Palace spa it was a terrible shock. I went home and, I'll be honest, I threw up. Leyla didn't see me, though, I made sure of it. I wasn't ready for that. But in spite of the fact that her appearance was a shock, I'd be lying if I said I didn't know about her and Faruk. I saw her sitting on his knee in his office. It made me furious to see her with him. I watched her and then I confronted her one night in the hotel garden after one of their lovemaking sessions. I said I knew she was having an affair and I needed to speak to her. They always met on a Saturday night and a Tuesday if they could, and the next Saturday was the twenty-first, which was perfect for me. I told her to get Faruk to leave the spa first, which she did. Then she let me in. And even after all that time, she still wanted me. I could see it in her

393

eyes. You know, when her family made her have an abortion, I still loved her; I even put flowers on her doorstep for her birthday. Why? Was I a fool? She was such a slut!' For a moment his face fell. 'A beautiful, beloved slut.'

'You killed her in the plunge pool.'

'The Mayans called them cenotes, the water holes into which they would hurl their sacrifices.'

'Yes, you or one of your Mesoamerican experts told me,' İkmen said. 'In amongst royal blood and heart-ripping . . . But if you respected and had sympathy for the Maya, why did you emulate the very worst elements of their culture? You liked them . . .'

'They were convenient,' he said. Even his lawyer looked taken aback.

'And you were full of rage and vengeance, weren't you?' İkmen said. 'Rage at Leyla's family, who had rejected and humiliated you.'

His face went red. 'They're a danger to all of us. Doesn't matter whether we love or like them, that's irrelevant. Don't you see?'

İkmen ignored him and looked down at his notes. 'And John Regan. A nephew of Abdurrahman Şafak, who was also related to Hatice Öz . . .'

It took a moment for the professor's anger to blow itself out, and then he said, 'Hatice saw the old man from time to time, her mother's cousin. He was furious because he got a letter from John Regan asking if they could meet and talking about a romantic book he wanted to write about Sultan Abdülhamid II. Regan thought the old man could help him. It was nauseating. Abdurrahman didn't reply. But then he got another letter from Regan, this time from a Karaköy address. Hatice had already told me that the old man had made his servant girl pregnant, and had got her to take the kid to the abortion clinic, and so we wanted to make room for him in our scheme. But then there was this silly Englishman.'

'Mr Regan fought you,' Ömer said.

'Yes. I did almost exactly the same thing as I did when I killed Abdurrahman Efendi.'

'Which was?'

'I got into the building hours before I needed to be there. In the case of John Regan, he was out when I got in. The kapıcı at that building is always drunk. He was in the street laughing with some other drunk. I asked to go in; he didn't even look at me, just waved me inside. I waited in an empty apartment. Then, when Regan came home, I knocked on his door and said I was one of his neighbours. He just let me in.'

Ömer frowned. 'Did you work with anybody?' he said. 'We had reports of a gypsy outside the synagogue opposite.'

The professor gave one of his eerie smiles. 'Oh, he was one of Şukru Şekeroğlu's. Şukru was having me followed and watched.'

'And you knew?'

'By that time, yes. We'd spoken. He'd told me he knew that I'd killed Levent Devrim.'

'He didn't try and stop you?'

'He needed money. He'd seen me kill once, and he suspected I'd killed more than once, so he wanted to see what I'd do next. He wanted to get as much as he could out of the situation. Those watching me didn't know why they were doing so. That's what Şukru told me. And subsequent events have not proved him wrong. So far no other gypsies have beaten a path to my door.'

'He blackmailed you?'

'He knew that all he had to do was point a finger at me and, true or not, his accusations would ruin my career. So yes, he began to blackmail me.'

'Until you drugged him and then killed him. Then you burned his body on some waste ground in Aksaray.'

'It's a shithole. Nobody cares. I waited until the next twenty-first of the month. It amused me.'

'Be that as it may. Where did you get the intravenous benzodiazepine our doctor says you must have used on Şukru and later on Inspector Süleyman? I doubt it was prescribed to you.'

'No. I have tablets. The liquid and the needles came from Hatice. She used to be a nurse. She still knows people.'

'You mean she *knew* people . . .'

'If you will.' He cleared his throat. 'Almost everyone I have killed has been either a particularly ghastly member of that parasitical family or corrupt.'

'John Regan was neither.'

'No, but if his book had become popular, it would have been more exposure for that family. John Regan was stupid.'

'If that were a crime, Professor, then half the world would be slated for death,' İkmen said.

He shrugged. 'But Şukru came in useful. Made you think you'd had your twenty-first of the month murder and then along came another one.'

İkmen sat back in his chair. He was desperate for a cigarette, and toyed with the idea of going outside for a while, but he also wanted this over with and the professor was being candid, to say the least. 'So let me get this right,' he said. 'You can now live with yourself because you've killed all these people?'

'In the past, unwittingly, I promoted them. Now I'm not.'

'Yes, but your career, the fame you love so much is over now.'

'My career, yes, my fame . . .' He laughed. 'Well that, I think you will find, will live on.'

396

'So you can be a legend in your own mind while you clean up shit and piss and get buggered in Silivri Prison,' İkmen said.

'I killed a madman, an adulteress, a fool, an old man who raped a young girl and an ancient paedophile. Another man tried to blackmail me and so I killed him. What was I supposed to do?'

'You also killed my sergeant, and you killed Hatice Devrim too, didn't you? Selçuk Devrim didn't kill her; he couldn't have.'

This time he didn't answer straight away. In fact he looked anywhere but at İkmen's face before he spoke, and when he did, it was in an entirely different tone.

'The problem was,' he said, 'that Hatice only ever did what she did to please me. She hadn't necessarily wanted her brother-in-law to die, but when she found out I'd murdered him, if anything she loved me even more than she had before, because she thought I'd done it for her. She happily bribed the servant girl to leave Abdurrahman Efendi's front door unlocked for me the afternoon he died. Her politics were always left-wing, but I don't know whether she actually hated her family as much as she claimed to do. She wanted to please me . . .'

'She did what you asked her and still you killed her.'

'When she found out that Selçuk had known about our affair for some time, Hatice hoped he'd ask her for a divorce. But he didn't. He didn't want one, she did, and what was more, she wanted to be with me all the time. I didn't want that. I could also see that she was starting to lose her nerve, becoming a weak link.'

'You couldn't have that.'

He smiled. 'I couldn't live with one of that family, not really, not for ever, not after what they'd done to me.'

'You'd have lived with that family for Leyla İpek. Professor, a lot of men make girls pregnant and then get thrashed by their families,' İkmen said. 'A lot of men are never allowed to see those girls ever again. Leyla İpek suffered just as much, in fact more than you did, because she had the abortion.'

'Leyla was not humiliated. Her Uncle Beyazıt Süleyman beat me with a whip as if I were some sort of lackey!' He flung his hands in the air as if suddenly impatient with everything. 'Hatice wanted me all the time and I didn't want that! I couldn't have done that! But then that is what the Ottomans do, isn't it? They can't help themselves. They take and take and drink you dry like vampires! That's what they did to this country for centuries!'

İkmen felt a long, thick shudder run down his back. 'Civilised people do not solve their problems by killing,' he said.

'*They* did, the Ottomans. That was always how they solved their differences! How could we live with that in this country again, eh? We should have killed them when we deposed them, like the Russians did with their tsar.'

İkmen said nothing. Since the end of communism in Russia, the last tsar, Nicholas II, and his family had been canonised.

'Yes, I killed them all,' the professor said. 'I waited behind the lift on the ground floor for Abdurrahman Şafak's English guest to go and for the maid to leave the door unlocked, and then I went in and I butchered him. I walked through the back door in the steps of his rent boys to kill Rafik İpek, and if I had been able to do so, I would have killed his nephew Mehmet Süleyman too. I'm being honest with you and I'm not ashamed or sorry. I expect you think that's really "disordered" and "mad" of me, don't you? I expect you'll have every bloody psychiatrist in the country poking about in my brain. Well, won't you?'

Çetin İkmen didn't answer. Ömer showed him his watch, and after a moment, he nodded. He spoke to the academic and his lawyer. 'I am going to be seeking prosecution on eight counts of murder, including that of Sergeant Farsakoğlu, and one of the attempted murder of Inspector Mehmet Süleyman. You, sir, are never going to get out of jail. And yes, you're right, I am going to request psychiatric assessments.'

Cem Atay, smiling again now, shook his head sadly. 'Are you?'

'Yes.' İkmen stood up and leaned across the table. 'Sadly, and this is just my opinion, you, Professor, have probably increased public sympathy for the Osmanoğlu family more effectively than any of your documentaries ever would have done. I wouldn't be surprised if they really are invited back to run the country after this. I'd call your project a failure. Now Sergeant Mungan and I have a funeral to go to.'

Chapter 35

Mehmet Süleyman hadn't been obliged to drive Arthur Regan to the airport for his flight back to London, but he'd wanted to. He parked up and then walked with him to the smoking area outside International Departures. The whole airline security madness began as soon as one walked through the doors, and anyway the policeman wanted to have a cigarette.

'I can't thank you enough for what you did for me and for John,' the old man said as he put his suitcase down on the pavement.

'I wish we could have protected him,' Süleyman said. 'I wish we could have stopped his death.'

'But you found his killer.'

Süleyman shook his head. 'I cannot decide whether Professor Atay is crazy or evil. He is certainly deluded.'

'You don't think your family will ever rule this country again?'

Süleyman smiled. It hurt a bit because his nose was still a little swollen from first being broken by the professor and then rebroken by the surgeon, who had made it look like his 'old' nose again. 'No,' he said. 'Our time has passed. Some people might like to call themselves new Ottomans and dream about a Turkish empire, but it will not happen. You know, when I looked through the professor's genealogies, I found that I am related, if distantly, by blood to the Şafak family.'

'And so to John!'

'And so to your son, yes,' he said. 'I wish I could have known him.'

'I wish you could have known him too. He was a nice man.' Arthur went quiet for a moment, and then he said, 'So you're quite recovered now?'

'I am very well, thank you,' Süleyman said. 'Although sad.'

'You lost a colleague,' Arthur Regan said. 'A nice lady as I recall her. A terrible waste.'

'I had known Sergeant Farsakoğlu for a very long time,' Süleyman said. 'And I was not always as kind as I should have been to her.' His eyes misted, and Arthur Regan put a hand on his shoulder.

'I am sure that if you were unkind it was not intentional,' the Englishman said. 'We all do things we are not proud of. I go over the last conversation I had with John sometimes, endlessly wondering what I could have said that would have been kinder or more loving. Our last moments with people are what they are. You are a good man.'

Süleyman smiled. 'Only sometimes.'

'That is about the best that any of us can hope for,' Arthur Regan said. He offered his hand to Süleyman. 'I must go home and put my life back together.'

Süleyman took the old man's hand and shook it. 'And I must stay and make sure that Inspector İkmen doesn't work himself to death.'

'He's sticking to his decision not to retire, then?'

'Oh yes,' Süleyman said. 'They are getting him a new sergeant soon and he says he will work on until he feels that he can leave.'

'Which will be never.'

'I imagine so.' He smiled again, and then, just briefly, the two men embraced.

As Arthur Regan passed through the glass door and into the terminal he said, 'When I come back next time, I will buy you a drink and we will toast my son. Maybe make a toast to your family, even!' Then he said, 'You do drink?'

Süleyman laughed. 'I am an Ottoman, Mr Regan, I do as I please.'

The house opposite the Şekeroğlus' place, the one that used to double as a drinking den, came down in minutes. The wrecking ball, a mindless sphere of concentrated force, flattened it and then smashed it into its own cellar. Gonca, a cigarette in her hand, watched it come down. Her father, sitting in the living room at the back of his property, was, she knew, watching that film of Şukru again. He had no interest in anything but images of his dead son.

Neither Gonca nor anyone else had told the old man the whole truth about Şukru. A couple of the men he'd used to follow Professor Atay around had turned up at the house asking for money not to talk to the press. But when she'd told them that her lover was a policeman, they'd quickly melted away. After all, even if they were entirely innocent of any crime, they all knew that if they ended up in a police station, almost anything could happen. Not that she'd seen much of her policeman lover in recent weeks. But she could understand that and she was fine with it. Ayşe Farsakoğlu had been a big part of his life both personally and professionally, and it was going to take time for the emotional wounds he had suffered after her death to heal.

She knew that he felt guilty. Had he been conscious, maybe he might have been able to save her. But he'd been entirely helpless. Gonca was just happy that he was alive and that finally, the person who had killed poor mad Levent Bey had been brought to justice. She'd heard that since the professor had been arrested,

Hamid had stopped having nightmares. If only she could say likewise. Tarlabaşı haunted her.

With the houses opposite down, it wouldn't be long before the developers came for her father's house. He'd been offered money, which he wouldn't take, and a flat in some new development, which he also wouldn't accept. And she agreed with him. But where, when Tarlabaşı did eventually gentrify from its ragged head to its bare toes, would or could they go? The question was of course rhetorical.

In Balat there was an artist's studio and a great big house in a garden filled with terracotta pots and olive oil cans full of flowers. Although she shared her home with two teenage sons, a daughter and a grandson, Gonca did have space for a life of her own. And when Mehmet visited, it was always as if it was just the two of them. But she had a lot of family in this house in Tarlabaşı. There was her father, her two older, widowed sisters and now Şukru's widow and her children, all nine of them. She couldn't see them out on the street, none of them.

She looked at the destruction and she smoked. Once the ball had stopped swinging, a group of workmen with wheelbarrows came to start removing the rubble. One of them, a man probably in his fifties, showed his appreciation of her cleavage with a smile and a widening of his eyes. But she wasn't in the mood.

'In your dreams, you destructive bastard!' she yelled at him, and then she threw her cigarette butt into the street and disappeared inside.

Fatma had been as fine as she could be with the five thousand lira he'd sent from their savings to some family they didn't know in Anatolia. He'd given Suzan Arslan's family the money in memory of Ayşe Farsakoğlu because he knew she'd liked the girl and he couldn't bear the thought of her mother dying without a fight. Because that was how Ayşe had died, without a murmur, and he knew how unlike her that was and it weighed upon him. The aborted retirement had been another thing, however.

She'd said, or rather screamed, 'So when are you going to retire, then? At seventy? Eighty? When you die?'

He'd said what he believed, which was, 'I don't know.' Then he'd assured her that his carrying on in the police in no way affected their planned purchase of central heating. It was at that point that Fatma had thrown a vase at him.

Now this was supposed to be his day off, but he'd come into the station to get some peace and be somewhere away from those eyes that bored into his guilty soul like instruments of torture. He'd thought that, in a way, his wife would have been glad not to have him under her feet all day long. But he also knew that what had happened to Ayşe and to Süleyman had unnerved her. She didn't want him to die.

'İkmen.'

He hadn't heard anyone come in. He looked up and saw Ardıç. 'Hello, sir.'

With some difficulty Ardıç lowered himself into the chair on the other side of İkmen's desk. 'About retirement . . .' he began.

İkmen held up a hand. 'My mind's made up, sir,' he said. 'My postponement has been agreed.'

'Not yours!' he said. 'You'll go on for ever. You think I didn't know that? No, mine.'

'Yours?'

'Yes,' he said. 'I spoke to you about it some months ago.'

'Oh yes.' İkmen remembered. 'You're going to be replaced by some religious—'

'My successor will start in October. A three-month handover period. Allah, she'll need it!'

He waited for some sort of reaction. But then he remembered

404

that İkmen was still not himself after Ayşe Farsakoğlu's death. He wouldn't be for a while. He said, 'What I'm trying to tell you, İkmen, is that your new commissioner is not going to be a man of high religious sentiment after all but a fifty-year-old lady from Gaziantep called Hürrem Teker.'

'A woman. That's good.' İkmen smiled. 'We need more women.' He suddenly looked alarmed. 'But she's not . . .'

'Religious? No. They call her "the Stormtrooper" in Antep,' Ardıç said. 'As tough as leather. Single. Real career woman.'

İkmen knew the type, or thought he did. He had a cousin who was out of that old republican, heavily secular tradition. He rather liked them.

But then Ardıç said, 'Good to look at, too.'

'Really?'

'Oh don't look so surprised, İkmen,' Ardıç said. 'It isn't just the little covered girls, the models and the pneumatic TV stars who can be beautiful. Your new commissioner is a stunning woman, although what she'll make of that little boy Süleyman has from Mardin I do not know.'

'Ömer Mungan? He's a good officer, sir. He started slowly. I think the city was a bit of a shock to him at first . . .'

'Yes, they all worship odd things down there, don't they?' he said. 'The devil and snakes. Antep being just west of Mardin, Commissioner Teker will know all about it.'

'Doubtless.' İkmen had suspected for some time that Ömer Mungan probably did adhere to some unusual and probably incomprehensible religion – so many in Mardin and its environs seemed to. But then he paused for a moment to really look at the fat man in front of him. In one way or another he'd known him for over forty years. 'I'll miss you, Commissioner Ardıç,' he said. 'You've always been a fair man. That's rare.'

Ardıç wasn't often either flustered or embarrassed, but this was one of those rare occasions. 'You'll manage,' he said. 'A handsome woman to look at. You'll have your work cut out keeping her away from Süleyman!'

İkmen ignored his superior's attempt at levity. 'You have often protected me, against your better judgement, and I know that you've sometimes been punished for it. I can only thank you from the bottom of my heart, Ersin Ardıç Bey.'

No one ever used Ardıç's first name. İkmen wondered as he saw the fat man's face redden with embarrassment whether he'd realised anyone even knew it.

'Ah well, İkmen, that is very generous of you.'

'It is my pleasure, sir.'

The commissioner began the long process of standing up. İkmen always wanted to help him, but he never had and he never would. Ardıç for all his fat, had dignity. 'So, er, now that we have Professor Atay in custody, we are, er, business as usual, I imagine, İkmen.'

'I do hope so, sir,' İkmen said.

Ardıç eventually managed to achieve verticality. 'So, well,' he said, 'my retirement, just between us at the moment.'

'Of course, sir.'

Ardıç assumed a very stern expression. 'No such luxury for you, İkmen.'

'No, sir,' İkmen said. And then, just before the commissioner left his office, he added, 'Thanks be to Allah.'

Ardıç turned, smiled, and then burst out laughing.

Acknowledgements

Two books really helped during my research into the Maya and all things 2012. They were *The Maya* by Michael D. Coe (8th Edition), which really goes into depth about all aspects of Mayan life, including the Long Count calendar. Another excellent guide was *The Everything Guide to 2012* by Mark Heley. This achieved the amazing feat of making the Long Count calendar comprehensible to me.

Now you can buy any of these other **Barbara Nadel** titles from your bookshop or *direct from her publisher*.

FREE P&P AND UK DELIVERY
(Overseas and Ireland £3.50 per book)

The Inspector İkmen Series:

Belshazzar's Daughter	£7.99
A Chemical Prison	£8.99
Arabesk	£8.99
Deep Waters	£8.99
Harem	£8.99
Petrified	£8.99
Deadly Web	£8.99
Dance with Death	£8.99
A Passion for Killing	£6.99
Pretty Dead Things	£8.99
River of the Dead	£8.99
Death by Design	£7.99
A Noble Killing	£8.99
Dead of Night	£8.99
Deadline	£7.99

The Hancock Series:

Last Rights	£8.99
After the Mourning	£6.99
Ashes to Ashes	£7.99
Sure and Certain Death	£7.99

TO ORDER SIMPLY CALL THIS NUMBER

01235 400 414

or visit our website: www.headline.co.uk

Prices and availability subject to change without notice.